Bound by Fate

The Key Stone Pack Series Book 1

Aisling Elizabeth

Copyright © 2023 by Aisling Elizabeth

All rights reserved.

No portion of this book may be reproduced in any form without written permission from the publisher or author, except as permitted by U.S. copyright law.

The story, all names, characters, and incidents portrayed in this production are fictitious. No identification with actual persons (living or deceased), places, buildings, and products is intended or should be inferred.

ISBN: 9798857412435

Book Cover Design: Aisling Elizabeth

Contents

Acknowledgments	VII
Dedication	VIII
Content Warning	IX
The Keystone Prophecy	1
Chapter 1	3
Chapter 2	10
Chapter 3	17
Chapter 4	25
Chapter 5	32
Chapter 6	37
Chapter 7	44
Chapter 8	53
Chapter 9	59
Chapter 10	66
Chapter 11	73
Chapter 12	81

Chapter 13	88
Chapter 14	96
Chapter 15	103
Chapter 16	109
Chapter 17	116
Chapter 18	121
Chapter 19	129
Chapter 20	136
Chapter 21	142
Chapter 22	150
Chapter 23	158
Chapter 24	165
Chapter 25	172
Chapter 26	179
Chapter 27	186
Chapter 28	191
Chapter 29	196
Chapter 30	202
Chapter 31	208
Chapter 32	214
Chapter 33	223
Chapter 34	233

Chapter 35	242
Chapter 36	248
Chapter 37	254
Chapter 38	260
Chapter 39	268
Chapter 40	274
Chapter 41	281
Chapter 42	286
Chapter 43	293
Chapter 44	299
Chapter 45	306
Chapter 46	312
Chapter 47	319
Chapter 48	325
Chapter 49	332
Chapter 50	340
Chapter 51	346
Chapter 52	352
Chapter 53	360
Chapter 54	371
Bound by Rivalry	383
Read where it all began	385

About Aisling Elizabeth	387
Also By Aisling Elizabeth	389

Acknowledgments

First to my Higher Power Puzzle Pieces, Sydney and Rach, your support is amazing. And to all of my puzzle pieces, even though you aren't named you still mean the world to me.

I couldn't do this without the team that I have that supports me. Kayla my assistant, who should really be called my boss, Rach my on hand Editor, Amanda for getting the word out about my books and Nicole for helping me plan an amazing launch party for this book.

Also, my support system is essential to me being able to work the way I do. Again, Kayla for making sure I eat. Mark for being my "research partner" and telling me to rest. Jes and Naomi for the amazing motivation and friendship. Michael Evans and Emilia Rose for making me feel like part of the family and introducing me to so many amazing authors and readers. There are more I am sure, and I do love you all.

Finally and the most important are my children. You are the reason I do everything in this life.

Dedication

To Cassandra and Hunter (IYKYK)

Content Warning

First, this is a dark paranormal romance book, so it deals with dark themes throughout. The series will also get considerably dark as it progresses as well. Please ensure you read the warnings and take care of your mental health.

This book contains elements of and/or mentions of:-
PTSD and Truma
Panic Attacks
Kidnapping
Violent attacks
Sexual, physical and mental assault
Death
If you feel I have missed a potential trigger then please message me at aish@aislingelizabeth.com and I will ensure it is added.

Second. This book is set in the UK and written in British UK, so if any of the spellings look funky, that could be the reason. This series is also a re-imagining of another series (The Dark Essence World) which is now no longer available. There will be some key elements that are the same or similar but it is a different and, in my opinion, a much better written story.

Happy reading, and don't forget the tissues.

The Keystone Prophecy

From The Dark Prophecies - Visions from the Essence of the Fates

In the world where shadows blend with light,
A maiden of twenty-five shall rise from the night.
Descendant of Diana, Queen of Witches and Beasts,
Half witch, half wolf, her lineage in the least.

From an alpha's might and a priestess concealed,
Her ancient bloodline to the goddess revealed.
Though the paths of magic run deep in her veins,
Her true power's asleep, bound by invisible chains.

For the key to her strength, the heart's true desire,
Lies in a bond, set passionately on fire.
Born of two worlds, she's a hybrid so rare,

AISLING ELIZABETH

Destined to change fates, with power to bear.

She'll encounter a man, from realms dark or light,
His submission to her, sets their spirits alight.
For in their union, the scales shall tip,
Balancing power, in a tight-knit grip.

If he's born of the light, the world finds its peace,
If of darkness, then shadows may never cease.
But remember this well, for as stories unfold,
The key to their fate, in their hands, they do hold.

Butterflies emerge, symbols of transformation,
Guiding their journey, without hesitation.
Balance is crucial, for the stakes are so high,
The gods watching closely with a vigilant eye.

So, heed this prophecy, for as legends declare,
Love and choice rule over despair, with Diana's care.

Chapter 1

Erica

The ancient, creaking floorboards of the old house groaned beneath my feet as I paced around the small room. The city's polluted air wafted through the cracked window that overlooked a bustling street. It had been two years since we moved into this crumbling relic of a home, but it never felt like mine. The walls were painted with secrets and memories, some tainted with pain, while others whispered of love long forgotten. It seemed pointless to even bother to decorate when at any moment we might need to pack up and leave. The joy's of living in hiding with the threat of being hunted down at any moment.

It didn't help with my own personal circumstances. Being a werewolf who couldn't shift was like living in a prison within myself. My body yearned to run, to feel the wind blow through my fur, to taste the freedom that came with four legs instead of two. But my wolf wouldn't come forth – she remained dormant, hidden beneath layers of guilt and trauma. And so, I was stuck in this human form, unable to protect those I cared about most.

"Erica," Trenton's deep voice called from the doorway, snapping me out of my thoughts. His piercing blue eyes softened when they met mine.

"You're overthinking again." "Am I?" I mused, keeping my gaze level with his. The Alpha of what was left of our pack had been both my rock and my shield ever since tragedy struck us all. Trenton Hughes was more than just a leader; he was family.

"Come downstairs," he beckoned, turning to leave before pausing. "We have much to discuss." His words hung heavy in the air, like the weight of an unseen storm. I followed him down the rickety staircase, taking in the familiar sight of Becca, his human Luna, standing by the fireplace. Her kind grey eyes flickered with warmth as she smiled at me. She had taken me in when my parents were killed, and despite everything she had lost, our friendship had only grown stronger.

"Imogen and Beck are on their way home," Becca informed us, her eyes momentarily drifting towards the door as if she could sense their presence.

"Good," Trenton replied, his strong arms folding across his broad chest. I noticed the worry etched into the lines of his face. "Is everything alright?" I asked, unable to quell the concern in my voice. "Let's wait for the twins," he said, settling into a worn armchair. "We'll talk then."

Moments later, Imogen and Beck burst through the door, their cheeks flushed from laughter as they chatted between them.. They were twenty years old, young, spirited, and fiercely protective of their family. Their resemblance to both Trenton and Becca was undeniable; Imogen with her father's striking blue eyes, and Beck with his mother's warm smile.

"Imogen, Beck, take a seat," Trenton instructed, his tone heavy with authority. I met the twins' gazes as both of them reacted to their father's tone, and I knew that whatever news he had wasn't good. As the twins settled onto the sofa opposite us, I clenched my fists, anger boiling beneath my skin. This never-ending cycle of fear and danger felt like a noose tightening around our necks, threatening to strangle the life from us. It wasn't long before we were joined by Marshall, Trenton's beta and his wife Charlene. I knew now for sure that what Trenton had to say wasn't good.

"We've received news that our pack has been found again," Trenton said, his voice almost a whisper. My heart skipped a beat, and an icy chill washed over me. Fear clenched at my chest like a vice; the possibility of another attack was terrifying.

"Are you sure?" I asked, my voice trembling.

"Unfortunately, yes," Marshall confirmed, his expression grim. "We have reliable sources who've reported that there have been some people asking around about us. They're closing in on us."

"Then we need to act immediately," Beck declared, his eyes lit up with fierce determination. "We must plan our next move and ensure the safety of our family."

"Agreed," Trenton nodded. "We've survived this long by relying on each other, and we'll continue to do so. No matter what it takes."

As the room fell silent, I couldn't help but feel a sense of foreboding. Despite our determination and courage, the knowledge that our enemies were drawing near threatened to shatter the fragile peace we had built. But we would not go down without a fight. I owed that much to those who had given their lives for ours. The weight of responsibility hung heavy on my shoulders as our pack's future teetered on the edge. I looked around at the faces of those who had suffered so much already. Nineteen years ago our, then thriving three hundred plus, pack had been attacked, it had resulted in a horrifying massacre. My parents had been among those killed, as had Christian, Trenton and Becca's oldest son. He'd died protecting me, and the weight of his sacrifice weighed heavily on my heart every day. Marshall, our pack's Beta, had also lost his first wife Amy in that brutal attack. What was once a powerful pack was reduced to nothing more than a small group of rogues, since it was the law that a pack could only be established if they had their own land to claim. As far as I remembered, ours was a wasteland of the spilt blood and burnt-out buildings of our home. The guilt gnawed at me like a relentless beast, for I knew that each person here had experienced loss and pain and couldn't help but think that it was because of me.

"I've been considering our options," Trenton said, breaking the silence that had settled over us like a dark cloud. "There is a potential location for us to move to."

"Where?" I asked, anxiety curling its tendrils around my heart.

"More north, near the coast," he continued. "It's remote and well-hidden. We've never lived there before, so they shouldn't be expecting it."

"Sounds promising," Becca chimed in, trying to sound upbeat, but I could see the worry etched into the lines of her face.

"Is it safe?" Imogen asked with a tremor in her voice.

"Nothing is truly safe anymore, sweetheart," Trenton replied solemnly. "But it's the best option we have right now."

"Then let's do it," I said with determination, clenching my fists to steady myself. "We can't afford to sit here waiting for them to find us."

"Agreed," Trenton nodded. "We must prepare ourselves and make this move as quickly as possible."

"Leave that to me," Marshall said.

"I can help," I offered, drawing on my resourcefulness and adaptability. It wasn't the first time we had to act quickly, and it sure as hell wouldn't be the last either. Trenton nodded with pride in his eyes.

"Thank you, Erica" Becca smiled warmly, her eyes filled with gratitude. "We are lucky to have you with us."

"Believe me, the honour is mine" I replied, though the guilt still gnawed at my soul.

"Erica," Marshall said, placing a hand on my shoulder. "We can do this. Together."

"Right" I nodded, taking a deep breath to steady myself. "Let's get to work."

"What can we do?" Beck asked and Becca smiled.

"You can help me pack," she said. Imogen groaned and rolled her eyes.

"Packing duty," she complained. "Surely we can do more than that." I bit back a smile as I glanced at Marshall who was also trying to keep a straight face.

"Do as your mother says," Trenton said, a warning in his tone. Imogen rolled her eyes again and stood up with a huff.

"It sucks being a human," she muttered to herself as she stormed out of the room.

Later that night Trenton, Marshall and I surrounded the battered wooden table. There was a map spread across it and a circle where Trenton had said was the potential location.

"Alright," I began, my voice low and steady. "We need to plan this move carefully. Our enemies are relentless, and we can't afford any mistakes." My fingers traced the contours of the map, marking the path to our new sanctuary.

"Erica's right," Trenton chimed in, his voice commanding and firm. "We'll need to split into groups for transportation, taking different routes to avoid detection."

"Imogen and Beck can go with me in the van," Becca offered, her eyes filled with maternal concern. "We can take the coastal route, less populated areas."

"Good idea, I will take the motorcycle," Trenton said, his jaw set in determination. "It's faster and more manoeuvrable in case I need a quick escape."

"Then I'll go in the car with Erica and Amy," Marshall said with a nod. "We can take the forest route, it'll give us more cover."

"Maybe I should travel with Becca and the twins," I said. Before they had died my father was the pack Gamma, and his job was to protect our Luna and Alpha's children. With him gone, that duty fell to me. I saw Trenton and Marshall glance at each other before Trenton smiled at me.

"No, we need more space for our belongings in the van," he said. "You are best in the car with Marshall."

"But then Becca is left with no protection," I argued.

"Becca can look after herself," Becca said from the doorway with a smile. "Do as Trenton says sweet girl, it's for the best." I saw a look cross her face and looked around at Trenton and Marshall. I could tell that there was something being left unspoken, and I didn't like it. How was I meant to protect our family if I didn't have all the information?

"Perfect," Trenton said after I grudgingly nodded. "Now, let's discuss supplies."

"Imogen and I will pack food and water for the journey," Becca volunteered. "Enough for everyone, just in case we get separated."

"Beck and Amy can continue to pack our belongings," Marshall added.

"And I suppose there is no point even going to work tonight," I said. I felt surprised that I was kinda disappointed about that. But between my job at Red Bank, a supernatural only bar and my growing little graphic design side hustle, I was starting to actually feel like I could actually maybe have something like a normal life. At least the design stuff was online so I could continue that wherever we were, as long as I had the internet.

"No," Trenton said. "Keep everything as normal, at least until I get back. We don't want to draw attention to ourselves." Marshall and Becca nodded, and I smiled.

"How long will you be gone?" Marshall asked Trenton.

"I'm not sure," Trenton replied as he reached over to Becca to give her a hug. "A week at the most."

"I don't like you going on your own," Becca said, and I nodded to echo her concern.

"I'll be fine," Trenton said as he forced an attempt of a reassuring smile to his face. He hugged Becca tighter and nodded briefly to Marshall.

"Well, I suppose I should get ready for work then," I said. I started to make my way out of the room when Trenton stopped me.

"Erica," he called, and I turned to face him again. I caught another strange exchange between him and Marshall.

"Yeah?" I asked, suddenly feeling anxious.

"When I get back..." he trailed off and then looked at Becca and Marshall again. Becca patted his arm and Marshall nodded. He turned back to look at me. "When I get back, I think we should sit down and have a conversation. There are some things that I think it is time you should know." I looked between the three people but no one spoke any further.

"Like what?" I asked.

"Not now," Trenton said. "I really must be going. But I promise, when I am home, that we will talk." He walked over and kissed my forehead before pulling on a jacket and heading to the door. Becca followed him and they hugged in the doorway. I felt Marshall's hand on my shoulder as I watched the couple saying goodbye.

"Don't worry kid," he said. "Everything will be okay." I knew he was trying to be reassuring but I couldn't shake the feeling that danger was already closing in on us. Time was running out, and soon we would be forced to face our enemies whether we liked it or not.

Chapter 2

Erica

The sultry scent of magic and blood hung heavy in the air as I wiped down the polished mahogany bar. Victor Reynard's supernatural establishment was an oasis amidst the chaos of the world outside. The dimly lit, plush interior provided a sanctuary for all those looking to escape their mundane lives or simply indulge in the company of like-minded creatures.

Victor, a 300-year-old vampire with the wisdom and cunning of the ages, had a knack for attracting the most diverse clientele. From ethereal nymphs nursing goblets of glittering nectar, to hulking werewolves drowning their sorrows in mugs of foamy ale, we welcomed any and all who passed through our doors.

"Erica, love, be a dear and fetch me another bottle of that exquisite O negative from the cellar, would you?" Victor called out, his voice smooth as silk and just as compelling.

"Of course," I replied, tossing the rag over my shoulder and making my way towards the hidden door at the back of the room. As much as I hated to admit it, working for Victor had its perks. The pay was excellent, and he treated me more like a confidante than an employee.

The hinges creaked open as I entered the cellar, the cool dampness a stark contrast to the warmth of the bustling bar above. As I reached for a bottle, the sound of the entrance bell chimed, signalling a new arrival.

"Jasper, long time no see!" came Victor's voice from above. Curiosity piqued, I quickly grabbed the bottle and ascended the stairs.

"Ah, Erica, perfect timing," Victor purred as I emerged from the cellar, the bottle clutched tightly in my hand. "Allow me to introduce Jasper Blackwood." My eyes locked onto the newcomer, taking in his tall, lean frame and tousled blond hair. His blue eyes sparkled with an intensity that was both alluring and unnerving. He had an air of authority that made the hairs on the back of my neck prickle, but his smile was warm and disarming.

"Nice to meet you," I said, forcing a smile as I offered my hand. Jasper took it, his grip firm and reassuring.

I could tell that he was an Alpha werewolf as soon as our hands touched, and a powerful one at that. And that concerned me. I hadn't seen him in the bar before and I didn't like that at all, especially with Trenton being on high alert. It wasn't unusual for pack wolves to come into the bar, but the Alphas rarely made an appearance, which suited me just fine. I didn't like Alphas, apart from Trenton, of course. They were often territorial and demanding. I had my fair share of unmated Alphas deciding that as a rogue wolf that I would be an adequate mate for them, and I had no plans for that at all. The idea of living in a structured pack with all their rules and shit was not for this wolf. I was happy being a rogue, despite the reputation rogues had, and I was happy with the freedom that came with it.

"And this is Kieran, Jasper's Beta," Victor said with a flourish of his arm as he gestured to another man. I realised that I was still holding Jasper's hand and let go quickly as my face flushed with embarrassment. Jasper seemed to have a knowing smile. I tried to turn my attention to the other man that was with him. He was slightly smaller, but just as lean as the Alpha standing next to him. His black t-shirt showed that much of his skin was decorated with tattoos, even up his neck.

"Guilty as charged," Kieran said in a thick Irish accent, his grin infectious. It was easy to see that their relationship was more casual and friendly than the typical Alpha-Beta dynamic. "Jasper, Kieran, please, make yourselves comfortable," Victor chimed in, extending his arms in a sweeping gesture. And with that, he disappeared into his private quarters, leaving me to tend to our guests.

"Can I get you gentlemen anything?" I asked, trying to keep the professional facade intact despite the pounding in my chest.

"Whiskey for me, please," Jasper replied, his voice deep and velvety. "Neat."

"Same for me," Kieran added with a nod and a wink.

"Coming right up," I said, turning to fetch their drinks. I could feel Jasper's eyes following me as I busied myself with their drinks.

"Here you are," I said, handing Jasper and Kieran their glasses with a smile. As they took their first sips, Jasper turned to me, his eyes still holding that unnerving intensity.

"Erica, we're actually here looking for some old friends of ours. They've fallen off the radar, so to speak. A group of werewolves who've chosen to go rogue. You wouldn't happen to know anything about them, would you?" His question was casual, but I could sense the weight behind it.

"Can't say I do," I replied cautiously, my heart racing as I wondered how much he knew. "Rogues tend to keep to themselves, don't they?"

"True," Jasper agreed, swirling the whiskey in his glass. "But I've heard that these rogues live in a pack of their own making. Surely that would stand out to an intelligent girl such as yourself." I swallowed hard, feeling my palms grow clammy. It was clear he was talking about my people, but why? Was this some twisted Alpha mind game, or did he truly not know who I was? I was silently begging the goddess for some sort of distraction, when I heard the bell for the door go off. Thank you goddess, I thought, until I turned and saw who had walked in. I smiled an apology at the two men and turned to deal with my next customers. Just before I could walk away, Jasper reached out and grabbed my hand.

"If you hear anything," he said, his gaze not leaving mine, "Would you let me know?"

"Of course," I lied, knowing full well I'd keep my distance from him and his questions.

At that moment, Heidi Matthews, a werewolf from one of the local packs banged her fist on the bar at the other end. Her piercing blue eyes scanned the room with disdain before settling on me. Her long black hair cascading over her shoulders like a dark waterfall. " Erica," she sneered, her voice dripping with sarcasm. "Do you actually work here or does being a dirty rogue mean that we all have to slum it?"

"Nice to see you too, Heidi," I replied dryly, not in the mood for her games. "What brings you to Victor's humble abode?"

"None of your business," she snapped, tossing her hair over her shoulder as she turned to face the other werewolves who had come in with her. "Just get me a gin and tonic."

"Right away," I muttered, rolling my eyes when her back was turned. I was used to her vapidness and her disrespect, she was the worst of the group that had just walked in. There were seven or eight of them, mostly girls, but a few men as well. They were all from the Silver Stone pack which was about twenty miles south of the city. I watched as they found two tables close to each other and as one of the men looked over at the bar as if he was searching for something. Our eyes locked, and he nodded in my direction. I nodded back slightly but kept my expression clear of emotion. I glanced over to the two men sitting at the other end of the bar and saw that Jasper was watching me. He raised an eyebrow at me with clear amusement on his face. I felt heat in my face as I blushed again.

"Oh, my goddess!" Heidi exclaimed. "Am I going to actually get my drink or am I interrupting your plans to increase your notches to your slut bedpost?" She pouted and leaned forward on the bar.

"Victor, why do you still have that skanky rogue still working here?" I laughed to myself at her using the term skanky, being that her dress was so short I didn't think it could be called a dress, showing just how classy she was. Her breasts practically poured out of her dress as she continued to pout at Victor.

"Victor, please will you serve me tonight?" she pouted at him, "I wouldn't want to catch rabies off that dog that you insist on keeping around." I rolled my eyes again.

"Yeah, you serve her, Victor," I called over. "Just watch out for crabs, from what I hear."

"You bitch!" she screamed, and Victor sighed dramatically, although I could see the glint of amusement in his eyes.

"Erica," he pleaded. I shrugged and smiled. I couldn't help it. This bitch wolf had been on my back almost as long as I worked here, and it was grating on me. What made it so much worse was the main reason she had a vendetta against me was making his way up to the bar as we spoke.

My heart lifted slightly as I turned to see Damon Pierce sauntering towards me, his dark hair perfectly tousled and a playful grin on his lips. He was tall and well-built, with deep brown eyes that always seemed to be dancing with mischief. Despite being the beta heir of a local pack, Damon had never shown any interest in asserting his authority over me. A refreshing change from the majority of werewolves I'd encountered in my life.

"Hey," I said, managing a genuine smile. "What brings you here? And on a school night I believe." I winked with a flirty smile that I knew would piss Heidi off.

"Thought I'd drop by and surprise you." Damon playfully reached out and took my hand, very much aware of the glare from Heidi. "You know, keep things interesting."

"Interesting?" I raised an eyebrow at him. That was one way to describe the current situation. I glanced down the bar again at the Alpha, knowing full well he was still watching me. Damon's eyes followed my gaze, and I saw his face harden as he saw the two men at the end.

"What the fuck is he doing here?" he hissed, and I looked at him in shock. It was rare that I saw anything but happiness on Damon's face.

"You know him?" I asked, and Damon looked at me before looking back down the bar.

"Yeah I do," he said. "And I don't like him." I looked down the bar again and Jasper was observing the exchange between Damon and me with undisguised interest. He glanced at Damon and I heard a growl coming from Damon in response. Jasper looked more amused by Damon's reaction. I saw his beta Kieran lean over and whisper something in his ear. Jasper laughed at whatever it was and Damon growled again.

"Who is he?" I asked Damon, "Why is he getting under your skin so much?" It wasn't just Damon I was concerned about, this Alpha had just been asking about my family, if I could get information on him then I could take it back to Trenton.

"It's complicated," Damon said. He then looked at me with concern in his eyes. "I don't trust him, and neither should you."

"Are you jealous?" I asked, arching an eyebrow.

"Of course not," Damon blustered, his cheeks reddening. "I just care about you, and don't want to see you get hurt."

"Then trust me to make my own decisions," I replied, trying to convey both my gratitude for his concern and my determination to handle the situation on my own.

"Fine," he relented, but his expression remained tense.

Damon took a big sigh and shook his head. He reached over the bar and took me by the elbow. He pulled me down to the other side of the bar, as far away from the two werewolves as he could before he spoke.

"Can we talk?"

"Sure," I replied, feigning nonchalance.. "What's up?"

"Look, I know tonight's been a bit... intense," he admitted, rubbing the back of his neck. "But there's something I've been meaning to ask you."

"Shoot," I said, folding my arms across my chest and bracing myself for whatever bombshell he was about to drop.

"Not here," he said and glanced down the bar. "Will you meet me tomorrow night? It's your night off right? Can I take you out for dinner or something?"

"I don't know," I said, suddenly feeling uncomfortable. He flashed his award-winning boyish charm smile.

"I'm gonna be staying over at the apartment," he said, and I sighed. The apartment was owned by the Silver Stone pack and was used by the upper ranks in case they needed a bed in the city. Or if they needed to house a potentially dangerous guest.

"Damon," I said, "I'm not sure that it's the right time." I was reminded of the fact that once Trenton got back from his trip, we could be out of here and I wouldn't see those beautiful brown eyes again.

"Please Erica, I really want to see you," he pleaded, and I grimaced. I tried to think of an excuse, but already knew I wouldn't find one.

"Fine," I said. The smile I got was bright enough to make me smile.

"Great," he said happily. "We can talk properly tomorrow." I smiled in return, although I was starting to feel nervous. I didn't like the sound of this. Whatever he wanted to talk to me about, I had a feeling that I wasn't going to like it.

Chapter 3

Erica

I APPLIED THE LAST of my makeup in the mirror while Imogen sat on my bed watching me. I glanced over at her and frowned.

"Don't you have anything better to do?" I asked, and she grinned.

"Nope," she said, "So when will we get to meet this guy?" she asked, wiggling her eyebrows.

"Why would you meet him?" I asked, "I told you, it's nothing serious. And even less serious now that we will be moving pretty soon." Imogen pulled a face. She hated moving around more than the rest of us.

"Tell me about it, I just want to put down some good roots you know," she said with a sad look on her face. "I'm just hoping dad finds somewhere with a garden this time, my plants are dying in those stupid pots." Imogen was such a green thumb, she had been since we were young. Imogen filled the apartment with plants, each one cared for by her.

"I'll keep my fingers crossed," I said, and she smiled.

"So back to the Beta babe," she said, and I groaned, "do you think he will ask this time?" she asked and I pulled a face.

"I sure as hell hope not," I replied. Whilst I had been spending time with Damon over the last few months, I was very aware that he seemed to have changed somewhat. He seemed more demanding for my time and quick to defend me when that bitch friend of his started with her shit talk.

"He said he wanted to talk to me about something important," I said with a frown, and Imogen scrunched her face up.

"Yeah, that sounds like it won't be fun," then she perked up. "But what if he asked you and then you could put down some roots yourself?" I shook my head. I had a strong feeling that Damon wanted more than the arrangement we had, and he had alluded to me joining the Silver Stone pack before. I, of course, had no intention of doing that.

I hated packs and their structures, and wanted absolutely no part in them. Whilst we still considered ourselves the Moon Key pack, our pack was long since dead. You can be the biggest pack in the world, but if you don't have your own territory, then you were a rogue pack, and they were considered less than the omega rank in an established pack. The standard on rogues is that we were all loners, thieves, murderers, and traitors. It wasn't true. Some were, but some of us just didn't want to be ruled by one small group of people who seemed to inherit their rank and not earn it.

I sighed. I knew that the conversation was coming with Damon, and when he brought it up, well, then I would have to permanently end things with him. I was kinda just hoping that it would be after Trenton found us somewhere new. Or at least I was now. Telling Damon that I was leaving town would have been significantly better than outrightly turning him down. But in true sod's law fashion, he would want that conversation today. I was seconds away from cancelling on him, but I knew he would then attempt to come and see me at home, and I really couldn't have that happen.

I looked at Imogen and smiled weakly.

"Aw, don't worry about it," she said and jumped up and gave me a hug. "I mean, what's the worst that can happen, right?" I hugged her back, and I guessed she was right. I had been mentally preparing myself for this for weeks. And I'd be lying if I said I didn't care about Damon, but I had to keep myself at a distance. It was better for everyone.

It was an hour later, and I found myself standing in front of one of the more luxurious houses in the city. As the sleek black door swung open, my breath hitched in my throat. Damon stood there, his dark eyes danced with his usual hint of mischief. My heart raced as I hesitantly stepped inside, the chill of the city air, dissipating under the warmth of his gaze.

Damon closed the door behind me. The sound echoed through the luxury apartment, a symbol of isolation from the outside world. For now, we were alone, our secrets and desires locked away within these four walls.

As I walked further into the room, my senses were overwhelmed by the opulence surrounding us. Plush carpets cushioned my feet while modern art adorned the walls. A fire crackled in the corner, casting flickering shadows that danced with the night. Floor-to-ceiling windows offered a panoramic view of the city skyline, and the sleek furniture showcased modern design.

"Nice place," I muttered, trying to sound unimpressed, though I had to admit, it was stunning.

"Thank you," he replied, his tone light and playful. "I'm glad you agreed to meet me here." My heart hammered in my chest, betraying the calm façade I tried to maintain. I already knew why Damon wanted to meet me, and I knew I was going to have to disappoint him. I had been stupid to allow things to get to this point. But there was something about Damon that made me feel seen.

I sat down on the sofa while Damon headed into the kitchen. The first thing I noticed were the two wineglasses and the bottle of Sauvignon

Blanc chilling in an ice bucket on the coffee table. I arched my eyebrows at Damon as he walked into the room holding a plate of mini cheese pizzas.

"My favourite wine and my favourite snacks?" I asked, and he grinned.

"I like to think that I know you pretty well by now," he said with a wink. He placed the plate on the table and sat down next to me on the sofa.

"Look, Erica," Damon began, his tone serious and unwavering. "I want you to join my pack. I want you by my side, as my chosen mate." A bitter laugh escaped my lips as I stood up from the sofa and turned to face him, my green eyes narrowing.

"You can't be serious."

"Deadly serious," he replied, following me and stepping closer until our bodies were mere inches apart. "I've fallen in love with you, and I want to be with you."

"Love?" I scoffed, my mind reeling as I attempted to process his words. How could someone like him fall for a broken werewolf like me? It didn't make sense.

"Erica, please," he urged, his voice laced with desperation. "I just want you to be part of my life." I hesitated, torn between the burning desire to belong and the fierce need for independence that had become my armour.

"Damon, I can't just abandon who I am, what I've fought so hard to protect." He took a step closer, his dark eyes searching mine.

"You wouldn't be giving up your identity, Erica. You'd be embracing it, embracing us."

"Us?" I scoffed, my voice dripping with sarcasm. "You don't understand. Joining your pack would mean becoming an Omega, submitting to a hierarchy I never chose."

"Is it really about rank?" he questioned, his brow furrowing with concern. "Or is it about fear? Fear of letting go, fear of trusting someone again?" His words stung, but I refused to let him see how deeply they cut. Instead, I summoned my most defiant glare, meeting his gaze head-on.

"You think this is about fear?" I spat, bitterness coating my tongue. "My Gamma rank is all I have left from my parents, Damon. My past, my legacy... everything I am." A flicker of surprise flashed across his face before he schooled his expression once more.

"Your parents? Why didn't you tell me before?"

"Would it have changed anything?" I asked, my heart pounding in my chest.

"Erica, I..."

"Did you know?" I interrupted, my voice trembling with barely restrained anger. "Did you know I was a member of the Moon Key Pack?" The shock in his eyes was answer enough.

"I had no idea," he confessed, his voice barely audible. "Everyone thought you were all dead."

"Yet here I am," I replied bitterly, my throat tight with unshed tears. "A living ghost, clinging to the tattered remains of a life long gone." His hand reached out to cup my cheek, and for a moment, I allowed myself to lean into his touch, seeking solace in his warmth. But as the weight of the fear that lived inside me threatened to overwhelm me, I pulled away, refusing to let him see just how much I longed to surrender.

"Living in constant fear, Damon. That's been our reality," I said quietly, wrapping my arms around myself. "Hiding, running, never letting our guards down. It's like being hunted, even when we're not." His brow furrowed as he stepped closer to me, his dark eyes filled with concern and frustration.

"You don't have to live like that, Erica. Join our pack, let us protect you. We're stronger together."

"Stronger?" I scoffed, fighting back the urge to laugh bitterly. "You think being part of a pack will make me strong? It'll just make me dependent on you, on everyone else. That's not strength."

"Erica, it's not about dependence," he argued, his voice firm yet gentle. "It's about having a family who has your back, who supports you and helps you grow. Isn't that what you want?"

My heart clenched at his words, and for a moment, I allowed myself to imagine a life where I didn't have to hide or constantly watch over my shoulder. But that dream was nothing more than an illusion, something I couldn't afford to indulge in.

"Of course I want that," I admitted, staring into his eyes. "But I can't just abandon my family. They're all I have left. And they need me now more than ever."

"Your family can join too," he offered quickly, desperation creeping into his voice. I let out another bitter laugh.

"Really?" I asked. "You think you can convince your almighty Alpha to take in a bunch of rogues?" Damon looked conflicted for a moment but then fierce determination set in his eye.

"Yes," he nodded. "If that's what it takes, then I will make it happen." My heart hurt at his persistence, but I still shook my head.

"And our humans?" I asked, already knowing the answer. It was a strict pack law that humans were not allowed in packs unless they had some way to supernaturally protect themselves. Damon tried to hide the shock on his face but failed.

"Humans?" he asked.

"Yep," I nodded. "Four of them." I knew that there was no way, unless he was the Alpha himself, that he would be able to get four humans to be allowed in the pack.

"Maybe we could work something out. We could protect all of you. You wouldn't have to run anymore."

"Except we do, Damon," I said softly, rubbing my forehead as I tried to ward off the headache that threatened to consume me. "We think we've been discovered. We have to leave, find a new place to lie low. We would only be putting your pack in danger as well."

"Damn it, Erica!" he snapped, his anger finally boiling over. "Why are you so stubborn? Can't you see I'm trying to help you?"

"Help me?" I raised an eyebrow, my sarcasm returning full force. "Or help yourself by keeping me close?" His jaw clenched, and for a moment, I thought he'd argue further. But instead, he took a deep breath, his supernatural ability to calm himself evident in the way his anger dissipated as quickly as it had come.

"Fine," he said quietly, his voice strained. "If that's what you want, I won't try to stop you."

"Thank you," I whispered, feeling tears prick at the corners of my eyes. I knew how much it cost him to let me go, but I couldn't give up my family – not even for him. I sat back down suddenly feeling emotionally drained.

The silence between us was heavy, like a suffocating fog that crept its way into my heart. I clenched my fists, feeling the cool leather of the sofa beneath me, trying to ground myself in the moment. Finally, I felt Damon's eyes on me and seconds later he broke the silence.
"When do you leave?" he asked quietly.
"Next week, I think," I said.
"Next week?" he echoed, his shock evident in the way his eyes widened. "But that's... Are you sure there isn't another way?"
"Believe me, if there was, I'd take it," I whispered. "But I can't risk my family's safety. I won't."

"Erica..." His voice was barely a whisper, filled with pain and longing. And as our eyes met, locked in an unspoken understanding, I knew that this was a decision we'd both have to live with, no matter how much it hurt. And I knew that I had to get out of this place before the pain suffocated me.
"Goodbye, Damon," I said, turning away from him for the last time, my heart heavy with the words.
"Erica, please," Damon's voice cracked with emotion as he grasped for my hand. "Don't go. We can figure something out. Just give me a chance."
"Stop," I whispered, even as I felt the familiar heat of desire stirring within me. "We both know I can't."
"Alright," he relented, his voice barely audible. "But if you're going to leave me, at least give me tonight."
"Tonight?" I asked, my voice breathless.
"Let me show you how much you mean to me," he murmured, his hand reaching up to cup my face. "So that no matter where you go or what happens between us, you'll always carry a piece of me with you."
"Dammit, Damon," I whispered, my heart breaking even as I felt myself giving in to the urge to be close to him one last time. "Why do you have to make this so bloody difficult?"

"Because I love you, Erica," he said simply, his eyes never leaving mine. "And I refuse to let you go without a fight."

"Fine," I agreed, my voice shaking as I leaned in to capture his lips in a fierce, passionate kiss. "You can have tonight. But tomorrow, I'm gone." As his strong arms wrapped around me and pulled me against him, I lost myself in the heat of his embrace, knowing that every moment we spent together just made leaving that much harder.

Chapter 4

Erica

I awoke to the gentle warmth of sunlight filtering through the floor-to-ceiling windows, painting the room in hues of gold. Snuggled securely in Damon's arms, I couldn't help but feel comfortable and safe for just a moment. His steady heartbeat and the rise and fall of his chest lulled me into a sense of contentment that I hadn't felt in ages. My thoughts drifted to the passion that had engulfed us both last night. The way Damon's hands had explored every inch of my body, his touch igniting a fire within me that I hadn't known existed. His lips traced a path along my collarbone, while his fingers danced over my most sensitive spots, sending shivers down my spine and causing me to gasp in pleasure.

"Erica," he'd whispered into my ear, his breath hot against my skin. "You're so beautiful." As he entered me, our bodies moving together in perfect harmony, and we lost ourselves in each other time and time again, the intensity of our connection growing stronger with every thrust, every moan, every whispered word of encouragement. And when we finally collapsed together around 5am, our limbs tangled and our hearts racing, I felt sated and happy. But as quickly as it came, the guilt washed over me like ice water. My family was out there, facing the dangers of being hunted, while I selfishly allowed myself to seek solace in the arms of a man who I would probably never see after today.

"Last night..." I murmured, more to myself than to him, thinking back on our conversation.

"Erica?" Damon stirred beside me, his dark eyes still glazed with sleep. "You okay?"

"Sort of," I replied, forcing a smile onto my lips. "I was just thinking about our talk last night." He shifted, propping himself up on one elbow to meet my gaze.

"You said you'd be leaving soon?"

"Right." I nodded, biting my lip as I worried that I might have revealed too much information. My voice wavered as I added, "I shouldn't have told you that." He offered me a reassuring smile, one that seemed to say he understood my vulnerability. But at the same time, those dark eyes of his held a flicker of concern.

"Hey," he said softly, cupping my face with his warm hand. "It's okay. You can trust me, Erica."

"Can I?" The question slipped out before I could stop it, mingling with the air between us as a mix of hope and doubt. My heart raced in my chest, fearful of the consequences of putting my faith in someone else, in anyone that wasn't my pack.

"Erica." Damon's voice was firm, his eyes never leaving mine as he spoke with quiet conviction. "I would never do anything to hurt you or your family. You have my word." His sincerity touched me deeply, but the fear and suspicion that had been ingrained in me for so long refused to dissipate entirely. I wanted to believe him. God, how I wanted to trust him, but the stakes were too high. I couldn't afford to let my guard down. Not now. Not with everything on the line.

"Thank you," I whispered, the words tasting bittersweet on my tongue. "But I still need to go. My family... they're probably worried sick."

"Stay for just a little longer?" His request was gentle, more of a plea than a demand. It was one that tugged at my heartstrings, threatening to unravel the tightly wound knot of self-preservation that I had been clinging to for so long.

"Dammit, Damon..." The words escaped me like a sigh, equal parts frustration and longing. I knew that I should leave, that every moment spent here was a risk, but the temptation to give in to the desire that danced between us was almost too much to bear.

"Please," he murmured, pressing his lips softly against mine, stealing what little resolve I had left. As we kissed, I felt the last vestiges of my resistance slip away, carried off by the tide of passion that surged within me. And for a single, fleeting moment, I allowed myself to be swept away by it, lost in the depths of his embrace while the world outside faded into oblivion.

The insistent buzzing of my mobile phone on the nightstand yanked me from my passion, and I was once again flooded with guilt. How could I have let myself get so carried away, knowing that my family was in danger? They needed me, and yet here I was, wrapped up in Damon's arms like some lovesick fool.

"Shit," I muttered under my breath, the weight of my actions crashing down upon me like a tidal wave. Reaching for my phone, I saw a string of missed calls and texts from my Becca and Marshall, their words laced with worry and fear. "Erica, where are you?" one text read, while another simply said, "Please answer, it's important."

"Are you okay?" Damon asked, his voice thick with lust. I could feel his concern, even through the haze of guilt that clouded my mind.

"Y-yeah," I stammered, not quite meeting his gaze. "I just... I need to go."

"Go?" he repeated, blinking in confusion as his expression dropped into concern. "But we were just-"

"I know," I interrupted, my voice barely more than a whisper. "But my family..." I trailed off, unable to even try to explain.

My phone buzzed again, and I sighed. As I tried to slip out of bed, Damon's arm tightened around me, pulling me back into his warm embrace. He nuzzled my neck, his breath tickling my skin as he spoke with a teasing lilt in his voice.

"Where do you think you're going, darling? Trying to escape me before I've had my fill?" I couldn't help but laugh at his playful tone, despite the heavy guilt that weighed on my chest.

"Damon," I protested, squirming in his grasp, "I really need to get home." He sighed but didn't loosen his hold on me. Instead, he began to press soft kisses along my throat, causing shivers to race down my spine. The sensation was both electrifying and maddening, reminding me of the passion we had shared just hours earlier.

"Come on, Damon. Stop it," I urged him, trying to sound stern even as my heart raced in response to his touch. "My family needs me." At the mention of my family, he paused mid-kiss and pulled away, studying my face. Despite my protests, I couldn't help but notice the disappointment clouding Damon's eyes.

"I'm sorry," I murmured, the words barely audible as they escaped my lips. "I never meant for any of this to happen. I shouldn't have stayed."

"I'm glad you stayed," he whispered, and I reached and cupped his face with my hand.

"So am I," I said, "Or at least part of me is." I leaned in for a kiss and he willingly complied. As I moved away, a mischievous glint flickered in his gaze. Before I could say anything further, he silenced me with another searing kiss, his hands sliding up my sides as he twisted around to loom over me. Trapped beneath him, I felt powerless to resist, and part of me didn't want to.

"Erica," he whispered against my skin, his breath hot on my neck as he trailed kisses downward. My heart pounded in tandem with each press of his lips, my body betraying me as it responded to his touch. I tried to focus on my family, on the urgency that had woken me in the first place, but the sensations Damon elicited were all-consuming. When he reached my breasts, I gasped, unable to suppress the shudder that coursed through me as he nipped at my sensitive flesh with his teeth. It was maddening, intoxicating, and utterly irresistible – and I hated myself for it.

"Dammit, Damon," I groaned, torn between wanting to push him away and urging him closer. "This isn't fair."

"Life rarely is," he murmured against my skin, his voice laced with a blend of amusement and desire that only served to fan the flames within me. As he continued his torturous actions, the line between right and wrong blurred, the guilt and responsibility that had driven me from his embrace fading beneath the onslaught of need that threatened to overwhelm me. I knew I should be fighting, that I couldn't afford to indulge in this momentary pleasure, but the mounting desire was impossible to ignore.

"Please," I whimpered, as much a plea for him to stop as it was an encouragement for him to continue. My body quivered beneath his touch, and I could feel my resolve crumbling with each passing second.

"Tell me what you want, Erica," he urged, his voice husky with lust as his teeth grazed my nipple, sending a jolt of pleasure straight to my core.

"Goddess, I don't know," I admitted, the words barely more than a breathless sigh. "All I know is that I can't think straight when you're touching me like this."

"Then don't think," he whispered, capturing my lips in another searing kiss as his hand slid down my stomach, igniting a trail of fire in its wake. "Just feel."

"Damon, I really need to..." My words faltered as he trailed his fingers along my side, his touch eliciting goosebumps across my heated skin. The protest died in my throat when his hand dipped between the curve of my thighs, sending shivers down my spine.

"Stay with me, just a little longer," he whispered seductively against my ear, his breath hot and tantalising. My heart raced in my chest, torn between the desire pulsing through me and the gnawing guilt that urged me to leave.

"Fine...a little longer," I conceded, my voice barely audible amidst the haze of passion that clouded my thoughts. A triumphant smile spread across Damon's face as he pressed his body closer to mine, the feel of him electrifying every nerve ending.

"Good girl," he murmured, his lips tracing the contours of my jawline before capturing mine in a searing kiss. His tongue danced along my lower lip, coaxing it open, before delving deeper into the recesses of my mouth. Our tongues entwined, the taste of him igniting a fire within me that threatened to consume us both.

With practised ease, Damon shifted his weight, settling between my thighs. The sensation of his rock-hard cock pressing against my slick folds sent jolts of pleasure radiating through my core. As our bodies brushed together, the friction had me arching against him, desperate for more.

"God, Erica, you drive me wild," he groaned, his dark eyes filled with lust and desire. The way he said my name, full of raw need, sent my mind reeling, and all coherent thought fled from my brain.

"Please, Damon," I begged, my hands gripping his shoulders tightly, nails digging into his flesh. "I need you."

"Anything for you, darling," he vowed, his voice thick with carnal intent. And with that, he began to tease my entrance with the head of his cock, causing me to gasp at the delicious contact. My body trembled in anticipation, and every inch of me yearned for him to fill me completely.

"Say it again," he commanded, his eyes locked onto mine as he continued to stroke himself against my throbbing core.

"Please... Damon... I need you inside me." With a growl, Damon plunged forward, burying himself deep within me. The sudden fullness had me seeing stars, and I couldn't help but cry out at the exquisite sensation. He paused for a moment, allowing me to adjust to his size before starting a slow, deliberate rhythm.

Our bodies moved together like a well-choreographed dance, each thrust driving me closer to the edge of oblivion.

"God, you feel incredible," Damon panted, beads of sweat forming on his brow as he drove into me with increasing force. As much as I wanted to respond, to tell him how amazing he felt too, my voice had abandoned me, replaced by a chorus of moans and whimpers that served as testament to the pleasure coursing through my veins. And as we lost ourselves in each other's embrace, the world outside our little cocoon ceased to exist, leaving only lust, desire, and the sweet taste of surrender.

I was nearing the edge when I was pulled from my climax by the sound of a door closing. Both Damon and I froze in place as we heard footsteps.

"Hey Damon? Sorry to interrupt, but this is important," I heard, and I saw a look of concern cross Damon's face.

"Who-" I began to ask, but the door burst open and I gasped as the scent of gingerbread and open fire invaded my senses.

"I hope all are decent in h-" The deep, jovial rumble was cut mid sentence as the feeling that I could only describe as everything clicking into place and becoming complete flood through my body.

"Oh my goddess," I whispered as I knew in that instant that the fated mate bond had snapped into place. I looked up at Damon, my eyes widening in shock. I saw his own eyes widen as he realised what had just happened. A growl sounded to our side and a single word was uttered.

"MINE."

Damon barely mouthed the words, "Oh fuck," before he disappeared in a blur from above me and went crashing into the wall.

Chapter 5

Liam

The city scenery blurred as I drove faster than I should have, my jaw clenched in frustration. God, I hated this place. The noise, the filth, and the chaos of it all was suffocating. But I had no choice but to come here. After the look on my father's face when he and Gregg arrived home this morning. They left quickly yesterday afternoon after my father had received a phone call. I tried to ask what was happening but my father said he would explain when he got back. All I knew was that a friend of theirs needed help.

I had been sitting at breakfast with my mum and sister when they had returned. My mum felt the distress and upset as soon as he entered the pack gates. It was less than half an hour before my mum mind linked me to come down to the Alpha office. To say I was shocked when I entered the office was an understatement. The place was a mess. My fathers large mahogany desk was smashed against one wall and books and papers were everywhere. My father was sitting in his leather desk chair nursing what looked like a large glass of whisky in his hand, his posture and expression screaming defeat. Gregg was standing next to him with his hand on my father's shoulder. He had a gift of calming down my father, and it looked like it was working overtime right now. It was a gift that his son Damon, my best friend and future Beta shared and it came in handy more than once, especially when I lost my temper.

My father had quickly explained that an old friend of his had been in trouble. They had gone to help him but had got there too late and the people after him had caught up to him and killed him. My father said that they needed to find the rest of his friend's pack as a matter of urgency but all he knew was that they were in the area. He told me to get Damon and it would be all hands on deck to find these people and bring them to safety. I hadn't asked any more questions. I had jumped in my car and left for the city straight away.

As I drove deeper into the city, my mind couldn't help but drift back to the conversations Damon and I had shared about the woman he was seeing. It wasn't like him to get so wrapped up in someone; he was usually all about casual flings and one-night stands. But this woman, she seemed different.

"Liam! You've got to meet her, man," Damon had gushed to me one evening at our pack's training grounds. His eyes were lit up with excitement as he spoke, a rare sight for someone who usually kept his emotions in check. "She's bloody amazing."

"Really?" I asked, raising an eyebrow. "What makes her so special?"

"Everything!" He exclaimed, throwing his hands in the air. "She's smart, funny, and gorgeous."

"Sounds promising," I conceded, genuinely curious about this mystery woman who'd captured my best friend's heart.

"Promise, man." Damon grinned, taking a swig from his water bottle. "I'm actually thinking about petitioning for her to join the pack."

"Wow, that serious, huh?" I couldn't help but feel impressed. This was uncharted territory for him.

"Yeah," he admitted, rubbing the back of his neck sheepishly. "I even, uh... I think I might love her, Liam." Hearing those words from Damon's mouth sent a shock through my system. Love? That was a powerful emotion, especially for a werewolf. We didn't throw that word around lightly. As the Alpha heir, I knew the significance of such a commitment.

"Love, huh?" I mused, clapping him on the shoulder. "Well, if she's that important to you, then I trust your judgment. Just be careful, alright? Things are complicated right now."

"Trust me, I know," he replied with a grimace. It was hard knowing that bringing someone into the pack could give them a death sentence, but time was already running out and my father believed that more pack members would actually help us deal with this cloud that we have been living with my whole life.

As I snapped back to the present, my grip on the steering wheel tightened. I had to get him away from his new lover and back home. With a determined sigh, I pressed down harder on the gas pedal, my mind racing alongside the speeding car. I just hoped that whatever awaited us back at the pack wouldn't shatter the fragile happiness my best friend had finally found.

As I pulled up to the safe house, my thoughts were a storm of concern and frustration. I didn't want to interrupt Damon's date; he deserved this happiness after everything we had all been through. Exiting the vehicle, I strode towards the private elevator, my heart pounding in my chest. My wolf, Musk, stirred within me, restless and eager all of a sudden. Its excitement was contagious, and despite my reluctance to disturb Damon and his date, I couldn't help but feel a spark of anticipation. The more steps I took toward the elevator, the stronger that connection became. I tried to suppress it, knowing full well that letting the beast loose in a moment like this could lead to disaster.

"What is wrong with you?," I said to him in my head, feeling my pulse race as the elevator doors slid open. "You are being weird." Musk just replied with a grunt and carried on his restless pacing. The elevator doors opened once more, revealing the sleek, modern hallway of the safe house. I strode forward, my footsteps echoing against the polished floor as my wolf's restlessness continued to grow. There was something in the air, a tension that set my nerves on edge and made it difficult to focus. I couldn't shake the feeling that something monumental was about to happen.

I entered the access code on the keypad, my fingers trembling slightly. As soon as the door clicked open, I was assaulted by the most intoxicating scent I'd ever encountered. It was like a burst of citrus, sweet and tangy, and it seemed to wrap around me, urging me towards the closed bedroom door. My wolf's excitement grew exponentially, its desire to track down the source nearly overwhelming.

"Easy, boy," I murmured under my breath, trying to keep him in check. I forced myself to take in the rest of the apartment first, hoping to regain some semblance of control. Clothes were strewn haphazardly across the floor, a trail of discarded garments leading from the front door to the bedroom. An uneaten pizza sat abandoned on the coffee table, flanked by an unopened bottle of wine. It was clear that whatever had transpired between Damon and this woman tonight, it had taken priority over everything else. I couldn't help but grin at what fun he must be having. It had been a while since I had let loose. I still had my fair share of fun but I was more cautious about it after what happened with Jessica.

"Hey Damon, Sorry to interrupt. But this is important," I shouted as I approached the closed bedroom door, my heart pounding in my chest. Even without my werewolf hearing, the sounds of pleasure emanating from behind the door were unmistakable.

"Sorry dude," I muttered under my breath, feeling a pang of guilt for barging in on my best friend's intimate moment. But there was no time for hesitation. Whatever had happened during my father's trip, it needed immediate attention.

With a deep breath, I pushed open the door and bellowed, "I hope all are decent in h-" My words caught in my throat as the intoxicating citrus scent hit me full force, sending an overwhelming wave of completion through my entire being. My pulse raced and every nerve in my body seemed to awaken, as if charged with electricity. It felt like I'd been existing in a world devoid of colour, and suddenly everything around me was vibrant and alive. The heady sensation left me momentarily disoriented, the world narrowing down to that potent aroma and its source.

"Fuck, what is happening?" I muttered to myself, trying to make sense of the sudden onslaught of emotions coursing through me. This wasn't just some ordinary attraction; this was something deeper, more primal. And as much as I didn't want to get my hopes up, a small voice in the back of my mind whispered that it could only be one thing, my fated mate.

My eyes focused on the source of my salvation and the first thing I saw was the bright red hair. Then the scene in front of me cleared and fogged up at the same time. Internally I knew what I was seeing. My best friend, and the woman he told me he loved. But the possessive side of me came to the front and all that mattered was that someone else was touching my mate. The red anger clouded my eyes and I let out a growl.

"MINE," I growled. I focused on my target and threw myself at the man who dared to try to take what was mine.

I hit his body with the force of mine and we both went crashing into the opposite wall. Before we had even landed, I had my hand fisted and began to punch the person who threatened my happiness. I was vaguely aware of him trying to defend himself, and I could hear screaming, but it was all lost in the anger I was consumed by. Then I felt someone grab my arm and electricity ran from their touch through my whole body. I whirled on the offending party and came face to face with a pair of vivid green eyes that shined with anger themselves. Then everything else came into focus as the citrus scent invaded me again. I started to feel the rage rush away as I focused on my beautiful fated mate. From the way her long red hair fell against the soft white skin of her naked flesh. A growl left my mouth again as another red rage flooded into me. Even as I was aware of my mate shouting at me, I was only really focused on her beautiful body and the mass of lust that was coursing through my veins.

"Mine," I growled again and saw her eyes widen seconds before I lunged at her.

Chapter 6

Erica

Tingles raced through my body, making my skin prickle with an electric heat I'd never known before. My heart thudded against my ribcage, as if trying to escape its confines. The world around me faded into nothingness, leaving behind only the sensation of this powerful, inexplicable connection.

"Wh-what is this?" I whispered, breathless, unable to tear my gaze away from the man across the room. From what I could see he was tall, broad-shouldered, and radiated an aura of raw power. And he was undeniably, impossibly beautiful. My fated mate. This couldn't be right. I wasn't supposed to have a fated mate, not when I couldn't even shift. It had always been my greatest shame, being a werewolf who couldn't become a wolf. Yet there was no denying the magnetic pull that drew me towards this stranger. But the bubble shattered as I saw the stranger's fist connect with Damon's face. Rage surged through me, fierce and fiery, as I watched Damon crumpled on the floor, barely even defending himself.

"Stop it!" I screamed, launching myself at the attacker. "How dare you attack someone like that, and a Beta as well!" My hands balled into fists, ready to fight for Damon's safety. I grabbed the man's large arm just as he was about to punch Damon again. The man snarled and instantly whirled to face me. His eyes were stormy, filled with fury. But then something shifted within them, and I felt the power of our fated mate bond surging between us. It was an overwhelming force that neither of us could resist, and suddenly, the anger in his eyes melted away, replaced by a hunger I'd never seen before. My heart hammered against my chest, betraying me. I couldn't deny the connection between us, no matter how much I wanted to.

The man looked me up and down, and looked like he was taking in every detail. I glanced at Damon, who was just lowering his arms. I could see his face was already bruised down one side and there was blood from somewhere, not that I could tell where. He was holding himself like his left side was injured.

"Who the fuck do you think you are?" I shouted at the guy angrily and he stood up. I pushed him, or tried to as my hands hit solid mass and he barely looked like a fly had buzzed by him. He was watching me with an almost amused look and it just made me more angry, so I shoved at him again.

"You can't come storming into someone's room and start pounding on them! What were you, born in a cave?" His mouth twitched into what looked like it was threatening to be a grin.

"Oh, you think this is funny, do you?" I had just met my fated mate, but I was so angry that I clenched my fist and punched him in that smirking, perfect jaw of his.

Or I tried, at least. His reflexes kicked in and he grabbed my wrist before I could make contact. He glared at me as I struggled to pull my arm back.

"Liam," Damon gasped from the floor, wincing in pain. As soon as I heard the name, my eyes widened. Liam? Damon's best friend, future Alpha of the Silver Stone pack, one of the largest packs in Europe. An Alpha. I hated Alphas. I backed away. He looked back at me as I did and he looked me up and down again. His eyes flashed the light gold of the Alpha rank and I realised I was naked. He ran his tongue over his lips briefly and my eyes were drawn to the action, focusing on them as my mind flooded with images of kissing them, biting them, feeling them all over my body. My heart hammered in my chest as I stared at him, the Alpha heir, my fated mate. The room seemed to close in on me, and my nakedness suddenly felt like a glaring vulnerability. Panic surged through me, and I instinctively tried to back away from him.

"Mine," he growled once more, his voice dark and possessive. He lunged towards me in an instant, his strong arms wrapping around me before I could even react. My scream was muffled by his lips pressed against mine, forceful and demanding, leaving no room for resistance. The moment our lips met, something within me clicked into place, and I was powerless against it. Lust flooded my body, making me ache for him, my traitorous desire betraying my own convictions. It was as if bolts of electricity coursed through my veins, igniting a fire deep inside of me, a fire that only he could quench.

"Please," I whispered between heated kisses, my voice barely audible even to myself. It wasn't a plea for him to stop, but rather an unspoken acknowledgement of the undeniable connection between us. He responded with a low, throaty growl, his hands roaming over my body with teasing caresses that left me trembling. There was a primal hunger in his eyes, one that both terrified and excited me in equal measure.

"Perfect," he murmured against my skin, his breath hot on my neck as he nipped and kissed his way along my collarbone. The bond between us was all-consuming, its magnetic pull overriding any sense of self-preservation I may have had.

In one swift motion, Liam backed me up against the wall, lifting me off the floor with ease. As if drawn by a force beyond my control, I wrapped my legs tightly around his waist and clung to him, our lips locked in a passionate dance that left me breathless.

"Goddess, you're perfect," he whispered, his voice ragged as his hands explored every inch of my body. My heart pounded wildly in my chest, the line between pleasure and pain blurred beyond recognition. As my world narrowed down to the intoxicating sensation of his touch, I couldn't help but wonder what this meant for us, for our future. I was meant to be leaving next week. But in that moment, lost in the dizzying whirlwind of desire, fear, and longing, it didn't matter. All that mattered was the unbreakable bond between us, a bond that had been forged by fate and sealed with a single, desperate kiss.

A sudden flash of memory pierced through the haze of lust and desire, jolting me back to reality. My mind was flooded with images of Alphas from my past. The one who had tried to kidnap me and killed my parents when I was only five years old; the one who had manipulated me into joining his pack at eighteen; the night in the alleyway with that dangerous Alpha just a few years ago. But the memory that hit me the hardest, extinguishing the flames of passion that had been consuming me, was of Christian, the Alpha heir who had died protecting me. Suddenly all I could see in my mind was his cold dead eyes staring at me accusing me. The weight of that loss pressed down on me, heavy and suffocating, as Liam's hands continued their exploration of my body.

"Stop!" I choked out, shoving against Liam's chest with all my strength. The force of my push caught him off guard, and we both toppled to the floor. As he tried to regain his balance, I scrambled away from him, still naked and trembling.

"I can't do this, I have to go."

"Wait, what's happened?" He reached for me, concern etched across his handsome face. I flinched away from his hand and tried to back up further. His face changed to panic, and he shook his head.

"No, you can't leave," he growled as he grabbed my legs and pulled me across the floor back to him. "You are my mate." My chest heaved with panic as I tried to shove Liam away from me, desperate for any chance of escape. He grabbed my wrists in an iron grip, halting my efforts and pinning me to the floor.

"Get off me, you bloody bastard!" I screamed, my voice raw with fear and rage. "Baby, calm down," he growled, his eyes darkening.

"Stop!" I could feel his Alpha command try to invade my senses, but I pushed back against them and growled back at him. His eyes widened, and the arrogant bastard's expression shifted into a sudden, triumphant grin.

"Oh baby," he whistled, "Damn!" I glared at him and growled again. I could feel every muscle in my body taught, ready to jump into action. My survival senses were activated and struggled against his hold.

"Damon, get over here now," he called, the Alpha tone still clear in his voice. I saw Damon appear cautiously in my field of vision. He was battered and bruised and blood was running down his face. I could tell that it hurt to move. He was watching the Alpha carefully, but then he glanced down at me and his eyes widened.

"What the fuck!" he exclaimed, and the Alpha grinned.

"Yeah," he said proudly, like he had some shiny new toy. "Do your thing, but just her arm, nowhere else."

"But it only works on... oh!" he said and looked back down at me again. He reached out towards me and both me and Liam growled. Damon threw Liam a concerned look.

"Sorry," Liam said, and Damon shook his head. His hand touched my arm, and I growled again. Then I felt something. Like a cool sensation flowing into me, my eyes widened as I tried to struggle away.

"It's okay baby," Liam whispered. I could feel my whole body relax as the cooling whatever it was seemed to put out my anger, and I felt more calm. Damon took his hand away and then stepped back out of view and Liam slowly removed his hold on me.

"What the fuck was that?" I exclaimed, sitting up, and Damon chuckled and then winced and held his side. Liam watched me carefully.

"You alright?" he asked, and I scowled at him.

"No, I'm not alright," I snapped. "I'm naked on the goddamn floor and I need to get home to my family."

"Sorry baby," he said, shaking his head, "I can't let you leave."

"Liam," Damon said with a warning tone, "Let her go for now." Liam glared at Damon and growled.

"But I can let you get dressed," he said, turning back to me.

"Well, thank you," I replied sarcastically, "And stop calling me baby." Liam raised an eyebrow at me, clearly amused. I wanted to punch the smug look off his face but instead I hurried through the hallway and into the bathroom. Grabbing my clothes, I quickly pulled them on, every movement laced with urgency. I needed to get out of here as quickly as possible. I had seen my phone light up again as another call had come in. Something must be wrong for them to call me this much.

Taking a deep breath, I stepped back into the hallway to face them. Liam's predatory smile greeted me, while Damon leaned against the wall, wincing in pain from his injuries. My heart twisted at the sight of him, but my determination to escape remained steadfast.

"Baby, erm I mean Erica," Liam murmured, reaching out for me. He pulled me into his arms, and against my better judgement, I let him. The fated mate bond stirred within me, urging me to give in to the longing that threatened to consume me.

"Please," I whispered, pretending to submit, even as my mind raced with possible escape routes. "I need to go home."

"Stay," Liam insisted, locking his eyes on mine, the intensity of his gaze sending shivers down my spine. I knew what he wanted, for me to surrender myself to him completely, body and soul. But I couldn't do it. Not yet, not when there were so many unanswered questions.

"Okay," I murmured, feigning acquiescence, "but first..." I brought my knee up into his crotch with all the force I could muster, causing him to double over in pain. His grip on me loosened, and I seized my chance, wrenching myself free from his embrace. He yelped in pain and I pushed him over while he was clutching his jewels and glanced at Damon. He was laughing so hard that tears streamed down his face. He saw me look and raised his hands in surrender. Good, he knew what was good for him and would not stop me.

My legs carried me back home, driven by an urgency that clawed at my insides. As I burst through the front door, my lungs burned with exertion, but the sight that awaited me made me forget about the pain. Becca sat on the couch, her face streaked with tears, while Marshall stood beside her, his expression a mix of relief and grief. My heart clenched at the sight, dread settling heavy in my stomach.

"Erica..." Becca choked out, her voice raw with emotion. "Goddess I'm glad you're safe. I was worried about you, but... but..."

"Becca," I whispered, reaching out to comfort her as she dissolved into sobs once more. My gut told me that something terrible had happened, and I braced myself for the blow.

"Erica," Marshall said quietly, stepping forward. "It's Trenton. He's... he's gone."

"Wh-what do you mean?" I stammered, praying it wasn't true.

"Car accident," he replied, his voice barely audible. "They found him this morning." My knees buckled under the weight of the news, my world collapsing around me. The man who had been like a father to me, who had always protected me and my family, was gone.

Chapter 7

Liam

My heart hammered in my chest as I searched the darkening, damp streets for any sign of my mate. My breaths came out in ragged puffs, and my frustration mounted with each passing second. She was out there somewhere, and it was my responsibility to find her.

"Erica!" I shouted once more, my voice echoing off the brick walls around me. "Please, just come back!" But there was no response, save for the distant howl of sirens and the steady patter of the rain. I gritted my teeth, my wolf's possessiveness clawing at my mind like a ravenous beast. The scent of her tantalising skin still lingered on my hands, and it took all my restraint not to shift and hunt her down. I slammed my fist against the brick wall, cursing under my breath. The pain that shot through my arm did nothing to dull the anguish in my heart. I glanced up and down the street again desperately, but there was no sign of her. Should I keep looking? But I had no idea which direction she had gone in.

With a growl of defeat, I made my way back to the apartment, my boots squelching in puddles as I went. When I stepped inside, the sight that greeted me was one of pain and despair. Damon sat hunched on the sofa, his face twisted with pain from the injuries I'd inflicted on him in my blind rage. Now that I wasn't under the fog of a possessive jerk, I felt bad.

"Shit, man," I muttered, taking in the bruises and bloodied cuts that marred his usually handsome face. "I'm really sorry about what happened earlier." Damon forced a weak smile, but his dark eyes held an unmistakable hurt.

"It's fine," he said, although I could tell from his tone that it wasn't.

I reached out to help Damon up from the sofa, but the image of him entwined with my mate in bed assaulted my thoughts. An involuntary growl escaped my lips, causing Damon's face to pale even further.

"Whoa!" Damon said, pulling his hand back. He glared at me, and I closed my eyes and took a deep breath. It wasn't helping. I was on edge. Not only seeing them together infuriated me. But now my mate was running around the goddess damn city unprotected.

"Sorry," I mumbled, shaking my head to dispel the unwanted image.

"Listen Liam, I didn't know. You know that…" He trailed off as I growled at him. He needed to drop the subject until I could think clearly. He might be my best friend, but I still couldn't get that image of them together out of my head, and I wouldn't hesitate to rip him apart right now. He pulled himself to his feet and then backed away, his hands in the air.

"Jus put some fucking clothes on," I growled at him, my alpha tone accidentally coming through. He nodded and grabbed some jeans from the floor, wincing in pain, before limping into the bathroom.

"And hurry, because we need to get back home," I called through the door.

"Yes, Alpha," I heard through the door. That hurt for a moment. I had never pulled rank on him, but I guess I had just kicked the shit out of him.

I waited impatiently for Damon to return from the bathroom. He finally did, and although the black shirt and jeans covered the majority of the body wounds, it was obvious by the way he walked and the display of purple bruises decorating his face, exactly how far I actually went. With a deep breath, I decided to address the more pressing matter at hand.

"We need to find my mate and bring her back to the pack. And soon because my father needs us both."

"Sure, just one thing, well, two actually," he said, and I raised my eyebrows, waiting for him to continue.

"First off, how do you plan to find her? And should you find her, I highly doubt she will come back willingly."

"What do you mean, how am I going to find her? You know her address, right?" I asked, and he shook his head.

"Nope, she never told me," he said. Dammit! What the hell was I going to do? I gritted my teeth, frustration boiling within me. The thought of Erica out there alone, possibly in danger, sent a sharp pain through my chest. My wolf paced restlessly inside me as I fought to suppress the urge to go charging back into the streets in search of her.

"Damn it," I muttered under my breath, running a hand through my hair. "Then we're back to square one."

A faint buzzing sound caught my attention. I followed the noise, stepping into the bedroom where Erica's scent still lingered, intoxicating and electric. On the nightstand, a phone vibrated with an incoming call, the screen displaying someone called Marshall. Who was Marshall? Was he another boyfriend? I growled at the thought of yet another man's hand on my mate.

"Got something?" Damon called from the doorway, snapping me out of the endless possessive urges that were cycling through my brain. I looked down to see the call had ended and there was a picture of my mate with some blond girl on the screen. I held the mobile up so Damon could see it.

"Erica's phone," I replied, pocketing the device. "Maybe Kaitlyn can dig up some information on her whereabouts." My sister Kaitlyn was barely eighteen but there wasn't much she didn't know about computers. If anyone could get into the phone, then she could.

"Let's hope so," Damon murmured, and we made our way out of the apartment, our footsteps heavy with the weight of our mutual frustration and concern.

The drive back to Silver Stone pack territory was spent in uncomfortable silence, the air thick with tension as we navigated through the winding roads of the English countryside. The lush green fields rolled by like waves, broken only by the occasional stand of trees or stone walls that marked property boundaries. It was a stark contrast to the city we had just left behind, but it was a landscape that spoke to the wildness within us, the part of us that longed to run free under the moonlit sky. As we continued our journey, I couldn't help but let my mind wander to Erica. What was she doing right now? Was she safe? My wolf growled deep inside me, a constant reminder of my responsibility to protect my fated mate.

Finally, we reached the pack grounds, and we waited in silence as security opened the gates and then I drove down the long drive into the territory. We were lucky to have such a big pack territory. There were even some commercial businesses here. Most packs had to attach to a town of sorts so that they could get daily supplies, but we were one of the few packs that were self-sufficient. I turned at the waterfall and headed towards the pack house. The pack house and the two boarding houses were separated from the rest of the territory by a river that ran through our land. A lot of the pack activity happened there, but the family homes and the commercial side were in the main part of the territory or the next valley. And we were lucky that our whole ground was nestled within a couple of valleys, making it a lot easier to protect our borders.

I crossed the river at the main bridge and turned past the main park and up to the pack house. The two boarding houses were for single pack members, one for civilian members, and one for the pack warriors. There was a third boarding house off territory, which was for when we held special events like the mating balls. My father encouraged socialisation, and we had our fair share of events, mostly with the intent of me finding my mate in time, but also so our pack members met other packs and potentially find their mates too.

I smiled at myself as I pulled up to the pack house that stood at the head of the park. Now that I have found my mate, I wouldn't need to attend these events. I jumped out of the car and looked around at all the activity, pack members going about their business, happy that I could soon introduce them to their future Luna. I knew my dad was keen to retire from his position as Alpha and pass on the title to me. And I was keen to take the position and be the best Alpha that I could for my people. But I couldn't help but feel a pang of apprehension. Would Erica ever see it as her home?

"Welcome back," Damon said with a forced smile as we walked slowly up the pack house steps, the gravel crunching beneath our feet. The moment we set foot inside the pack house, I tried to offer my assistance to Damon. His injuries were a painful reminder of my own inability to control my emotions when it came to my mate. But he just shrugged me off, his eyes dark with a mixture of pain and anger.

"Leave it, Liam," he snapped. "I'm going to my room. I'll be back down soon."

The pack house housed the ranked families. I shared the top floor with my parents and my sister Kaitlyn and then the second floor split between Beta Gregg, his mate Astra and Damon, and our Gamma Gideon and his family. Then the first floor housed the main offices and the ground floor was where the grand hall was, as well as a few common rooms for pack members to hang out in.

I watched as Damon limped his way up the stairs and sighed. The guilt gnawed at me as I turned in the opposite direction, making my way towards my father's office. I couldn't believe how much of a mess this was. I had heard so much about the girl that Damon had been seeing at the bar in the city. About how much he liked her and how he even wanted her to be his chosen mate. If I had just gone with him once, then this could have been a lot less messy. I sighed. There was nothing I could do about it now.

I headed into the house and nodded at a few of the pack members that I passed and headed upstairs to the first floor. I walked down to my father's office and knocked before walking in. The heavy wooden door creaked open, revealing the familiar sight of high bookshelves and the new desk. Everything was back in place if my father hadn't lost it a few hours ago.

"Finally, you're back," my father, Declan, said, his piercing gaze fixed on me. To his side stood Gregg, Damon's father, along with Gideon, our pack's Gamma, and his son Jacob. Grayson, the pack's Warrior Commander, leaned against one of the bookshelves, his arms folded across his chest.

"Is everything alright?" I asked, feeling the weight of their stares and the tension in the room.

"First things first," Declan replied, his voice firm yet laced with concern. "Why did it take so long for you to bring Damon home?" My heart raced as the truth clawed its way to the surface, demanding to be shared.

"I've found her," I said, my voice barely above a whisper. "My fated mate." A collective gasp filled the room, followed by a flurry of congratulations and back-slapping. The Curse that plagued our pack could finally be broken, but only if I bonded with my mate.

"Congratulations, man." Gregg got up and came over and patted me on the back. "Can't wait to meet her. Where is she from?" I grimaced slightly.

"Erm, I met her in the city," I said, and they all looked confused.

"But you went to pick up Damon," Gregg said. "When did you have time to go shopping for your mate? And by the way, where is that son of mine?"

At that moment, the door swung open, and Damon limped into the room, his face bruised and swollen from our earlier encounter. My heart ached at the sight of him, guilt gnawing away at me like a ravenous beast. He glared at me, pain and betrayal etched in his dark eyes.

"Jesus, what the hell happened to you?" Gregg demanded, rushing to his son's side. His eyes flicked between Damon and me, piecing together the truth.

"Ask your future Alpha," Damon spat, his voice thick with hurt and anger.

"I... I lost control," I confessed, my voice barely audible. "When I saw them together, my wolf took over. I didn't mean to hurt him." But even as I said it, I knew there was no excuse for what I'd done. "My mate was with Damon?"

"Wait! Erica? She's your mate?" Jacob blurted out. "Aw man, you're fucked." He started laughing. My father walked over to Damon and handed him a glass.

"I made it a double," he said as Damon took it from him and settled back into the chair next to me. I looked at Jacob, who was still chuckling to himself.

"What do you mean by fucked?" Both Damon and Jacob grinned.

"Erica is erm.." Damon started.

"That girl is feisty. She's gonna chew you up and spit you out," Jacob said, and started laughing again, clearly enjoying my predicament. "She won't be easy to handle."

"Jacob!" Declan warned, giving him a stern look.

"Sorry, Alpha," he replied, only half-heartedly.

"She squares up against Heidi all the time in the bar," Damon said. "They hate each other."

"And I have seen her kick guys twice her size out without batting an eyelash," Jacob said.

I sat and listened with pride as they told tales about my mate. She was certainly amazing Luna material.

"Well, where is the girl?" Gideon asked, "When do we get to meet her?" and I looked down.

"I don't know," I said and Damon laughed.

"She kicked him in the balls and ran off," he said, and Jacob burst out laughing again. I glared at Damon, and he shrugged. I guess I deserved that. I turned to my dad, and he nodded.

"Don't fret, son. We will do everything in our power to find your mate. But first, we must attend to the situation at hand."

"Right," I muttered, forcing myself to focus on the present.

Alright, everyone," my father announced, commanding the attention of the room. "Before we can focus on finding our new Luna, there's another situation we must deal with." My heart ached at the thought of delaying the search for my fated mate, but I knew better than to question my father's judgement. I clenched my fists, struggling to keep my frustration in check.

"Gregg and I went to help an old friend who was being hunted by his enemies," my father continued, his voice heavy with sorrow. "Unfortunately, we arrived too late. We found him dead, brutally tortured for several hours before he finally succumbed to his injuries." Shock and anger rippled through the room like a tidal wave. The air thickened with tension as our pack's leadership absorbed the horrific news. My own grief and rage boiled beneath my skin, threatening to unleash the beast within me.

"His pack is now in danger from the same monsters who killed him," my father said, his eyes blazing with determination. "We must find them before the enemy does."

"Who are they?" Gideon asked, his face etched with concern.

"Remnants of the Moon Key pack," my father replied, the words heavy with significance.

We all knew about the Moon Key pack. They had been a thriving pack one day and then wiped out in a cruel attack the next. It had been almost twenty years since it happen and my father had taken the news really badly. We had been working with the pack to protect them and my father felt like their demise was his failure. But as far as anyone knew, the entire pack had been wiped out. By the sounds of the way my father was talking that wasn't entirely true.

"Gregg and I have been helping them stay hidden for the past decade or so." I glanced around the room, taking in the expressions of shock that mirrored my own. How could a pack, thought long extinct, still exist? Who were these survivors, and why had my father kept their existence a secret?

As I wrestled with these questions, I noticed Damon's sudden shift in demeanour. His face was pale, his eyes wide with fear. Something about the Moon Key pack had struck a chord within him.

"Damon," I growled, unable to mask my impatience. "What's wrong?"

"Erica," he whispered, his voice barely audible. "She's one of them." My heart thundered in my chest, the revelation sending a jolt of adrenaline through my veins. My fated mate was not only connected to the pack we were now sworn to protect but was also in danger from the same ruthless enemies.

"Then we have no time to waste," I declared, my voice hard and resolute. "We need to find Erica and the Moon Key pack before it's too late." As I looked around at the men who had stood by my side for years, I knew that together, we would face whatever darkness lay ahead. For our pack, for my mate, and for the future we all fought so desperately to protect.

Chapter 8

Liam

The rain outside my window blurred the world beyond, like a veil of sorrow shrouding my thoughts. I paced my father's office, unable to shake the image of Erica's face from my mind. The weight of the curse bore down on me; the knowledge that I had to bond with a mate before I turned thirty or the entire pack would perish. But now, it wasn't just the curse that troubled me; it was her. My father and the others in the room had been talking for the last thirty minutes while I did everything I could just to keep myself and my wolf calm. Something kept niggling at the back of my mind, like it was trying to come forward.

"Well, this certainly complicates things," Gregg said, and I heard Gideon huff.

"That's an understatement."

"I don't see how," Damon snapped, "We needed to look for the Moon Key pack, now we have a more pressing reason to."

"That's true," my father said, "But with Trenton's death I fear that the rest of the pack may try to make a rash decision and disappear before we have a chance to find them."

"Then what the fuck are we doing sitting here and discussing it for?" Damon slammed his fist on the table. I turned in time to see him wince from his injuries.

"Well first off," Gregg said, "You aren't going anywhere until you've had yourself checked over at the hospital." Damon glanced up at me quickly and then huffed.

"I'm fine," he mumbled.

I still felt guilty about what I did, and I knew that he was pissed at me, but I wasn't too worried about lasting damage. As werewolves we healed quickly, but if any bones were out of place they would need to be re-broken and healed properly.

"Maybe you should go and get seen," I said and Damon glared at me again.

"Trying to get rid of me, already?" he snapped. I closed my eyes and took a deep breath.

"Fuck Damon," I said. "How many more times do I have to apologise?" Surely he understood. Or maybe he didn't, I'm not sure I would have until today. The power of the fated mate bond was like something I had never experienced and couldn't even begin to explain it. It was like my entire world had narrowed down to that beautiful redhead goddess. She had got her claws into me like a cat.

"Enough, both of you," My father said, his Alpha tone edging his command. We both bowed our heads slightly and complied.

Cat? Whatever it was that was at the back of my mind seemed to brighten. Musk huffed in my head.

"Kitten," he growled and an image of a little girl or maybe four or five leapt into my mind.

"Kitten," I said out loud and everyone looked at me confused. Then it hit me like a wave and a flood of memories and emotions smashed into me all at once.

"Dad," I said with a grin that I couldn't contain. "Moon Key pack. That is the first time I came on pack business with you, right?" My father furrowed his eyebrows but nodded.

"Kitten," I said again, and I was met with blank confusion, all apart from Damon whose eyes widened.

"Holy shit," he said and everyone looked between us. He looked up at me. "Are you sure?" he asked, and I nodded. I was as sure as I was that I was standing here.

"Someone wanna share with the studio audience?" Jacob asked, and I turned to my father.

"Remember the little redhead girl, she was the Gamma's daughter. She used to follow me around everywhere." I could see the realisation in my father's eyes as Damon huffed.

"Ha," he said, "Follow you around? You encouraged her all the time." I grinned at him and he grinned back.

"I called her Kitten because she would hide and then try to pounce on me," I said, "She would puff out her chest and declare she wasn't a kitten, but a fierce wolf."

"Well, I'll be damned," Gregg said with a grin. My father was also grinning and shaking his head in disbelief.

"I have heard of rumours that there can be signs of a fated bond in childhood, but i never quite believed it," my father said.

My thoughts sobered up almost instantly.

"Dad," I said, and he nodded.

"I know, son," he replied. "We will find her and bring her home, I promise."

"Good luck with that," Damon muttered, and I narrowed my eyes on him.

"What's that supposed to mean?"

"It means that Erica hates packs, and Alphas for that matter. Something about a bad experience with a pack. You'll need more than the fated bond to convince her," Damon said and then looked down and mumbled. "I certainly couldn't."

"This is different," I said. "This isn't just some infatuation, it's the fated mate bond. You wouldn't understand." Damon looked back up at me and I could see anger in his eyes.

"Is that it?" he hissed, "Because I haven't found my fated mate, I don't know what love is?"

"Yeah something like that," I said, and he growled.

"Did it ever occur to you that love without the bond is more genuine love?" Damon snarled. "You don't even know her, I do. You think that just because some all seeing power has connected you too that your love is more valid?" He was practically spitting the words.

"Are you saying that you love my mate?" I growled and stepped forward. Out of the corner of my eye I could see my father and Gregg both move, ready to intercept. Damon shot up out of his chair and growled at me.

"Is that what you want to hear?" he snarled, "Yes, I am in love with Erica, and it rips me apart knowing that she is my best friend's mate. It might take me a while to deal with that, so get off my damn back already." My wolf snarled in my head and anger boiled around me as I rushed forward and grabbed Damon around the throat. I launched him across the room and he smashed against the wall before crumpling to the ground. I felt people grabbing my arms as I tried to lunge for him again.

"She is my mate," I snarled trying to pull away from whoever was restraining me.

"And don't I bloody know it," Damon snapped as he pulled himself back to his feet, with the help of Jacob. He winced as he tried to stand up straight. "And you are treating her like some possession. Did it ever occur to you that she would be in more danger with you than without?" The question hit me like a ton of bricks.

"After what happened with Jessica, maybe Erica is better off disappearing and keeping the hell away from the lot of us," Damon carried on before shrugging off Jacob's arm and storming out of the room The words stung with bitter truth. I had already lost one mate because of this damn curse. Was he right? Was I being selfish? I looked at my father and shook my head.

"I.." I couldn't form the words in my head. I sat in a nearby chair and dropped my head into my hands. I could hear movement around me and heard my father dismiss everyone. Soon the room was silent, and I was sure that I was alone. I rubbed my hands over my face and looked up to see my father sitting patiently on the edge of his desk.

"Is he right?" I asked. "Am I being selfish?" My father grimaced slightly.

"Son, the bond is powerful," he said. "And yes maybe it is selfish, but there is also a reason why you and Erica were paired by the goddess. I have to believe that this is meant to be. To help both of our communities."

He walked back around and sat back behind his desk.

"But Damon is right about one thing. Erica won't come easily. I am all too aware of the traumas she has experienced."

"Like what?" I asked. The idea that my beautiful mate has gone through anything traumatic made me want to hurt someone.

"A few years ago, Gregg and I were called by Trenton. One of his children had been manipulated into joining a pack that trafficked supernatural creatures. They kept her prisoner, and it took a coordinated effort from her old pack, myself, and Gregg to extract her from that situation. I didn't know then but from the age, I reckon it was Erica." Declan's jaw tightened. "If so, then she has every reason to distrust Alphas and want nothing to do with packs. You'll have to prove you're different if you want her to accept you."

Rage simmered in my veins, directed at the bastards who had hurt her. At the same time, it made sense now why Erica had been so wary of me. Of any Alpha. My wolf snarled inside me, wanting to hunt down each of those responsible for her suffering. I balled my hands into fists, struggling to contain my anger.

"How could anyone do that to her? She didn't deserve that."

"No, she didn't." My father's eyes were hard as flint. "None of the girls we found there did. The conditions that we found them in were horrendous." I could tell from the way he spoke he was still haunted by the incident. I couldn't even imagine how my mate would be dealing with it.

"What happened to the pack?" I asked. I was ready to go and tear them limb from limb.

"We managed to disband them, although the Alpha disappeared before trial at the Conclave," My father said. I growled at the thought. How could the Conclave lose someone like that? They were supposed to be the ones protecting the supernatural community.

My father spoke again, pulling me from my anger.

"Which is why you must proceed carefully. Erica has been through enough trauma to last several lifetimes. If you pressure her or make her feel threatened in any way, she will flee from you and never look back."

"I would never hurt her," I said through gritted teeth.

"I know your heart is in the right place, son. But you must understand, Erica's experiences have likely made her quick to perceive threats where there are none. You'll have to earn her trust, prove you want to protect her rather than control her. It's the only way she'll even consider bonding with an Alpha again."

Bonding. My heart clenched at the thought, even as hope sprang anew. My father believed Erica and I could be mates, if I handled the situation right. I inhaled a steadying breath and met his gaze.

"Then we'll have to change her mind."

"Be careful, Liam." My father's gaze was steady, full of warning. "Forcing a mate against their will is unethical and will only make things worse in the long run."

"I won't force her," I bit out. "But I will protect her, whether she wants me to or not. She is my mate, and her safety is my responsibility now." I stood and began to pace, too restless to remain still. "We have to find her before they do. Or before her and her pack run again."

"We'll find her," Declan said. "But remember, Erica is not a possession. She is a person, and she deserves your respect. If you want any chance at winning her over, you must approach this with care and compassion." I sighed, rubbing the back of my neck. He was right, of course.

My wolf saw Erica as ours to claim, but I had to remember the woman she was, strong, independent, untrusting of Alphas. This was not going to be easy. But for her, I would try.

"I'll be careful," I said. "But if it comes down to her safety or her freedom, her safety will always come first." Declan studied me for a long moment, then dipped his head.

"Very well. We'll begin planning a search party at once. The hunt for your mate begins now."

Chapter 9

Liam

The lingering scent of my mate's citrus scent haunted my shirt as I went to take it off. I wasn't ready to let go of that scent just yet. I had come up to my room on the top floor to change but I couldn't get the memory of her out of my head, the curves of her body pressed against mine as I held her in my arms. I was worried sick. Erica was in danger, not just from the curse that threatened to destroy my pack, but because of who she was. As a member of the Moon Key pack, Erica had enemies, and if anyone discovered how much she meant to me...I couldn't bear to think about it.

I fished the mobile phone from my pocket and pressed the button to wake up the screen. There had been no more missed calls in a while, which made me think that at least she had got home to her family. That was a slight relief at least. I smiled at the picture of my smiling mate for a moment, although even in the image I could tell her eyes were haunted with memories that no person should have. I sighed and headed down the hall to my sister's room.

I stood outside the room and knocked.
"Come in," Kaitlyn called through the door and I opened the door with a smile. My sister was sitting in a beanbag type thing with her laptop on her

knees. She looked out of place all in black in her very pink princess themed room. She looked up and smiled.

"Hey," she said. "You're back. I want to go to Brews tonight, but dad said no, can you convince him for me?" She sweetened her smile and widened her eyes like she did when she wanted something. It didn't work as well with so much black eyeliner as it used to. Barking Brews was the only bar on pack territory. Most of the pack chose to stay on territory to drink so it was easier to get home. The pack was pretty much in the middle of the English countryside and it was difficult to get to the city for most. It was especially impossible for our Omega ranks who couldn't leave the territory, and of course for my sister, who as the Alpha's daughter was one of the most protected werewolves in the pack, even if she hated it.

"Sorry," I said. "I kind of agree with dad right now. There is a lot going on. We need the guard." Kaitlyn screwed her face up before huffing and muttering to herself that she could take care of herself.

"I know you can," I said. "But it's dangerous right now, especially now that I found my mate." Kaitlyn's eyes lit up, and I smiled. I knew that little bit of information would make her forget her sulking.

"Your mate?" she asked excitedly, "Seriously, are you sure? Is she here? Can I meet her?"

"Yes, seriously," I said, "I am sure, and no she isn't here so you can't meet her yet."

"Well, where is she?"

"Erm..." I ran my hand through my hair and cringed. "She kind of ran away from me." Kaitlyn laughed.

"Goddess, I love her already," she said. "Do you know where she is?" I shook my head but then held out the phone.

"But I am hoping you can help with that."

"You stole her phone?" Kaitlyn's eyes widened.

"No of course not," I said, "She left it when she ran off. I was hoping that you could hack it, or something."

"You want a location right?" Kaitlyn looked at the phone and then leaned over to a drawer in her desk and pulled out a wire. She plugged it into the phone and then into her laptop. The screen lit up again and my eyes were drawn to the picture once again.

"Which one is she?" my sister asked, and I pointed Erica out to her. "Oh, nice a redhead. Cute as well." She began tapping on her laptop.

"How long will it take?" I asked and Kaitlyn grinned.

"Are you in a hurry or something?" she asked. But then her expression sobered up. "I get it," she said sincerely. "Once you meet your mate, it's all or nothing." I raised an eyebrow at her.

"Speaking from the voice of experience there?" I asked, and Kaitlyn blushed and quickly shook her head.

"Of course not," she blurted, and I smiled. I already knew my sister had a secret. I suspected she had found her mate when she turned eighteen four months ago. I also knew she would tell when she was ready.

"Anyway, give me an hour and I will have the information you need." Then she looked at me.

"That quick," I said. "You're a genius."

"Damn straight I am," she replied. I leaned down to kiss her head and turned to walk out of the room.

"Mind link me when you get something," I said, and she waved her arm. I was almost out the door when Kaitlyn called again.

"Liam?"

"Yeah?" I looked back, and she had a big grin on her face.

"I'm happy you found her," she said, and I grinned.

"Yeah, so am I."

With time to spare until Kaitlyn could get into the phone I decided it was time to go apologise to Damon. I went downstairs to the Beta and Gamma floor of the pack house, but his room was empty. I linked him, asking if we could talk. He cursed at me before shutting me out with a harsh force that must have taken some effort to shut down an Alpha link. A quick mind link to Gregg told me he was at the hospital, so I left the pack house and walked in that direction, which was located behind the training grounds. It seemed like I had done some serious damage.

My feet stomped on the ground as I marched, fuming just thinking about the Shadow Night pack and their tyrannical rule. My heart ached for Jessica and the many other victims who had been taken by their malicious Alpha, Jasper Blackwood. He was responsible for all of this, his acts of terror against us and neighbouring packs filling me with white-hot hatred.

It felt wrong. I had promised to keep Jessica safe, and yet here I was, putting Erica in the same position. My pack of over three thousand wolves would be affected by the curse if I didn't honour that promise and mate and mark with a compatible wolf before my thirtieth birthday, or they would all die. But as much as I couldn't risk losing them, I couldn't bear to see anyone else hurt like Jessica did either. It was a terrible dilemma.

My journey around the world had been filled with dark, magical encounters. I had spoken to wicked witches, powerful shamans and brutal witch doctors, but even when I was granted an audience with the Conclave. But, despite my cousin Ethan being on the board, they coldly refused to help with our insignificant problems. Now, however, I'm filled with joy because I've finally found my true mate, and I have less than five months before our bond has to be sealed forever.

I strode through the hospital doors, anxiety churning my gut. What if Damon refused to see me? What if he couldn't forgive me for attacking him? I wanted to blame my rage on him being with my mate. But the simple fact was, I was a dick who let his emotions and shit get the better of him. Kaitlyn was right. The mate bond fucked with your head. I was thinking from my heart, or in this case from my dick, and I felt threatened that Damon knew my mate more intimately than I did. I couldn't even blame it on being worried or protective. Not fully anyway, even with the curse.

I smiled sweetly at the receptionist and got the room number for where Damon was. The place was small compared to a standard hospital, but we were a wealthy pack and we had a good healthcare system for our people. I found the room quickly and knocked lightly before walking in.

Damon was sitting on the hospital bed looking annoyed, which only got worse when he saw me.

"Can't you take a bloody hint?" he snapped. "Or have you come to finish me off? I reckon I've got a part round the side that you haven't hit yet." I was immediately flooded with guilt again. Goddess, I really was a dick. I noticed Gregg, who was sitting in the visitor chair pretending to be asleep, raised an eyebrow. Damon was always the fun loving one. I was the angry, irrational one. I knew I really fucked up but the way he was reacting.

Gregg sighed dramatically, before opening his eyes.

"As much as I would like to watch another squabble, I'm tired," he said standing up. "I'm going home to my mate." He leaned over and patted Damon's shoulder lightly. "Do as the doctor says. If she says you stay the night, then you stay the night. Understand?" Damon grumbled to himself but nodded to his father. Gregg walked over to me and nodded his head.

"Try to get along now," he said, and I grimaced but also nodded. With one last look around Gregg let himself out of the room.

The room fell into an awkward silence. I fumbled with a loose string on my shirt while Damon scowled into space.

"You have to stay the night?" I finally asked and Damon scoffed.

"Like you care," he snapped.

"Of course I care," I said. "I'm a dick, I know. I'm sorry."

"No arguments here."

"Dude, I am trying here," I snapped. "But the stress is not helping. It's not an excuse, I fully own my dickish nature." Damon looked over at me. He met my eyes and held them for a few seconds before nodding.

"Fine," he grumbled, "You're a dick. But I get that it's kind of tense as well." I felt my body relax as I walked over to him.

"So, we're good then?" I asked tentatively. Damon stood up from the bed and winced at the pain. I went to help him and didn't even see his fist until it had connected with my face. Pain shot through my head as I stumbled back and I glared up at Damon. He stood holding his side with one hand and flexing the other, that had just hit me. He nodded briefly before lowering himself back to the bed.

"Now we're good." I couldn't complain, I guess.

I sank into the chair beside his bed, a smile tugging at my lips happy that we had at least started to sort things out. I knew we hadn't got through everything, but we both knew that there were bigger, more important things going on.

"Find anything useful on the phone?" Damon asked, and I shrugged.

"I just gave it to Kaitlyn before I came here," I said and he nodded.

"She'll sort it out." He struggled to find a comfortable position on the bed. "Kaitlyn's resourceful." I resisted the urge to help him, knowing he wouldn't appreciate being coddled.

"Aye, she is. Best hacker I've ever known." We sat and talked about plans of what we could do to find Erica. Damon suggested that we go back to the bar where she worked but I had a feeling that she wouldn't return there. We continued to brainstorm until I felt the buzz of a mind link. I opened up to my sister's voice.

"You can bring me a large bar of chocolate to say thank you," she sang through the link, making me smile. I thanked her and told her I would be right there.

"Kaitlyn came through?" Damon asked, and I nodded,

"Sounds like it," I said. "Are you going to be okay?"

"Of course I am," Damon scoffed. "Go get what you need to bring your girl home." I nodded at him and smiled.

Just as I was about to walk out the door, I stopped without turning.

"Damon?"

"Yeah?"

"Do you really love her?" The question was painful to ask, but I had to know.

"Yeah." His voice sounded sad and his own hurt was clearly evident. I said nothing for a moment.

"Good," I finally said with resolve. "That means that you will protect her."

"With my last dying breath," he responded with the clearest certainty.

I nodded and walked out of the room.

Chapter 10

Erica

As I stood in front of the mirror, my green eyes staring back at me, I couldn't help but feel a knot forming in my stomach. The black dress seemed to swallow me whole, amplifying the darkness that surrounded us since Trenton's death. Imogen entered the room, her usual fierce expression softened by her own grief.

"Are you ready?" she asked, her voice cracking slightly. I nodded, my hands trembling as I tried to smooth down the fabric of my dress.

"Imogen," I said hesitantly, "I'm scared. I'm terrified of being hunted again. We need to leave this place." She sighed heavily, her gaze dropping to her father's picture on the dresser.

"I know, Erica. I don't want to move either, but we have to keep our family safe, especially now that Dad's gone."

As we continued to prepare for the funeral, I could see the pain and uncertainty etched across Imogen's face. I knew she was struggling just as much as I was, if not more. Her eyes met mine in the mirror, and I could see the unspoken questions burning behind them.

"Erica," she began cautiously, "About your new mate. Do you think if you accepted the bond, you might be safer? That way, you wouldn't have to hide with the rest of us." The thought had crossed my mind, but I couldn't abandon Imogen and our family. I shook my head, feeling the weight of my decision settling over me.

"No, Imogen, I can't leave you guys. You're my family too." My voice broke, betraying my fear and resolve. "Please, don't tell anyone about my mate. It's too risky." Imogen's jaw clenched, but she nodded begrudgingly.

"Alright, Erica. I'll keep your secret. But we need to be careful, now more than ever."

"Thank you," I whispered, feeling the weight of our shared grief and determination binding us together like iron chains. We had survived so much already, but the darkness lurking on the horizon threatened to consume everything we held dear. And as we prepared for Trenton's funeral, I knew that only our loyalty and love for one another would guide us through the treacherous path ahead.

A firm knock on the door pulled me from my thoughts. Beck, Imogen's twin brother, stood in the doorway with a solemn expression.

"It's time to go," he said quietly, his voice thick with emotion.

"Alright," I replied, my heart twisting with grief as we left the sanctuary of the room. We climbed into Beck's car, the atmosphere heavy and oppressive. As the vehicle started, I gazed out the window, watching the familiar landscape pass by. The drive to the service was emotional, but quiet, each of us lost in our own memories and pain. My thoughts wandered back nineteen years, to when I had lost my parents. It felt like a lifetime ago, yet the ache of their absence never truly faded. A deep sadness settled over me as I considered how much they had missed, and all the things I wished I could share with them. Tears pricked at my eyes, but I stubbornly blinked them away, focusing instead on the here and now.

We arrived at the service, and I took a shaky breath before stepping out of the car. The attendants were a mix of werewolves and humans, some in the know, but some not. Becca approached me with a warm smile despite her red-rimmed eyes. Even in her grief, she looked beautiful, wearing a tailored black dress and simple black heels. Her almost white blond hair was loose around her shoulders and her blue eyes sparkled from unshed tears. She looked so fragile. I wanted to rush to her and protect her from the pain that I could only imagine she was feeling. As my father was originally the Gamma, it was his job to protect the Luna and Alpha Pups, a role that would normally be passed on to the Gamma's son. I knew I wasn't a male wolf, and didn't even have access to my wolf, but I trained to ensure that I could take the position when the time came. As Imogen and Beck were born human, then technically the responsibility didn't cover them, but that would not stop me.

"I'm so sorry my Luna," I whispered as Becca pulled me into a hug. She pulled away and shook her head.

"You don't need to call me that anymore." She smiled at me.

"What?" I was confused.

"My dear, sweet Erica," she said. "I am no longer Luna of this pack. Right now, other than you and Marshall, there isn't really a pack left." I was shocked. I knew that as a human, she technically couldn't hold the title any more but she had been my Luna and caregiver all my life and I wasn't going to accept anything else.

"I don't care about the rules," I said defiantly. She laughed, although it was a sad laugh.

"Oh Erica, you beautiful girl, if only you knew." She pulled me into a hug and whispered, "It has and always will be a pleasure to serve you."

"Thank you, Becca" I managed, touched by her words. But there was something about her tone that confused me, as if there were a secret hidden beneath her praise. I couldn't dwell on it, though, as Beta Marshall appeared beside us, his presence grounding and reassuring.

"Erica," he murmured, pulling me into a tight hug. "He's in heaven now, with your parents, Amy and Christian." My chest tightened at the mention of their names, the weight of our losses nearly unbearable. "He can finally tell them how proud he is of them and how much of an amazing woman you have grown into." I could only nod and hug him tighter as I tried to hold back the tears. I released him and moved to gently hug his wife Charlene too before moving aside to allow the twins to greet Beta Marshall and Charlene.

The service began, and as we honoured Trenton's life, I couldn't help but feel the pain of all those we had lost along the way. Each name, each memory, a fresh wound in my heart that never seemed to fully heal. But amidst the grief, there was a fierce determination, an unbreakable bond between us forged through hardship and loss. We were a family, bound by loyalty and love, and no matter what darkness lay ahead, we would face it together. The Officiant stood at the front, his voice steady as he recounted Trenton's life.

"Trenton was a man who loved hiking and all things nature." A soft chuckle rippled through the crowd, those in the know sharing a knowing glance. The irony of a werewolf loving nature wasn't lost on us.

"His love for his family knew no bounds," the Officiant continued. "Nineteen years ago, we suffered the tragic loss of his son, Christian, as well as his brother Nathaniel and sisters-in-law Andrianna and Amy." He paused, allowing the heavy weight of their names to settle over the gathered mourners.

"Though not brothers by blood, Trenton and Nathaniel shared an unbreakable bond that brought our community together." I stared at the ground, my heart aching with the pain of loss and guilt. I missed my parents deeply, and the knowledge that Christian had died protecting me was a burden I couldn't escape. I felt so alone, despite being surrounded by the people who mattered most to me.

"Let us remember the love they shared and the memories they left behind," the Officiant concluded, his words echoing through the solemn air.

The service finally ended, and one by one, werewolves approached the casket to say a last goodbye. I waited until the end, not trusting my emotions enough to join the procession. Marshall appeared at my side, his solid presence a comfort.

"It's time, little one." Little one. A term of endearment he hadn't used in decades. I peered up at him but he remained implacable. With a fortifying breath, I approached the casket and placed a hand on it.

"Thank you," I whispered. "For everything." A single tear slid down my cheek as I turned away. The finality of this moment carved a hole inside me, one that would never quite heal. I only hoped Trenton could finally rest, free of the demons that had haunted him in life.

After the service we began the sombre journey back to the house for the informal wake. As we arrived, I couldn't shake the feeling of unease that settled over me. The house was filled with people, some familiar and others less so. My instincts screamed at me to be on guard, to watch for any hint of danger lurking in the shadows.

"Erica," Marshall murmured, placing a hand on my shoulder. "You should try to relax a little. We're among friends here."

"I know, but I can't help it," I admitted, my gaze darting around the room, searching for any sign of threat. "I feel like there's danger nearby. I can't let my guard down."

"Trust your instincts," he advised, his eyes softening with understanding. "But remember, we're here for you, and we'll face whatever comes our way together."

"Thank you, Marshall," I whispered, grateful for his unwavering support. But the unease continued to gnaw at me, a dark cloud hovering over what should have been a time of shared grief and remembrance. I knew that I couldn't ignore this feeling for long, but for now, I had to focus on honouring Trenton and the family we had lost. As the wake continued, I tried my best to mingle and accept condolences graciously. But beneath the surface, my heart raced, and my senses remained alert, ever vigilant against the shadows that seemed to close in around us.

The time for the ritual last run approached, and my nerves frayed as werewolves began to file outside. The scent of their excitement was palpable, a mixture of anticipation and grief. Despite the sombre occasion, they would honour Trenton's memory by running together one last time in his name. My heart ached with the longing to join them, but I knew that wasn't an option, not when my secret threatened to be exposed.

"Erica, are you alright?" Imogen asked softly, her blue eyes filled with concern.

"Fine," I lied, feigning a smile. "Just... a little overwhelmed."

"Let's step outside for some fresh air then," she suggested, guiding me toward the door.

As we emerged onto the porch, I attempted to slip away from the crowd under the guise of seeking solitude. But fate had other plans.

"Oof!" I collided with a solid mass of muscle and stumbled back. The scent hit me before I could even process the sight in front of me, a powerful Alpha, his presence commanding the space around him.

"Apologies," he said smoothly, extending a hand to steady me. His voice sent shivers down my spine, and my heart pounded with recognition: Alpha Declan Anderson of the Silver Stone pack. Liam's father.

"Erica, isn't it?" he asked as I looked around frantically for any sign of Liam, a cold sweat broke out across my brow. "Are you not joining the run, young one?" His piercing gaze bore into mine, and I struggled to find my words.

"Um, I-" Before I could stammer out an explanation, Becca appeared at my side, her presence radiating strength and protection.

"Erica's been through a lot lately," she interjected, placing a reassuring hand on my shoulder. "She's emotionally tired and needs her rest."

"Ah, I see," Declan responded, a subtle hint of scepticism in his tone. "Well, my condolences for your loss. I hope you find the peace you need."

"Thank you, Alpha Anderson," Becca replied, her voice steady as we watched him walk away. I swallowed hard, hoping against hope that today would pass without any more unexpected encounters or revelations. The weight of my secret felt heavier than ever, but with a family like Imogen and Becca by my side, I knew I had to keep fighting, to keep surviving. For now, I could only focus on honouring Trenton's memory and praying that the shadows lurking just beyond our reach would remain at bay.

With a shaky breath, I excused myself from Becca's side and made my way upstairs to my room. The air felt heavy with tension and sorrow, but I couldn't afford to let my guard down. I closed the door behind me, leaning against it for a moment as I listened carefully for any footsteps or whispers in the hallway. Silence greeted me, offering a small reprieve from the chaos below. The encounter with Alpha Declan had left my nerves frayed, his presence an ominous reminder of the dangers that still lurked nearby. If Liam was here too... No, I couldn't risk bumping into him again. I needed to leave, to find some place safer for both me and my makeshift family. Determined, I grabbed a duffle bag from the closet and began to shove clothes inside, not bothering to fold them neatly. My thoughts raced with each passing second, weighing the risks and potential consequences of my sudden decision. It wasn't just about my safety; Imogen, Beck, and the others depended on me too. The stakes were higher than ever, and I couldn't afford to fail them.

My hands trembled slightly as I zipped up the duffle bag, my heart pounding in my chest like a caged animal desperate to escape. My ears strained for any hint of danger, but all I heard was the distant murmur of conversations from the wake downstairs. So focused on the task at hand, I failed to notice the sound of my door opening until it was too late. An angry growl reverberated through the room, making me jump and spin around, clutching the duffle bag protectively to my chest. My heart threatened to leap out of my throat as I found myself face to face with the source of my fear: Liam.

"What the hell do you think you're doing?" he snarled, his brown eyes blazing with fury. The air around us crackled with tension, threatening to suffocate me as I stared back at him, struggling to find the words to explain myself. All the while, the question loomed over us like a storm cloud, heavy and foreboding.

Chapter 11

Liam

I stood at the back of the hall with my father, watching as people paid their last respects. My all black tailored suit felt uncomfortable and stiff, and the sweet scent of citrus teased me and my wolf. I saw as the beautiful sight of red hair came into view. I had purposely avoided looking for her since we came into the room. I knew that the moment I saw my beautiful mate that my thoughts would be consumed with only her.

My sister had found the location of Erica's house from the phone. She had got all the information off of it just in time. An hour later the phone erased itself. Kaitlyn said she was impressed with the software and there was clearly someone who knew what they were doing in their pack. That made sense given that they had spent their whole lives as ghosts.I wanted to go straight over and get my mate but my father had forbidden me to do so. He said that we would need to approach things delicately, whatever the fuck that meant. This was why we came to the funeral. Just my father and me, so as not to draw too much attention to ourselves.

My body stiffened and my wolf urged me to go to my mate, but instead I watched as she hesitated before another man approached her. He was older, maybe my father's age. Not that you could tell with werewolves. He laid a hand on Erica's shoulder. I felt my wolf pace inside me.

"Mine," he grunted. I never even realised I was growling until my father took my arm.

"Do I need to order you to leave?" he asked sternly. I shook my head quickly. I knew my father didn't even want me to come with him today, but the thought of not being near my mate was ripping me apart inside.

"I'm fine," I said through gritted teeth. I could tell from the side eye he gave me that he wasn't convinced.

My mate was standing at the front of the room now, with her hand on the casket. The waves of sadness coming from her hurt my heart, and I wanted nothing more than to wrap her in my arms and take away the pain. My father nudged me and I looked over to where he was looking. The man that had just been with Erica was now standing with a small blond girl with pixie like features. I recognised the girl from the image on Erica's phone. Both of them were watching my father and I. My father nodded to the man and he made his way over to us.

"Alpha Anderson," he said as he reached us and held out his hand. "What an honour to see you here." My father shook his hand and smiled sadly.

"Beta Hayes," he replied. "I am truly sorry for your loss. Trenton was a good friend. I am so sorry that I couldn't get to him in time." Beta Hayes nodded in response. My father turned and gestured to me.

"This is my son Liam," he said, and I held out my hand to the man.

"Beta Hayes," I said. "It is a pleasure to meet you."

"Please call me Marshall," he said and shook my hand. "Will you both be joining us for the last run?"

"Yes, we would be honoured to," my father said, nodding. "I would like to talk to you about the future of your pack, and how we can help." Marshall visibly stiffened at my father's request and I felt as he closed down his expression.

"Well, I am sure we can figure something out," he said quickly, but then forced a fake smile on his face. "But for now I must see to my family." He turned and walked off into the crowd before either of us could respond.

I turned to my father with a panic settling into my stomach.

"Dad," I said, and he held up his hand.

"Give me some time."

"We don't have time," I snapped. "You heard what Damon said. They are planning on disappearing again." My wolf growled in my head and I wanted to join him.

"And if we act rashly, then they will disappear and so will their trust in us," my father responded. I knew he was right, but I was terrified of my mate leaving me before I could convince her that she could rely on me.

We followed the other mourners back to the house where they were holding the wake. Today was the first time that I was seeing it and the general disrepair and state of the place was awful. You could tell that the, practically falling down, townhouse on the edge of the city was decorated as a home, but it certainly wasn't good enough for my mate to be living in. Is this how she has lived for her whole life? We entered the home with my father insisting that I keep a low profile while we were there. I just wanted to watch my beautiful mate as she nervously made her way through the crowd.

About two hours later everyone began to make their way outside for the last run. I was excited to finally see my mate shift into her wolf. I knew then that when she saw my wolf that she would understand that we were made for each other. But it wasn't until I went in search that I found her talking with my father. She had another woman that looked like an older version of her friend with her and from what I could pick up from the conversation I could tell that my mate was tired. I watched as the two women walked back into the house and approached my father.

"You met her?" I asked with a grin, "She is amazing isn't she?" My father smiled at me and nodded.

"She truly is something, he replied.

"I can't wait to see her wolf," I said and my wolf yipped in my head in agreement. My father frowned a little and looked towards the house.

"I am afraid that won't be tonight," he said and my heart dropped.

"What? Why not?" I asked. For someone to miss the last run of an Alpha was considered rude, for a member of their own pack to miss it was a sign of disrespect.

"Her Luna said that she had been excused due to emotional stress," my father said, although I could tell that he wasn't all that convinced. He shook his head and smiled at me. He waved to the group of people disappearing into the woods behind the house.

"Shall we?" he asked. "This old wolf could do with a good leg stretch."

"You go ahead," I said looking back at the house. "I'll follow in a moment."

"Liam," my father warned, and I forced a smile on my face.

"I promise I will be good." Again he didn't look convinced, but he nodded anyway.

I headed into the house as my father headed towards the woods. The house was practically empty now, with all the werewolves out for a run, and the other supernaturals and humans outside to pay tribute as well. I could smell my mate's scent all over the house. There were other smells, but they all paled in comparison to her intoxicating aroma. I explored the downstairs, looking at pictures of the family. My mate was in a few of the pictures and she was always smiling, but it never seemed to reach her eyes.

Finally, I found myself at the bottom of the staircase and hesitated briefly before making my way up them. I unconsciously followed the scent of citrus to a closed door where the scent seemed to be the strongest. I deliberated over knocking but decided against it. I quietly opened the door and my senses were instantly flooded with the most delicious citrus. It was so strong I could practically taste the juices.

The first thing I saw was my mate standing with her back to me. Her room was a whirlwind of activity, clothes and personal belongings strewn haphazardly across the floor. Then I noticed she was pushing things into a bag on her bed, and the realisation hit me like a sledgehammer. She was packing clothes. She was running away. She was leaving...me.

I growled before I could help myself and I saw Erica whirl around to face me. The look of pure fear on her face.

"What the hell are you doing?" I snarled and stepped forward into the room. Erica froze in place for a moment, only her eyes darted around the room like she was looking for a weapon, or to escape. Then her features flooded with anger.

"I could ask you the same thing," she snapped, and I growled again. "Who do you think you are coming into my house like that?"

"I am your goddess damn mate," I snarled and stepped forward again. I could see the hesitation in her face and smell the fear from her. My logical self tried to reason with me and calm down, but my irrational side was stronger and I couldn't let my mate leave me. Not when it took me so long to find her.

"Erica, please," I pleaded, feeling the weight of her past trauma in her eyes. "I know it's difficult, and I know you have been through a lot."

"You don't know anything about me and what I have been through," she snapped at me. "You come here and just assume that some magic bond will make everything better, well the world doesn't work like that."

"It does if you let it," I whispered. "I swear on my life that I will protect you from anything, any Alpha that tries to hurt you." I saw her flinch at the words and her eyes widen slightly. Then the bitterness flooded back in.

"Will you protect me from yourself?" she asked bitterly, her eyes shining with unshed tears. "You're an Alpha too. How do I not know you aren't just like all the others? All I have seen so far is anger and demanding from you."

"Erica..." I began, my voice cracking at the raw truth in her words. But she didn't give me a chance to respond.

"It's best if I leave," she whispered, her voice thick with emotion. "I need a fresh start, somewhere away from all of this. A safer place for me and my family."

"Please, don't go," I whispered, my desperation mounting as I watched her methodically pack her life away. The room seemed to shrink around me, suffocating me with the realisation that I was messing everything up and I was losing her.

"I know I'm an Alpha, and that terrifies you. But I swear, I will do everything in my power to show you who I really am, to show you how much you mean to me." She hesitated for a moment, I could tell that the mate bond was warring with the trauma inside of her. Finally, she let out a shaky breath and tears flooded down her cheeks.

"I can't, Liam. I just can't. I'm sorry."

The room seemed to close in around me, smothering me with the weight of my own helplessness. A torrent of frustration and anger surged through my veins, like molten lava threatening to erupt. My fists clenched, knuckles turning white as I fought to contain the tempest within.

"Damn it, Erica!" I exploded, my voice cracking under the strain of my emotions. "I need you! I love you more than I've ever loved anyone, and the thought of losing you is tearing me apart!" Her body stiffened, and she took a step back, visibly flinching at my outburst. The sight of her fear sent ice-cold shame flooding through me, dousing the flames of my anger. "Erica, I'm sorry," I choked out, horrified at my own inability to control my emotions.

"I didn't mean to..."

"Stop, Liam," she whispered, her voice trembling. "Just... stop." And with that, she turned away from me, resuming her packing as though I wasn't even in the room.

The air grew thick between us, heavy with unspoken words and regrets. I watched helplessly as my fated mate and yes even though I barely knew her, the woman I loved slipped further and further away, the chasm between us growing wider by the second. It was a torment beyond anything I'd ever known, this desperate struggle to hold on to her even as she slipped through my fingers like sand. And as the weight of my powerlessness crushed me beneath its merciless heel, I knew in my heart that I would do anything, anything at all, to keep her with me.

In that moment, as Erica turned her back on me, something inside me snapped. The tidal wave of fear, frustration, and anger that had been building up for days, weeks, even, finally shattered the dam that held it at bay, and I found myself drowning in the flood.

"Erica," I growled, my voice low and dangerous. The sound seemed to reverberate throughout the room, echoing off the walls like a thunderclap. "Look at me." She hesitated briefly but didn't turn around. The defiance in her stance only served to fan the flames of my rage, and I could feel the beast within me stirring, clawing at the bars of its cage.

"Enough!" I roared, losing control of my emotions completely. In one swift, fluid motion, I crossed the room and grabbed her by the arm, wrenching her around to face me. Her eyes widened in surprise and fear, but she didn't cry out. She refused to give me the satisfaction of knowing that she was afraid.

"Let go of me, Liam," she whispered, her voice shaking despite her brave front. "Please. Let me go."

"Never," I snarled, tightening my grip until I could feel the delicate bones of her wrist grind together beneath my fingers. "You're not leaving me, Erica. Not now. Not ever."

"Y-you're hurting me," she stammered, tears welling up in her green eyes.

"Good," I spat, my heart twisting painfully in my chest at the sight of her pain. But I couldn't back down. I couldn't let her go. Not when so much was at stake.

I reached out with my free hand and grabbed a handful of her red hair, yanking her head back so that her throat was exposed. The scent of her fear was intoxicating, drowning out all rational thought and leaving only the primal need to claim her, to make her understand that she was mine.

"Stop fighting me, Erica," I hissed, my breath hot against her skin. "You belong with me. Why can't you see that?"

"Because it's not true," she whispered, tears streaming down her cheeks. "I don't belong to anyone. Not you, not your pack. I'm not some possession for you to control."

"Damn it, Erica," I snarled, unable to contain the seething torrent of emotions that threatened to tear me apart from the inside out. With a swift movement, I swung us both around and let go. She went crashing into the wall and crumpled to the floor. I knelt down beside her as she struggled to get to a sitting position.

"It's for your own good," I whispered. Her eyes widened again as I grabbed another handful of her hair. I quickly used my hold to slam her head against the wall. She yelled out briefly before going silent. I looked to see her eyes closed, and she was no longer struggling. I swept her off her feet, stood up, and threw her over my shoulder. She hung lifelessly against me and for a brief second I hoped that she was comfortable.

I grabbed the bag that she had been packing and then made my way through the house, quietly and quickly. I sent a quick mind link to my father to say that I was heading home and would send someone with another car. I placed my beautiful mate into the back seat of the car and went and got in the driver's seat. I started the engine of the car and made my way with my mate out of the city and back home.

Chapter 12

Liam

"Damn it," I muttered under my breath as I accelerated through the pack territory. The night was dark and unforgiving, much like the situation I had found myself in. My grip on the steering wheel tightened with every passing mile, my knuckles turning white from the pressure.

"I did this for you, can't you see? It's for your own good." In the backseat, Erica lay unconscious, her red hair splayed across the seat like a fiery halo around her head. I couldn't help but feel a pang of guilt at the sight of her vulnerability, but it was quickly overshadowed by my determination to protect her. She needed me more than she realised, and I would do whatever it took to keep her safe, even if it meant proving her right about Alphas hurting her.

As I approached the pack house, I slowed the car down, relieved to see that no one seemed to be around. The last thing I needed was an audience for my actions. Pulling up to the front door, I turned off the engine and took a deep breath before stepping out into the chilly night air. Carefully, I opened the back door and gently lifted Erica out, wrapping her in a blanket to shield her from the cold. Her body felt so fragile in my arms, yet I knew her spirit was anything but. As I carried her inside and up the stairs to my room, I couldn't help but marvel at the woman I held. So strong and fierce, yet plagued by a past filled with pain and betrayal.

Laying her down on my bed, I brushed a strand of hair away from her face and pressed a gentle kiss to her forehead. The urge to stay close to her, to protect her, was overpowering. But I knew I had to give her some space. With a sigh, I closed the bedroom door and locked it securely. I pulled a chair up to the bed, my eyes never leaving her form as I sat down, waiting for her to wake up.

"Please understand, baby," I whispered, my heart heavy with the burden of responsibility and love. "I'm doing this because I can't bear the thought of losing you." The room was silent, save for the rhythmic sound of her breathing. And as I sat there in the darkness, watching over her, I couldn't help but feel like both her guardian angel and her personal demon, torn between my need for control and my desire for her happiness.

"Forgive me, baby," I murmured, my voice barely audible. "I just want to keep you safe, even if it means hurting you in the process." And with those words lingering in the air like a ghost, I continued my vigil, hoping that when she woke, she would somehow understand the depth of my love and the lengths I would go to protect her.

As I sat there, watching Erica's peaceful slumber, I couldn't help but marvel at her ethereal beauty. Her red hair fanned out across the pillow like a halo of fire, accentuating the porcelain skin that seemed to glow in the dim light of the room. The gentle rise and fall of her chest as she breathed was mesmerising, the very picture of serenity. Yet, I knew that beneath this calm facade lay a tempest, a fiery spirit that would undoubtedly be unleashed when she awoke and realised what had transpired. I imagined her green eyes blazing with fury, transforming her from an angelic vision to a vengeful force of nature.

"Baby," I whispered, my fingers itching to brush her hair back from her face. But I resisted the urge; it wasn't my right, not after what I had done.

A soft groan escaped her lips, and I tensed in anticipation. Her eyelids fluttered open, revealing hazy, disoriented eyes that slowly focused on me.

She reached up to cradle her head, wincing as her fingers brushed against the tender skin where I had struck her.

"Where am I?" she croaked, fear creeping into her voice as the reality of her situation dawned on her.

"Baby," I began, trying to keep my tone calm and soothing. "You're in my pack house. I brought you here for your own safety." Her eyes narrowed, and she attempted to scoot away from me, pressing herself against the headboard.

"Safety? You hit me and kidnapped me, and now you're saying it's for my safety?"

"Please, just let me explain," I pleaded, desperate for her to understand. My heart clenched at the sight of her trembling form, and guilt washed over me like a tidal wave.

"Stay away from me!" she demanded, her voice cracking as she tried to put more distance between us.

"Baby, please, I know how this looks, but I swear I only did it because I love you and want to protect you," I insisted, my hands outstretched in a futile attempt to calm her. Her breathing was ragged, and I could see the battle raging within her, torn between wanting to believe me and fearing the truth of her situation. But I knew that my actions had wounded her deeply, and there would be no easy path to forgiveness.

"Let me go, you psycho!" Erica screamed at me as she jumped up from the bed, her fear morphing into a fiery rage. "You're just like all the other Alphas, thinking you can control everyone!" Her words cut through me like a dagger, as I truly believed I was doing this for her own good. She couldn't see that my actions were driven by love and an overwhelming need to protect her.

"Baby, please listen to me," I tried again, desperate for her to understand my motives. But she was having none of it, her green eyes blazing with fury and defiance.

"Stay the hell away from me!" she spat, "And stop calling me baby." she moved towards the door in a frantic attempt to escape. Her hand reached for the handle, only to find it locked. A wave of panic washed over her face, and I could sense a deeper, hidden trauma resurfacing in her reaction. Her breathing began to become shallow.

"Please, Liam, let me go," she pleaded, her voice breaking as tears streamed down her cheeks. "I can't be trapped in here. Please." My heart shattered at the sight of her, so vulnerable and afraid. Doubt crept into my mind, making me question whether I was really doing the right thing. As her fated mate, it was my duty to protect her and keep her safe, but had I gone too far?

"Erica, I promise you, I'm not trying to hurt you," I whispered, reaching out to her with trembling hands. "But I couldn't let you leave without giving me a chance. I need to keep you close to ensure your safety." But my words seemed to fall on deaf ears as her sobs grew louder and more heartbreaking.

"Unlock the door, Liam," she begged between sobs, collapsing onto the floor in a flood of tears. "Please, just let me go."

"Erica," I sighed, my voice heavy with sorrow and regret. "I'm sorry, but I can't." And as I stood there, watching my mate cry out in pain, I couldn't help but wonder if I had become one of the very monsters I was trying to protect her from.

I approached slowly so as not to scare her anymore. My heart ached as I knelt down beside my mate, gently pulling her trembling form into my arms. Her sobs tore through me, each one causing a wrenching pain in my chest. I told myself that this was for her protection, but the pain etched on her face made me doubt my convictions.

"Shh," I murmured, trying to soothe her. "I won't let anything happen to you, baby. Please, just trust me." As her body shook against mine, I closed my eyes and breathed in her amazing citrus scent, trying to calm myself and absorb some of her strength. Little did I know that her resourceful mind was already miles ahead of me.

"Baby, I'm so sorry," I whispered against her hair, hoping for some semblance of forgiveness. But her response came in the form of a sudden knee to my groin, catching me completely off guard.

"Ah!" I gasped, collapsing to the floor in agony, my hands instinctively flying to protect the sensitive area.

"Sorry, Liam, but I can't trust you," she spat. I barely registered the flash of her foot before it connected with my head, dazing me further. I watched in a haze as she unlocked the door and darted out into the hallway, her red hair streaming behind her like flames.

Rage boiled inside me, overpowering the pain of her betrayal. She had tricked me again, and I couldn't allow her to escape. Clenching my teeth, I pushed myself up from the floor and gave chase, growling with fury. My feet pounded against the hardwood floors, echoing through the empty hallway. As Erica reached the stairs, I lunged forward, tackling her to the ground before she could descend.

"Run all you want, sweetheart," I snarled into her ear, pinning her beneath me. "I'll be the big bad wolf if you want me to be, and I will always catch you."

"Get off me!" she screamed, struggling against my hold. Her green eyes blazed with defiance, making her even more captivating.

"Listen to me," I growled, desperation beginning to seep into my voice. "I'm not the enemy here. I'm just trying to protect you."

"By kidnapping me and locking me up?" she shot back, her voice crackling with anger. "You're just the same as all the others." My chest tightened at her words, and I knew that I had to make her see the truth. But how could I convince her when my actions spoke louder than any words ever could?

"Baby, please," I pleaded, searching for the right words in a sea of doubt. "Give me a chance to prove myself. I can't let you go now, but I swear on the life of my pack that I'll do everything in my power to keep you safe and earn your trust."

"Your promises mean nothing to me, you crazy bastard," she hissed, tears glistening in her eyes. The weight of those words crushed me, and I knew that I was losing her, before I had even got her, perhaps forever. And yet, as much as it pained me, I couldn't let her go; not when the darkness threatening our world was still lurking just beyond our reach.

As I hoisted Erica over my shoulder, her body squirmed and writhed in a futile attempt to break free. Her fists pounded against my back, each strike an echoing reminder of the trust I'd broken.

"Put me down, you bastard!" she screamed, her voice like a dagger stabbing at my heart. But I couldn't let her go, not now, not when I knew the danger that awaited her outside these walls.

"Erica," I growled, trying to keep my voice steady despite the rising tide of anger within me, "I am just trying to protect you. Trust me when I say your wellbeing is at the centre of my thoughts."

"Trust you?" she spat, her words dripping with venom. "I'd sooner trust a snake." The bitter sting of her words fuelled my temper as I carried her back to my bedroom, my grip tightening around her waist. I threw open the door, my nostrils flaring with each breath, and tossed her onto the bed.

"Stay," I commanded, my voice dark and menacing. Erica growled in response, a feral sound that sent shivers down my spine. Her green eyes flashed with fury, defiance burning within them like wildfire. As I watched her lunge for the door, my instincts kicked in, and I lunged after her.

"Going somewhere?" I taunted as I grabbed her by the arm and threw her back onto the bed. The impact caused her hair to fan out around her like a halo of fire, making her look more like a fury than the angel I saw earlier.

"Get away from me!" she snarled, her face contorted with rage. "You are nothing but a monster, just like the rest of them!" Her accusations cut deep, I was her goddess given fated mate. How could she not see that I was different? That I only wanted to protect her?

"Baby," I whispered, my voice raw with emotion, "I'm not like them. If you'd just give me a chance–"

"Never!" she interjected, her voice rising in pitch. "And stop calling me BABY." The last was in a ragged scream "You're just another Alpha who thinks he can control me, but you'll never break me. You hear me? Never!" As her words continued to rain down on me like a torrent of daggers, I knew that no matter how much I tried to convince her, she would never believe me. And in that moment, it felt like the world had finally tipped off its axis, sending me spiralling into the darkness.

In a flurry of desperation, I managed to slip past Erica and slammed the door shut just before she could reach me. The sound of her body colliding with the solid wood reverberated through the hallway, followed by the relentless banging on the door as she screamed and shouted from inside the room.

"Let me out, you bastard!" she yelled, her voice cracking under the strain of her anger and fear. "You'll pay for this, Liam! I swear!" I stood there, my back pressed against the door, trying to catch my breath as I listened to her cries.

A twisted sense of satisfaction welled up within me, at least I'd managed to contain her, for now. My heart raced as I struggled with the responsibility I felt towards my pack and the love that burned for this fierce woman who fought me at every turn.

"Baby, please," I whispered, knowing she couldn't hear me over her own screams. "I'm doing this for your own good." But deep down, a gnawing uncertainty began to take root. Was I truly doing what was best for her, or was I becoming just another Alpha who sought to exert control over someone weaker? Was I only this desperate because I have a curse to break.

As I turned away from the door, still grappling with my conflicting emotions, I found myself face-to-face with my father, our Alpha, standing at the end of the hallway with a glare that could have frozen hell over. His eyes bore into me, full of fury and disappointment, and it became painfully clear that he was not happy with the scene that had just unfolded. "I think we need to talk?" he growled, his voice dripping with contempt.

With a heavy heart, I nodded in acquiescence, unable to meet his gaze. As I walked away from the locked door that separated me from the woman I loved, the sound of her sobbing cries echoing through the hall, I couldn't help but fear that I had lost her trust forever.

Chapter 13

Liam

The office seemed to close in on me as my father's voice boomed, his dark eyes fixed on me with an intensity that matched the storm brewing outside.

"What were you thinking, Liam?" my father shouted, throwing his hands up in disbelief. "Kidnapping her, and from a funeral? You've gone too far this time!" I could feel the heat rising in my cheeks, anger and frustration intertwining like the roots of an ancient tree. My fists clenched at my sides as I tried to defend myself.

"I went to see her," I said, my words coming out sharp and desperate. "She was packing her clothes, Dad. She was going to leave before I even had a chance to show her I'm a good man, her fated mate." My heart ached as I recalled the fear and distrust in Erica's green eyes when I approached her earlier. The scent of her light red hair still lingered, taunting me, reminding me of what I might lose. She was strong-willed and cautious, traits that both drew me to her and made it difficult for her to trust someone like me.

"Erica wouldn't listen to reason," I continued, my voice cracking under the weight of my emotions. "I couldn't just let her go, not without trying everything I could to make her see that we belong together."

My father's expression softened for a moment, but his eyes remained dark and stormy. He knew the importance of finding our fated mates, especially for me, but he was also acutely aware of the responsibility that came with being an Alpha. His grey-streaked hair seemed to carry the weight of every decision he'd ever made for our pack, and I knew he wanted better for me.

"Kidnapping her isn't the way to prove your worth, Liam," he said, his voice low and heavy with disappointment. "You need to earn her trust, show her that you can protect and care for her. This... this is only pushing her further away." The truth of his words stung like a slap to the face. I knew my actions were reckless, the result of an impulsive anger born from a lifetime of feeling trapped by the curse that plagued our pack.

But it was more than that, it was my fear of losing Erica before I even had a chance to know her, to love her.

"I know," I whispered, my voice breaking as I fought back tears. "I just... I didn't know what else to do. I felt so powerless, Dad. And now I've only made things worse."

"Well, that's an understatement," my father snapped. I clenched my fists, trying to control the anger boiling inside me as my father continued to berate me. My heart pounded in my chest, and I could feel the muscles in my jaw twitching with every word he spoke.

"Kidnapping Erica and hurting her is hardly a way to show that you can keep her safe!" he scoffed, his dark eyes filled with disappointment. "You're being irrational and irresponsible. This is not how the future Alpha of our pack should behave!" My blood roared in my ears as I struggled to maintain control over the beast within. The wolf inside me snarled at the injustice of it all. He just didn't understand what was at stake. I couldn't let Erica slip through my fingers.

"Erica is my fated mate!" I shouted, my voice cracking with emotion. "She was going to leave, Dad! It wasn't just me who would lose out, without my mate, I'd never be able to break the curse!" I stared at him, my chest heaving as I tried to catch my breath.

The air in the room felt thick and oppressive, suffocating me as I waited for his response. The scent of my own fear mingled with my father's disappointment, creating an unbearable atmosphere that made it difficult to think. My father's gaze bore into mine, searching for any signs of weakness or doubt. I could see the pain behind his eyes, the worry that consumed him for our pack and our future.

But there was something else there too, a flicker of understanding that gave me hope.

"Even if she is your fated mate, Liam," he said slowly, his voice softening slightly, "you cannot force her to love you. You cannot make her accept you by kidnapping her and causing her pain." His words cut deep, like a knife slicing through my already battered heart. I knew he was right, but the thought of losing Erica was unbearable. The weight of my actions and their consequences pressed down on me, making it difficult to breathe. How could I fix this? How could I make her see that I wasn't just a monster, but a man who wanted nothing more than to love and protect her? I swallowed hard, forcing down the lump that had risen in my throat.

"What am I supposed to do, Dad?" I asked, my voice barely audible.

"Show her who you truly are," he replied, his tone firm but not unkind. "Prove to her that you can be the Alpha our pack needs, and the man she deserves." He laid a hand on my shoulder, squeezing gently in a gesture of support.

"But most importantly, Liam," he added, his eyes locking onto mine with an intensity that left no room for doubt, "give her a choice."

My father's words echoed in my head as I stared into the darkness of my soul, searching for the strength to do what was right. I didn't know if I could let Erica go, but I couldn't keep her prisoner either. It was time to face the consequences of my actions, and fight for the woman I loved.

The lingering disappointment in my father's eyes cut like a blade, sharper than any weapon. Before I could try to explain further, the door to the office burst open and Damon strode in, followed closely by Gregg. Their faces were etched with concern and fury.

"Alpha, what the hell is going on?" Damon demanded, his dark eyes blazing. "I heard Liam took Erica from her home." My father's gaze never left mine.

"Yes, he did," he confirmed, the disappointment clear in his voice. I clenched my fists at my sides, my nails digging into my palms as I fought to keep my own rage in check.

"Is she okay?" Gregg asked, his voice tight with worry.

"Erica is understandably upset," my father replied, shooting me another disappointed glance before turning to address the two men.

"Liam has locked her in his room for now."

As if on cue, the phone on my father's desk rang, its shrill tone slicing through the tense atmosphere. He picked it up, his eyes narrowing as he listened to the panicked voice on the other end. I could feel the hairs on the back of my neck prickling, my instincts screaming that something was wrong.

"Marshall," he said, trying to soothe the beta of Erica's pack. "Calm down. Yes, we know about Erica." At the mention of Beta Marshall's name, my heart dropped like a stone. The realisation that I had caused even more chaos than I'd intended sank in, and I felt my insides churn with a mixture of guilt and frustration.

"Look, I understand how you feel," my father continued, glaring at me as he spoke. "But I assure you, Erica is safe. Liam acted impulsively, and we're dealing with the situation." I could almost hear Marshal's anger crackling through the phone line, and it took all my self-control not to lash out. My wolf prowled beneath my skin, its frustration mirroring my own. Love and responsibility warred within me, the weight of my actions bearing down on my soul. I had taken Erica in a desperate bid to keep her close. But in doing so, I had only driven her further away, and brought the wrath of her pack down upon us all.

"Marshall, hold on a second," my father said, pressing a button to put the call on speakerphone. The room fell silent as everyone listened intently.

"Look, I'll be straight with you," he continued, his voice heavy with the weight of responsibility. "Liam took Erica from her home."

"Are you kidding me?" Marshall roared through the phone, his voice laced with fury. "You let your son kidnap her?"

"Marshall, I assure you that we're handling the situation," my father replied, trying to keep his own anger in check. "But I understand how you feel, and-"

"Understand? You think you understand?" Marshall cut him off, his voice rising. "Becca and I are coming over right now. We want answers, Declan, and we want Erica back."

"Marshall, please—" my father began, but the line went dead before he could finish. With a sigh, he glared at me once more before sinking into his chair, the disappointment in his eyes cutting deeper than any physical wound. I clenched my fists, my nails digging into my palms, struggling to contain the turmoil raging within me.

We all sat in uncomfortable silence for about an hour before my father's office door opened, and Kaitlyn, my younger sister, walked in, followed by my mother, who held her head high, projecting an air of calm authority. Their arrival only added to the already tense atmosphere.

"Hey, Liam," Kaitlyn said, her eyes narrowing as she looked at me. "What's going on? It sounds like there's a wild animal locked in your room." Damon couldn't help but snort at the comment.

"That's one way to put it. Your brother went all caveman on his fated mate and kidnapped her. She's locked in his room right now." My face flushed with a mix of embarrassment, anger, and shame as my sister stared at me, her mouth agape. My mother, however, regarded me with a quiet disapproval that somehow managed to cut deeper than Kaitlyn's shock.

"Really, Liam?" she said softly, the disappointment evident in her voice. "Is this who you want to be? The kind of Alpha who resorts to force instead of understanding and compassion?" I wanted to defend myself, to tell them that I was trying to protect Erica, but the words caught in my throat. I knew they were right, and it hurt more than I could bear. The burden of love and responsibility weighed heavily on my shoulders, crushing me beneath its relentless pressure.

As the room remained tense and silent, I couldn't help but feel the enormity of my actions closing in around me. I had acted out of fear, driven by a desperate need to keep Erica close and break the curse that plagued our pack. But I knew that in doing so, I had only pushed her further away and risked causing irreparable damage to the fragile bonds between our packs. And as much as it pained me, I realised I had no choice but to face the consequences of my actions, no matter how daunting they might be. A mind link buzzed through from the warrior on guard at the gate.

"Alpha Declan, your guests have arrived."

"Finally. Show them in," my father ordered through the link before shutting it down again. He knew as well as I did that this situation was far from simple, and the arrival of Erica's pack members would only complicate matters further.

As Marshall and Becca stormed into the office, their faces contorted with fury, I could practically feel the heat radiating off them. They were like living embodiments of righteous anger, and I knew that facing them would be akin to walking through fire.

"Where is she?" Marshall demanded, his voice like thunder rolling across the sky. "We want her back now!"

"Please," my father replied, attempting to defuse the situation with a calm authority. "I assure you, I am dealing with this matter. But there are complications."

"Complications?!" Marshall spat, his eyes blazing with a mixture of rage and disbelief. "What could possibly be more important than returning Erica to us?" My heart hammered against my chest as I fought to find the words, knowing that they would either save or damn me. And then, without thinking, I blurted out the truth that had been gnawing at me since the moment I'd laid eyes on Erica:

"She's my fated mate!"

The room fell silent as Becca and Marshall stared at me, their expressions a mixture of shock and confusion. It was clear that they had no idea about the connection that bound Erica and me together, and I could see them struggling to process this new information.

"Even if that's true," Marshall said finally, his voice heavy with barely contained rage, "that doesn't give you the right to kidnap her, lock her up, and take away her freedom!" I knew he was right, but the thought of losing Erica, of letting her slip through my fingers like grains of sand, filled me with a desperate, primal fear. My wolf snarled inside me, urging me to fight for what was mine, but my human side knew that I had to be better than that. I had to show Erica that I could protect her not just from the dangers lurking in the shadows, but from my own worst instincts as well.

"Please," I whispered, my voice cracking under the weight of my emotions. "Let me make this right." Marshall and Becca exchanged a glance, their faces unreadable. And as the seconds ticked by, the tension in the room grew thicker and heavier, until it felt as though the very air itself was pressing down on me, threatening to crush me beneath its suffocating burden.

"Fine," Marshall gritted his teeth, "but Erica's fate still remains her choice. You must let her go."

"Under the extenuating circumstances, with your pack being hunted, she'll be safer with the Silver Stone pack," my father interjected, his voice steady and authoritative.

After another half hour of arguing and no conclusions my father finally sighed heavily. The guilt was eating my up that I had caused this level of mess for everyone.

"I suggest we call in the Conclave to mediate this situation if we really can't deal with it ourselves," my father finally said.

"Very well," Marshall conceded after a tense moment, "but I want to see Erica now."

"Of course," my father replied before turning to Damon. "Would you please escort Erica here?" My blood boiled as I watched Damon nod in agreement, clearly eager to reunite with Erica, my fated mate. The urge to snarl at him was almost too strong to resist, but I managed to reign in my temper as I clenched my fists tightly.

"Sit down and shut up," my father ordered quietly, his voice dripping with authority. I obeyed begrudgingly, feeling like a caged animal as I stared at the closed door that separated me from Erica.

The air in the room grew heavy with frustration and anger, a tangible pressure that weighed down on all of us. I tried to focus on the sound of my own heartbeat, steady and determined, as a reminder of my purpose, to protect Erica and break the curse that had plagued our pack for far too long. But as the seconds ticked by, I couldn't escape the gnawing ache deep within me, the fear that I'd pushed Erica too far. That despite our connection, she would choose to walk away, leaving me and my pack to face an uncertain future alone. As I waited for Erica's return, I closed my eyes and drew in a deep breath, allowing the scent of the forest through the open window to calm my frayed nerves. For now, all I could do was hope, and pray, that she would see the man beneath the rage, the Alpha who longed to protect her even from himself.

Chapter 14

Erica

I slumped at the edge of Liam's bed, my limbs heavy with exhaustion. For the past few hours, I had unleashed my fury on his room. The once pristine space was now a battlefield of broken furniture, torn clothes, and shattered objects. My rage had temporarily numbed the pain inside, but as the adrenaline began to fade, a cold wave of loneliness replaced it. My knuckles throbbed from punching through the wooden dresser, and my lungs burned as I tried to steady my breathing. This wasn't how things were supposed to go. I never wanted any of this.

As the sound of the door unlocking reached my ears, my body tensed. A low growl rumbled in my throat, the only defence I could muster in my weakened state. Through narrowed eyes, I watched Damon hesitantly poke his head around the door. His dark eyes widened at the sight of the wreckage before him. It seemed he hadn't expected me to take my anger out on the room. He stepped cautiously into the chaos, meeting my glare with an uncertain look.

"Wow, Erica," he said, glancing around the destroyed room. "I knew you were pissed, but this is... impressive." His attempt at humour fell flat, and I didn't bother responding. Instead, I focused on the sharp sting of betrayal that twisted in my gut. How could he even look me in the eye after what Liam had done?

"Erica," he started, taking a slow step towards me. Panic flared in my chest, and I instinctively shrank back, pressing myself against the cold wall. A wave of shame washed over me as I realised just how much my reaction had affected him.

"Hey, it's okay," Damon said softly, his dark eyes filled with concern. He paused, giving me space to process what was happening.

"Alpha Declan sent me. You're not in any danger, I promise."

"Easy for you to say," I muttered, glaring at him. "You didn't get kidnapped by your so-called fated mate." The bitterness in my voice surprised even me.

"Listen, Erica," Damon continued, undeterred by my hostility. "Liam's actions were completely out of line, and he's going to pay for it. The Alpha is furious with him."

"Good," I spat, my hands balling into fists at the mention of Liam's name. "He deserves it."

"Alpha Declan wants to talk to you," Damon said gently, extending a hand to help me up. With great reluctance, I allowed him to pull me to my feet, but the moment I was standing, I ripped my hand from his grip.

"Lead the way," I growled, my voice dripping with unspoken venom. As I followed Damon out of the room and into the unknown, one thought echoed loudly in my mind: I would not let myself be anyone's pawn ever again.

Following Damon's lead, we stepped out of the wrecked bedroom and into the grand hallway of the pack house. As we walked, I couldn't help but take in my surroundings, the anger still simmering beneath the surface. The place was undeniably impressive – a vast expanse with high ceilings, intricate mouldings, and polished wooden floors that echoed our footsteps. It had an air of understated luxury without losing its homely feel.

"Seems like you guys live pretty well here," I remarked bitterly, not knowing if it would make any difference to my current situation.

"Alpha Declan believes in providing for his pack," Damon replied. He led me down a series of wide corridors adorned with paintings and tapestries that depicted the pack's history. I could tell we were in the Alpha family's private quarters, a fact confirmed when we descended three flights of stairs to a more formal, office-like setting.

We stopped in front of a large wooden door with a brass plaque that read 'Alpha Declan Anderson.' I hesitated, my heart pounding in my chest as I anticipated what lay beyond the door.

"Go on," Damon encouraged gently, gesturing for me to enter. Taking a deep breath, I pushed open the door and stepped inside. The first thing I noticed was Alpha Declan sitting behind a massive desk, his dark eyes filled with a mixture of compassion and sympathy. To his right stood Beta Gregg, a silent and imposing presence. Liam sat off to one side, looking like he wanted to say something, but a glare from me silenced him. His expression shifted to one of guilt and pain. Last, I spotted Becca and Beta Marshall. They both looked worried but relieved to see me, their familiar faces providing a small measure of comfort in this tense situation. Relief coursed through me as I rushed to Marshall and Becca, my only lifelines in this sea of uncertainty.

"Please," I begged, gripping their arms tightly, "take me home. I can't stay here." Becca's blue eyes filled with sympathy as she gently touched my hand.

"Erica, it's not that simple. Are you and Liam truly fated mates?"

"Absolutely not." I spat the venomous words, glaring daggers at Liam.

"Erica!" Liam shot up from his seat, clearly upset by my response. " I was trying to protect you!"

"Protect me?" I whirled around to face him, rage bubbling inside me like a volcano on the verge of eruption. "A fated mate wouldn't force his will on another. You're just a psychotic bastard!"

"Enough!" Alpha Declan's authoritative voice cut through our heated argument like a knife. He looked at me with an apologetic expression.

"I'm sorry for the way Liam handled things, but the fact remains: you share a fated mate bond with him."

"Then I'll reject him," I retorted, refusing to accept my fate so easily. Liam's eyes widened in anger, but I didn't care. I wanted my freedom back.

"Silence, Liam," Alpha Declan warned, sensing his son's outburst before it could happen. Turning his attention back to me, he continued,

"We've contacted the Conclave to mediate this situation."

"Couldn't I just go home?" I pleaded, my voice wavering as the weight of my circumstances threatened to crush me. I needed some sense of normalcy, some semblance of safety.

"Erica," said Marshall softly, placing a steadying hand on my shoulder, "it's best to let the Conclave handle this. Trust us."

"Trust?" That word felt like a foreign concept now. But as I looked into Marshall and Becca's eyes, I realised they were all I had left. With a heavy sigh, I reluctantly agreed to wait for the Conclave's decision.

An hour later, the atmosphere in the Alpha's office had shifted dramatically. The Conclave had arrived, and their power was immediately palpable. I could feel it prickling my skin like static electricity, causing the hairs on the back of my neck to rise. Their leader, Coleman Browning, stood at the head of the group like a lion among wolves. He exuded an overwhelming sense of authority, his mere presence commanding the attention of everyone in the room.

The Conclave was run by a group of highly powerful supernatural beings called the Alchemists. Little was known about them, even within the supernatural community. They were shrouded in mystery, but one thing was clear: they were not to be trifled with. These enigmatic figures looked just like normal human beings but their blank expressions, dark tailored suits and enigmatic postures seemed to absorb the light around them, making it difficult to focus on anything but them. Their very presence seemed to glow with an otherworldly luminescence that sent chills down my spine. They were the judge, jury and executioner of pretty much any situation within the supernatural community. But they were particular about what they actually got involved with, and I was all too aware of their overall belief that werewolves and other shifters were just animals to them.

"Alpha Declan, please recount the situation involving your son and Erica," Coleman Browning requested, his voice resonating throughout the room.

"Of course," replied Alpha Declan, straightening his posture as he began. "Erica is a rogue werewolf-"

"Rogue?" I interrupted, and the Alpha glared at me. I didn't let it faze me. "There are two members of my pack right here." Browning regarded me like something on his shoe and then looked at both Marshall and Becca.

"Your pack?" he asked. "What is the name?"

"The Moon Key pack," I said defiantly. Coleman glanced at Marshall again and then back to me.

"And where is your territory, young one? Who is your Alpha? How many shifters are in your pack?" he shot the questions at me knowing that I wouldn't have the answers.

"Well, erm..." I hesitated.

"Our Alpha has just passed away," Marshall replied. "And we do not hold any territory at the present time." He glanced at me with a weak sad smile. "Only Erica and I are the remaining shifters." Coleman watched him for a few moments before nodding.

"So you hold no land, no alpha and have only two shifters?" he asked. I put my head down, worried that I might say something stupid. "I think that it is fair to say that Alpha Declan's description is an accurate one. Please carry on Alpha."

"But-" I said, annoyed at being brushed off like some child.

"Erica," Becca scolded, and I put my head down again. It was no use, the almighty prick wasn't listening, anyway. Browning watched me for a moment and then nodded at Alpha Declan to carry on. The alpha glanced at me with sympathy but then continued.

"As I was saying," he said, "Miss Hallows has formed an incomplete fated mate bond with my son Liam. She had planned to leave the area due to danger, but Liam panicked and kidnapped her."

As the Alpha continued to recount the events, Coleman watched intently, occasionally asking a probing question or two. His gaze never wavered, and I couldn't help but feel increasingly uncomfortable under his scrutiny. It was as if he could see through me, peeling back every layer until my soul lay bare before him.

"Thank you, Alpha Declan," Coleman said finally. "We will hold a private hearing with you and Beta Gregg as Mr Anderson's representatives, and Beta Hayes and Luna Hughes as Miss Hallows' representatives." I swallowed hard, my throat feeling like it was lined with sandpaper. The mere thought of having my fate decided by these mysterious beings was terrifying, but I had no choice. I glanced at Becca and Marshall, hoping to find some reassurance in their faces, but they seemed just as tense as I felt.

"Very well," agreed Alpha Declan, his voice betraying a hint of trepidation. "We will abide by your decision."

As the Alchemists filed out of the room to conduct their private hearing, a heavy silence settled among us. I couldn't help but feel like a lamb being led to slaughter, my future hanging in the balance. But then again, I thought bitterly, that's exactly what I am. I clenched my fists, trying to push away the anger and fear that threatened to overwhelm me. No matter what happened next, I knew one thing for certain: I would not go down without a fight.

The door clicked shut, leaving me alone with Liam and Damon. It felt like the air had been sucked out of the room, replaced by a suffocating tension. I glanced at Liam, trying to determine if he was even sorry for what he'd done. He opened his mouth, attempting to speak, but I cut him off.

"Listen, Liam," I snarled, "if you ever speak to me again, I'll rip your tongue out and shove it up your ass." The colour drained from his face, and he quickly clamped his mouth shut. A half-smile tugged at Damon's lips, and he attempted to make light of the situation.

"Oh, this is so fun," he muttered sarcastically. I shot him a glare, and he sighed, running a hand through his dark hair.

We all lapsed into an uncomfortable silence, the weight of the situation bearing down on us like a crushing force. My thoughts raced, anxiety gnawing at the edges of my mind, wondering what would happen next.

Time crawled by at a snail's pace, each minute feeling like an eternity. The sun began to rise outside the window, casting a weak, gloomy light across the room. I sighed, shifting in my seat as my muscles ached from hours of sitting.

Finally, the door swung open, and the Conclave, Alpha Declan, Beta Gregg, Becca, and Marshall returned. My heart leapt into my throat as I searched their faces for any hint of what had transpired. Becca's eyes were red and swollen, and neither she nor Marshall would meet my gaze.

"Can we go home now?" I asked tentatively, hope flickering in my chest. Coleman Browning stepped forward, exuding power and authority that seemed to fill the entire room. I shrank back slightly, suddenly feeling very small and insignificant.

"Mis Hallows," he began, his voice firm yet somehow compassionate. "The decision has been made. By supernatural law, the Alpha heir Liam Anderson has a right of ownership through the fated mate bond, and you are to stay with the Silver Stone pack." His words echoed in my ears like a death knell, and I felt as if the ground had been ripped out from beneath me. Anger, betrayal, and despair swirled within me like a hurricane, threatening to rip me apart. This couldn't be happening. I wouldn't let it. Deep down, I knew there was nothing I could do. I was trapped, bound to a man and a pack I barely knew, and every ounce of freedom I'd fought so hard for had just been snatched away.

Chapter 15

Erica

The air in the room felt heavy, suffocating me as I tried to wrap my head around what had just happened. My heart pounded in my chest, a mixture of fear and rage threatening to burst from within me. This couldn't be happening. It wasn't fair. They were taking me away from my birth pack, tearing me from the only connection I had left to my parents.

"You can't do this. You can't just rip me away from my family like this." I said, my voice shaking with emotion. My green eyes locked onto Coleman Browning's stony gaze. He was the mouthpiece of The Conclave, the one delivering this heart-wrenching decree.

His tone was solemn but firm. "This is the final decision of The Conclave. You must adhere to it or suffer the consequences." The threat in his voice echoed through the room, chilling me to the bone. It was a reminder of how powerless I truly was in this situation. He turned to Alpha Declan and declared, "The matter is resolved. There is no more need for The Conclave to be here." With one last look of compassion, he excused himself and the other Conclave members from the room, leaving me to face my new reality.

I glanced over at Alpha Declan, my emotions boiling beneath the surface. His dark, almost black eyes bore into mine, unwavering. He was the one who would now hold power over me; the thought made me sick to my stomach. How could I trust him when I knew so little about him? And why was he so insistent on taking me from my family?

"Please," I begged, unable to keep the desperation from my voice. "There has to be another way. Let me stay with my pack." Alpha Declan remained silent, his expression unreadable.

The silence that followed the Conclave's departure was deafening, pressing down on me like a suffocating weight. I could feel my heart pounding in my chest, each beat a reminder of the life I was about to leave behind. My entire world had crumbled around me, and I couldn't find the strength to pick up the pieces. Alpha Declan cleared his throat, drawing all eyes to him.

"I think it's time," he announced, turning to Marshall with a nod.

"Please, don't do this!" I cried out, desperation clawing at my throat. I turned to Marshall and Becca, pleading with them to intervene.

"You can't let this happen. You can't just give me away like I'm some... some object!" Becca's blue eyes filled with tears as she reached for my hand.

"Erica, you have to trust us," she whispered, her voice thick with emotion. "We're doing this for your own good. We all want what's best for you." But I couldn't listen, wouldn't listen. How could they possibly know what was best for me when they were ripping me from the only family I'd ever known?

"You're taking me from my pack and stripping me of my Gamma rank! This is barbaric!" I spat, glaring at Alpha Declan.

"Rank?" Alpha Declan scoffed, his dark gaze unyielding. "As a rogue, you don't technically hold a Gamma rank, Erica."

"Rogue?!" I bristled, anger flaring within me. "You have no right to discredit my pack like that!"

"Your 'pack' holds no territory, has no Alpha or alpha heir, and of the two werewolves left, one can't even shift due to deep-rooted trauma," he replied coldly, his words an icy dagger to my heart. My hands clenched into fists, and I fought back a fresh wave of tears. It felt like the world was crushing me, pushing me under with each cruel revelation. My heart pounded as I stared at Alpha Declan, the betrayal digging its claws into my chest. How could he know my secret? That I couldn't shift? My gaze darted towards Marshall, who shook his head, silently denying any involvement. Liam's shocked expression confirmed that even he hadn't known.

"How did you know?" I whispered, my voice trembling with fury and hurt. He met my eyes without flinching, his own dark orbs full of a cold calculation.

"I figured it out at the funeral when you didn't take part in the last run. The pain in your eyes that you couldn't shift was clear." His words hit me like a blow to the stomach. He had been watching me during one of my most vulnerable moments. And now, he held the power to rip away my last remaining connection to my pack.

"Please don't do this," I begged, unable to keep the despair from my voice. But it was no use. Alpha Declan turned back to Marshall and nodded.

"I, Declan Anderson, Alpha of the Silver Stone pack, request that you, Beta Marshall Hayes, acting Alpha of the Moon Key pack, relinquish control of pack member Erica Hallows to my pack." The formality of his words only heightened the raw emotion coursing through me.

With a scream, I lunged at him, desperate to make him feel even a fraction of the pain he was causing me. But before I could reach him, powerful arms snatched me from the air and held me tight.

"Let me go!" I thrashed against the iron grip, my vision blurred by angry tears. But there was no escaping the vice-like hold.

"Erica," Liam's voice cut through my rage, filled with concern and helplessness. The grip of Beta Gregg's powerful arms threatened to crush the breath from my lungs. Panic and fury coursed through me, granting me a surge of strength that I used to thrash against his hold. But my efforts were futile; he was an immovable force.

"Stop," Beta Gregg whispered into my ear, his breath hot against my skin. The command carried with it an icy wave of calm that washed over my body, extinguishing my rage like water dousing a flame. My legs buckled beneath me, and I crumpled to the floor in a heap of despair, tears streaming down my face. I barely registered Marshall's presence as he knelt beside me, his voice thick with regret.

"I'm so sorry, Erica," he said, placing a hand on my shoulder. "I wish there was another way."

"Please, Marshall," I choked out between sobs, clutching at his shirt. "Don't do this to me. Don't let them take me away from our family." Marshall looked pained, but he slowly stood up and faced Alpha Declan, his expression steely.

"I, Beta Marshall Hayes, accept your request and relinquish control of Erica Hallows to the Silver Stone pack."

A scream tore itself from my throat as the bond to my pack stretched taut, then snapped like a frayed rope. It felt as though my heart had shattered along with it, leaving me hollow and broken. With venomous hatred burning in my eyes, I glared at Marshall, feeling betrayed by the man I'd once considered family. My gaze shifted to Liam, who watched me intently, his face etched with concern and sorrow. In my heart, I knew that joining the Silver Stone pack would only bring more pain and suffering. I'd rather be completely alone than part of a pack that didn't value loyalty and family.

"Never," I whispered, steeling myself for the consequences of my decision. "I'd rather be a rogue than submit to any of you." I spat, the anger and betrayal fuelling my defiance.

"I, Erica Hallows, declare myself a true rogue and reject Alpha Liam Anderson as my—"

"NO!" Liam's scream cut through the air, interrupting me before I could finish. His voice was filled with anguish, but I refused to back down.

"Enough!" bellowed Alpha Declan, his fury only matched by the power of his Alpha command. It slammed into me like a tidal wave, forcing me to my knees and stealing the breath from my lungs.

"Submit to me now, Erica," he demanded, his eyes cold and unyielding.

"Go fuck yourself," I snarled back, defiance shining in my green eyes despite the crushing weight of his command. A flicker of regret crossed his face, gone as quickly as it appeared.

"I'm sorry, but I didn't want it to come to this." With that, he backhanded me so hard that I went crashing across the room, slamming against the wall with enough force to rattle my bones. Pain exploded through me, and I struggled to push myself up, gasping for breath.

Alpha Declan was suddenly beside me, the full weight of his Alpha power and command focused on me. I screamed, feeling as if I were being torn apart from the inside out. He was relentless, demanding my submission once more. Through blurred vision, I saw Liam struggling against Gregg and Damon, desperate to reach me but held back by their combined strength. Becca sobbed in Marshall's arms, her cries cutting through the chaos like a knife.

"Please, Erica, just submit!" Marshall called out, his voice cracking under the strain of his emotions. But I couldn't, wouldn't, give in to the man who had ripped me away from my family.

"Never," I whispered, though the pain threatened to choke me. "I won't submit to you." "Enough!" Declan roared again, his power intensifying until I thought I would shatter into a million pieces. "NO!" Liam's scream echoed through the room once more. I thought for a moment that I was going to pass out from the immense pain slamming into my body but then the oppressive weight of Alpha Declan's power suddenly lifted, and I could breathe again. The pain that had me in its clutches moments before was gone, replaced by a dull ache throughout my body.

As I gasped for air, my vision slowly returned to focus on Declan kneeling beside me.

"Erica," he said softly, his eyes filled with regret. "If you submit to me, I will do everything in my power to keep you safe and help you find out why you can't shift." His words were an unexpected lifeline thrown to me in the midst of my torment, but I hesitated, unsure if I could trust him.

"Please, Erica." Marshall's voice came from across the room, thick with emotion. "Give in. I'll look after our family for you. You don't have to suffer like this any longer." I glanced over at him, tears streaming down my face, as the memory of laughter and camaraderie with my pack flooded my thoughts. How could I leave them behind? But what choice did I have?

Declan had made it clear that he wouldn't back down, and I couldn't bear the thought of enduring more pain, not just for myself, but for everyone who cared about me. A tearful sob escaped my lips, the weight of my decision bearing down upon me. I looked into Declan's dark eyes, searching for any semblance of compassion or understanding. I looked at Liam again and then back at Alpha Declan.

"I'm not agreeing to mate with anyone," I said, and the Alpha chuckled.

"That's acceptable," he replied.

"What!" Liam exclaimed, and the Alpha held up his hand to him.

"You said you wanted to earn her love, well now you have the chance," he said.

"Good luck man," Beta Gregg chuckled, and I glanced up at him and he winked at me. I couldn't help a small smile. I also saw Damon smother a laugh.

"Erica?" the Alpha asked, drawing my attention back to him. "As a rogue joining our pack, you will join as an Omega. Do you understand that?"

"Dad, no!" Liam exclaimed, which earned him a glare from his father. I looked at Liam and nodded before looking back at the Alpha.

"I understand," I said. Even losing my Gamma rank would be better than being tied to and controlled by an Alpha mate.

"Then I ask you again, will you submit to me as your new Alpha?" Finally, emotionally drained and tired beyond belief, I surrendered.

"I... I submit," I whispered, choking on the words that sealed my fate. It felt as if I'd signed away my soul.

Chapter 16

Erica

I sat on the edge of the leather couch in Alpha Declan's office, my hands clenched tightly together in my lap. The silence was deafening and my heart ached with a sense of despair that settled like a heavy stone in my chest.

"Erica," Becca said softly, her blue eyes brimming with tears. "You'll be okay here. We'll all adjust to our new lives, and we'll still be a family, no matter what." I glanced over at her, noting the way her voice cracked and how she clutched at the locket around her neck, the same one Trenton had given her.

Though she tried to sound reassuring, I could see the pain in her eyes, mirroring my own.

"Becca's right," Marshall chimed in, his tone more steady but with an undercurrent of sadness. He gave me a half-hearted smile and continued, "Besides, I'll have your clothes and belongings sent over in the next couple of days. You won't be without your things for long."

"Thanks, Marshall," I muttered, feeling the weight of their impending departure pressing down on me. Their words were meant to comfort, yet the thought of being separated from them only added to the sense of abandonment gnawing away inside me. I looked around the room, taking in the dark wood furniture and shelves filled with old books, trying to distract myself from the emotions threatening to overwhelm me.

"Hey," Becca said, reaching out to squeeze my hand gently. "We'll still be in touch, okay? You're not going to lose us. We're just... moving forward, that's all."

"Moving forward," I echoed, the words tasting bitter on my tongue. In that moment, it felt like I was being left behind while everyone else moved on to something better.

"Erica," Marshall said, placing a hand on my shoulder and giving it a reassuring squeeze. "I know this is hard, but you'll find your place here. You're strong, and you're not alone. We'll still be there for you, just in a different way."

"Sure," I replied, swallowing the lump in my throat and forcing a weak smile onto my face. But deep down, I couldn't help but feel like I was losing everything that had once mattered to me.

The sound of the door creaking open pulled me from my thoughts. Beta Gregg stepped into the room, his movements quiet and cautious. I could tell he was trying to be considerate of our emotions, but his presence only reminded me of the reality I needed to face.

"Erica," he spoke softly, his eyes filled with concern. "Your room has been prepared for you. Perhaps you could use some rest after all that's happened." I glanced at Becca and Marshall, noticing the bags under their eyes as well. We were all exhausted, emotionally and physically. But the thought of going to a new room in this strange place filled me with dread.

"Thank you, Gregg," I murmured, struggling to keep my voice steady. "I'll... I'll go now."

Together, we made our way out of Alpha Declan's office and into the dimly lit hallway. The early morning sunlight cast eerie shadows on the walls as we slowly walked toward the entrance of the pack house. My heart felt heavy, each step taking me further away from the life I had known. As we stepped outside, the cool morning air sent a shiver down my spine. I spotted Marshall's car parked nearby, its dark exterior dull in the gloomy light. A fresh wave of tears threatened to spill over, and I tried to blink them back.

"Marshall, Becca," I choked out, my voice barely above a whisper. "Please say goodbye to Beck, Imogen, and Amy for me. And... and tell them I'll be in touch."

"Of course, Erica," Marshall replied, his eyes filled with sadness. "We'll make sure they know you're thinking of them."

"Stay strong, Erica," Becca added, her own tears streaming down her cheeks. "You've got this. We believe in you." Their words of encouragement fell on my deaf ears, as my mind was consumed with the thought of losing them all. I couldn't help but wonder if I would ever find a sense of belonging again.

"Erica," Alpha Declan's voice broke through my haze of grief, his tone surprisingly gentle for someone who was used to commanding an entire pack. He took Marshall's hand in a firm shake, nodding solemnly to him.

"I will make sure your family is safe and protected. You have my word as Alpha."

"Thank you, Alpha Declan," Marshall replied, his voice thick with unshed tears.

"Take care, Erica," Becca whispered, her blue eyes clouded with sadness. I could see the fear and helplessness she felt mirrored back at me, and it only served to intensify my own emotions.

"Goodbye, I love you." I managed to choke out, wrapping my arms around them in a tight embrace. It felt like I was saying goodbye to more than just two family members; I was saying goodbye to my old life, my old pack, and everything that had given me a sense of security and belonging.

As they pulled away from me, their faces etched with pain, I couldn't hold back the sobs any longer. Tears streamed down my cheeks, and I wiped them away angrily, hating how vulnerable I felt in front of everyone. But there was no hiding my grief.

"Come on, Erica, I promise it will be alright," Alpha Declan said softly, placing a tentative hand on my shoulder. I shrugged it off, not wanting his comfort. The moment Marshall's car disappeared down the road, a wave of desolation washed over me. The last remnants of my old life were gone, and all that remained was the cold, unfamiliar world of the Silver Stone pack. I was alone, utterly and completely.

"Erica," Alpha Declan said quietly. "I know this is hard, but you're not alone here. We'll help you through this. You're part of our pack now."

"Am I?" I snapped, the anger bubbling up inside me. "Because it sure doesn't feel like it."

"Give it time," he replied, his voice soft but firm. "You'll find your place here. I promise." But as I stared into the darkness where my friends had vanished, all I could think was that the promises of an Alpha meant nothing to me. All they had ever brought me was pain and betrayal. Tears blurred my vision, the pack house entrance swimming before me as I struggled to breathe through the anguish that gripped my chest. The chilly early morning air stung my cheeks, but I barely noticed it; my world had been reduced to a whirlwind of grief and confusion.

I barely even noticed Alpha Declan's eyes glaze over until he spoke. "I've called for a Warrior," he said. "He will escort you to your accommodation." My heart throbbed painfully in my chest at the reminder that I was now alone in this unfamiliar place. A part of me wanted to scream, to lash out at the unfairness of it all, but my body felt too heavy, weighed down by the crushing weight of my sorrow.

"Erica," Liam's voice came from behind me, soft with concern. I stiffened, refusing to turn around to face him. He stepped closer, hesitating for a moment before continuing. "You should get some rest. I'll take you to my room." His words lit a fire within me, igniting my anger and giving me the strength to whirl around and glare at him.

"I hate you," I spat venomously, my green eyes blazing. "I never want to lay eyes on you again."

"Erica," Liam began, reaching out to me, but I recoiled from his touch, my fury burning hotter than ever.

"Give her some space, Liam," Alpha Declan said quietly, his dark eyes watching the exchange with a mix of concern and understanding. Liam clenched his jaw, frustration and hurt flickering across his handsome face before he stormed off, leaving me alone with Alpha Declan and my own roiling emotions.

As if summoned by the tense atmosphere, a warrior appeared at the pack house entrance. His presence brought me no comfort, but at least it meant I wouldn't have to be alone with Liam, or the Alpha, any longer.

"Take Erica to her quarters," Alpha Declan instructed, his voice carrying a note of finality. The warrior nodded and gestured for me to follow him. But I couldn't seem to move, like moving would confirm that this nightmare was happening. I just looked up at the warrior blankly. The warrior guard stood tall and lean, his blond hair falling into his eyes as he flashed a cheeky smile in my direction. I'd never met him before, but something about his energy piqued my curiosity despite the overwhelming grief that consumed me.

"Erica, this is Grant," Declan introduced, his dark gaze fixed on mine. "He'll escort you to the Omega houses where you'll be staying."

"Give her time to settle in," Declan said softly, his words seemingly directed at both Grant and myself. I looked at him blankly, still trying to process everything that had happened.

"Of course, Alpha," Grant replied, his blue eyes meeting mine with an almost playful glint. I couldn't tell if he was genuinely trying to lift my spirits or just oblivious to the storm of emotions raging inside me. It dawned on me that as an Omega, I would be expected to take on the menial tasks like cleaning and serving. The thought of being relegated to such a position infuriated me, but my emotional exhaustion prevented any protests from escaping my lips.

"Are you okay?" Grant asked, breaking the silence that hung between us like a thick fog.

"Since when do warriors care about Omegas?" I retorted, my voice dripping with sarcasm. I was too tired to put up a facade, and my anger bubbled just below the surface. "Hey, I'm just trying to help," he defended himself, the playfulness in his voice replaced by sincerity. "I guess you're going through a lot right now."

"Thanks for the reminder," I muttered under my breath. It seemed that everywhere I turned, someone was there to remind me of the hellish nightmare I now found myself in.

"Look, I get that you're angry," Grant said, his eyes locked on mine. "But sometimes it helps to have someone to talk to."

"Is that your job now?" I snarled, barely able to contain my frustration. "To be my shoulder to cry on?"

"Maybe," he replied with a hint of a smile, the corners of his mouth tugging upwards ever so slightly. "Or maybe I'm just trying to be a friend." I didn't respond, the concept of friendship feeling like a distant memory in this cold, unfamiliar world. But as much as I wanted to shut him out, some part of me couldn't help but wonder if there was more to this warrior than met the eye.

"Grant, flirt on your own time," Beta Gregg called out as he walked up to us. Grant seemed to laugh at the beta's words and the two fell into a quiet conversation.

As they shared their exchange, I found myself staring blankly at the world around me. The weight of my new reality felt like an anchor dragging me down into the depths of despair. My chest tightened with unshed tears, and I barely noticed when Beta Gregg approached.

"Erica," he urged gently, "follow Grant. You need some rest."

"Rest?" I scoffed internally. As if sleep could somehow erase the pain that clung to me like a second skin. But I couldn't argue, not when my body felt so heavy and my thoughts swirled like a hurricane in my mind. Was this what shock felt like?

"Come on," Grant said, trying to engage me in small talk as we began our trek towards the Omega houses. "I promise it's not as bad as you think."

"Really?" I snapped, my patience wearing thin. "Because it feels pretty damn awful right now." I muttered bitterly, unable to bite back my anger any longer.

As we walked down the path, the pack house loomed behind us like a dark spectre. A sudden urge to look back washed over me, and there, standing at the window, was Liam. Our eyes met, and I could feel the sting of his hurt through our bond. But as my gaze lingered on his brooding figure, something inside me hardened. I couldn't bring myself to care.

Chapter 17

Erica

One Week Later

It had been a week since my world had fallen apart. The room I found myself in was small and sparsely furnished, a far cry from the lavish spaces provided to higher-ranking pack members. It was tucked away in the omega quarters, a place where those of us who didn't quite fit in were relegated. The walls were a dull grey, almost as though they were meant to dampen any flicker of hope that might emerge within me. A single bed with plain white sheets occupied one corner of the room, while an old wooden dresser stood against the adjacent wall. In another corner, there was a tiny desk with an equally tiny chair, both looking like they had seen better days. The only window in the room was high up near the ceiling, its small size allowing just enough light to filter through.

As I sat on the edge of the bed, my hands clenched into fists, I couldn't help but feel a tidal wave of anger and despair crash over me. How did I end up here? Why did fate choose to play such a cruel joke on me? My stomach twisted with nausea at the thought of food, and my eyes were heavy with sleeplessness. Dark circles marred my usually vibrant green eyes, giving them a hollow, haunted appearance. Sleep had become a luxury I could no longer afford, as nightmares continued to plague me relentlessly when I closed my eyes.

"Damn it!" I cursed under my breath, my voice hoarse from disuse. I felt like a caged animal, trapped within these four walls, unable to escape the torment that followed me. The sense of loss weighed heavily on me, choking off my ability to breathe freely. But the idea of leaving this small space made me want to curl up inside myself. I missed having a family, and the loyalty that came with it. But now, I was alone, left to face the demons that haunted me day and night.

I paced the small room, my bare feet padding softly against the cold wooden floor. Each step I took was a reminder of the prison I found myself in, and with every passing moment, my anger and despair grew. My chest tightened as though it were being squeezed by an unseen force, and tears threatened to spill from my eyes.

"Get a grip, Erica," I muttered to myself, wiping away the traitorous tears before they could fall. "You're stronger than this." But even as I tried to convince myself of my own strength, my heart ached with the knowledge that I was just one lone wolf against a world that seemed determined to break me. And despite my best efforts, I couldn't shake the feeling that I was losing the battle, slowly succumbing to the darkness that threatened to consume me whole.

Damon had been to visit me a few days ago, or maybe it was months. Time seemed to lose all meaning here. He told me that he had been called away on some urgent pack business and was off again for a few more days. I couldn't shake the feeling that Damon's disappearance was somehow connected to my current situation. But he wasn't my only visitor.

"Erica?" Liam's voice came through the door, hesitant but persistent. This was his third attempt to visit me, and like the previous times, I didn't respond. I couldn't bear to face him, not when my emotions were so tangled, threatening to unravel at the slightest provocation.

"Go away," I muttered, my voice barely audible even to my own ears.

"Please, Erica," he pleaded. "Just let me in. We need to talk." I clenched my fists, nails digging into my palms. My heart twisted in pain, wanting to believe that he truly cared, but fear of betrayal held me back.

"What's there to talk about? We are nothing to each other."

"Erica, please don't say that," he insisted. "I just want to help. Please, let me in." I hesitated, my resolve wavering. But ultimately, I couldn't bring myself to open the door, to let him see just how broken I was.

"Leave me alone, Liam," I said, my voice cracking with emotion. "I don't need, nor want, your pity." With those words, I heard him sigh heavily and walk away, his footsteps echoing in the silent hallway outside. But the feelings of hurt still lingered through the bond. I leaned my back against the door, sliding down to the cold floor as sobs wracked my body.

"Damn it," I whispered, wiping away my tears with the back of my hand. "Why does everything have to be so complicated?" But no answer came, only the oppressive silence, a constant reminder of the isolation that had become my reality.

"Erica," a voice interrupted my thoughts and despair, pulling me back to reality. It was Grant, he had made a habit of visiting and I guessed that he had been assigned to me by Alpha Declan as a sort of companion and protector. He stood in the doorway, his dirty blond hair tousled, concern etched on his face. His blue eyes met mine, filled with an empathy that made me uncomfortable.

"Hey," he greeted softly, stepping into the small room. "I thought you might want some company."

"Thanks," I muttered, not entirely sincere. As much as I appreciated his presence, it only served as a constant reminder of my own captivity. Grant was kind-hearted and compassionate, but the fact remained that he was here because Declan ordered him to be.

"Look, I know you don't want me here," he said, sensing my unease. "But I just want to help you through this. You don't have to face it alone."

"Help?" I scoffed, my anger bubbling to the surface. "You can't help me escape, can you? Because that's all I really want."

"Erica, I –" he began, but I cut him off.

"Save it," I snapped. "Your words are useless if they're just going to keep me locked up in this prison."

"It doesn't have to be a prison," he said. It's not so bad here. "Trust me, I have been in worse places." He had a haunted look in his eyes when he said that. One that I recognised all too well from the person who I saw in the mirror. Grant sighed and ran a hand through his hair, clearly at a loss.

"Alright, I understand. I won't push you. But if you ever need someone to talk to, I'm here."

"Great," I muttered sarcastically, turning away from him.

Despite my harsh reaction, I couldn't deny that a small part of me was grateful for his efforts. He had tried everything, from bringing me my favourite snacks to telling me stories of the pack's history, in an attempt to distract me from my misery.

"Erica, please," he implored. "I just want to see you smile. I bet you are really pretty when you smile."

"Smile?" I repeated bitterly, my eyes filling with tears. "How can I smile when all I feel is pain?"

"Maybe we can find a way to ease that pain together," he suggested quietly, placing a gentle hand on my shoulder. "You don't have to suffer alone."

"Like it or not, Grant, I am alone," I whispered, shaking his hand off and staring at the cold, wooden floor. "And until I can escape this cage, that's how it's going to stay."

A few days after Grant's last attempt to cheer me up, I found myself sitting on the edge of my bed, staring blankly at the grey painted walls of my small room. My mind was numb, and my heart ached with despair. All I wanted was to be free, to escape this hellish prison, but the more time passed, the more that dream seemed impossible. There was a soft knock on my door, breaking me from my thoughts.

"Erica," came Grant's voice from the other side. "May I come in?"

"Door's unlocked," I mumbled, not caring enough to argue or push him away. The door creaked open, and Grant stepped inside. His dirty blond hair was messy, and there were dark circles under his bright blue eyes, a sign that he hadn't been sleeping well either. He didn't say anything at first, just stood in the doorway, observing me with a mix of concern and determination.

"Hey," he finally said, offering me a small, tentative smile. "I, uh, have some news for you."

"News?" I scoffed, rolling my eyes. "Unless it's about me being released, I don't care."

"Actually," he hesitated, "it's about Alpha Declan. He wants to see you." My heart skipped a beat, and I could feel the blood draining from my face. The mere thought of facing the Alpha filled me with dread. In the past, my encounters with Alphas had never ended well, and I had no reason to think it would be any different this time.

"Are you serious?" I snapped, my voice shaking with anger and fear. "Why the hell does he want to see me?" Grant shifted uncomfortably, clearly reluctant to deliver the message.

"He didn't say, but it sounded important. He asked me to bring you to him."

"Important?" I snorted, my chest tightening with anxiety. "I doubt that. What business would be so important that he would need to discuss it with a lowly Omega." Other than the fact that I was fated to his son and heir, I thought to myself. But I wasn't about to share that piece of information.

"Erica," Grant said softly, stepping closer and placing a hand on my shoulder. "I know you're scared, but maybe this is an opportunity for you. If you talk to him, perhaps you can convince him to let you go."

"Like he would ever listen to me, besides the situation is way too complicated for any chance of that happening," I muttered, averting my gaze. Grant inclined his head in curiosity.

"In what way?" he asked, and I shook my head.

"I don't want to talk about it."

I exhaled. I was already feeling the world was burning around me, what fresh hell could the Alpha think of now. I guessed there was only one way to find out.

"Fine," I agreed reluctantly, my heart pounding in my chest. "Let's go see what the Alpha wants."

Chapter 18

Erica

I sighed in resignation, my shoulders slumping as I trailed behind Grant. My eyes narrowed, making my reluctance clear, and my lips pressed into a thin line. The last thing I wanted was another encounter with Alpha Declan, but it wasn't like I had much of a choice.

As we walked through the pack grounds, I couldn't help but take in the flurry of activity around me. Werewolves of all ages bustled about, some sparring in the practice area in the distance, while others carried out various tasks with a sense of purpose. Laughter and conversation filled the air, weaving an undercurrent of camaraderie that made me feel even more like an outsider. My presence didn't go unnoticed. A young werewolf with dirt smeared on his face paused mid-play, curiosity glinting in his eyes as he tilted his head. Another, a woman with sleek black hair, eyed me warily before whispering something to her companion, who then shot me a disdainful look. The weight of their gazes made my skin crawl, and I resisted the urge to wrap my arms around myself.

"Can you walk any slower?" Grant asked, shooting a glance over his shoulder.

"Sorry," I muttered, quickening my pace despite my reluctance. "Just taking in the sights, I guess."

"Trust me, You'll get used to it, eventually. They will too," he said, his tone laced with bitterness.

"Promise?" I asked, the word slipping out before I could stop it. Grant hesitated, then gave me a small, reassuring smile.

"I promise." The words did little to quell the unease churning in my stomach, but I managed to nod and follow him the rest of the way in silence. Every step felt heavier than the last, weighed down by the knowledge of what awaited me in Alpha Declan's office. I'd been through enough to know that whatever it was, it wouldn't be pleasant.

"Here we are," Grant announced as he stopped in front of a heavy wooden door. "Ready?" "About as ready as I'll ever be," I replied, forcing a tight smile onto my face. The truth was, I wasn't ready at all. But there was no turning back now.

Grant pushed the heavy wooden door open, and we stepped inside. Alpha Declan sat behind a massive oak desk, his hands clasped together as he eyed me with an unreadable expression. Beta Gregg stood to his right, arms crossed over his broad chest, his gaze more curious than hostile. Liam leaned against the far wall, a warm smile gracing his handsome features as he took in my presence. It was clear they each held their own opinions of me, and I braced myself for whatever interrogation or confrontation might come next.

"Ah, Miss Hallows, thank you for joining us," Alpha Declan said, his voice smooth but commanding. "Please take a seat." He indicated a leather chair in front of his desk. I sat in the chair and looked down at my hands while fumbling with my fingers. I could feel the Alpha's eyes on me but I was refusing to look up. I really wanted to get this over and done with so I could go and wallow in the misery that my life had become.

"That'll be all Grant, thank you," the Alpha said without looking up at the door. I turned and looked around at Grant in fear. He wasn't staying? He shot me a weak smile but then nodded to the side.

"Yes Alpha," he said and closed the door, leaving me alone with the three imposing men.

I glanced around nervously and noticed Liam watching me intently. He straightened up from the wall and took a few steps towards me, his brown eyes softening with genuine concern.

"How are you holding up, Erica?" he asked, attempting to bridge the gap between us. But I wasn't quite ready to let him in. My body stiffened, and I looked away, focusing on a spot just past his left shoulder.

"I'm fine," I muttered, not bothering to hide the edge in my voice.

"Are you sure?" Liam pressed gently. "It can't be easy, being thrust into a new pack like this."

"Like I said, I'm fine." My words were sharp, like shards of glass that I hoped would deter him from prying any further. I couldn't afford to let my guard down, not when the stakes were so high.

"Alright, then," Liam conceded, stepping back with an air of disappointment. I knew I'd hurt him, but I couldn't allow myself to feel guilty for it. Not now. Alpha Declan cleared his throat, drawing the attention back to himself.

"We have some matters to discuss, Erica," he stated, his dark eyes boring into mine. I looked back at him and tried not to back down.

"Like what?" I asked, my voice unsteady. What fresh hell did he have for me now?

"I understand that you've been spending most of your time confined to your room." He leaned back into his chair, steepling his fingers. "Is everything alright?"

"Peachy," I snapped, not bothering to hide the sarcasm. My anger bubbled beneath the surface, threatening to spill over. "I mean, aside from being ripped away from my old life and dropped into this one." Declan frowned, clearly taken aback by my outburst.

"I know this transition hasn't been easy for you," he admitted, leaning forward again. "But it's important that you make an effort to integrate with the pack. You can't spend your entire life hidden away in your room."

"Can't I?" I retorted, crossing my arms over my chest defensively. "I have no choice about being stuck here. What difference does it make where I sit and stare at the walls?"

"Erica," Alpha Declan said firmly, his tone brooking no argument. "You are not stuck here. But you must understand, we need to protect you. To do that, we need to know where you are and what you're doing."

"Protect me?" I snorted derisively. "Or control me?" Declan's jaw tightened, and I could tell he was struggling to maintain his patience with me. I knew I was pushing him, but the constant feeling of helplessness had worn me down. It was hard not to lash out when I felt so trapped.

"Both, if necessary," he said finally, his voice like ice. "But my primary concern is your safety, Erica. You may not believe that right now, but in time, I hope you will."

"Sure thing," I said with a roll of my eyes. Did he really think that I would believe this bullshit?

Despite the anger simmering in my chest, I couldn't help but notice the Alpha's struggle to maintain his composure. He clenched his fists by his sides, and the muscles in his jaw twitched with suppressed emotion. It was clear that my defiance made him uncomfortable, but he was determined to keep a level head.

"Erica," he began, carefully choosing his words. "I understand your frustration, and I'm not asking you to blindly trust us. But as your Alpha, it is my responsibility to ensure your safety and the well-being of all pack members." His dark eyes locked onto mine, unwavering, as he continued. "Each member must do their part to ensure the productive running of the pack." I snorted again. I knew where this was going.

"So where do I pick up my toilet brush then?" I asked, venom dripping from my voice.

"Toilet brush?" Apparently I had confused the Alpha.

"Well, the job of a lowly Omega is to clean up after the rest of the pack, right?"

Alpha Declan closed his eyes and took in a deep breath. If I could see inside his head right now, I'd reckon he'd be counting to ten right now. Finally he opened his eyes and forced a tense smile onto his face.

"If you were to accept the fated bond with my son," he said and I saw Liam perk up out of the corner of my eye, "Then you would retain your

Gamma rank, at least until you completed the bond and then you would likely move to an Alpha rank." Liam looked hopeful, But I couldn't think of anything worse.

"I'd rather clean the toilets," I said with a derisive snort. Liam looked furious, which satisfied me to no end. I also noted Beta Gregg trying to hide a chuckle. I could see where Damon got his humour from. I even saw the corners of the Alpha's mouth tug up slightly.

"Very well," he said, "I am sure we can find some suitable work for you."

He then took a brown file from the side of his desk and opened it up. He began reading through it. I watched as his eyes moved from left to right. Did he have information on me? Like what was he reading?

"What exposure have you had in the shifter community?" he asked not even looking up.

"Well, not much." I said, "We kept to ourselves and we were rarely around other supernaturals while I was growing up, until I started working at the bar. Alpha Trenton wasn't happy, but he said it was better than somewhere else. He said he knew Victor, the owner from before."

"And dating?" the Alpha asked. Liam growled behind him and I rolled my eyes. Alpha Declan shot him a glare, and he stopped.

"Erm, not much I guess," I said. "What little exposure I've had wasn't pleasurable experiences."

"Is that where your distrust of Alphas comes in?" I really didn't want to go into one of the traumas of my life, but I suspected that I didn't have a choice.

"Well yes," I said. "When we were attacked when I was little, the Alpha tried to kidnap me." I shot Liam a glare, and he looked away with guilt on his face. "Then there were a couple of bad experiences when I was older, one when I was eighteen-"

"Oh yes, the Frost Bite pack," he said, and my eyes widened.

"That's in the file?" I asked, and the Alpha smiled sadly at me.

"Yes, but..." he looked over at Liam and then at the Beta behind him. "Beta Gregg and I assisted Alpha Trenton and Beta Marshall in getting you away from and dealing with those disgusting vermin." Liam growled as he spoke and I could tell that he was trying to maintain his composure.

"I never knew that," I whispered. I looked back at the Alpha and saw that he was watching me with a sad look. "Thank you." I didn't know what else to say to a man who helped to rescue you from being whored out by a bunch of bottom feeders. The Alpha nodded before looking back down at his papers.

"And you've never shifted, never heard the voice of your wolf?"

"Voice, no." I shook my head. "But I have shifted once, I think." He looked surprised.

"When?"

"When I was twenty, I was attacked." I told the story of my first and only potential shift and the Alpha was writing it all down.

"I was out one night and I could feel someone following me," I said, my mind flashing back to that night. "He was an Alpha rogue who had scented that I was unmated and tried to claim me."

"And you shifted and stopped him?" The Alpha asked.

"I guess so," I said with a nod. "I can't fully remember it. I remember being really scared as he attacked but then blacking out. When I woke up I was covered in blood and there were a few bits of, well I guess him, left scattered around."

"So you are not sure if you shifted or not?" he asked and wrote something down. I shrugged and shook my head.

"I'm not sure what else could have happened," I replied.

"And you also can't hear the voice of other wolves?"

"Huh?"

"Mind linking, dear."

"How did you know?" I was both impressed and concerned at the knowledge he had on me.

"I was watching you with Beta Marshall," he said. "There were plenty of opportunities for you to have a private conversation, but not once did your eyes cloud."

"Oh."

"Tell me, do you hear me now?" His eyes glazed over and I listened intently, but all I could hear was a slight buzzing sound. His eyes cleared up again, and he looked at me expectantly, but I shook my head, disappointed.

His eyes glazed over again and this time I noticed that the Beta's eyes also glazed. Clearly, they were having a conversation about me. After a few moments, their eyes cleared again, indicating their private conversation was over. The Alpha looked back down at the file and then back at me.

"It's not that you don't have a wolf. You think you have shifted." He looked at Liam again. "And there is other evidence as well, so your wolf is there," he explained. "But there appears to be some sort of interference in you two being able to connect."

"Oh," I huffed. He looked amused at my response.

"It could be because of the trauma from the attack, or it could be living with humans all these years." I scowled at that.

"What would living with humans have to do with it?"

"Werewolves are pack animals, we call to each other. If you had been in a pack, around other wolves, then your wolf could have been coaxed out of whatever hole that she is stuck in," he mused. "It's further supported by the knowledge that you could shift when your life was in danger."

"But it's not like I don't have wolf abilities," I stated. "I still have strength and speed, and my hearing is as good as any wolf."

"Yes, and they are all physical attributes. Even as pups, we have strong bodies, but our wolves don't surface until late teen years. The wolf is all mind connected." I had never seen that connection before.

"But I believe with immersion within the pack, we will soon be reunited with your other half." He smiled reassuringly. Part of me hoped it would be that simple.

While I thought over what he had said I noticed that he had gone back to reading the papers again.

"I see you never attended university?" he said finally, and I shook my head.

"That's right sir, moving around a lot and keeping ourselves hidden meant there was little opportunity to go to a university." He looked up over the top of the file, a strange look on his face.

"Interesting." He looked back down at the file. "Would you have liked to have gone?" The question shocked me. Nobody had ever asked me that before. It had never even been a conversation. Even Imogen and Beck didn't consider it.

"I don't know," I said with a shrug. "I think I did okay, given the situation."

"Ah yes," he said, flipping through the paper. "I saw you had a business of your own."

"Not really," I said, "It was just a little thing to help with money and all." The Alpha looked back up at me with a stern look.

"I have seen your work Miss Hallows, even spoken to some of your former clients. You have genuine talent, don't discredit yourself."

"Oh," I said and then internally cursed myself. I was beginning to sound like a right chump. Alpha Declan looked amused at my frustration with myself.

"Good business sense is hard to find in this world," The Alpha said. "Which is why I might have an interesting offer for you."

Chapter 19

Erica

"What offer?" I asked with caution. I might be new here, but even I wasn't stupid to think that you could get something for nothing.

"Well, we have several pack owned and run businesses." He picked up a thick file and held it out to me. I looked at the file and then back at him without taking it. He raised his eyebrows in disapproval, not moving his hand. I just stared at the file, and I could tell he was getting annoyed again and the tension in the room was building.

"Just take the damn file," the Beta growled and my eyes snapped to him and I saw he was glaring at me.

I huffed again and went to snatch the file, but the Alpha held onto it. I looked into his eyes and saw a warning glint in them that made me want to shrink into the chair. I closed my eyes and lowered my head and he made a satisfied sound in his throat before letting the file go.

I opened up the file and in it were brochures and leaflets and paperwork from several businesses, some of which I had heard of and some I hadn't. I looked up at the Alpha, a little confused. I wasn't really sure why he was showing me all this.

"I want you to use your business talents for the businesses within our pack." the Alpha said. "I feel that would be a more fitting purpose for you than..." he glanced up at Liam, "Cleaning toilets." Liam frowned at the comment and I felt my own lips tug up into a half smile. I also noticed that Beta Gregg chuckled too. Still his offer surprised me, considering I had been in the pack for a week, and it wasn't the smoothest of transitions. But I couldn't deny the allure of putting my skills to good use. I always like the idea of working more on my design stuff, but I felt the requirement of helping out with money more.. My curiosity piqued, I raised an eyebrow at him.

"Really? And what's in it for me?" I asked, unable to keep the scepticism out of my voice.

"Should you accept this new role," Alpha Declan continued, ignoring my tone, "you'll be upgraded to a mid-family rank, and of course, would receive a generous salary."

"Hmm," For Alpha Declan to know that I was involved in any sort of business, no matter how small, made me cautious. Did he want me in the pack for something other than mating with his son? It would explain why he so readily agreed to my request to not be forced to complete the mate bond.

"This would afford you some more privileges within the pack that an Omega rank doesn't have."

"What's the catch?" I narrowed my eyes suspiciously at him. He smirked, and I knew I wouldn't like the next part.

"As a mid family rank who is unmated, you will live in one of the unmated pack houses up here. I am expecting you to make a concentrated effort to spend time with pack members of your own age." I frowned, the thought of mingling with these wolves leaving a sour taste in my mouth.

"No offence, Alpha, but I'm not exactly the social butterfly type." He chuckled, a low rumble that made the hairs on the back of my neck stand on end.

"I understand that, Erica. But you might find some of the activities beneficial. For example, warrior training."

"Warrior training?" My interest was piqued, despite myself. Learning to protect myself had always been something I craved, especially considering my inability to shift into my wolf form. Maybe this could be my chance to finally gain some power. My heart raced at the prospect, a flicker of excitement igniting within me. I hated feeling weak, vulnerable. Warrior training would give me the tools I so desperately needed. But something didn't feel right. It seemed like everything was a little too easily given.

"If I accept this new role and become a mid-family rank... would I be able to leave the pack grounds?" His dark eyes narrowed as he considered my question. The silence between us was heavy, a tangible weight pressing down upon my shoulders.

"Normally, yes," he finally answered, his tone guarded. "Mid-family members have more freedom than Omegas do. However, in your case, you will still be restricted to the pack grounds." I gritted my teeth, trying to suppress the anger bubbling up inside me. Of course, there were strings attached, conditions to be met.

"Is that really necessary?" I snapped, unable to contain my frustration any longer. "Why can't I have the same freedoms as everyone else?"

"Erica, it's for your protection," he insisted, his voice firm yet not unkind. "You are valuable to the pack, and we cannot risk losing you."

"Protection?" I laughed bitterly, the sound hollow even to my own ears. "That's a nice way of saying you're keeping me trapped here like a caged animal."

"Please understand," Alpha Declan implored, his expression softening. "I know it feels that way, but believe me when I say it's for your own good." I scoffed, my arms crossing defensively over my chest. For my own good. How many times had I heard those words before? They were nothing more than a thinly veiled attempt to control me, to keep me in line.

"So let me get this straight," I said slowly while trying to fight the rage that was building up in me again. "You expect me to move away from my family and use my talents to line your pockets?" I was so angry that I couldn't see straight. "And you still want to hold me prisoner in this godforsaken place?" I was standing and shouting by the end of that. I threw the file with the brochures onto the desk, only they slipped everywhere and went flying.

"Thank you for the offer, but I respectfully decline," I spat.

The tension in the room was palpable. Liam stood frozen in place, eyes wide with fear. I could feel the rage radiating from the Alpha's body as he seethed, muscles tense and veins bulging. His eyes seemed to have turned a liquid gold hue, and he exuded a power that made both of us tremble. Suddenly, with a flurry of motion, the Alpha lunged forward and grabbed me, throwing me across the room with a force that knocked the breath out of me. I crashed against the wall with a thud, and before I could react, the Alpha was on top of me, his face mere inches from mine. His hot breath blasted against my skin as he snarled and growled with anger, and I felt my body quaking with fear.

The Beta edged towards us slowly, not wanting to cross the Alpha's path or anger. There was something about the Alpha's anger that seemed primal and almost supernatural, and it made us both afraid. I closed my eyes tightly, hoping this nightmare would end quickly.

"You have been repeatedly disobedient, and I will not tolerate this kind of behaviour from someone who is not much older than a pup." He dropped me to the floor, towering over me.

"You might have got away with this kind of shit in your old life and that sorry excuse for a pack you were in, but you are in my pack now and you will follow my rules, or I will really show you what it is like to spend your life as a prisoner when I throw you into the dungeons. DO I MAKE MYSELF CLEAR?" My blood ran cold, and I started shaking, but I nodded my head, quickly sending a fresh wave of pain slammed into me from the movement and I winced.

The Beta had come up behind the Alpha and placed his hand on his shoulder. The Alpha looked at it and took a breath before turning back around and walking to the desk.

"Get back in the chair," he snapped, sitting back down in his own chair. Liam offered me a hand to help me up off the floor. I took it and winced as I lifted myself up. Thank the goddess that I still had werewolf healing, but I was still gonna hurt. I limped back to the chair and sat down tentatively, biting my lip to stop myself from crying yet again today. Liam followed me and sat in the chair next to me. I could tell that he wanted to lean over and offer some sort of comfort, but at that point, I was glad that he didn't. Instead, he sat there and glared at his father.

Once I was seated, the Alpha started speaking again with a menacing calm. His hands were spread out before him as he leaned forward intensely with a pointed look in his eye.

"You have two options, Miss Hallows." His voice seemed to linger and hang in the air before coming down like thunder over me. "Option number one, you accept my generous offer with my terms and enjoy most of the benefits of the new rank. I aim to coax out your wolf with the help of the wolves in the pack." He glanced at Liam with an icy stare.

"I believe the best bet is for you to connect with your fated mate, because their wolf will have the strongest chance of connection. So I suggest spending some time with my son... even in a platonic setting." His gaze pierced into mine as he challenged me to refuse him.

"Option number two, you indeed reject my offer and keep your omega rank, and you will still be commanded to work on the businesses at no pay. Only you will have full Omega restrictions, including having your quota of omega duties on top of the business work." My eyes widened in disbelief.

He looked slightly to his side, and I glanced at the Beta, whose eyes were glazed for an instant. The Alpha smirked.

"And of course, with an Omega rank, you would need express permission from me if you want to train to fight." I shot daggers at the Beta as the tears started falling down my cheeks. I was conflicted about the idea of allowing myself to fall into the fated bond and all it entailed. On one hand, I had an undeniable attraction to the sheer power and strength of Liam. The fated bond caused everything around him to be dull while he shined. But on the other, I was terrified that if I allowed that bond to be formed, I would no longer be able to protect myself or those I loved. Maybe it would be best to go rogue, escape from here, and never look back.

It was like the Alpha heard my thought, although I don't know how, and a glint of something terrifying passed through his eyes.

"And be warned, child, if you attempt anything like you have been planning."

"I have no idea what you are talking about," I tried for defiance but cringed when I saw the flash of gold in the Alpha's eyes again.

"Don't play coy with me, Erica. I know you've been trying to get Grant's help to escape." My stomach dropped and anger coiled within me like a snake ready to strike. Betrayal stung like an open wound, but I forced myself to remain calm, my jaw clenched tight.

"Grant wouldn't –" I began, only to be cut off by Alpha Declan.

"Grant has loyalties to this pack, and it seems he values them more than any misguided attempt to help you run away," he said coldly. I bit back a snarl, despising the fact that he was right. Grant had chosen his loyalty to the pack over our connection, leaving me exposed and vulnerable. I couldn't decide whether I was more furious with him or with myself for ever trusting him in the first place. I should have known not to trust someone here.

"Fine," I spat out, unable to keep the bitterness from my tone. "You've made your point. I won't go anywhere without your permission."

"See that you don't," Alpha Declan warned, his expression unyielding. "Because if you do try, you will be severely punished. Even if you get past the border guard, I will send out my best trackers after you, and I will have you dragged back here. You will be restrained in silver chains in the dungeons for as long as I see fit." I couldn't help the sob that came as I buried my head in my hands. How had my life turned to this in such a short time? No, I refuse to stop fighting. I will play along until I get my chance, so I looked back at the Alpha with determination. He was still sitting there, leaning forward on his desk, his chin resting on his entwined hands.

"I have one condition of my own," I declared. His only acknowledgement was a raise of his eyebrows.

"No one knows," I stuttered slightly and my voice cracked. "About my wolf, or the fated bond, I mean." I looked over at Liam and saw him looking at me. He still looked upset, but nodded his head.

"That's okay," he said. "I plan on proving myself to you, anyway. I can be quiet until then. But I ask for something in return." I looked at him expectantly and waited.

"Please give me a chance." I looked at him for a moment before nodding my head. He nodded back and smiled, his eyes showing his happiness. I couldn't help the smile back. I looked back at the Alpha, who was quietly watching our exchange, and I bowed my head in submission.

"Please, Alpha," I whispered. I looked back up and was surprised to see what looked like sadness in his eyes. He nodded his head slightly.

"You have my word. No one else knows unless you tell them." I felt relief sweep through me, I didn't even realise how much this had been worrying me.

"Then I accept your offer."

Chapter 20

Liam

I SAT IN THE chair next to Erica and watched her intently. I hated to see the tears that fell down her beautiful cheeks as my father commanded her life like it was just another piece on his board. It was so out of character for him as well. Obviously he was thinking of his pack, and of Erica, but he seemed to be going about it in an unusually harsh manner. It took everything I had not to go for him when he threw my mate across the room. That and Gregg mind linking me and telling me to stay still.

"Then I accept your offer," Erica said, bringing me back to the room from my mind. I smiled at the thought of working with her on the business. I already worked alongside my father, and Erica probably didn't realise it yet, but this meant that we would be spending more time together.

"Wise choice," my father said. His eyes flickering to me before settling back on Erica.

His eyes glazed over, and a few seconds later, a knock came at the door. Genevieve Sinclair, or Gen as we called her, entered. Gen was a kind-hearted member of our pack, always ready with a smile and a helping hand. Her blond hair cascaded down her back, framing blue-green eyes that sparkled with warmth and good humour. She appeared petite, yet possessed a strength that belied her delicate features. Like most members of the Silver Stone pack, I found it impossible not to like her.

"Alpha Declan, you requested for me?" she asked cheerfully, giving a slight bow.

"Remind me of your name again, dear?" my father asked, even though I knew full well that he knew who she was.

"It's Gen, sir. Genevieve Sinclair."

"Are you related to Amaury Sinclair?"

"Yes sir, I am. He's my papa," she proclaimed with a big smile.

"That's good. He's a good man, your father." Amaury was one of our top warriors. He was just barely beaten out for the Commander role by Grayson Thompson, and that was probably because every single one of Grayson's six children were amazing warriors. Gen smiled proudly.

"Gen. I have a task for you," he replied, his voice firm but not unkind. "This here is Erica, she is a new pack member."

"Oh how lovely," Gen beamed, clearly excited to help. Turning towards Erica, she extended her hand.

"I'm looking forward to getting to know you, Erica." I observed Gen's infectious excitement, I noted the concern etching itself onto Erica's face. She seemed almost wary of the bubbly young woman before her. My father's words only served to increase her unease.

"Gen will be your guide and help you settle into your new room," he informed Erica, who looked as if she were swallowing a bitter pill. I couldn't quite put my finger on why she appeared so reluctant, but I knew that pushing her would not yield any answers.

"Thank you," Erica managed to say, her voice strained but polite. "I just need to gather a few things first. Has there been any word from Marshall about sending my belongings?"

"Actually, your things arrived the other day," Gen replied brightly, seemingly oblivious to Erica's distress. "They've been waiting for you in your room." The annoyance flared in Erica's green eyes as she processed this information. It was as though she had suddenly realised that my father had already decided her role within our pack, without consulting her.

"Can we go now?" Erica asked through gritted teeth before my father dismissed them with a nod. She followed Gen out of the room, her shoulders tense as she tried to maintain composure. The door slammed shut, echoing through the office like a gunshot. As soon as they were gone, I turned to glare at my father, my feelings clashing inside me like a storm.

My father sat with his chin resting on his hands, watching the door for a moment.

"I like her," he said, leaning back in his chair. Gregg grinned and came and sat in the chair next to me.

"She sure is a feisty one," he replied with a chuckle, his eyes flicking to me for a moment before returning to my father. "She'll be an interesting addition to our pack."

The casual conversation grated on my nerves, and I clenched my fists at my sides. Finally, my father acknowledged my silent fury, his dark eyes narrowing as they met mine.

"What's on your mind, Liam?" I couldn't contain my anger any longer.

"You went too far," I snapped, my fists clenched at my sides. "Throwing her against the wall like that? What were you thinking?" My father's dark eyes met mine without flinching.

"I was testing a theory, Liam," he replied coolly.

"Her reaction to danger is telling, and it's important we understand her fully."

"By treating her as an enemy?" I shot back, my blood boiling. My father glanced at Gregg who shook his head.

"What would you have done if your dumbass plan had worked?" Gregg asked him. Plan? I looked between the two of them.

"What Plan?" I asked.

"I mean, yeah, you scare the shit out of her and her wolf shows up and protects her." Gregg said, and it finally clicked for me. My father was trying to see if he could trigger a shift.

"Well done." Gregg carried on, "But then you would be facing a super pissed off wolf who would be looking for your throat." My father grinned sheepishly and shrugged.

"I thought that's what you're here for?"

"Oh, hell no. You poke the wolf, you get eaten." He laughed. "I'm here to protect you from external threats, not your own stupidity."

"It was worth a try." My father shrugged again. I got the theory behind it but I still didn't like the way he went about it.

"At least we managed to help Marshall and his family relocate to a new place." My father nodded. Gregg had been involved in the move north for the remaining members of their pack, although at this point the only werewolf left was Marshall.

"We've done what we can for them so far, but we need to ensure their safety," my father said.

"During my time with them," Gregg said, his gaze thoughtful, "I noticed the little blond one, Imogen. She seemed particularly close to Erica. If anyone would come looking for her or try to help her escape, it'd be her."

"Then we'll keep an eye on them," Declan decided, his tone final. "They may not realise it yet, but they're better up there away from all this." As much as I hated to admit it, they had a point. Erica's old pack had been weak and vulnerable, easy prey for someone wanting to take advantage.

It was bad enough that Damon had told me that he'd seen some of the Shadow Night pack in the bar in town where Erica used to work, including that bastard Jasper Blackwood, who apparently had taken quite the interest in my mate. The last thing we needed was him finding out that Erica was my fated mate. That would put her in way more danger. That was why even though I wasn't happy about keeping our bond a secret, I was willing to do so for now until Erica trusted me to protect her.

The door creaked open, casting a shaft of light across the dimly lit room. My mother, Fallon Anderson, Luna of the Silver Stone pack, stepped into the office, her soft hazel eyes searching each of our faces. I felt my heart swell with love and worry as she approached. Her normally radiant face was marred by the lines of stress and sorrow that had become a constant presence over the years.

"Is everything all right?" she asked, her voice laced with concern as she looked at us. "I heard raised voices."

"Everything's fine, Fallon," my father assured her, his expression softening for a moment as he met her gaze.

"Mum," I breathed out, unable to contain the mix of emotions coursing through me. "You don't need to worry about us."

"Of course I worry, Liam," she replied gently, placing a warm hand on my shoulder. "Especially when it comes to you."

Her touch sent a pang of guilt through me. It wasn't fair that she blamed herself for the curse that loomed over me like a dark cloud. But no matter how many times we tried to tell her otherwise, she couldn't shake the belief that it was her fault.

"I just..." I trailed off, struggling to put my thoughts into words. "I hate seeing you suffer because of me." my mum smiled sadly, her fingers brushing a stray lock of hair from my forehead as she spoke.

"It's not your fault either, Liam. We've been over this before." And we had, countless times.

The curse had been placed upon me while my mother was pregnant with me, by a man named Felix Blackwood, father to Jasper Blackwood and former Alpha of the Shadow Night pack. Felix had harboured feelings for my mother, and when she met my father, her fated mate; he took it hard. The curse was his twisted way of making her suffer for a choice that wasn't even hers to make. My parents told me about the curse when I was nineteen. At first I was confident in Diana the Moon Goddess's plans and said that my fated mate would appear. But by the time I was twenty-three, and she still hadn't arrived, I started to worry. I even attempted to take a chosen mate, which ended in the worst possible way. After that, I declared that the Moon Goddess would decide my fate and I would only complete the bond with my fated mate.

I have travelled the world, visiting more packs than I could count. Going to all the mating balls and other events that I could. Officially, I was working on pack business, networking within the werewolf community, but the aim was simple: find my fated mate before my 30th birthday. We were getting close, less than half a year, and I had been searching for some other saving grace, or some way to break the curse. I thought again about how I had so little time left. What would happen if I told Erica about the curse? Would she bolt? Or would she complete the bond to save my pack? For some reason I suspected that she would do the second. But I didn't want her to be with me through some sort of duty. I wanted her to realise how amazing the bond could be between us. One look at my father and mother was enough to confirm that the mate bond really was something beautiful. I wanted Erica to see that, and I was willing to take the risk and wait to prove it to her. The last thing she needed was to be forced to be used for other people's gain. I suspected that was something she was used to, and I didn't want to be one of those people.

I glanced up at my father who was whispering something in my mother's ear.

"Dad," I said, and they both looked over. "Can we keep the curse quiet from Erica, just for now?"

"Are you sure that is wise?" Gregg asked. I glanced at him and then back at my father.

"I don't want her to feel like we only want her to save ourselves," I said "I'm trusting that this is the right way. Please?" My father looked to be thinking about it for a moment, but then nodded.

"Okay son," he said, "If you are sure."

"I am." Now all I needed to do was to convince my fated mate that the bond was worth her trust. That was easy, right?

Chapter 21

Erica

Heat swirled in my chest as the realisation struck me. Alpha Declan had orchestrated everything, from assigning me to work for the pack businesses, to predicting I would agree to his plan. My hands clenched into fists as I felt the bitterness of being manipulated once again by an Alpha.

"Is everything alright, Erica?" Gen asked, her brow furrowed in concern.

"Fine," I gritted out through clenched teeth. "Just peachy." I slammed the door to the office behind me, following Gen out of the pack house and into the grounds.

The sun glinted off the windows of two large buildings that flanked the main pack house, a well-manicured park situated between them. Laughter floated on the breeze as children played tag on the lush grass, their happiness mocking the turmoil simmering inside me. Families lounged on picnic blankets, sharing food and conversation. The scene was like something out of a damn postcard, and it only fuelled my anger.

"Everyone seems so... happy," I muttered with more than a hint of sarcasm.

"Of course they are," Gen replied, oblivious to my inner storm. "Alpha Declan runs a tight ship, but he also knows how important it is for everyone to feel at ease and connected."

"Right," I said, rolling my eyes. "Because being a puppet-master brings everyone closer together."

"Erica, I'm sure you've been through a lot," Gen said gently, placing a hand on my shoulder. I fought the urge to shrug it off. "But give this place a chance. It's not what you think." I wanted to scoff, to tell her I knew better than to trust Alphas and their grand plans. But instead, I swallowed my words and forced a smile.

"Sure thing. Thanks."

As we continued walking through the picturesque scene, my mind raced, analysing every detail and interaction around me. I knew from experience that things weren't always what they seemed, and I wouldn't let myself be played like a pawn in Declan's game. But for now, I'd play nice and see where this path led. And if it turned out to be just another cage, well, I'd find a way to break free. I always did.

Gen guided me toward one of the two large buildings that flanked the park.

"This is one of the unmated accommodations," she explained, gesturing to the modern-looking structure before us. She pointed across the park to the other building.

"That's the other one. Over the bridge, you'll find some of the family residences, along with the hospital and training grounds. Further down in the next valley is another residential area and the commercial district."

"Commercial area?" I raised an eyebrow, my curiosity piqued despite my lingering anger. "Yep!" Gen nodded enthusiastically. "We have a whole shopping centre and even a cinema on pack grounds. Our territory is pretty much like its own small town."

"Great," I muttered under my breath, not quite able to keep the cynicism from my voice. "Just what I've always wanted: to be trapped in a self-contained werewolf paradise."

"Erica, it's not as bad as you're making it out to be," Gen insisted, her tone patient but firm. "There's a real sense of community here. We all work together, support each other, and have some fun while we're at it."

"Sure," I replied, forcing a smile on my face even though I couldn't shake the feeling that there was more to this place than met the eye. "Sounds wonderful."

As we approached the unmated accommodation building, I took note of the people around me, observing their interactions with one another. They did seem genuinely happy, laughing and chatting as if they didn't have a care in the world. But I knew better than to judge a book by its cover, and I wasn't about to let my guard down just because the scenery was pleasant.

"Come on," Gen encouraged, leading me inside the building. "Let's get you settled in. You can see for yourself that this place isn't as bad as you think."

"Alright," I agreed, following her into the building while silently promising myself that I'd keep my wits about me.

The sun cast a warm glow over the building's modern facade as we reached our destination. I glanced up, taking in the three floors of geometric glass windows and sleek lines that seemed to defy the natural world around us. Despite my misgivings, it was hard not to be impressed.

"Welcome to your new home," Gen announced, spreading her arms out wide. "Each floor houses different members of the pack, with the top floor reserved for the high-family rank." She gave me a sidelong glance, her eyes twinkling with amusement. "That's where we'll be."

"But I'm not high-family," I said. Gen just shrugged and mentioned that Alpha Declan wanted me to be comfortable.

"Of course," I muttered under my breath, fighting the urge to roll my eyes. It figured that Alpha Declan would want to keep me close, even if it meant putting me among the elite.

We stepped inside, greeted by the hum of conversation as people milled about the open-plan lobby. Wide windows flooded the space with natural light, casting vibrant colours across the polished concrete floors and minimalist furniture.

"Downstairs is the common room, along with the gym and laundry facilities," Gen explained, gesturing towards a staircase leading below ground level. "Upstairs is where all the fun happens."

"Can't wait," I deadpanned, earning a smirk from her. Despite my cynicism, I had to admit that the place had a certain charm to it. But then again, appearances could be deceiving.

We took the stairs to the top floor, and at the top there was what looked like a long hallway. Gen led us halfway down to another sleek wooden door and smiled as she unlocked it, allowing me to walk in. I found myself in a spacious apartment filled with modern furnishings. Floor-to-ceiling windows framed the living area, offering a breathtaking view of the surrounding landscape. The kitchen boasted gleaming stainless steel appliances, while the lounge consisted of plush couches arranged around a sleek coffee table.

"Your room's this way," Gen said, guiding me down a hallway lined with abstract paintings. She stopped at a door and pushed it open, revealing a room that was easily three times larger than the one I'd just vacated.

"Wow," I breathed, momentarily taken aback by the sheer amount of space. The bed was covered in soft linens, its headboard upholstered in a rich purple fabric. A matching armchair sat in the corner, next to a floor lamp that cast a warm glow over the cosy reading nook. A modern desk held a new laptop and mobile phone, while suitcases and boxes were neatly stacked against one wall.

"Feel free to make yourself at home," Gen said, her expression genuine. "You deserve it."

"Thanks," I replied hesitantly, my fingers itching to explore my new surroundings. But beneath the gratitude lay a spark of anger, a reminder that all of this had been orchestrated by Alpha Declan, who seemed intent on controlling every aspect of my life. And as much as I wanted to enjoy the comforts of my new room, I couldn't shake the feeling that I was dancing to his tune.

"Erica," Gen said softly, placing a hand on my shoulder. "It's okay to let your guard down sometimes. Just because things are going well doesn't mean it's a trap."

"Maybe," I conceded, although I didn't entirely believe her words.

"Take your time to settle in," Gen said, passing me a packet of information before leaving the room.

"I'll be around if you need anything," she said as she closed the door behind her.

Finally alone, I surveyed my new surroundings, my heart heavy with mixed emotions. On one hand, it was comforting to have a space to call my own, but on the other, the thought of Alpha Declan's involvement gnawed at me. With a sigh, I began unpacking the suitcases and boxes, half-expecting them to hold more surprises from the Alpha. To my relief, they contained only my belongings, clothes, books, and the few trinkets I'd managed to hold on to over the years. As I placed my small collection of romance books on the bookshelf, my eyes drifted back to the shiny new laptop and mobile phone on the desk. The sleek devices seemed out of place amongst my well-loved possessions, and I couldn't help but feel a pang of resentment towards their unknown benefactor. A note attached to the laptop confirmed my suspicions:

"Welcome to your new home - Alpha Declan."

"Of course," I scoffed, rolling my eyes. Was there any aspect of my life he didn't plan to meddle in?

Flipping through the contacts on the phone, I discovered that several members of my family were already programmed in. My thumb hovered over Imogen's name, my heart pounding as I remembered the last time we'd been together, and then Liam kidnapping me at the funeral, and the gut-wrenching fear I'd felt as we'd been torn apart.

"Here goes nothing," I whispered, pressing the call button and praying for a familiar voice.

"Erica?" Imogen answered on the second ring, her tone laced with equal parts hope and disbelief.

"Is that really you?"

"Hey, Imogen," I said softly, feeling tears prick at the corners of my eyes. "It's me."

"Goddess, Erica, I've been so worried," she confessed, her voice trembling with emotion. "Ever since that bastard took you away, I just... I didn't know what to think."

"Believe me, I'm not thrilled about it either," I replied bitterly. The memory of that day still sent shivers down my spine, and I knew it would be a long time before I could put it behind me.

"But you're okay now?" she asked hesitantly. "You're safe?"

"Safe is a relative term," I mused, glancing around the comfortable room that felt like a gilded cage. "But yeah, for now, I'm okay."

We spent the next hour catching up on everything that had happened since we'd last seen each other, the good, the bad, and the downright confusing. Though the distance between us was vast, our conversation flowed effortlessly, as if no time had passed at all. And in those moments, I found solace in the knowledge that, despite the obstacles we faced, our bond remained unbroken.

"Promise me one thing," Imogen said, her voice filled with determination. "No matter what happens, don't let them break you. Stay strong, Erica."

"I promise," I whispered, my heart swelling with love and gratitude. "I won't let them."

"Tell me what's going on at home," I asked, trying to distract myself from the oppressive weight of my new surroundings. "I want all the juicy details." Imogen laughed softly, her voice a warm balm on my frayed nerves.

"Well, we moved to the northern English-Scotland border. You won't believe the house we're living in now, it's way better than the old one. It's bigger, brighter, and there's even a full garden for me to work with."

"Really?" I said, a genuine smile tugging at my lips as I pictured Imogen happily tending to her plants, her green thumb working its magic.

"Yep," she confirmed. "And you know how Beck's always been into swimming? Well, there's a pool just down the road, and he's loving it."

"Sounds like you're all really flourishing," I mused, inwardly marvelling at how the twins had managed to find their passions amidst the chaos that was our lives. It was a testament, perhaps, to the resilience of the human spirit.

"Definitely," Imogen agreed. "But you know what would make it even better? Having you here with us."

"Trust me," I replied, my voice thick with emotion. "I wish I could be there too."

"I know you do," she said softly. "Just promise me we'll see each other again soon, okay?"

"Promise," I whispered, sealing the vow with the unspoken understanding that neither of us knew when, or if, that day would come.

"Good," Imogen sighed, her voice tinged with relief. "Now go get some rest, Erica. We'll talk again soon."

"Thanks, Imogen," I murmured, feeling a swell of gratitude for the unwavering support she'd always offered me. "Take care of yourself."

"Always," she replied, her voice resolute. "You too." With a final goodbye, I hung up the phone and let it slip from my fingers onto the bed. The room, which had seemed so warm and inviting just minutes before, now felt cold and empty, a stark reminder of the gulf that lay between me and those I held dear.

A soft knock at the door pulled me from my thoughts, and I blinked back the tears that threatened to spill over.

"Come in," I called, trying to keep my voice steady. Gen poked her head around the door, a warm smile on her face.

"Hey, Erica. It's getting late, and I was wondering if you'd like some dinner?" I glanced out the window and realised with a start that the sun had dipped low in the sky, casting long shadows across the pack grounds. Time had slipped away from me as easily as sand through fingers.

"Yeah, sure," I agreed, welcoming the distraction.

"Great, come on," Gen said, beckoning for me to follow her into the living area.

As I stepped out of my room, I noticed two other girls lounging on the plush couches. Their eyes flicked up to meet mine, curiosity mingling with cautious optimism.

"Erica, this is Frankie and Verity," Gen introduced, gesturing to each girl in turn. "Frankie's our other roommate."

"Nice to meet you," I said, nodding at them both. My guard remained up, but I didn't want to seem rude.

"Welcome to the madhouse," Frankie quipped, her black hair tipped with purple falling over one eye as she grinned mischievously. The tattoos snaking up her arms hinted at a rebellious streak, yet her gaze held warmth.

"Thanks," I replied, forcing a small smile onto my lips, even as my heart ached for the familiar faces I'd left behind.

"Hey, I've got an idea," Frankie suggested, her eyes lighting up. "Why don't we all go to Barking Brews to celebrate Erica's arrival?" She looked at me, "It's a pub here on pack grounds."

"Sounds fun," Verity agreed, her white-blonde hair framing her pale grey eyes. Her voice was soft, and she seemed to have a quiet, timid feel. Her and Frankie, seemed almost opposites of each other. I hesitated, torn between wanting to maintain my distance and the undeniable allure of friendship. The question lingered in the back of my mind: could I trust these people? But then again, what choice did I have? This was my life now, whether I liked it or not. And perhaps, just for tonight, I could allow myself a moment of reprieve from the weight that settled on my shoulders.

"Alright," I conceded, feeling a flicker of hope ignite within me. "Let's do it."

"Awesome!" Frankie cheered, clapping her hands together in excitement. "Let's get ready, then."

As we dispersed to prepare ourselves for the night ahead, I couldn't help but wonder if this might be the first step toward building new bridges, or if it would only serve to remind me of everything I'd lost. Only time would tell, but for now, I resolved to make the most of the opportunity before me. After all, as Imogen had reminded me, life went on, and so must I.

Chapter 22

Erica

The heavy wooden door of Barking Brews creaked open as we entered, the warm and lively atmosphere washing over us like a tidal wave. The pub had an undeniably rustic charm with its exposed brick walls, dim lighting, and mismatched wooden tables and chairs. A DJ booth played in the corner, the energetic rock music pulsating through the air and making my heart race.

Gen, Verity, Frankie, and I had dressed to impress for our night out. Gen wore a sleek black dress that hugged her curves, paired with knee-high boots. Verity opted for a more casual look, her white blond hair cascading down her back, contrasting against her dark leather jacket and jeans. Frankie, true to her alternative style, sported a purple crop top under a studded vest, her tattoos on full display. As for me, I went with a simple but sexy black skinny ripped jeans and a red low cut top that matched my fiery hair.

"Erica, there's someone I want you to meet!" Gen shouted over the music, pulling me toward the crowded bar where a tall brunette stood, her eyes sparkling with excitement.

"This is Kaitlyn!"

"Hey, it's so great to finally meet you!" Kaitlyn gushed, extending her hand. "I've heard all about you from Liam!" Confusion settled on my face, why would Liam share anything about me? Kaitlyn leaned in closer, her voice barely audible above the din.

"Don't worry, your secret's safe with me. I'm Liam's sister." Great, just what I needed, another Anderson with insider knowledge about my situation. My guard heightened, but I decided to play along, offering a tight-lipped smile. Kaitlyn seemed genuine enough, but trust wasn't something I handed out easily.

"Thanks," I replied cautiously. "It's nice to meet you too."

As we chatted, I couldn't help but feel an odd sense of friendship with these girls. They all had their own baggage and secrets, but for one night, we could forget about them and just enjoy ourselves.

"Come on, let's get a drink!" Frankie suggested, her eyes scanning the bar like a predator searching for prey. We all nodded in agreement, after all, it was going to be a long night, and I needed some liquid courage if I was going to navigate through this pack's treacherous waters.

As we stood by the bar, nursing our drinks and laughing at Frankie's animated story, I couldn't help but feel a sense of belonging. It was strange and unfamiliar, but not unwelcome. My thoughts were interrupted by the sound of high heels clicking against the wooden floor, their owner strutting toward us like an angry peacock.

"Seriously, I need to vent." Heidi announced to us as though we had been waiting for her arrival.

"Some bitch just stole the job I went for, working with the Alpha!" She tossed her shiny black hair over her shoulder, her amber eyes narrowing with contempt.

"Really? That's terrible," Gen replied, eyeing me nervously.

"I didn't sleep with Jamie for the fun of it! Whoever she is, I'm going to rip her eyes out when I find out who it is." Heidi's hands clenched into fists, her anger palpable. She hadn't noticed me yet, so I decided to put an end to her rant before it escalated further.

"Actually," I interrupted, tapping her on the shoulder with a smirk, "I'm the 'bitch' you're looking for." Heidi's head snapped around, her eyes widening in surprise before narrowing into a glare.

"You? Why is this rogue bitch even on pack land?"

"Heidi. meet Erica. Erica, this is Heidi." Gen interjected, trying to defuse the situation.

"We've met," I said coldly, and Adelaide glared at me. I could feel her aggressive essence coming off her in waves and she was directing them at me, like she was challenging me.

"Erica's joined the pack," Frankie said, clearly enjoying herself. "And yeah, she got the job."

Heidi's face turned an interesting shade of red, her nostrils flaring as she processed this new information. She growled and stepped forward again, so she was right in front of me. She was a good few inches taller than me and she glowered down at me, and I could swear I could see her wolf behind her amber eyes.

"I want to know what you did to steal my job out from under me," she sneered. I couldn't help the cunning grin that formed on my lips.

"Well, I obviously didn't sleep with Jamie, because that didn't get you shit, now did it?" I heard the gasps behind me and a laugh from Frankie. Heidi's nostrils flared in anger.

"Who the fuck do you think you are to talk to me like that?" she fumed. "You are nothing but some omega trash who got fucking lucky." Even though I was no longer officially Gamma rank, I could still feel the power I was born into. Being stripped of it in name doesn't take away what the goddess gives you at birth. I allowed that power to course through my veins right now. I stared deep in her eyes and growled.

"Do I feel like an omega, bitch?" Heidi visibly recoiled, her bravado crumbling at the sight of my true nature. Realising she had underestimated me, she tossed her shiny black hair over her shoulder and stormed off with a snide comment.

"This isn't over, slut. Just remember, everyone has secrets."

The tension in the air dissipated as she disappeared into the crowd. I rolled my eyes and turned to find Frankie practically vibrating with excitement.

"Erica, that was the best thing I've ever seen!" she exclaimed, her dark eyes sparkling with admiration. "Heidi needed taking down a peg or two, and you just became my favourite person!"

"Thanks, I guess," I said, trying to brush off the praise. I never cared much for the spotlight, especially when it came to confrontations. But there was something gratifying about standing up to Heidi and showing her I wasn't someone to be pushed around.

"Seriously, though, that was badass," Frankie continued, her grin infectious. I couldn't help but smile back, feeling a sense of camaraderie with this rule-breaking pack member who seemed to have my back.

As we shared a laugh, I sensed someone approaching. A presence suddenly appeared beside me, causing Frankie's grin to widen even more.

"Looks like you've got a shadow," Frankie teased, nodding toward the figure beside me. I glanced over to find Grant standing there, his blue eyes dancing with mischief and a cheeky grin plastered across his face.

"Seems like you're already causing trouble," he said, his tone light and flirtatious.

"Me? Causing trouble?" I replied sarcastically. "I think you have that backwards, Grant. You're the one who ratted me out to the Alpha when I was trying to escape." He shrugged nonchalantly, his grin widening.

"Maybe I just wanted to keep you around." His words were playful, but something in his gaze told me there might be a kernel of truth hidden beneath the flirtation. Despite my irritation, I couldn't help but smile at his flirting. There was something about Grant's carefree demeanour that drew me in, and I found myself wanting to let down my guard, if only for a moment. But I couldn't forget that he had betrayed me, even if his intentions weren't malicious.

"Anyway," I said, forcing my expression back to neutral, "I'm not looking for trouble. It just seems to follow me wherever I go."

"Isn't that the truth?" Grant laughed, his eyes twinkling as they met mine.

But our moment of levity was short-lived, as a dark cloud seemed to descend over the room. Across the bar, I caught sight of Liam glaring in our direction, his handsome face twisted into a scowl. He was watching Grant and me with an intensity that sent a shiver down my spine.

Suddenly, he pushed through the crowd and made his way over to us.

"Grant," Liam said coldly, his voice dripping with disdain, "shouldn't you be on duty or something?" The tension between them was palpable, and I couldn't help but wonder what had caused such animosity. I knew Liam had a possessive streak when it came to me, but this felt like something more, something rooted in their shared history.

"Relax, Alpha," Grant replied, his tone casual but his eyes wary. "I'm just enjoying some time off with my friends."

"Your 'time off' seems to coincide with mine a little too often for my liking," Liam snapped, his gaze never leaving Grant's face. Grant's jaw clenched as the tension between him and Liam continued to escalate. With a frustrated huff, he threw back the rest of his drink and stormed off, leaving me standing there with Liam's dark gaze boring into me.

"Excuse me," I muttered, attempting to sidestep him and put some distance between us. But Liam had other plans, seizing my arm and pulling me around a corner, away from the prying eyes of our friends.

"Hey!" I snapped, yanking my arm free from his grasp. "What the hell do you think you're doing?"

"Erica," he growled, his voice low and dangerous. My heart pounded in my chest, partly out of anger but also, frustratingly, out of attraction. His close proximity was doing things to me that I didn't want to acknowledge.

"Leave me alone, Liam." My voice shook slightly, betraying my growing unease. Instead of listening, Liam suddenly closed the gap between us, pushing me against the wall and kissing me fiercely. Instinctively, I tried to push him away, furious at his audacity. But as his lips moved hungrily against mine, my resolve began to crumble, and soon I found myself melting into his embrace, my hands gripping the fabric of his shirt.

His scent, an intoxicating mix of gingerbread and fire, enveloped me as our lips danced together, each kiss more passionate than the last. I hated how good this felt, how easily my body responded to his touch. It wasn't fair, especially when I'd already made up my mind about not giving in to the mate bond.

As we kissed, I couldn't help but wonder what this meant for my future with Liam, and how much longer I could resist the powerful connection between us. The thought both terrified and excited me, leaving me breathless and wanting more, even as I knew I shouldn't. But instead of pulling away, I found myself only craving more of him, and hating myself for it. My mind raced as Liam's hands roamed over my body, his touch leaving a trail of fire in its wake. I run my fingers over his back. I can feel the heat radiating from his body and the hardness of his muscles. I curl my fingers into his t-shirt and pull him in closer. The rough scratch of his beard, the warmth of his body, the softness of his lips. His hands are like the softest velvet, gripping me like they're brand new. I gasped as Liam's lips left mine, and he trailed a line of flames down my neck. His hands continued to explore my body, and I felt the warmth and desire radiating from them. The sensation was so intense that I wanted to cry out in pleasure, but I held back, knowing that I shouldn't give in just yet. His lips finally reached my collarbone, and he gently nipped at the exposed skin there. Instantly, a jolt of electricity shot through me and I shuddered with pleasure. His hands moved lower on my body, causing me to moan softly as he touched me in all the right places.

His mouth urgently met mine again. Our kiss was electric, almost like a drug, and I felt myself growing more and more addicted with each passing second. I could no longer deny the attraction that burned between us, and it only seemed to intensify as we explored each other with our mouths. Liam's hands moved possessively over me, igniting a fire inside of me that threatened to consume us both. He was demanding yet gentle, setting my skin on fire wherever he touched. The sensations were overwhelming, and I found myself longing for even more. Time seemed to stand still as we clung to each other desperately, exploring every inch of each other with our tongues. I felt as though I had been transported to another world where nothing else mattered but this moment between us. Every sensation combined into an intoxicating blend of pleasure and desire that left me wanting more and more of him. We were lost in each other, completely unaware of the world around us. Just when I thought I couldn't take any more, his fingers slipped beneath the waistband of my jeans. He expertly explored every curve of my body until I was trembling with anticipation and desire for more. It didn't matter that we were in a public place, and anyone could walk around the corner and see us at any moment. My skin burned wherever he touched, sparking an inferno inside me that threatened to consume us both. His hands moved in slow circles over my hips and stomach before sliding upward toward my chest. He slipped his hands into my bra and cupped my breasts in his palms and gently massaged them until I moaned with pleasure. His lips trailed kisses down my neck as he moved his hands back down to explore the rest of me. Everywhere he touched felt like pure bliss and I found myself arching into him, desperate for even more contact. With each caress, he seemed to be reminding me of just how much he wanted me and it only made me want him even more. Before long, we were both lost in a haze of desire and longing for each other, our bodies intertwined in passion-fuelled abandon.

"Erica," he whispered into my ear, his breath hot against my skin. "You need to remember that you're mine. You might not agree yet, but I won't hesitate to kill any man who dares to touch you like this." And just like that an emotional bucket of cold water drenches the fire in me.

"Who the hell do you think you are?" I snapped, trying to regain control of my emotions. "I'm not your property."

Ignoring my protests, he continued to kiss my neck, nipping gently at my marking spot. The sensation sent a thrill down my spine, and I hated myself for enjoying it. Liam was claiming ownership over me, and despite my anger, I couldn't deny the pull between us. As if sensing my internal struggle, Liam pulled back slightly, smirking at my flushed appearance.

"It's only a matter of time, baby. You can fight it all you want, but you can't escape what fate has planned for us." His words stung, making me feel trapped and powerless. But instead of lashing out, I just clenched my fists, biting back tears of frustration.

"You don't know me, Liam. Don't you dare presume to know what I will or won't do."

"Time will tell," he said with a smug grin before walking away, leaving me standing there, a mess of conflicting emotions.

Annoyance and anger warred within me, battling against the undeniable attraction I felt for Liam. I tried to tell myself it was just the bond, that I didn't actually want him. But as I leaned against the wall, trying to calm my racing heart, I couldn't help but feel a nagging sense of doubt.

"Damn you, Liam Anderson," I muttered under my breath, wiping away a stray tear. As much as I wanted to deny it, there was a part of me that feared I might be falling for him, and that terrified me more than anything else.

Chapter 23

Erica

The first rays of sunlight filtered through my curtains, warming my face and bringing me back to consciousness. I blinked into the light, taking a moment for the haze of sleep to dissipate. It was Monday morning, and despite the whole being-forced-into-working-for-the-pack-businesses thing, I couldn't help but feel a surge of excitement. My design side hustle had been fun, but this... this was something else entirely. A real business setting, with all its challenges and opportunities.

"Alright, Erica," I muttered to myself as I swung my legs over the edge of the bed, "Time to show them what you're made of."

I padded across the room to my closet, the carpeted floor comfortable beneath my feet. As I stared at the array of clothes hanging there, I couldn't shake the feeling that somehow, none of it would be good enough. I needed to make a strong first impression, not just because my position here was tenuous at best, but also because of the heavy weight of imposter syndrome pressing down on my chest.

"Ugh, why is this so hard?" I groaned, rifling through the hangers. Each outfit seemed to scream that I didn't belong, that I'd be found out as soon as I stepped foot in the office. But I pushed those thoughts aside, reminding myself of the strengths I brought to the table, even if they were different from those around me.

"Alright," I murmured, finally settling on a sleek black pantsuit with a dark green blouse that complimented my red hair and green eyes. "You've got this, Erica. You're strong, resourceful, and damn good at what you do."

As I dressed, I tried to focus on the positives. Sure, I might not be able to shift like everyone else. And yes, my past experiences with Alphas left me more than a little wary. But that didn't mean I had nothing to offer. And it certainly didn't mean I should let my fear define me.

"Okay," I said, taking a final glance in the mirror and smoothing down my hair. "Let's do this." Taking a deep breath, I left my room and ventured into the unknown, determined to prove that I belonged here, with or without the abilities of my fellow pack members.

Stepping out of my room, I was greeted by the sight of Gen, cheerful as always, sweaty from her gym session. Her enthusiasm seemed to fill the room, making it hard not to smile in response.

"Morning, sunshine!" she beamed, a towel draped over her shoulder. "Ready for your first day at the big, bad pack office?"

"More like nervous," I admitted, rubbing my palms on my pantsuit to dry them off. "But yeah, I think I'm as ready as I'll ever be."

"Great! You want some breakfast?" She gestured to the table, laden with an assortment of cereals, fruit, and toast.

"Uh, no thanks," I said, feeling slightly queasy at the thought. "I think I'll just... take a walk to clear my head before work."

"Suit yourself," Gen said, shrugging and scooping up a spoonful of yoghurt. "But you know what they say about breakfast being the most important meal of the day."

"Right," I muttered, grabbing my bag as I headed for the door. "Thanks, Gen."

The morning air was cool and crisp against my skin as I began my slow walk toward the main pack house. The grounds were still quiet at this hour; the sun casting long shadows across the dewy grass. It felt peaceful, almost serene, and I tried to soak up that tranquillity to quell my nerves. As I walked, I couldn't help but marvel at how different life had become since joining this pack. Sure, there were challenges, like my inability to shift and my distrust of Alphas, but for once, I felt like I could carve out a place for myself here. A place where I belonged.

"Who would've thought," I mused, watching a rabbit dart across the path in front of me. "Erica Hallows, working for the pack and... maybe even making friends." With each step, my anxiety seemed to lessen, replaced by a growing determination. This was my chance to prove my worth, to show that I had something valuable to contribute, and I wasn't going to let it slip away.

"Alright," I said under my breath as the pack house came into view, its imposing facade bathed in golden morning light. "Let's do this."

Hesitating at the entrance of the pack house, I took a deep breath and braced myself for whatever lay ahead. As I stepped inside, a guard stationed near the door nodded at me in acknowledgement.

"Morning," I mumbled, racking my brain to put a name to his familiar face.

"Good morning, Erica," he replied warmly. "You're looking for the pack offices, right? They're on the first floor."

"Thanks, um... sorry, I can't seem to remember your name," I admitted sheepishly. He chuckled.

"No worries, it's Wesley. But you can call me Wes."

"Right, Wes. Thanks again." With a small smile, I headed for the stairs as he wished me a nice day.

Reaching the first floor, I ventured into the main office. The open-plan space was filled with sleek, modern desks, all currently unoccupied. I couldn't help but feel a tad overwhelmed by the sheer size of the room, not to mention the responsibility now resting on my shoulders.

"Get it together, Erica," I muttered under my breath, feeling the weight of my own insecurities pressing down on me. "You've got this."

As I hesitated in the doorway, the sound of footsteps caught my attention. A dark-haired woman emerged from a side room, her confident stride making me feel even more out of place.

"Hey there," she called out, her warm smile doing little to ease my nerves. "You must be Erica. I'm Lucy, Alpha Anderson's personal assistant."

"Hi, Lucy," I responded, trying to muster up some confidence. "Nice to meet you."

"Likewise! Welcome to the pack offices. You're actually one of the first people here today, so you'll have some time to settle in before things get busy."

"Thanks," I said, grateful for the small mercy. As I glanced around the room, I couldn't help but wonder what challenges awaited me in this new environment – and whether I'd truly be able to rise to the occasion.

"Let me give you a quick tour," Lucy said, gesturing for me to follow her. She walked around the office with an air of authority, explaining the layout and daily schedule as I trailed behind, trying to absorb everything she was saying.

"Over there is the conference room," she pointed out, "where we hold our weekly staff meetings. And down that hallway are the private offices for upper management." I took in the sleek, modern design of the space, glass partitions, ergonomic chairs, and state-of-the-art computers adorning each desk. It was impressive, no doubt, but it only served to fuel my sense of being an imposter in this world.

"Any questions so far?" Lucy asked, turning to face me.

"Uh, no, I think I'm good," I replied, hoping that my expression didn't betray the whirlwind of emotions swirling inside me.

"Great," she smiled, clearly oblivious to my internal turmoil. "Now, let's get you settled in."

Lucy led me to a desk near the centre of the room, where she picked up a brown envelope with my name scrawled across the front. Handing it to me, she explained,

"This contains your employment contract, as well as your passwords, logins, and company bank card."

"Bank card?" I echoed, eyebrows raised in surprise.

"Yep," Lucy replied casually. "All company directors have access to the financials. It's part of your role here."

"Directors?" My heart skipped a beat, and I could feel the anxiety bubbling up within me.

I couldn't help but gape in horror as Lucy pointed out the part of the contract that named me a company director in training. The words seemed to leap off the page, taunting me with their implications. My chest tightened, and I suddenly felt like I was suffocating under the weight of my new title. I mean, Director, what in the actual fuck, I had been in the pack a week. This felt like yet another play to mess with my head.

"Come on," Lucy said, unfazed by my reaction. "Let me show you your office." I followed her, still clutching the envelope and feeling like an imposter.

The office was impeccably modern, with sleek lines and minimalist decor. It looked like a space designed for someone far more important than me.

"Here we are," Lucy announced, gesturing toward a glass-walled office with a stunning view of the grounds. My name was already on a gleaming silver plaque next to the door. It added to the sense of unreality, making me feel like I'd walked into someone else's life.

"Wow," I breathed, barely able to process the fact that this was all mine.

"Pretty nice, huh?" Lucy grinned. "You'll get used to it soon enough. Now, if you need anything, just give me a shout. Otherwise, good luck settling in!"

"Thanks," I mumbled, still reeling from the shock of it all as Lucy walked away.

I hesitated outside the office, feeling the weight of expectation bearing down on me. My stomach churned with anxiety, but I forced myself to step through the door and take in my surroundings. As my eyes swept over the polished surfaces and state-of-the-art technology, I felt a sudden presence behind me, and my heart skipped a beat.

Turning around, I found myself face to face with Liam, who was dressed in a stunning tailored black suit. The fabric clung to his perfectly sculpted body, accentuating the broadness of his shoulders and the defined curve of his biceps. The suit was cut in such a way that it highlighted his narrow waist and muscular thighs, leaving no doubt about the power that lay beneath the elegant exterior. As my eyes traced the lines of his body, I became acutely aware of how hot he looked. It was as if the suit had been designed specifically to showcase his rugged handsomeness and raw masculinity. My cheeks burned with embarrassment when I realised I'd been caught staring. Liam's eyes sparkled with amusement as he caught my lingering gaze.

"You know, it's considered rude to stare," he teased, his voice smooth and warm like rich chocolate. My cheeks flushed crimson, and I stammered, trying to find the right words.

"I, uh... I wasn't staring. I was just admiring your suit," I mumbled, feeling my embarrassment grow by the second.

"Uh-huh," Liam replied, clearly not buying my flimsy excuse. "Well, in that case, consider yourself lucky. I usually reserve this level of stunning attire for special occasions." His grin widened, making me all too aware of how close we were standing.

"Right," I said, forcing a laugh to diffuse the tension building between us. My heart raced, pounding in my chest like a trapped bird desperate to escape. This wasn't good; I couldn't afford to let him get under my skin like this. I cleared my throat and decided to change the subject.

"So, what brings you to the office? Are you here to keep an eye on me?" I asked, trying to inject some cynicism into my tone. Liam shook his head, his expression turning serious. "No, Erica. I'm here because I work in the business too. And I'm looking forward to working very closely with you." His words sent a shiver down my spine, but I refused to let my emotions show. Instead, I focused on the practicalities.

"What exactly will we be working on together?" I inquired, raising an eyebrow sceptically.

"You'll see soon enough," Liam replied cryptically. "Just trust me when I say that our collaboration will benefit both the pack and our businesses." I wanted to believe him, but my natural distrust of Alphas made that difficult. Still, I couldn't deny the allure of working alongside someone as captivating as Liam. Maybe, just maybe, this would turn out to be the opportunity I'd been waiting for, if I could keep my guard up and resist his undeniable charm. Or maybe it would just be another big clusterfuck and I would fail miserably.

"Fine," I sighed, trying to sound nonchalant. "I guess we'll see how this goes."

"Trust me, baby," Liam said, his voice low and sincere. "You won't regret it." I rolled my eyes at his pet name. I had given up telling him to stop using it.

As I watched him walk away, I couldn't help but feel a strange mixture of anticipation and dread settling in my stomach. This partnership could either make or break me, and only time would tell which outcome awaited me.

Chapter 24

Liam

The moment I told Erica we'd be working together, I couldn't help but notice the blush that spread across her cheeks. Her light red hair framed her face as she glanced down at the floor, attempting to hide her attraction to me. It brought a smirk to my lips, and I revelled in the effect I had on her. She was struggling to maintain her composure, and it only made me want her more.

"Are you okay?" I asked, raising an eyebrow as she fidgeted with her fingers.

"Y-yes," she stammered, not quite meeting my gaze. "I didn't expect we'd be working so closely."

"Neither did I," I admitted, though secretly enjoying the prospect. "But I'm glad we are."

Just then, a knock sounded at the door. Lucy, my father's assistant, entered the room. Her eyes darted between us for a moment before she addressed Erica.

"There's a meeting starting soon in the main conference room," she informed her.

"Thank you, Lucy," I said, earning a nod from her before she left the room. Erica looked flustered, her green eyes wide as if she'd been caught off-guard. She bit her lip nervously, and I couldn't help but imagine how it would feel to have those lips wrapped around my cock. I shook the thought away, knowing now wasn't the time for such fantasies.

"Come on," I said, offering her a reassuring smile. "We don't want to be late."

As we walked through the halls, Erica muttered under her breath, "I can't do this."

"Hey," I said, stopping her in her tracks and making her look up at me. "You're going to do amazing." Her eyes held a mix of gratitude and disbelief, but she nodded hesitantly. The vulnerability in her gaze made my chest tighten, and I couldn't help but reach out to brush a strand of her hair behind her ear. The contact sent a shiver through her, and it took everything in me not to pull her into my arms and claim her then and there.

"Thank you, Liam," she whispered, her breath warm on my skin.

"Anytime," I said, the words barely audible as we continued our way to the conference room. My mind raced with thoughts of Erica as we walked, and I knew it would be difficult to keep those desires at bay. But for now, I had to focus on the task at hand - and that meant keeping my hands off Erica for just a little while longer.

The moment we entered the conference room, I could feel the tension in the air. I glanced at Erica, noticing her green eyes widen as she took in the scene before her. My father stood tall and imposing at the head of the table, his dark eyes scanning the room with authority. As he caught sight of us, he gave a curt nod and motioned for us to sit in the two empty seats near him.

"Welcome," he said, his voice deep and commanding. "We have much to discuss." I guided Erica to her seat, my hand lingering on her lower back for just a moment longer than necessary. The room was packed with various pack staff members, all seated and waiting for the meeting to commence. Through our mate bond, I could sense Erica's anxiety rising, her heart racing like a trapped bird in her chest.

"Alright, let's begin," my father announced, his eyes flicking between Erica and me as he started the meeting.

As the discussion began, I couldn't help but steal glances at Erica, watching how she tried to maintain her composure despite being overwhelmed. I wanted to comfort her, to let her know I was there, and that she didn't have to face this alone. Beneath the table, I reached over and placed my hand on hers, giving it a gentle squeeze. Her fingers felt warm and delicate under mine, and it took all my restraint not to interlace them together. Her gaze met mine, and I flashed her a reassuring smile.

"Thanks," she whispered, squeezing my hand back. I could see the gratitude in her eyes, and my chest swelled with pride that she was starting to trust me.

"Of course," I replied, turning my focus back to the meeting but keeping my hand on hers. As the discussion continued, I felt the burning need to be closer to Erica, to feel her body against mine, to taste her lips and claim her as my own. But I knew I had to be patient, to wait for the right moment to show her just how much she meant to me.

"Before we conclude this meeting," my father announced, "I'd like to welcome a new member to our pack's executive team. Erica Hallows will be joining us to help manage and expand our businesses." He paused, scanning the room before adding, "You may have heard she has unique experience and skills that will prove invaluable to our pack. We'll be holding an evening event in her honour on Saturday." The murmurs of approval and curiosity filled the room, but as I glanced at Erica, I could tell she was far from thrilled with the announcement. Her green eyes flickered with apprehension, and her lips pressed into a tight line. I squeezed her hand again under the table, hoping to reassure her that I would be there for her every step of the way.

"Thank you, Alpha Declan," Erica said, her voice steady despite her visible unease. "I look forward to working with all of you and contributing to the pack's success."

"Here, here!" a few of the pack members chimed in, toasting Erica with their water glasses.

I casually let my hand slide up her leg, holding my breath, wondering if she'd push me away. But she didn't. Instead, her breath hitched ever so slightly, and the look in her eyes was one of curiosity mixed with desire. My hand continued its journey up Erica's leg, fuelled by her silent encouragement. Her breathing grew heavier, and she closed her eyes, leaning into my touch.

"Erica," I murmured as I began to rub between her legs over her clothes, teasing her with slow, deliberate motions. I could feel her growing warmer beneath my hand, and it only served to stoke the fire that burned within me.

"Please, Liam," she whispered, her voice barely audible over the sound of our laboured breaths. My inner wolf howled in response, eager to claim what was rightfully ours. The scent of her arousal filled the air, intoxicating me with its heady sweetness.

"Meeting adjourned," announced my father, jolting us both back to reality. With one final squeeze of her thigh, I withdrew my hand reluctantly, knowing that now wasn't the time nor the place for what we both craved.

"Come on," I muttered, my voice husky with unspoken desire. I stood up and pulled her to her feet, guiding her through the office as I tried to ignore the way my body screamed for more.

We reached her office, and as soon as the door clicked shut behind us, all semblance of control shattered. I pinned Erica against the door, my hands tangling in her hair as I captured her lips in a passionate kiss. She responded with equal fervour, her fingers digging into my shirt as she pulled me closer, desperate for contact. Our tongues tangled together, exploring, tasting, claiming.

"Mine," I growled, claiming Erica's lips in a searing kiss that left no room for doubt. She was mine - now and forever. My mate. My everything.

"Goddess, Liam," she moaned into my mouth, her hips grinding against mine. I growled low in my throat, overcome by the heady mix of her scent, taste, and touch. My hands roamed her body, memorising the curves and dips as though they were a map to some undiscovered treasure.

"Erica," I whispered against her lips, my voice rough with need. "I can't wait any longer."

"Neither can I," she replied, her green eyes darkened with lust. And in that moment, we both surrendered to the passion that had been simmering just beneath the surface for far too long.

My mind raced with the intensity of the moment as I roughly tugged on the buttons of Erica's green blouse, snapping them off one by one. The material fell open, and her breasts spilled from the lacy confines of her bra, pale mounds tipped with dusky pink that begged for my attention. My mouth closed over one pert nipple, sucking hard enough to leave a mark. Erica cried out, her hands fisting in my shirt. I soothed the ache with my tongue before moving to her other breast, intent on branding every inch of her skin. She moaned softly; the sound sending shivers down my spine and fuelling my inner wolf.

"Erica," I growled, and continued leaning in to take one of her nipples into my mouth, sucking and teasing. My other hand travelled down her body, finding the fastening of her pants suit and slipping inside. I could feel the heat radiating from her core, and my fingers brushed against the damp silk of her panties. Her arousal was evident, making me even hungrier for her.

"Liam," she panted, tearing her mouth from mine. Her pupils were blown wide with desire, lips kiss-swollen and parted invitingly. "Please." The needy whimper undid me. I lifted her, carrying her to the desk and laying her back atop the smooth wood surface. Papers and pens clattered to the floor, forgotten.

"Please, Liam," she whispered, her voice thick with need.

"Are you ready?" I asked, my voice strained with the effort it took to hold back.

"More than ready," she breathed, a lustful glint in her eyes. I pushed her pants down, laying kisses along her legs as I revealed more of her soft skin. Her scent grew stronger, driving me wild with desire. Reaching her drenched panties, I slipped them aside and her glistening folds were flushed pink, swollen and ready. Torturing us both, I dragged a single finger through her slick folds before burying my face between her thighs.

"So wet for me, mate. So perfect." I circled her clit with deliberate strokes, watching her come undone for me. She gasped, her fingers curling into my hair and pulling me closer, urging me on.

"Goddess, Liam, yes!" she cried out, her hips bucking against my face. The taste of her arousal filled my senses, intoxicating and addictive. I couldn't get enough of her, every flick of my tongue, every breathy moan only stoking the fire within me.

"Erica," I murmured against her, my voice a low growl of need. "I want to taste you, feel you... every part of you."

"Then do it," she whispered, her body trembling with anticipation. As we continued to explore each other's bodies, our connection deepened. Our shared lust melded with something deeper, something raw and primal that spoke to the very core of who we were as werewolves. And as I looked into Erica's eyes, I knew that there was no turning back – we were bound together, not just by desire, but by fate itself. Her hands fisted in my hair as I pushed two fingers into her tight channel, growling at the feel of her clenching around them. She cried out, shattering around my fingers in climax. I lapped at the flood of arousal coating my hand, savouring her taste. My cock throbbed almost painfully, desperate to be inside her. Her cries echoed through the room, leaving no doubt in anyone's mind that I was claiming her as mine.

"Goddess, Liam, please..." she moaned, her green eyes filled with raw need.

As I worked my way up her body, our lips met in a passionate kiss, our tongues dancing together as I lined up my cock with her entrance. The connection between us flared, an unbreakable bond forged by lust and fate.

"Claim me," she whispered against my lips, her breath ragged. With a deep groan, I thrust into her, filling her completely, our bodies joining as one. The sensation was electrifying, every nerve ending alight with pleasure. I could feel her warmth, her slick arousal coating my throbbing length. Our bodies moved together, driven by the primal urge to mate, to claim each other as ours.

"Erica... fuck, you feel incredible," I growled, my hands gripping her hips as I drove into her harder, deeper. My wolf yearned for her, desperate for the union that would bind us together forever. And as I looked into her eyes, I knew she felt the same.

"Take me, Liam," she panted, her nails digging into my shoulders. "Show them all that I'm yours." I set a brutal pace, unable to control the frenzied rutting of my wolf. Our harsh breaths and the slap of skin filled the room, accompanied by broken moans and growls. She met each thrust eagerly, writhing beneath me. I hooked her leg over my arm, changing the angle to drive in deeper. Her inner walls fluttered and clenched, rippling along my length. My mouth found the marking spot on her neck and I sucked the skin between my teeth. I fought the urge to claim her fully, knowing that she wasn't ready. Erica stiffened beneath me with a wail, drenching my cock in another release. The rhythmic pulsing of her climax triggered my own, hot spurts flooding her channel.

"LIAM!" The sound of my father's voice jolted me out of my erotic reverie. I blinked, disoriented, and realised that I was still seated in the conference room. The meeting had never left, and neither had I. Everyone, including Erica, stared at me with a mix of confusion and amusement.

"Is there anything else you'd like to add?" My father's grin held a knowing glint, as if he understood the nature of my daydream.

"Uh, no," I stuttered, feeling my face flush with embarrassment. "No, that's... that's it."

"Very well," he said, clapping his hands together. "That concludes the meeting." As everyone filed out of the room, my father leaned in close, whispering,

"Try to keep your fantasies to yourself next time, son."

"Right," I murmured, desperately trying to hide my raging boner as my father laughed and exited the room. Erica spared me one last glance, her cheeks flushed and her eyes curious before she too disappeared from view.

"Fuck," I muttered under my breath, cursing my overactive imagination and the undeniable pull that Erica had on me.

Chapter 25

Erica

"I am not wearing pink," I declared, eyeing the dress Verity held up for me. The four of us, Verity, Gen, Frankie, and I, were in our apartment, preparing for my Welcome Ceremony. The air was thick with excitement and anticipation, mingling with the scent of wine that filled our glasses.

"Fine, how about this one?" Gen offered, holding up a deep emerald green dress that seemed to shimmer with each subtle movement.

"Much better," I said, smiling at her choice, feeling it was more fitting for the occasion. As we continued to get ready, I felt an undercurrent of nerves bubbling beneath the surface. Alpha Declan had invited several other Alphas, putting me directly in the spotlight. It was a far cry from the life I was used to, and the prospect of being watched so closely made my stomach twist uncomfortably.

"Erica, you've been awfully quiet tonight," Verity observed, her pale grey eyes studying me intently. "How has your first week at the new job been?"

"Good, actually," I replied, trying to sound nonchalant. "I'm still adjusting to everything, but it's been nice to have some semblance of routine." My thoughts drifted to Liam, who I'd been working alongside all week. Every time our eyes met or our hands brushed against each other, I felt a jolt of electricity between us. Being around him made my heart race and my mind swirl with conflicting emotions.

"Speaking of adjusting," Frankie chimed in, smirking as she applied her dark lipstick, "We've noticed you've been spending quite a bit of time with Grant lately. Anything going on there?"

"Nothing like that," I brushed off the comment, suddenly feeling defensive. "He's just been helping me settle in, that's all." Though it wasn't entirely untrue, I couldn't ignore the connection I felt with Grant, but it was a complicated situation. One I wasn't quite ready to face.

"Anyway," Gen interjected, sensing my unease and changing the subject, "Frankie got a new tattoo this week. Show her, Frankie!" As Frankie rolled up her sleeve to reveal an intricate design, I felt a small wave of gratitude towards Gen for redirecting the conversation. The atmosphere lightened as we continued to discuss our lives, both within and beyond the pack.

The night wore on, and my nerves grew with each passing moment. I knew I couldn't avoid my fate any longer, so I took a deep breath, bracing myself for the evening ahead. Surrounded by the fierce women I'd come to call friends, I tried to focus on the present, allowing their support to steady me as I prepared to step into the unknown.

Finally, we were all ready for the event. Verity looked stunning in a floor-length silver gown that seemed to shimmer with her every movement, accentuating her pale grey eyes. Frankie had chosen a daring black dress with purple accents that matched her hair and revealed her impressive tattoo collection. Gen wore a beautiful deep blue gown that complemented her warm skin tone and framed her curvy figure perfectly. As for me, I settled on an emerald green velvet dress that hugged my body just right, showing off my curves without feeling overly revealing. The fabric felt luxurious against my skin, and I couldn't help but feel a small sense of pride at how well it suited my red hair and green eyes.

"These events are amazing, and a real highlight," Gen remarked as she adjusted her earrings. "I mean, this isn't even one of our major celebrations, and the Alpha has invited Alphas from other packs!"

"Wow," I breathed, trying to quell the butterflies dancing in my stomach. "No pressure, then."

"Erica, you'll be fine," Verity assured me with a gentle smile. "Just remember, we're all here to support you."

"Besides," Frankie chimed in, grinning mischievously, "if things get too overwhelming, we can always sneak away for some liquid courage."

"Frankie!" Gen scolded, though I could see the amusement in her eyes. With one last deep breath to steady my nerves, we left the apartment and made our way across the park toward the pack house where the event was being held.

As we walked, I noticed that many other pack members were also heading in the same direction, families and children included. There was an air of excitement and happiness surrounding everyone, and I couldn't help but be swept up in the infectious atmosphere.

"Look at little Tommy," Verity said, pointing to a young boy who was practically dragging his parents along in his excitement. "He's been talking about this event all week."

"Let's not forget the gossip that will come from tonight," Frankie added with a smirk, earning a knowing chuckle from Gen. As we approached the pack house, I marvelled at the grandeur of the building, its exterior adorned with intricate carvings and glowing lanterns. My heart pounded in my chest, the anticipation and nerves threatening to consume me. But as I glanced back at my newfound friends, their faces filled with excitement and support, I knew I couldn't let my fears hold me back.

"Ready?" Verity asked, squeezing my hand reassuringly.

"Ready," I replied, my voice barely above a whisper. With determination fuelling each step, we entered the pack house together, ready to face whatever the night had in store for us.

Stepping into the main hall of the pack house instantly took my breath away. The grand space was adorned with deep purple and blue drapes that cascaded down from the high ceiling, while shimmering gold accents added an air of opulence. Crystal chandeliers hung above us, casting a soft, warm glow throughout the room. The walls were lined with tall windows, their heavy velvet curtains pulled back to reveal the moonlit night outside.

"Wow," I whispered, unable to find any other words to express my awe.

"Alpha Declan always goes all out for these events," Gen explained, her eyes sparkling as she took in the lavish decorations. "It's important for the pack to come together and celebrate our unity." As we made our way through the hall, I couldn't help but notice the intricate details of the table settings – delicate crystal glasses, polished silverware, and exquisite floral arrangements adorned each place setting. It was clear that no expense had been spared, and I couldn't help but feel a mix of gratitude and trepidation at being the centre of such an extravagant event.

"Erica!" Gregg called out, approaching us with a wide smile. His wife and fated mate, Astra, stood by his side, her black hair cascading down her shoulders like a waterfall of moonlight.

"You look absolutely stunning tonight."

"Thank you," I replied, feeling a blush rise to my cheeks. "You both look incredible as well."

"Where's Damon?" Gregg asked, scanning the room for him.

"I'd bet he's off in some broom closet with a girl, as per usual." Astra rolled her eyes good-naturedly. "Honestly, I wouldn't be surprised. That boy never seems to tire of chasing skirts." I couldn't help but laugh at their banter, though my nerves were still threatening to get the better of me.

As our conversation continued, my eyes darted around the room, searching for Liam. I hoped to avoid him, knowing full well that his presence would only add to my anxiety.

"Relax, Erica," Gen whispered, noticing my tense demeanour. "We're all here for you, and we'll be by your side every step of the way tonight." Her words brought me a small measure of comfort, but as the time for the ceremony drew nearer, I couldn't help but feel the weight of what was to come bearing down on me. With each passing moment, the hall filled with more pack members, their excited chatter and laughter only serving to amplify my fears. Yet, amidst the sea of faces, I knew I could count on my newfound friends to help me navigate the treacherous waters that awaited.

The noise over the speakers jolted me from my thoughts, and Gregg leaned in to say,

"It's time for the ceremony, Erica. Come with me." I followed him through a dimly lit corridor to a back room already occupied by Alpha Declan, his Luna and wife Fallon, and Liam. My heart skipped a beat as I caught Liam's gaze – those dark brown eyes held an intensity that sent shivers down my spine.

"Ah, Erica, allow me to introduce you to my lovely Luna, Fallon," Alpha Declan said with a warm smile as he gestured toward the elegant woman beside him. Her black hair cascaded around her shoulders like a cloak, and her vibrant amber eyes sparkled with excitement.

"Erica, it's a pleasure to finally meet you. I've heard so much about you," Fallon gushed, clasping my hands in hers. The warmth of her touch was reassuring, but there was something cryptic in her eyes that made me uneasy.

"You're going to be an incredible addition to our pack."

"Thank you, Luna. That means a lot to me," I replied, trying to sound more confident than I felt. Just then, Kaitlyn burst into the room, her cheeks flushed and her chest heaving as if she'd run a marathon. Alpha Declan's expression soured, but Kaitlyn seemed unfazed by his disapproval. She rushed over to me, beaming.

"Erica! I'm so glad I made it in time!"

"Better late than never, right?" I joked, attempting to deflect the tension in the room.

"Indeed," Alpha Declan interjected, his voice stern yet measured. "Now, Erica, let me explain the ceremony to you. I'll be guiding you through what you have to say, so don't worry. We'll get through this together."

"Thank you, Alpha," I murmured, my stomach twisting into knots at the thought of standing on stage before the entire pack. As we prepared to go on stage, Liam approached me, his eyes never leaving mine.

"Erica, you look beautiful tonight," he said softly, his compliment catching me off guard.

"Thanks," I stammered, feeling heat rise to my cheeks, but my thoughts were a whirlwind - was this just another tactic to control me? Or was there something genuine in his words? Conflicting emotions warred within me, each fighting for dominance as I struggled to maintain my composure.

"Alright, everyone, let's get this show on the road," Alpha Declan announced, ushering us toward the stage.

Alpha Declan and his Luna, Fallon, stepped onto the stage first, their presence commanding the attention of everyone gathered. Gregg followed behind them, his stride confident as he took his position at the Alpha's side. The crowd hushed as Declan began to speak.

"Tonight, we come together as a pack, as a family," he proclaimed, his voice echoing throughout the hall. "Loyalty is what binds us, trust is what unites us, and strength is what drives us forward." My heart raced as I watched from the wings, feeling more like an outsider than ever before. Liam and Kaitlyn stood beside me, their expressions conveying a mix of anticipation and concern.

"Please welcome Erica Hallows to the stage," Alpha Declan announced, gesturing for me to join him. Taking a deep breath to steady myself, I stepped into the blinding lights, feeling as if I were walking into the lion's den. My eyes scanned the crowd, noting the curious gazes that seemed to bore into my soul. As I reached the centre of the stage, Liam and Kaitlyn followed suit, providing a semblance of support in this overwhelming moment.

"Erica Hallows, you stand here before Alpha Declan Anderson of the Silver Stone pack, who bears witness today. What say you?" Gregg called out, his voice firm and unwavering. Swallowing hard, I struggled to find my own voice amidst the turmoil within me.

"I... I renounce my former allegiance to the Moon Key pack and seek acceptance into the Silver Stone pack," I managed to choke out. An icy sensation shot through my veins as the bond to my old pack snapped, leaving me breathless with loss and sorrow.

"Let it be known," declared Alpha Declan, his eyes locked on mine. He raised his arm, calling for the ceremonial knife. Gregg dutifully retrieved it and handed it to the Alpha.

"Erica Hallows, do you vow to be loyal to the Silver Stone pack, placing the safety and concerns of the pack above all others?" Alpha Declan asked me, his voice reverberating throughout the hall. I took a deep breath, trying to calm my racing heart.

"I do," I replied, my voice stronger than I felt.

"Then let us proceed," he said solemnly. He grasped the ceremonial knife and sliced his palm, blood welling up and glinting in the dim light.

"Erica Hallows, I offer you sanctuary and acceptance in the Silver Stone pack. Do you submit to the blood bond?" My hands trembled as I reached for the knife. It's cold handle pressed against my fingertips, a stark contrast to the warmth of the blood that stained its blade. With a mixture of fear and determination, I pressed the steel into my own palm and winced at the pain.

"I, Erica Hallows, submit to the blood bond of the Silver Stone pack." Alpha Declan's hand, heavy with authority and command, covered mine, and our blood mingled together. A sudden surge of power raced through me, electrifying and unexpected. The connection forged between us was palpable, like a live wire jolting every nerve. I glanced at the Alpha, and his eyes widened in surprise, mirroring my own shock.

"Erica Hallows," he announced, his voice steady despite the unique sensation, "as the bond forms from blood, I officially recognise and accept you as a member of the Silver Stone pack." He turned to face the audience, still gripping my hand firmly.

"I announce Erica Hallows, formerly of the Moon Key pack, now bound by blood to the Silver Stone pack." The room erupted in cheers and applause, but their excitement was muted by the lingering sense of loss within me. My old life, my former pack, had vanished like a wisp of smoke, leaving me adrift and uncertain.

"Erica Hallows," Alpha Declan said softly, his eyes meeting mine with sincerity, "I officially welcome you to the Silver Stone pack." A new bond began to form within me, tendrils of connection and belonging weaving together as I officially joined the pack. The sensation was both exhilarating and terrifying, a testament to the weight of my decision.

As the Alpha released my hand, I attempted to make my way offstage, but my legs felt weak, and I stumbled slightly. Just then, Fallon stepped forward and enveloped me in a warm embrace. Her whispered words, full of warmth and understanding, brushed against my ear,

"Welcome home."

Chapter 26

Erica

The evening event was in full swing, and I found myself feeling awkward as I tried to mingle with the other pack members. Their well-meaning welcomes and congratulations felt overwhelming, making me acutely aware of my outsider status, but I knew I had to make an effort to fit in with my new pack. As I stood by the edge of the dance floor, sipping a drink and trying to blend into the shadows, Liam approached me, his dark brown hair cascading to his neck, framing his ruggedly handsome face. I could feel my body tense up just being near him; he was the Alpha heir after all, and it was impossible to escape the imposing aura that surrounded him.

"Erica, would you like to dance?" he asked, his brown eyes meeting mine with an intensity that sent a shiver down my spine. My instinct was to refuse, but the last thing I wanted was to disrespect the Alpha heir. So, I reluctantly agreed, setting down my drink and letting him lead me onto the dance floor.

As we danced, our bodies moved in sync, and I couldn't help but feel the sexual tension that simmered between us. Liam's strong arms guided me effortlessly through the intricate steps, and I found myself struggling to breathe under the weight of our unspoken desires. My heart raced, and

I couldn't deny the primal attraction I felt towards him, even though my mind screamed for me to resist. When the song finally ended, and we were both panting slightly from the exertion, Alpha Declan approached us with another man in tow. This man was classically handsome, with dark blond hair, blue eyes, and a well-built physique beneath his tailored suit. Liam's face lit up at the sight of him, and it was clear they shared a close bond.

"Erica," Alpha Declan said, drawing my attention back to him. "I'd like you to meet my nephew Alpha Ethan Anderson of the Rose Moon pack, just outside of London."

"Nice to meet you, Erica," Ethan said with a warm smile that instantly put me at ease. Even though he was an Alpha, his friendly demeanour and obvious affection for Liam made it difficult to maintain my usual wariness.

"Likewise," I replied, trying to hide my relief at the arrival of someone who could momentarily break the tension between Liam and me.

The laughter and clinking of glasses filled the air, creating a dizzying cacophony that only served to heighten my sense of overwhelm. I tried to focus on the conversation with Ethan, but my thoughts kept drifting back to the charged dance with Liam.

"Erica, are you enjoying the party?" Ethan asked with genuine concern, his blue eyes searching mine for an answer.

"Um, yes," I lied, forcing a smile. "It's just a lot to take in." Before he could respond, Luna Fallon, Alpha Declan's mate, appeared at our side, her authoritative presence cutting through the noise.

"Declan, it's time we leave the party," she said, her tone firm yet gentle. "Parties are a young person's game, after all." Declan nodded in agreement, and then turned to Liam.

"It's time, son," he said, and I could see the understanding pass between them, Liam would leave early to give me some space. My chest tightened with a mix of gratitude and disappointment.

"Of course, Father," Liam replied, his eyes still locked on mine. The intensity in his gaze made my heart race, and I struggled to maintain my composure.

"Good night, Erica," Declan said, offering me a nod of respect before he and Luna Fallon began their ascent up the grand staircase towards the Alpha apartments.

"Good night, Alpha Declan, Luna Fallon," I replied, watching as they disappeared from view. Liam lingered behind, hesitating for a moment, his dark eyes filled with longing. And then, with one last lingering glance, he followed his parents upstairs.

I stood there, staring after him, acutely aware of the emptiness that settled around me now that he was gone. While I was grateful for the reprieve from the overwhelming tension, I couldn't deny how much his absence affected me.

"Are you okay?" Ethan's voice pulled me back to the present.

"Yeah, I'm fine," I muttered, forcing my thoughts away from Liam. "Just... a lot happened today." Ethan nodded sympathetically, his eyes kind.

"It's never easy joining a new pack, but give it time. You'll find your place here."

"Thanks, Alpha Ethan," I said with a small, genuine smile.

The lively music and laughter of the pack members filled the air as I stood there, feeling a mixture of relief and loneliness. It was then that Verity and Gen appeared before me, their arms linked together, their faces alight with excitement.

"Come on, Erica! You can't just stand here all night," Verity urged, her white-blonde hair swinging as she tugged at my arm.

"Let's dance!" Gen chimed in, her usual reserved demeanour replaced by an infectious enthusiasm. Before I could protest, they whisked me onto the dance floor, and suddenly, I found myself caught up in the whirlwind of movement and energy. We danced, laughed, and shared stories, our friendship blossoming amidst the chaos of the evening.

As the night wore on, though, I began to feel the effects of having drank more than I'd eaten. Excusing myself from my friends, I wandered in search of sustenance, only to bump into Damon, quite literally.

"Whoa, easy there," he said, steadying me with strong hands around my waist. His dark eyes sparkled with amusement as he looked down at me.

"You look like you could use something to eat."

"Is it that obvious?" I asked, trying to hide my embarrassment behind a sarcastic smile.

"Maybe just a little," Damon teased, guiding me towards the kitchen, where an impressive buffet had been set up. He expertly filled a plate with an array of delicious-looking food, and I couldn't help but feel grateful for his presence.

"Come on, let's find somewhere quiet to sit," he suggested, leading me out to a secluded seating area under the stars. The cold night air felt refreshing against my skin as we settled down, and I eagerly dug into the feast before me.

As I ate, Damon spoke about Liam, his words sincere and earnest.

"I hope you give him a chance, Erica. He's a good guy, just... under a lot of stress."

"Is that supposed to excuse his aggressiveness?" I asked, my voice laced with skepticism.

"Maybe not," Damon conceded, "but it does explain it. Deep down, he has a good heart. You'll see." I chewed thoughtfully, considering Damon's words. Despite the turmoil and confusion I felt, there was something about Liam that had undeniably captured my attention. But could I open myself up to the possibility of trusting an Alpha again, especially one who seemed so volatile? I was still wary of the Alpha Heir but couldn't deny the spark that had ignited between us during our dance. It was Damon's words, however, that made me truly consider giving Liam a chance.

"Hey there, handsome" Heidi's sultry voice interrupted my thoughts, causing me to tense. She sauntered over to our table, completely ignoring my presence, and slid onto Damon's lap, her amber eyes locked onto his.

"Having fun?" she purred, running her fingers through Damon's hair and pressing herself against him. The overt flirtation and suggestive language left no room for doubt about her intentions.

"Um, I'll just go..." I muttered, pushing back my chair and standing up. Damon looked up at me with concern.

"Where are you going, Erica?" he asked, his dark eyes searching my face.

"Back to the party," I responded sarcastically. "I was enjoying my food, and I'd hate to throw it up."

"Erica, don't-" Damon began, but Heidi cut him off.

"Let her go, Damon. It's not like she'll be missed," she sneered, but Damon had already pushed her off his lap and was on his feet.

"Erica, wait!" he called, hurrying after me. Heidi's face twisted with fury.

"First, you steal my job, and now you're trying to steal my man? You really are a dirty rogue slut, aren't you?" she spat, her voice venomous.

"Excuse me?" I whirled around to face her, anger pulsing through my veins. "I'm not stealing anything from you, Heidi. Maybe if you weren't such a psycho bitch, people would actually want to be around you."

"Bring it on, rogue," she snarled, lunging at me. Her body collided with mine, sending us both sprawling to the ground. The air whooshed out of my lungs as we tumbled together, snarling and clawing at one another.

"Get off me, you crazy bitch!" I shouted, struggling to free myself from Heidi's grasp. But despite my best efforts, her grip only tightened, and I could see the malicious intent in her eyes. Heidi's nails dug into my skin, drawing blood as she tried to claw at my eyes. I dodged her attack and managed to land a punch on her jaw, momentarily stunning her. The pain and anger fuelled me, driving me to fight back with everything I had.

"Is that all you've got?" I taunted, ducking beneath her wild swing. "You're pathetic!"

"Shut up, rogue!" she snarled, lunging at me again. This time, I sidestepped her and grabbed her arm, using her momentum to send her crashing into a nearby table. Plates shattered, and food splattered everywhere.

"Leave me alone, Heidi. This isn't worth it," I warned her, trying to catch my breath. But she refused to listen, stubbornly advancing towards me once more.

"Like hell it isn't!" she spat, grabbing a handful of my hair and yanking my head back. Pain shot through my scalp, making my vision blur for a moment. Desperate, I slammed my elbow into her ribs, forcing her to release her grip.

"Enough!" Damon roared, finally tackling Heidi around the waist and pulling her away from me. She thrashed and kicked, still hurling insults at me.

"Get off me, Damon!" she screamed, but he held her firm, his dark eyes filled with disappointment and anger.

"Maybe if you stopped acting like a rabid animal, people would give a damn about you!" I snapped, feeling blood trickle down my face from a scratch near my eye.

"Erica, are you okay?" Gen and Kaitlyn rushed to my side, their concerned gazes taking in my injuries. Despite the pain and humiliation, I nodded, accepting their help as they guided me to my feet.

"Look what you've done, Heidi," Kaitlyn scolded, her eyes blazing with anger. "You've gone too far this time."

"Shut up, you Alpha brat!" Heidi spat back, still struggling to break free from Damon's grasp. "Enough of this!" a deep, commanding voice bellowed from across the room. All attention turned to the older, imposing man who strode towards us, fury etched on his face. I felt a shiver run down my spine as I realised this was Grayson Thompson, the Warrior Commander of the pack and Verity's father. I felt a mix of awe and fear. Despite my resentment towards authority figures, I couldn't help but be struck by the sheer power that radiated from him.

"Explain yourselves!" Grayson stormed over, his voice a growl that sent a shiver down my spine. His eyes bore into each of us in turn, demanding the truth. Heidi, still caught in Damon's grip, sneered and refused to speak.

In that moment, I knew it was up to me to set things straight. Taking a deep breath, I recounted the events leading up to the confrontation with as much composure as I could muster.

"Enough!" Grayson barked once I'd finished. He turned on Heidi, fury etched on his face.

"You should be ashamed of yourself! As a pack warrior and of higher rank, you ought to know better!" His gaze then shifted to me, and I could feel him trying to force me into submission with just the intensity of his stare. But I refused to bow down for something I hadn't done wrong. Something inside me snapped, and I met his gaze with a determination I hadn't felt in years. To my surprise, Grayson's expression softened ever so slightly.

"Impressive," he muttered under his breath. "I expect to see you in Warrior training. With some work, we might be able to clean up your fighting technique."

As if on cue, Grant appeared by Grayson's side, wearing a look of concern.

"I'll take her home and tend to her wounds," he offered without hesitation.

"Actually," Damon interjected, "I can do it." The tension between them was palpable, but Grant held his ground, adamant that he would be the one to escort me.

"Please, both of you," I sighed, rubbing my temples. "This isn't necessary,"

"Only been here a couple weeks, and already got two guys fighting over you," Heidi snarked, cutting me off. She paused for dramatic effect before delivering the final blow:

"Were you this much of a slut in your old pack too?" Rage coursed through me, and I lunged at her once more, but Grant was quick to grab my arm, pulling me back before I could reach her. Grayson, obviously displeased with Heidi's behaviour, ordered a couple of guards to take her to the cells. She begged him not to do it, but his decision was final.

"Grant," Grayson said sternly, "Take Erica home."

"Of course, sir," Grant replied, sending Damon a smug grin as he led me away from the chaos and towards my apartment. I looked back to see Damon storming off into the pack house.

Chapter 27

Erica

As I stumbled into my apartment, Grant's strong presence followed closely behind me. The place was empty; Gen and Frankie were still at the party, after me telling them repeatedly to go back and enjoy themselves. My emerald evening dress clung to my body, torn and ruined after my fight with Heidi.

"Let me take a look at those wounds," Grant said, his voice laced with concern. He began rummaging through the cabinets, searching for first aid supplies. I couldn't help but think how werewolves like us usually heal pretty quickly, but there was still a need to clean the wounds or the dirt would get trapped. It was times like these when being unable to shift was a frustrating reminder of my limitations.

"Erica, you should remove your dress so I can get to the wounds on your back," Grant suggested, trying to be gentle about the request.

"Fine, just give me a minute." I retreated into my bedroom, closing the door behind me as I peeled off the tattered remains of my once stunning gown.

"Come in," I called out to Grant. As he entered the bedroom, his strong hands gripped the first aid supplies, and I felt my heart race with anticipation.

"Thanks for doing this," I said softly, not meeting his eyes as I stood with my ruined dress removed, wearing only my black lace panties and matching bra.

"Of course, Erica." His voice was gentle and reassuring. He approached me, and I turned around, allowing him to see the extent of my injuries.

Without a word, he began cleaning my wounds, his touch surprisingly soft and tender. Despite the pain, a warmth spread through my body at his touch, and I found myself leaning into it. As Grant continued his ministrations, I felt him lean closer, his breath warm against my neck. He inhaled deeply, and I could hear him sigh contentedly.

"You smell so familiar, Erica," he murmured. "I can't explain it, but I feel incredibly protective of you." His words sent a thrill down my spine, and I couldn't help but agree.

"I feel something for you too, Grant. It's confusing and powerful, but I don't know what it is."

"Maybe we should find out," he suggested, his blue eyes locking onto mine. Slowly, he leaned in, his lips hovering just above mine. My breath caught in my throat, and my body screamed for me to close the gap between us. But something held me back.

"No, Grant, we can't. Things are complicated, and this isn't right."

"Complicated? How?" His brows furrowed in concern, but before I could respond, a thundering bang at the door startled us both.

"Erica!" The voice boomed from outside, and I knew immediately who it was. Liam.

The bedroom door burst open with a violent force, and Liam stormed in, the muscles in his shirtless torso rippling as he growled with fury. His grey sweatpants clung to his hips, accentuating his fine-tuned abs. My heart raced at the sight of him, torn between fear and desire.

"Get your hands off her!" Liam roared, grabbing Grant by the collar and hurling him against the wall. The impact made me wince, but Grant was quick to recover, springing to his feet with a snarl.

"Back down, mutt," Liam snarled, his brown eyes blazing. "Get out of here! That's an order from your Alpha!"

"Fuck that!" Grant spat, his blue eyes defiant. "I'm not leaving Erica alone with you while you're like this. You're dangerous!"

"Grant, please," I pleaded, my voice shaking. "It's okay. Liam won't hurt me."

"Really?" Grant looked at me incredulously, his distrust for Alphas written all over his face. "You expect me to believe that?"

"Enough!" Liam snapped, his anger boiling over. "Erica is my fated mate, and I would never hurt her!" My breath hitched at Liam's confession, and I could see the shock etched into Grant's features. Rage and betrayal flickered through his eyes, but he refused to back down. I clenched my fists, feeling both overwhelmed and caught in a storm of emotions I couldn't control. Horrified, Grant's eyes flickered between Liam and me, desperate for an explanation.

"Tell me it isn't true," he pleaded, his voice wavering with a vulnerability I'd never heard from him before.

"Grant... it's complicated," I whispered, my heart hammering in my chest as I tried to find the right words. He searched my face, and I could see the moment he decided to take that statement as confirmation.

"Complicated, huh?" The devastation in his voice cut through me like a knife, but it was quickly replaced by simmering anger.

"Well, tell me how it's complicated then!"

"Let me explain," I insisted, reaching out to touch his arm. But as soon as my fingers grazed his skin, he jerked away from me, his jaw clenched.

"Save it, Erica," he spat, his blue eyes like ice as they bore into me. I knew he wanted nothing more than to confront Liam, but instead, he stormed out of the room, leaving me feeling utterly exposed and vulnerable. I flinched as the apartment door slammed shut, and the sound echoed through the empty space.

My hands shook at my sides, and I couldn't quiet the chaos inside me. How had everything become so twisted and tangled?. It was as though I were watching my entire world crumble around me, and there was nothing I could do to stop it. As I turned to face Liam, I fought to regain control over my emotions. It felt like an impossible task, but I needed to find a way to navigate the mess that my life had become.

"Look what you've done, Liam!" I shouted at him, the anger boiling over inside me. "You promised not to tell anyone about our fated mate thing, and now you've broken that promise! How can I ever trust you?" His dark brown eyes flashed with fury as he retorted,

"I did promise to keep it quiet, but I'll be damned if I let my fated mate go fucking anyone else like a pack whore. I warned you I'd kill anyone who touched you, and Grant got off easy." My hand moved instinctively, slapping him hard across his face. The sound echoed in the empty room, leaving a stinging sensation in my palm.

"Nobody calls me a whore, Liam. Get out!" The Alpha heir growled, his muscular arms grabbing me roughly and slamming me against the wall. My breath caught in my throat as I stared into his enraged eyes.

"Don't hit me," he snarled, his grip tightening on my wrists. I tried to pull away from him, but his strength was too much for me to overcome. Feeling trapped and desperate, I attempted to hit him again. But Liam caught my hand effortlessly, pinning both my wrists above my head with just one hand.

"Fight all you want, baby," he whispered, his face inches from mine, "but in the end, you're mine." I struggled against his iron grip, feeling the heat of his body pressed against mine.

As Liam nuzzled into my neck, his teeth grazed my marking spot, sending shivers down my spine. I couldn't deny the arousal that pooled between my legs, even as my mind screamed for me to push him away.

"Maybe I should just claim you right now, complete the bond," he murmured against my skin, his hot breath making my heart race.

"Get off me, Liam!" I yelled, my body betraying me as it yearned for his touch. The intensity of my emotions was overwhelming, anger, fear, desire, and confusion all swirling together, threatening to drown me in their chaotic depths.

"Get off me!" I screamed, my body squirming in a futile attempt to escape his iron grip. But Liam's hold on me only tightened as his other hand slipped down between us, finding its way beneath my panties.

"Already so wet for me," he muttered, smirking against my neck as his fingers began to stroke and tease my clit. My body betrayed me, sending waves of pleasure coursing through me as I tried to fight the rising climax within myself.

"You can't deny how much you want this, Erica."

"Stop... please," I gasped, every ounce of my strength focused on not begging him to finish what he'd started. But even as the words left my lips, part of me craved his touch more than anything.

With a growl, Liam suddenly scooped me up and tossed me onto my bed. His weight pressed down upon me as he climbed between my legs, the hard, throbbing length of his cock straining against the fabric of his sweatpants. He captured my lips in a searing, passionate kiss, his hips bucking against mine with a desperate urgency that set my nerves aflame. The friction between our clothed bodies only intensified the pleasure coursing through me, pushing me closer and closer to the edge. And when it finally came, my orgasm tore through me like a wildfire, making me cry out into Liam's mouth as wave after wave of ecstasy crashed over me.

"Only I can make you feel like this," he whispered huskily into my ear, his breath hot against my skin. "You need to realise that you belong to me, Erica. I'm the one for you." Without another word, Liam climbed off me and strode out of the room, leaving me panting and trembling in the aftermath of my climax.

The sound of the apartment door slamming shut reverberated through the empty space, leaving me utterly alone.

"Fuck!" I screamed into my pillow, overcome with frustration and a sense of helplessness. I was falling hard for Liam, despite every fibre of my being telling me it was wrong, and I hated myself for it.

"Get a grip, Erica," I muttered, my voice muffled by the fabric. "You can't let him control you like this." But even as I tried to convince myself, loyalty, trust, desire, they all swirled together inside me, creating a storm of emotion I couldn't hope to contain.

"God, what the fuck am I going to do?" I whispered, tears stinging the corners of my eyes as I stared up at the ceiling, desperate for answers that refused to come.

Chapter 28

Erica

The morning sunlight filtered through the curtains, casting a warm glow on the kitchen table as I sat down with Gen and Frankie. We were all nursing our hangovers with steaming cups of coffee and plates full of scrambled eggs, bacon, and toast.

"Can't believe what happened last night," Frankie said, shaking her head. "Heidi had no right to attack you like that, Erica. I'm just glad she's locked up now."

"Me too," Gen chimed in, her expression concerned.

Their words brought a small smile to my face, but internally, my thoughts were still consumed by the events that had unfolded after the party. Liam had kicked Grant out even though he was helping me tend to my wounds, that infuriating Alpha heir. But I couldn't forget the feel of his lips on my throat and his fingers on my clit, expertly bringing me to orgasm. It was a confusing mix of anger and desire that gnawed at me.

"Hey, earth to Erica," Frankie waved a hand in front of my face, pulling me out of my thoughts.

"You okay?"

"Yeah, yeah, I'm fine," I assured them, trying to push the memory of Liam aside for now. "Just...still processing everything, I guess."

"Understandable," Gen said sympathetically. "We're here for you, though, no matter what."

"Thanks, guys," I replied, touched by their unwavering loyalty.

It was something I'd never take for granted, especially with people like Heidi lurking around every corner.

"Seriously, I wish I could've seen the look on her face when you took her down," Frankie grinned wickedly, her eyes sparkling with mischief. "She's always acted so high and mighty, like she's better than everyone else."

"Frankie, you're enjoying this way too much," Gen teased, but there was a hint of agreement in her tone.

"Damn right I am," Frankie shot back with a smirk. "Heidi's had it coming for a long time." I couldn't help but smile at their enthusiasm, even though my mind still raced with conflicting emotions. It was going to take some time to sort through everything that had happened, but at least I knew I could count on my friends to have my back. As for Liam, I'd deal with him and all the complications he brought into my life one step at a time. Frankie's laughter pulled me back into the present moment.

"Seriously, did you see her face? Priceless!" she cackled,

"Frankie, we get it," Gen smirked, shaking her head as she sipped her coffee.

"Hey, I'm just appreciating the minor victories," Frankie retorted, grinning unapologetically.

Suddenly, Gen's expression shifted. Her eyes glazed over, her spoon hovering mid-air as if time had stopped. After a few seconds, she blinked rapidly and looked at me with confusion etched across her features.

"Erica, why would the Alpha be mind linking me instead of you?" she asked, raising an eyebrow. I didn't really want to tell my friends that I was broken and couldn't do something as basic as shift into my wolf, or hear her.

"Erm... it's complicated," I said. Why did everything always have to be complicated? "What does he want?"

"He wants you to come to his office right away. He doesn't sound too happy." My stomach twisted into knots at the mention of the Alpha. Had word of my fight with Heidi already reached him? Was he going to punish me for standing up against her? My heart raced, but I forced a casual smile and shrugged.

"I'll explain later. That is, if I survive this meeting with the Alpha," I joked, trying to lighten the mood. Despite my attempt at humour, the unease continued to gnaw at me. Fighting another pack member wasn't taken lightly, even if it was someone like Heidi.

"Good luck," Gen offered sympathetically, her gaze concerned. Frankie chimed in with an encouraging grin.

"Kick some ass, just like you did last night!"

"Thanks," I muttered, pushing my half-eaten breakfast away and rising from my seat. As I walked away from the girls, my heart pounded in my chest. Despite their encouragement, I couldn't shake the feeling that things were about to get worse for me.

The pack house loomed before me, its imposing structure a testament to the power of those who resided within.

"Hey, Erica," Wes, the guard on duty, greeted me with a knowing grin as I passed him. "Well done for last night. Heidi needed putting in her place."

"Thanks," I mumbled, a blush creeping up my cheeks. I appreciated his support, but it only fuelled my anxiety further. If even Wes knew what had happened, it was likely the Alpha would be less than pleased. I steeled myself and continued towards the office. Alpha Declan's door stood before me, a barrier between me and whatever punishment awaited. My hand shook as I raised it to knock, the sound echoing ominously through the hall. His voice, stern and impatient, beckoned me inside.

"Come in." I hesitated, taking a deep breath before pushing the door open. The heavy scent of authority and dominance hung in the air, suffocating me. Alpha Declan sat behind his desk, a frown etched deeply into his features. Beside him, Beta Gregg stood with his arms crossed, the very picture of loyalty and strength. Across from them, Damon and Heidi occupied two of the other chairs. Heidi looked dishevelled, still clad in her tattered clothes from the previous night. She seemed to have been denied the luxury of cleaning up, which only served to heighten her resentment towards me. I couldn't help but feel a pang of satisfaction at the sight.

"Sit down, Erica," Alpha Declan commanded, his tone leaving no room for argument. Taking my place beside Damon, I felt his presence like a comforting wave, though his eyes remained fixed on the floor. I knew he was loyal to the pack, but how much of that loyalty extended to me? Damon offered me a sheepish grin as if to say, 'we'll get through this,' but it was quickly snuffed out when Gregg, his father, faked a cough, reminding him of the seriousness of the situation. I swallowed hard, preparing myself to face whatever was about to unfold.

"Now, I was saddened to hear of an altercation last night." He looked at the three of us one by one. "I will not tolerate this kind of behaviour in my pack. Tell me what happened last night," Alpha Declan demanded, his voice cold and unyielding. "Who started it?"

"Alpha, I-" I began, only to be interrupted by Heidi's voice. Heidi's demeanour changed in an instant. Gone was the dishevelled, bitter woman, replaced by a sweet and innocent victim.

"It was Erica, Alpha," she said with feigned vulnerability. "She attacked me without any reason. I was just spending some time with Damon here, and she went for me. I don't know, maybe she's bitter that he dumped her or something." She turned and put her hand on Damon's arm. I rolled my eyes, barely containing my annoyance. What a load of bullshit. Of course she did her best to lay it on thick. "You know me Alpha, I am not a violent person and just had to defend myself."

"Is that true, Erica?" Alpha Declan questioned, his dark eyes searching mine for any hint of deceit.

"Is it fuck," I said without thinking. Alpha Declan raised an eyebrow and Beta Gregg coughed again to hide a chuckle. Shit, try again Erica.

"Alpha, I didn't start it," I insisted, trying to keep my voice steady. "Heidi attacked me."

"Of course you'd say that," Heidi retorted, her facade slipping just a bit. She turned her attention to Damon, batting her eyelashes as if he would be swayed by such a pathetic attempt at flirtation.

"Damon saw everything. He will tell you what she did." All eyes fell on Damon, who seemed to shrink under the pressure.

"Damon?" Heidi's voice was sickly sweet. "Tell them." She looked back at the Alpha. "I had to spend the night in the cells," she sniffled. I looked at her in disbelief. She even had a fake tear rolling down one cheek. I could tell that Damon was struggling. Torn between loyalty to the pack and his growing feelings for me, he hesitated before finally speaking.

"I... I saw it, Alpha," he stuttered, avoiding eye contact with both Heidi and me. "Heidi started it." Heidi's face contorted with rage as she pointed an accusing finger at me.

"You're lying!" she spat, her voice dripping with venom. "You're just trying to protect your little girlfriend!" I fought the urge to snap back at her, knowing it would only escalate an already tense situation. Not that it needed any escalation. Heidi's snarl sent a shiver down my spine as she spun towards me, all pretence of innocence gone. Her eyes blazed with fury, and I could practically feel the heat of her anger radiating off her.

My instincts screamed at me to back away, so I did, trying to put some distance, and maybe a couple of chairs, between us.

"Look at you," Heidi sneered, stalking forward like a predator closing in on its prey. "So pathetic and weak." I swallowed hard, my heart pounding in my chest as I continued to retreat. The air in the room seemed to grow heavier, pressing down on me and making it difficult to breathe. Damon and Gregg were watching, but neither of them stepped in to intervene, they seemed as shocked as I was about Heidi's fury.

"Enough, Heidi," Alpha Declan warned, his voice low and dangerous. But it was clear that Heidi had no intention of heeding his command.

In an instant, Heidi lunged at me, shifting into her wolf mid-air. The transformation was fluid and terrifying, her body contorting as fur sprouted from her skin and her bones cracked and rearranged themselves. She became a massive, snarling beast, and I was her target. I screamed, throwing my arms up to shield myself as I braced for the impact. My body tensed, waiting for the inevitable pain of claws and teeth tearing into my flesh. I squeezed my eyes shut, refusing to watch my own demise.

Chapter 29

Erica

The sound of my own scream ripped through the air, a desperate cry for help that I knew wouldn't come. My hands flew up to shield my eyes, heart pounding in my chest as I braced myself for the pain of being torn apart.

A gust of wind whooshed past me, followed by a crash that shook the room. With trembling hands, I lowered my arms and found Gregg had shifted into his wolf form. His massive body had slammed into Heidi, stopping her attack just inches from where I stood. They were both on the floor, snarling and snapping at each other like rabid beasts.

"Submit!" Alpha Declan's command boomed through the room, powerful and unyielding. "Shift back, Heidi!" I knew all too well how much more painful a commanded shift was compared to a voluntary one. It was a forced submission, an assault on the very essence of our kind. But Heidi had brought it upon herself, and I couldn't find it in me to feel sorry for her.

Her screams echoed in my ears as she convulsed and writhed on the floor, her body contorting painfully as she returned to her human form. She was naked now, her dress having been shredded during her transformation. Gregg remained in his wolf form, standing guard over her shivering body.

"Erica," Damon whispered urgently, drawing my attention away from the scene. His dark eyes were filled with concern, but I saw something else there too, a flicker of admiration for my resilience.

My eyes fell upon a blanket draped across a sofa nearby. As much as I despised Heidi for what she had done, I couldn't let her suffer like that. I grabbed the blanket and approached her cautiously.

"Here," I said, offering it to her. But the hatred in her amber eyes was palpable and she growled at me, making Gregg snarl back in response.

"Fine!" I snapped, my own anger bubbling up inside me. "Freeze, for all I care!" Damon stepped forward then, placing a calming hand on my shoulder. He gently took the blanket from me and draped it over Heidi's trembling form, his eyes never leaving mine as he did so.

"Thank you," I whispered, feeling a mix of gratitude and shame for letting my emotions get the better of me.

The air was heavy with tension, and I could feel the anger simmering beneath the surface of everyone in the room. My heart raced as I clenched my fists at my sides, trying to keep my composure. A loud knock shattered the uneasy silence, and without waiting for an invitation, two men stormed into the office. One was older, heavyset, with a scowl that matched his imposing stature. The other was younger, fitter, a younger version of the first man. Their eyes, filled with rage, bore a striking resemblance to Heidi's.

"Who do you think you are, barging in like this?" Alpha Declan demanded, his voice booming across the room.

"Save your formalities, Declan," the older man spat back. "When I hear my daughter has spent the night in your cells, I don't wait for an invitation."

"This is Alpha to you," the Alpha snarled. "And I don't care what has happened, you still show me respect, Elder Aldrich." My heart skipped a beat as I realised these were Heidi's family members. I braced myself for the storm that was about to unfold.

Meanwhile, the younger man had knelt down beside Heidi, concern etching deep lines on his face.

"What have you done to her?" he demanded, glaring at Alpha Declan. Heidi continued to rock back and forth, a pitiful sight wrapped in the blanket. But as she caught my gaze, a smirk tugged at the corner of her lips. My stomach churned with disgust, she was playing them all like puppets.

"Pathetic," I muttered under my breath, rolling my eyes.

"Excuse me?" Elder Aldrich snapped, his gaze fixed on me. "Do you find my daughter's pain funny?" I wanted to scream the truth at him, to expose Heidi's deceit, but something held me back. Instead, I bit my tongue, my hands shaking with frustration. As the room continued to spiral out of control, I couldn't help but feel overwhelmed, trapped in a nightmare that refused to end.

"Enough!" Alpha Declan roared, his dominance radiating through the room. "This is not the time for petty arguments."

"Petty?" Elder Aldrich growled. "My daughter's well-being is far from petty."

"Your daughter," I thought bitterly, "is the cause of all this chaos." But again, I kept my silence, swallowing the bile that threatened to rise in my throat. It was becoming harder and harder to ignore the trauma that clawed at the edges of my mind, threatening to consume me whole.

"Let's get one thing straight," Alpha Declan said, his voice ice-cold. "I am still the Alpha, and you will respect my authority."

"Respect?" The word fell from Elder Aldrich's lips like acid. "That's something you have to earn, Declan. And right now, I see no reason to give it to you." As their exchange grew heated, I felt myself shrinking into the background, desperate to escape the maelstrom of emotions that swirled around me.

"Who the fuck is she, anyway?" Elder Aldrich barked, his gaze fixed on me with simmering fury. Gregg, still in his wolf form, growled at him, a deep rumble that vibrated through the air. I watched as both Elder Aldrich's and his son's eyes glazed over, clearly receiving a mind link. I glanced back down at Heidi, who was now smirking up at me, obviously providing them with information about my identity. As the connection between them ended, both men glared at me, their animosity palpable.

"Look," I began, trying to keep my voice steady despite the volatile atmosphere, "I don't have sympathy for your faking bitch of a daughter. If she hadn't attacked me twice already, and tried to kill me, then maybe I'd feel differently." My words were laced with bitterness, but I knew they were the truth.

The moment I finished speaking, the air around us crackled with tension and fury. Gregg, still in his massive wolf form, leapt in front of me, growling at Elder Aldrich with bared teeth. But Louis, like a coiled snake, lunged past Gregg and slammed me against the wall. His hand wrapped around my throat, effectively cutting off both my air supply and any hope I had of voicing my protests.

"Knew you'd be trouble as soon as I heard you were joining our pack," he snarled, his amber eyes filled with hatred. Panic swelled within me, threatening to drown out everything else. As much as I tried to fight him off, my hands clawing at his vice-like grip, the size difference between us was insurmountable.

"Get your hands off her!" Damon yelled, rushing over to my aid. He tried prying Louis' fingers from my throat, but the rage-addled man managed to knock him away with a swift elbow to the chest. Gasping for air, my vision began to blur, dark spots dancing at the edges of my sight.

"Women are good for one thing," Louis sneered, his free hand grabbing my breast, and I felt disgust rolling through me like a tidal wave. "Getting my dick wet. Time to show this little whore how it's done."

"No, you don't!" Damon roared, returning with renewed determination. In one swift motion, he yanked Louis into a choke hold, pulling him off me. The sudden release sent me crumpling to the floor, lungs heaving as they desperately sought oxygen.

"Stop it! All of you!" Alpha Declan's voice boomed through the room, silencing everyone.

Gasping for breath, and my body trembling with fear and violation. My heart pounded in my chest as fragments of a memory from years ago threatened to pull me under, a time that still haunted my dreams and left me gasping for air like a fish out of water.

"Alpha!" Damon shouted, his voice strained as he held Louis pinned on the ground. "Do something!" As my vision blurred, the scene before me seemed to slow down. Alpha Declan had Elder Aldrich cornered, his dark eyes burning with authority, while Damon's arms shook from the effort of keeping Louis restrained. The room felt thick with tension, the overwhelming force of the Alpha's power making it hard to breathe.

"Is this how you repay me, Aldrich?" Alpha Declan roared, his voice echoing through the room. "After I saved your pack and made you an Elder?"

"Declan," Aldrich spat, his face contorted with anger. "You should've never brought that girl into our pack. I warned you."

"ENOUGH!" Declan's rage erupted like a volcano, and the sheer force of his command sent Aldrich crumbling to his knees. "I am the Alpha, and it is my choice who joins this pack. Your insolence will not be tolerated!"

As the men continued their heated exchange, I struggled to keep the panic at bay, the sensation of Louis' hand around my throat and the ghostly grip of past memories threatening to suffocate me.

"Erica?" Damon's voice reached me, laced with concern. He'd managed to subdue Louis and now knelt beside me, his hands hovering uncertainly.

"Stay away," I choked out, my voice barely audible. My mind was a whirlwind of fear and anger, the memories of past traumas swirling together with the present and threatening to drown me.

"Erica, let me help you," Damon pleaded, his dark eyes filled with worry. But I couldn't let him close, not when every touch felt like fire on my skin and sent shivers down my spine.

With a heavy sigh, Alpha Declan turned away from Aldrich and addressed Heidi.

"You haven't learned your lesson," he said, his voice cold and stern. "You'll be escorted home to clean up, then taken back to the cells for three days."

"Please, Alpha," Heidi begged, desperation in her eyes. "Reconsider." He didn't even acknowledge her plea, turning instead to Louis.

"Attacking a pack member is unacceptable. You will also spend three days in the cells." The weight of his words hung in the air as he continued, "Both of you will lose your warrior status, and all three of you will be demoted to low-family rank." I watched Damon's eyes glaze over just before the Alpha's expression shifted to one of rage. My chest tightened, unsure of what had transpired between them through their mental link. In a swift motion, Declan lifted Louis by his throat, slamming him against the wall.

"I will not tolerate sexual assault on one of my pack members!" he roared. The fear that gripped me intensified at his words, my heart thumping wildly in my chest. He changed Louis' punishment to two weeks in chains, silver chains, the kind that would dampen a werewolf's abilities and inflict unbearable pain.

"Take them away," Declan commanded, and the guards rushed to obey.

As they dragged the siblings out of the room, I struggled to control the panic attack that threatened to consume me. Declan approached and knelt in front of me, his dark eyes filled with concern. My breath hitched when he touched my arm, causing me to flinch involuntarily.

"Erica," he said softly, but it was enough to shatter the fragile hold I had on my emotions. Tears streamed down my cheeks as flashes of past trauma crashed into my mind like tidal waves, overwhelming every inch of my being.

"Deep breaths," Declan instructed, his voice a lifeline in the storm of memories that threatened to drag me under. I tried to follow his guidance, but it felt like I was sinking deeper and deeper into the darkness that surrounded me. "Please," I whispered through ragged breaths, the world darkening around me, praying for an end to the torment.

Chapter 30

Liam

As I stepped onto the dew-drenched training grounds, the sun was just beginning to rise, casting a soft golden glow over the earth. My muscles ached from lack of sleep, but I pushed through it, focusing on the task at hand. Jacob, my future Gamma, stood across from me, his eyes locked on mine as we prepared to spar.

"Ready?" he asked, his voice steady and determined.

"Always," I replied, forcing a smile despite the storm raging inside me. We began our dance of power and agility, each strike carefully calculated and met with a parry or dodge.

But my mind kept drifting back to last night when I had burst into Erica's apartment, only to find her there with Grant. The anger still simmered within me, even though I knew deep down that she hadn't done anything wrong. In between thrusts and dodges, I couldn't help but recall how the situation had escalated, turning sexual and primal. How I had held Erica against the wall, showing her who her Alpha was and to whom she belonged. Her body writhed in pleasure, and she reached her peak without me even touching her intimately. A small flicker of guilt gnawed at me for being so rough with her, but satisfaction swelled in my chest knowing I was slowly wearing down her walls.

"Focus, Liam!" Jacob barked, snapping me out of my thoughts as his fist narrowly missed my jaw.

"Sorry," I grunted, ducking under another swing and countering with a swift kick.

"Your head's not in this, is it?" Jacob observed, eyebrows furrowed in concern.

"Let's just keep going," I muttered, avoiding his gaze and throwing myself back into the fight.

With each blow exchanged, I struggled to keep my emotions at bay, feeling both protective and guilty over Erica. Our bond was growing stronger, but I couldn't shake the feeling that I was treading on dangerous ground.

"Enough," Jacob said firmly, stepping back and lowering his fists. "What's going on, Liam? You're too distracted."

"Nothing," I lied through gritted teeth, my chest heaving with exertion. "Let's just do one more round."

"Fine," Jacob agreed, though his eyes still held suspicion. As we continued to spar, I tried to focus solely on the fight, but my mind refused to cooperate. Thoughts of Erica filled every corner of my consciousness, and I couldn't help but wonder if my actions had further damaged our fragile bond. Would she ever trust me enough to see past her fear of Alphas?

"Enough," I finally conceded, panting and wiping the sweat from my brow.

"You're right, I'm not focused." In a blur of motion, my body moved instinctively, and I flipped Jacob onto the ground with a heavy thud. He grunted in surprise, momentarily winded by the impact.

"Damn, Liam!" he exclaimed, staring up at me from the dirt. "What's got into you?" I offered him a hand and pulled him to his feet, brushing off his clothes in an attempt to regain some semblance of composure.

"Sorry, man," I muttered. "I'm just... distracted." Jacob laughed, rubbing his sore back.

"Let me guess, is this distraction a certain hot redhead?" My face grew warm, and I quickly looked away.

"Ah," Jacob nodded in understanding.

"Is she...?"

"Complicated," I finished for him, unable to find any other word to describe the tumultuous emotions she stirred within me.

"It's not just that," I said defensively, clenching my fists. "I'm not happy with Grayson. If Erica was hurt, he should've called me, not sent her home with some mutt of a warrior."

"Grant?" Jacob asked, raising an eyebrow.

"Exactly," I confirmed, anger bubbling beneath the surface. "But don't worry. He won't be a problem anymore. I spoke to my father last night, and we arranged for Grant to go away on a mission. I don't trust him near Erica." The mention of my father reminded me of the burdens that came with being the Alpha heir, and the weight of those responsibilities settled heavily on my shoulders. I glanced around the training grounds, the familiar sight doing little to ease the turmoil within me.

"Good call," Jacob replied, nodding in agreement. "We can't afford any distractions right now, especially with everything going on."

"Right," I agreed, though I couldn't help but wonder if removing Grant from the equation would truly make things any easier.

My thoughts drifted back to the previous night, the memory of our heated encounter still fresh in my mind. I could still feel the heat of Erica's skin beneath my touch, the way her body responded to my dominance. A mixture of guilt and satisfaction warred within me.

"Stay focused, Liam," Jacob warned, his voice pulling me back to the present. "We need you at your best."

"Of course," I replied, forcing a smile that didn't quite reach my eyes. "One more round?"

"Bring it on," Jacob challenged with a grin, and we resumed our sparring. But despite my best efforts, Erica's presence continued to haunt me. The powerful bond between us was undeniable, yet I couldn't shake the feeling that I had somehow failed her.

The air around us crackled with tension as we continued to spar. I tried to shake off the distraction, but my thoughts stubbornly clung to Erica and the events of the previous night.

"Let's finish this," I said, forcing myself to focus on the sparring match before me.

"Alright," Jacob agreed, still eyeing me warily as we resumed our positions. We danced around each other, exchanging blows and dodging expertly. Yet, even as I landed a solid hit against Jacob's shoulder, all I could feel was the lingering touch of Erica's skin beneath my fingers and the weight of my actions bearing down on my conscience.

Suddenly, I felt the familiar tingle of a mind link pushing through, snapping me back to reality. I opened my mind to Damon's voice, urgent and distressed.

"Liam, there's been an incident. Erica's having a meltdown." Annoyance flared within me, mingling with the guilt that already plagued me.

"What the fuck am I supposed to do?" I snapped back.

"Try being the Alpha she needs, not the one she expects," Damon replied, his words cutting through my frustration. "It's bad, Liam. She was attacked again." My heart clenched at the thought of Erica in pain, and I knew Damon was right. I had to be there for her, regardless of my own feelings. Turning to Jacob, I said,

"I have to go."

"Understood," he replied with a solemn nod.

As I sprinted away from the training grounds, I couldn't help but wonder if I was strong enough, not just physically, but emotionally, to be the Alpha that Erica truly needed. My heart pounding in my chest, I raced across the pack territory towards the pack house. The panic from Erica pierced through our mate bond like a thousand icy needles, urging me to move faster. As I ran, I cursed inwardly that we hadn't completed the bond yet, knowing it would be easier to feel her and provide comfort once we did. The wind whipped past me as I pushed myself to run even faster, my muscles straining with each powerful stride. My mind raced with thoughts of Erica's wellbeing and the fear that gripped her, making me wish for nothing more than to be by her side. Upon reaching the pack house, I didn't hesitate, bounding up the steps two at a time and bursting into the first floor offices without knocking. The scent of distress hung heavy in the air, only fuelling my sense of urgency further.

"Where is she?" I demanded, my voice rough and demanding, betraying the turmoil of emotions churning within me.

"Your father's office," someone replied, their voice barely registering as I zeroed in on the door.

Without waiting for permission or announcement, I threw open the door, my entrance sudden and unceremonious. As I burst into my father's office, my eyes quickly took in the chaotic scene before me. The room was a mess - overturned furniture and scattered papers signalling that something terrible had happened. My father stood with a grim expression, flanked by our pack doctor, Damon, and Gregg, who was clad only in shorts - evidence of a hasty shift back to human form. Their gazes were all fixed on one spot, and as I followed their line of sight, my heart clenched painfully. There, huddled on the floor, was Erica. Her once fiery green eyes were now glazed over with fear, her body shivering uncontrollably as she let out pitiful whimpers.

"Every time someone gets close, she freaks out," Damon said quietly, his voice strained with concern. "She just starts screaming."

"Something has triggered an old trauma," my father added, his expression sombre. "We need to help her, Liam."

"Tell me what happened!" I demanded, my voice shaking with barely contained fury. I needed to know who was responsible for this, who had hurt my mate so badly.

"Louis," my father replied, his gaze locking onto mine. "He sexually assaulted her." At that, my vision went red. The rage inside me surged, demanding retribution. Louis would pay for what he'd done. But first, I needed to help Erica.

Taking slow, measured steps toward her, I tried to calm myself, knowing that my anger wouldn't bring her any comfort. I focused on the bond between us - incomplete but still powerful, and sent waves of reassurance and love through it, hoping against hope that she could feel them too. I inched closer to Erica, my heart pounding in my chest as I tried to steady my breathing. The air around her seemed heavy with fear, and I desperately hoped that the familiar scent of our fated bond would bring her some comfort. With each step, I focused on projecting warmth and safety into the space between us, willing her to recognise me as her mate and not another threat.

"Erica," I murmured softly as I knelt beside her, my heart aching at the sight of her broken form. "I'm here, love. You're safe now." Her whimpers subsided slightly, but she remained huddled on the floor, trembling with fear.. Gently, I extended my hand towards her, my fingers brushing against her arm. She flinched and let out a soft whimper, but didn't scream. Relief washed over me, mixed with an overwhelming sense of protectiveness.

"Doctor," I said, keeping my gaze locked on Erica. "The sedative, please." Without taking my eyes off her, I held out my hand, feeling the cool syringe press into my palm. Carefully, I administered the sedative, watching as her tense muscles slowly relaxed under its effects. Just as she began to slump forward, I caught her in my arms, cradling her close to my chest.

"Let's get her to the hospital," I murmured, my voice thick with emotion. With Erica secure in my arms, I followed the doctor through the pack grounds, my mind racing with thoughts of guilt and responsibility. As we reached the hospital and settled her into a bed, nurses fluttered about, attaching fluids and monitoring equipment. I couldn't tear my eyes away from her pale, sleeping face, my hand gripping hers tightly. As the room quieted down and the nurses left us alone, I sank into a chair beside her bed, my mind replaying the events of the previous night. The memory of how rough I had been, of how I had asserted my dominance over her, twisted my gut with guilt. Had I added to her stress? Had my actions pushed her closer to this breaking point? The night wore on, and I remained by her side, my thoughts a swirling storm of anger, self-loathing, and the fierce need to protect her. As the first light of dawn began to creep through the window, I made a silent vow: I would be the Alpha she needed, the one she could trust and rely on. And together, we would forge a bond stronger than any darkness that threatened to tear us apart.

Chapter 31

Erica

My eyelids fluttered open, and a sharp gasp tore through my throat as I tried to sit up. Panic seized me as I registered the sterile white walls and the steady beeping of machines surrounding me. Disoriented memories flitted at the edges of my mind, but nothing concrete enough to explain why I was in a hospital bed.

"Wha...?" My voice came out as a weak croak, and I squeezed my eyes shut, trying to block out the overwhelming confusion. The sensation of warmth and safety enveloped me, pulling me away from the edge of panic. A familiar presence lingered nearby, tethering me to reality. Slowly, I opened my eyes and turned my head towards the source of that comforting feeling. There, slumped in an uncomfortable-looking hospital chair, was Liam. He appeared to have dozed off, yet his hand remained intertwined with mine. Despite the exhaustion etched on his face, there was no denying his rugged handsomeness. My eyes lingered on Liam's face, taking in the strong lines of his jaw and the curve of his lips. His dark brown hair fell across his forehead, adding a certain ruggedness to his appearance. I found myself entranced by the steady rise and fall of his chest, each breath a testament to his unwavering presence in my life.

As if sensing my gaze upon him, Liam opened one eye and raised an amused eyebrow.

"You know, it's considered a bit creepy to stare at someone while they sleep," he teased. I couldn't help but laugh, surprised by the genuine happiness that bubbled within me.

"I'm sorry, I just... I can't help it," I admitted, feeling the blush creeping up my cheeks. Liam sat up, squeezing my hand reassuringly.

"How are you feeling?" he asked, his voice laced with concern. I tried to gauge the question, how was I feeling?

"Thirsty," I replied, suddenly very aware of the dryness in my throat. In an instant, Liam was on his feet, grabbing a jug of water from the nearby table. He filled a glass and returned to my side, his movements swift and full of purpose. As he helped me sit up, I marvelled at the gentleness with which he supported me, a stark contrast to the powerful Alpha I knew he could be.

"Here," he said, holding the glass to my lips. The cool water provided sweet relief as it flowed down my parched throat. I drank greedily, grateful for the simple act of kindness.

"Thank you," I whispered once I had finished, allowing Liam to remove the glass from my trembling lips.

"Of course," he responded, his eyes never leaving mine. "I'll always be here for you, Erica." As I looked into his brown eyes, something inside me shifted. It was as if some long-buried part of me finally acknowledged the truth I had been trying to ignore: Liam was more than just my fated mate. He was my protector, my confidante... and maybe even the man I could learn to love. But for now, all that mattered was the gratitude I felt towards this remarkable individual who had saved me from my darkest fears. And as we sat there in the sterile hospital room, the beeping of machines provided a steady backdrop to our quiet conversation.

The more I drank and woke from the haze a newfound energy flowed through my veins as I felt quenched and revitalised. Liam's gaze remained on me, but his expression changed. He shifted uncomfortably in the chair, biting his lip as if debating whether to speak.

"Erica... I..." he started, hesitating before continuing, "I need to apologise."

"Apologise?" I furrowed my brow, not expecting him to say that.

"Yeah," he sighed, rubbing the back of his neck. "I've been so stupid, pig-headed, and selfish. I wanted to prove I was your perfect mate, but all I did was act like a complete dick." As he rambled, I couldn't help but smile at his sincerity. I reached out with my free hand, placing it on his arm to stop him mid-sentence.

"Thank you, Liam," I said softly, causing his eyes to widen in confusion.

"Thank you? For what?"

"During the trauma attack, I was trapped," I explained, my voice shaky as I recalled the experience. "I was struggling against the horrifying images, unable to break free. But I could feel you through the bond, reaching out to me, pulling me back to safety." Liam's cheeks flushed, and he looked down at our intertwined hands.

"That's what mates are for, Erica. We're meant to protect each other." His words stirred something within me, a warmth that spread throughout my chest. It wasn't just the mate bond that made me feel this way; it was Liam himself. Despite my initial reluctance, I found myself drawn to his strength, his compassion, and his unwavering determination to stand by me.

"Still," he continued, his voice barely above a whisper, "I'm sorry for how I've been acting. I want to do better, to be better for you."

"Thank you," I repeated, my heart swelling with gratitude. "I don't know what would have happened if you hadn't been there... and I'm glad I don't have to find out." A tentative smile crossed his face, and he squeezed my hand gently.

"I'll always be here for you, Erica. No matter what."

We sat in silence for a little while; the sun was shining in through the window and I could hear the warriors in the training grounds, which were next to the hospital. Finally Lian spoke

"Please, tell me what happened," Liam urged gently, his eyes filled with concern.

"I want to understand so I can help you." I hesitated for a moment, unsure if I was ready to relive the memories that haunted me. But as I looked into Liam's determined brown eyes, I felt a surge of courage. He deserved to know the truth, and maybe sharing my story could be the first step in healing.

"Years ago, when I was eighteen, I had a disagreement with Trenton," I began, my voice shaky. "He told me I couldn't leave the pack, but all I wanted was to find a place where I belonged. So, I ran away and joined another pack led by an Alpha who promised love and freedom." As I spoke, the images of that time flooded back into my mind. The hope I'd felt at finding a new family, the easy friendship I'd experienced with the other wolves, and the crushing reality when it all fell apart.

"Only, he wasn't the saviour I thought he was," I continued, tears welling up in my eyes. "He was running a werewolf trafficking ring, using his female wolves to satisfy the twisted desires of others... because apparently we could withstand more damage and heal faster." Liam's jaw clenched, his eyes darkening with fury.

"That monster..." he growled.

"Once I discovered the truth, I tried to escape," I choked out, hot tears streaming down my face. "But he caught me, locked me up, and... forced himself on me, calling it training for what was to come."

"Erica, I'm so sorry," Liam whispered, his own eyes glistening with unshed tears. He reached for my hand, holding it tightly as if to protect me from further harm.

"Eventually, Trenton and Marshall managed to rescue me," I continued, trying to regain my composure. "I believe your father was involved in the mission too."

"Really?" Liam's expression shifted from fury to surprise. "I remember him mentioning something about it, but he never gave any details. I'll have to ask him about it. If that bastard Alpha is still alive, I swear I'll hunt him down and make him pay for what he did to you."

"Thank you," I whispered, my heart swelling with gratitude for Liam's unwavering support. As Liam listened intently to my story, I could feel the fury radiating off him. His eyes were dark with anger and concern, and I knew that his protective instincts as an Alpha were kicking in.

"Erica, I'm so sorry you had to go through that," he said softly, reaching out to gently brush away the tears that continued to spill down my cheeks. The touch of his fingers sent electric shivers through me, a mixture of both pleasure and comfort. Despite everything, it felt safe to be near him.

"Thank you, Liam. But how can I ever repay you for helping me through this?" I asked, my voice cracking slightly under the weight of my emotions. He shook his head firmly, his brown eyes locking onto mine with a fierce intensity.

"You don't need to repay me, Erica. It's my duty as your mate to be there for you, to protect and care for you. Even if you decide not to complete our bond, I'll still be here for you. Always." The sincerity in his words warmed my heart, and I couldn't help but feel a surge of gratitude toward him. This man, this powerful Alpha heir, was willing to put his own desires aside just to ensure my safety and happiness.

"Erica, you are my everything," Liam whispered, his voice full of raw emotion. "I already love you more than anything in this world." My breath caught in my throat as I processed his confession. He loved me, truly and deeply, despite all the pain and turmoil we'd experienced together. The enormity of his feelings left me reeling, unsure of how to respond.

"Thank you, Liam," was all I could manage, my voice barely above a whisper. A part of me wanted to say the words back to him, to let him know that I could feel the stirrings of love growing within me as well. But I hesitated, still uncertain of the depth of my own feelings and the consequences they could have on our bond.

"Thank you for everything," I repeated, reaching out to take his hand in mine. The warmth of his skin against mine was a balm to my bruised soul, a reminder that there was still hope for us, for the powerful connection that had brought us together against all odds.

The weight of Liam's words echoed in my mind as I struggled to make sense of the whirlwind of emotions surging through me. Love? Could I truly love him? My heart raced at the mere thought, yet I couldn't deny the magnetic pull that drew me to him, a force far greater than simple attraction.

"Hey," I said tentatively, my voice shaking with uncertainty. "I have an idea." Liam looked at me with those warm brown eyes that seemed to see straight into my soul.

"Why don't we...go on a date? A real one – planned and everything." For a moment, his expression was unreadable, as if weighing the sincerity of my proposal. Then, a slow smile spread across his face, lighting up his features like the sun emerging from behind a cloud.

"I'd love that, Erica," he replied with genuine enthusiasm, squeezing my hand gently. "I promise it'll be the best damn date you've ever had." My heart swelled with gratitude as I studied the man before me, trying to reconcile the tender, caring Alpha heir with the arrogant, pig-headed wolf who had initially stormed into my life. Had our tumultuous past clouded my judgement, causing me to overlook the kind, devoted mate that he had the potential to become?

"Thank you," I murmured softly, my eyes brimming with unshed tears. It wasn't just for the promise of a perfect date – it was for the way he held my hand, the way he saved me from my darkest memories, and the way he gave me hope when all seemed lost.

"Erica," he whispered, leaning closer until his breath caressed my cheek, sending shivers down my spine. "I will do whatever it takes to make you happy. You deserve nothing less."

Chapter 32

Erica

The sun dipped low in the sky as anticipation tightened in my chest. It was the day of my date with Liam, and I couldn't stop the nervous energy from coursing through me. I paced around my room, clothes strewn across every surface, none of them were right for a mysterious outing that Liam had planned.

"Come on, Erica," Gen encouraged, picking up a black dress and holding it against me. "This one is perfect." I shook my head, feeling the weight of my light red hair swishing across my shoulders.

"Too formal." I glanced over at Kaitlyn who was sitting on my bed, "Did he give you any hints about what we're doing?" Kaitlyn shook her head.

"Not a word," she said, "And I asked a lot." Frankie smirked, her purple-tipped black hair falling over her eyes as she leaned against the wall.

"Well, it's not every day an Alpha heir is so keen on someone like us. Maybe he's taking you to a secret werewolf ball?"

"Very funny," I retorted, rolling my green eyes at her. Kaitlyn, who'd been quietly observing the chaos, finally spoke up.

"Erica, I think it's time you tell them the truth." My heart skipped a beat, and I hesitated. Kaitlyn was the only one who knew about the mate bond between Liam and me. But seeing the expectant gazes of my friends, I took a deep breath and revealed our secret.

"Liam and I are fated mates. That's why I joined the pack, but I didn't want to complete the bond until I knew for sure." The room erupted with excited squeals and supportive hugs. Gen looked at me with shining eyes.

"That means you'll be our new Luna!" My stomach twisted into knots at the thought, and I could feel the pressure settling on my shoulders.

"Oh Goddess, yeah, I guess so." My voice trembled, betraying my nerves.

"Hey, don't worry about that now," Verity said, her pale grey eyes softening. "Tonight is just about you and Liam getting to know each other better."

"Right," I nodded, taking a deep breath to calm my racing heart. Together, we sifted through the mess of clothes, and I finally settled on an outfit that I didn't totally hate. I stood in front of the mirror, giving myself one last look-over. I had chosen black skinny jeans and a purple off-the-shoulder top that hugged my curves just right. A nervous excitement bubbled inside me as I ran a hand through my light red hair, taming any stray strands.

"Erica, you look amazing," Gen reassured me with a smile.

"Thanks," I murmured, trying to quiet the doubts that nagged at me.

A knock on the door interrupted my thoughts. My heart leapt into my throat as Gen opened it, revealing Liam standing there like a vision. He was dressed in smart casual attire, his black jeans clinging to his muscular legs, and a tightly fitted black top that accentuated his broad shoulders and chiselled chest.

"Hey," he greeted us, a warm smile spreading across his face. His dark brown eyes met mine, and for a moment, time seemed to slow down. The air around us crackled with electricity, our fated bond pulling at my very core.

"Hi," I breathed, mesmerised by his ruggedly handsome features. The room felt suddenly too warm, and I could feel my cheeks flushing under his gaze.

"Erica, you look amazing," Liam said, echoing Gen's words from earlier. His voice sent shivers down my spine, and my stomach fluttered with anticipation. "I'm so happy we're finally getting this date."

"Me too," I replied, my voice barely above a whisper.

"Ready to go?" Liam asked, offering me his arm. I hesitated for a moment before looping my arm through his, feeling the solid warmth of his body against mine.

"Have fun, you two!" Verity called out, with a genuine smile.

"Goodnight, ladies," Liam said, nodding to each of them in turn.

"Goodnight," they chorused, with Gen, Frankie, Verity, and Kaitlyn all wearing matching grins.

"Bye, Erica!" Frankie added with a wink. "Don't do anything I wouldn't do!" I rolled my eyes, but I couldn't help the laughter that bubbled up inside me at her outrageous humour. As Liam led me out of the room, the sound of their giggles followed us, their playful teasing a reminder of the support they'd shown me earlier.

The cool night air brushed against my skin as we stepped outside the apartment building, and I couldn't help but shiver slightly. Liam noticed immediately and moved closer to me, his body heat a welcome comfort.

"Are you cold?" he asked with genuine concern in his voice. "I can grab you a jacket if you want."

"No, it's okay," I replied, not wanting to seem too fragile. "I'll warm up once we start walking."

"Alright," he said, still looking a little worried. "Just let me know if you change your mind." We walked away from the apartment building, and I expected Liam to lead me further into the pack compound. Instead, he guided me towards a hidden path behind the pack house. The trees around us seemed to close in, creating an intimate atmosphere that made my heart race.

"Where are we going?" I asked, curiosity getting the better of me.

"You'll see," Liam answered, a secretive smile playing on his lips. "It's my favourite place in the world." The sound of rushing water grew louder as we continued along the path, which followed the curve of a small river. The moonlight filtered through the trees above, casting dappled shadows on the ground beneath our feet. My senses were heightened by the anticipation of what lay ahead, and every new detail felt like a discovery.

"Almost there," Liam whispered, his breath warm on my ear, sending shivers down my spine.

As we rounded a bend, the sight before me took my breath away. The river had turned into a waterfall, its powerful cascade of water shimmering like silver in the moonlight. Liam guided me down a path to the bottom of the waterfall, and my eyes widened when I saw a blanket spread out beside the plunge pool, a picnic basket waiting nearby.

"Wow, Liam..." I breathed, unable to tear my eyes away from the stunning scene. "This is incredible."

"Only the best for you, Erica," he said softly, a tender expression in his eyes that made my chest tighten with emotion. I couldn't help but feel grateful for this beautiful moment, shared with a man who seemed to truly care for me. The world outside this hidden oasis faded away, leaving nothing but the powerful bond between us and the promise of an unforgettable night.

"Is this really your favourite place?" I asked, an incredulous smile playing at the corners of my mouth as I gazed around the enchanting scene.

"Absolutely," Liam confirmed, his eyes shining with sincerity. "I come here when I need to think or just escape for a while." He glanced towards the waterfall, a faint smile on his lips.

"There's also a hidden gap in the rocks over there," he gestured with a nod of his head. "I used to use it to slip off pack territory when I was a kid."

"Sounds like quite the adventure," I remarked, feeling a pang of affection for the young, rebellious Liam he had once been.

"Shall we?" Liam offered his hand, guiding me towards the blanket. I accepted, allowing him to lead me to our moonlit haven beside the plunge pool. The sound of the waterfall created a soothing, rhythmic backdrop as we settled onto the soft fabric beneath us. The picnic basket held a treasure trove of delights, including a bottle of red wine that Liam uncorked with practised ease.

"To a night of getting to know each other better," he toasted, and I couldn't help but feel a thrill of excitement at the prospect of learning more about this enigmatic man who had become such an important part of my life.

"Cheers," I agreed, clinking my glass against his before taking a sip of the rich, velvety liquid. We began to sample the delicious spread before us, from tender roast chicken to ripe, succulent berries. Each morsel seemed to taste even better than the last, and I marvelled at the thought and care that Liam had put into planning this perfect evening for us.

"Did you cook all of this yourself?" I asked, spearing a piece of grilled asparagus with my fork.

"Guilty as charged," Liam admitted, chuckling softly. "I thought it would be more personal that way."

"Colour me impressed," I complimented, feeling a warm glow of gratitude for his efforts. As we ate, our conversation flowed easily, touching on various topics from pack life to our favourite books and movies. I relished the opportunity to share parts of myself with Liam while also peeling back the layers of his own complex personality.

"Tell me something no one else knows about you," Liam suggested playfully, his brown eyes locking onto mine with an intensity that made my heart skip a beat.

"Alright," I agreed, taking a deep breath before revealing a long-held secret. "When I was little, I used to sneak out at night and pretend I was a wolf, running through the woods and howling at the moon." Liam's laughter was warm and genuine, his eyes crinkling at the corners as he grinned. "That's adorable," he declared, reaching over to brush a stray lock of hair out of my eyes.

"And now look at you, part of a pack and living the dream."

"Living the dream, indeed," I whispered, my heart swelling with gratitude and love for the man beside me, who had given me more than I could have ever imagined. As we continued to sip wine and share secrets beneath the silver light of the moon, I couldn't help but feel that this was the beginning of something truly magical, a bond stronger than any curse or challenge that might come our way. And in that moment, surrounded by the beauty of nature and the warmth of Liam's presence, I knew I was exactly where I was meant to be.

The last of the picnic remnants were tucked away in the basket, and Liam and I sat side by side on the plush blanket, the moonlight casting silver rays upon us. The sound of the waterfall created a soothing melody, enchanting me to the core. I glanced at Liam, his strong features softened by the gentle light, and my heart swelled with happiness.

"Tell me about yourself, Erica," Liam said, his voice low and inviting.

"Um, how about we play a game instead?" I countered, suddenly nervous about sharing my past.

"Let's play twenty questions."

"Twenty questions?" Liam raised an eyebrow. "How do you play that?"

"Each of us asks a question and both of us answer it. We each get ten questions. They could be about favourite things or stuff like that," I explained, hoping to keep things light and fun. Liam's eyes glinted mischievously, but he nodded in agreement.

"Sounds interesting. You go first."

"Alright, let's start," I said, feeling a strange mixture of excitement and apprehension. "What's your favourite colour?"

"Easy," Liam replied with a grin. "Dark green. Reminds me of the forest. Yours is purple right?"

"Yeah, how did you know?" I asked. He pulled at my top and smiled.

"I can be observant." He paused for a moment before asking his first question.

"What's your most vivid sexual fantasy?" I nearly choked on my own spit.

"Liam!" I exclaimed, blushing furiously. "That's not what I meant by 'favourites and stuff.'"

"Come on, baby," he teased, his eyes sparkling with mischief. "We're supposed to be getting to know each other, right? You can't expect me to pass up an opportunity like this."

"Fine," I muttered, trying my best to keep my composure. "I've always been intrigued by the idea of being intimate outdoors, surrounded by nature." It was true, although I'd never admitted it aloud before.

"Interesting," Liam mused, looking genuinely pleased. "I love to take control," he said while meeting my eyes, "To restrain you to my bed, and then you give over everything to me." I gulped at the thought of what this man could do if I let him. The longer he held my eyes the hotter I felt. Finally he broke the tension with a mischievous grin, "Your turn."

"Okay," I said, attempting to regain some control of the conversation. "What's your favourite book?"

"Dracula," he answered without hesitation. "Now, what's the most adventurous thing you've ever done in bed?" I couldn't help but laugh at his determination to keep things steamy.

"Well, there was this one time when I tried out some light bondage..." I trailed off, my face burning even brighter than before.

"Really?" Liam said, his voice low and smooth. "Sounds exciting."

"Alright." I took a deep breath, searching for a suitable query. "What's your favourite season?"

"Autumn," Liam answered without hesitation. "I love the changing colours, the crisp air, and the way everything feels alive before winter sets in. How about you?"

"Spring," I replied dreamily. "There's something magical about seeing the world come back to life after a long, cold winter."

"Good choices," Liam murmured, his eyes never leaving mine.

"Your turn again," I reminded him quickly, eager to shift the focus away from me.

"Alright," he said with a smirk. "What's the kinkiest thing you've ever wanted to try?"

"Are all your questions going to be about sex?" I asked, exasperated.

"Maybe," he replied, looking completely unrepentant. "You did say we're supposed to be getting to know each other, and I think this is a pretty important aspect of any relationship."

"Fine," I sighed, feeling both annoyed and intrigued by his persistence. "I've always been curious about role-playing."

"Ah, the allure of fantasy," Liam murmured, his eyes darkening with desire. "Tell me, what roles would you like to play?"

"Okay, that's enough!" I exclaimed, laughing despite myself. "Can we please move on to less... intimate questions?"

"Hmmm, maybe," Liam growled, and the sound went right to my centre. "I just have a few more questions."

"You're not playing the game right," I tried pouting in an attempt to regain control. How the hell did he turn this around on me?

"No, I'm playing to win. Ready, baby?" My body quivered with anticipation as I waited for Liam's next question. His tone, dripping with seductive promises, sent shivers down my spine and made me crave his touch all the more. Despite my nerves, I nodded eagerly, desperate for him to continue.

"Tell me," he whispered in my ear, "where on your perfect body do you like to be touched?" His words were like fire against my skin, and I struggled to compose myself as he trailed his fingers across my stomach.

"Is it here?" he murmured, placing his lips against the sensitive skin beneath my ear. "Or maybe here?" He nipped at the mark on my neck, sending waves of pleasure through every inch of me. Before I could even process what was happening, a moan escaped my lips. Liam chuckled darkly at the sound, clearly enjoying my response.

"Good to know, baby," he growled, promising so much more without saying a word.

"Do you want to know my answer, my love?" he whispered, and I felt like I was going to faint. His hand felt hot on mine as he placed it ever so gently against his hard abdomen, and I could clearly make out the shape of his forming erection pushing against the fabric of his boxers. "Li-Liam," I stammered, my cheeks growing warm in embarrassment. He smiled devilishly as he moved my hand lower towards the waistband of his pants, and then paused tantalisingly at the edge. He closed his eyes and ran my fingertips along the elasticated band and a shiver raced through me. He opened his gaze once more, hazy with passion and desire that made my pulse skyrocket.

"The tease of the waistline is enough to drive this wolf wild," he murmured, his voice low and rough as if barely holding back an animalistic urge. His hand locked around mine still pressing it against his body before slowly moving it down towards the waistband of my shorts. He sent a single finger inside the top of them and trailed it ever so lightly over my skin.

"Can you feel what I mean now, baby?" His words were soaked in longing that echoed within me until I thought I might burst from anticipation. My whole body shook uncontrollably with yearning for him. He pressed his lips to the soft skin of my neck, a possessive bite gracing its surface as he whispered in my ear,

"Ready for the next question, baby?" I shivered beneath his touch and struggled to speak, my voice barely more than a whisper.

"It - it's my turn." His lips curved into a wicked smile and he growled against my throat, sending a bolt of pleasure through me.

"I'm changing the rules," he murmured and I could feel his breath on my neck. He pulled away just enough to look me in the eye and said

"One last question, ready?" I nodded and before I could respond, his lips were back on my neck, sucking at my flesh as if he was trying to draw me into him.

"Baby, I can smell your arousal," he breathed against my skin. My heart raced, and I felt a throbbing between my legs that begged for him. He pulled away, meeting my gaze with an intensity that made me tremble. And then he asked me: "Want me to do something about it?"

Chapter 33

Erica

The moon cast a silvery glow over the waterfall, it's cascading water shimmering like liquid diamonds as it plunged into the pool below. In that singular moment, time seemed to stand still, and we were the only two beings in existence. Our connection was so strong, it felt like an electric current pulsating through us, binding us together with an invisible thread. Liam crashed his lips onto mine, claiming my mouth as if it were his territory. At the same time, his hand slipped into my jeans, his fingers seeking out the sensitive centre of my pleasure. When his touch connected with my throbbing clit, a cry tore from my throat, muffled by the passionate kiss. He used my reaction to plunge his tongue deeper, tangling with my own in a dance of desire.

"Your taste is intoxicating," he murmured between kisses, his voice husky with lust. He rubbed circular motions with his fingers, igniting a fresh wave of desire that threatened to consume me whole. I grabbed at his arm, my mind a whirlwind of confusion, did I want him to stop, slow down, or speed up? He seemed to sense my inner turmoil and pulled away from my mouth, moving instead to my neck where he nibbled at the crook where my mark would eventually go.

"Please, Liam," I begged, my voice barely above a whisper. The need for him coursed through my veins like wildfire, leaving me desperate for more of his touch.

"Patience, love," he replied, his voice both soothing and seductive. "Tonight, we will explore each other's bodies until the sun rises." His words sent a shiver down my spine, anticipation pooling in the pit of my stomach. I knew that this night was not only about passion and desire but also about the powerful bond between us, a bond that would soon be forged into something unbreakable by fate itself.

"Please, Liam," I moaned again, my voice hoarse with the intensity of my longing. "I can't wait any longer." He chuckled softly against my throat, the vibrations sending delicious shivers down my spine.

"You're so eager, baby. It's incredibly sexy." Despite the desire waves ripping through my body, I could still feel a stronger tension buried deep inside me, and I was going out of my mind at the thought of release. My nails dug into his strong shoulders as he continued to tease me mercilessly.

"Patience, baby," Liam growled against my ear, the sound sending shivers down my spine. He pulled his hand out of my jeans, leaving me aching for more. I couldn't help but growl at him in frustration.

Chuckling, he placed his hands on my hips and lifted me, flipping me so that I was straddling him. My sensitive core landed right on his rock-hard bulge, even through our clothes I felt it as I involuntarily ground against him. His hands tightened on my hips, stopping me from moving, and I glared at him with a mixture of annoyance and lust. He grinned at me, clearly enjoying the effect he had on me. Unable to resist the urge to wipe that grin off his face, I leaned down and crashed my lips back onto his. He eagerly accepted my kiss, his hunger for me evident as he deepened the embrace. One hand tangled in my hair, while the other slid down my side and onto my ass, squeezing gently and pushing me closer to his groin. I pulled away from his mouth, needing to catch my breath, and licked a clear line up his neck from the crook to his ear. I revelled in the salty taste of his skin, and he sighed, his eyes closed. I continued my exploration, laying kisses back down his neck and onto his collarbone, nipping at the skin playfully. His hand tightened in my hair as he groaned, encouraging me to continue. Smiling, I moved lower to his chest, shuffling down as he released his hold on my hair and ass, instead placing both hands on my sides to steady me. I reached his chest and flicked my tongue out, making contact with his nipple. His grip on my sides tightened as he groaned again, the sound driving me wild. I covered his nipple with my mouth and grazed it gently with my teeth, teasing him mercilessly. At the same time, I slid my hand down his torso and copied his earlier actions, running a finger along the waistband of his jeans. He groaned again; the sound sending waves of desire through me.

"Baby," he breathed, his voice thick with need. I paused in my ministrations, gazing up at him with a wicked smile.

"Patience, baby," I parroted back to him, my voice husky. "I want to enjoy this."

"Baby," Liam croaked out, his voice strained with desire.

I smiled at the effect I was having on him and continued my tortuous journey down his body, leaving a trail of feathery kisses and gentle nips in my wake. He had long since lost his grip on me, and now his hands were behind his head as he watched me with a lustful hunger burning in his eyes. The intensity of his gaze sent shivers down my spine, heightening the electrifying connection between us. As I reached the waistband of his pants, I pressed a gentle kiss right at the edge, letting my lips linger for a moment before teasingly running my tongue along the fabric. He threw his head back in a half groan and half growl; the sound echoing through the night air around us. His hand found its way back into my hair, gripping it possessively.

"Erica, goddess," he panted, his chest rising and falling rapidly with each breath. I couldn't help but revel in the power I held over him in this moment, a stark contrast to the vulnerability I felt just moments ago. My heart raced with anticipation, knowing that our fated love and powerful bond were leading us to an unforgettable crescendo.

"Please," he whispered, his plea barely audible yet filled with unbridled need.

"I said, patience, baby," I murmured, with a wicked grin that had him groaning. "Let's take our time and savour this."

My own desire surged through me, urging me to continue my exploration of his body. Liam's ragged breathing and desperate touches only fuelled my own desire, and I could feel the heat between us intensifying with every passing second. The waterfall's mist clung to our skin, adding a sensual layer to our passionate dance.

"Erica," he breathed, his voice filled with a mix of love, need, and something else, a primal intensity that sent shivers down my spine.

"Tell me what you want," I whispered, pausing my teasing ministrations to gaze into his eyes, searching for the raw truth within them.

"Make me yours," he growled, his request sending waves of desire coursing through me. Liam's grip on my hair tightened as he half-growled, half-groaned my name.

"Oh goddess Erica, what are you doing to me?" His voice was raw, filled with need and a hint of vulnerability. I paused my teasing ministrations, looking up at him with a wicked grin, our eyes locked.

"Shhh, I want to enjoy this." my voice dripping with sensual playfulness. He chuckled in response, his breath hitching as I resumed tracing the waistband of his pants with my tongue, each slow, deliberate stroke igniting something primal within both of us. The moonlight bathed us in its silvery glow, casting shadows that danced along with our passionate movements. The heady scent of the surrounding forest mixed with our own intoxicating scents, creating an atmosphere ripe with desire and anticipation.

"Erica," Liam whispered, his hands now roaming my body, following the curves of my hips, the swell of my breasts, as if trying to commit every inch of me to memory. My heart swelled with love for this man who had broken through my defences, who had touched a part of me I never knew existed - or perhaps was too afraid to acknowledge. My fingers trailed along his chiselled chest, marred with the scars of battles fought, both physical and emotional. I felt something stir within me, aching to be released. But it wasn't time yet, and I didn't know how. For now, we would continue our dance, two souls intertwined, bound by fate and the undeniable pull of our love.

"Please, Erica," Liam begged, his voice strained with desperation. "I can't take any more."

"Trust me," I murmured into his ear, taking the lobe between my teeth before gently releasing it. Our eyes met once more, and I saw the surrender in his gaze. He nodded, accepting my unspoken promise to push us both to new heights of pleasure.

"Good," I purred, resuming my tantalising exploration of his body.

"Patience" seemed to be the theme of the night, and yet, as I gazed up at Liam with his pants now unbuttoned, I couldn't help but feel that same impatience surging through me. He looked down at me with a mixture of pride and hunger in his eyes as I raised my eyebrows at his impressive size.

"Like what you see?" he taunted, a wicked grin playing on his lips.

"Very much so," I replied, unable to keep the desire out of my voice. The waterfall roared in the background, an apt metaphor for the torrent of emotions coursing through us both. I leaned in and pressed a gentle kiss to the tip of his erection, flicking my tongue against it. Liam's breath hitched, and I knew I was affecting him just as much as he affected me. Taking his head into my mouth, I began to move down his shaft, taking him in deeper with each motion. I settled there for a moment, relishing the feeling of him filling my mouth, before slowly pulling back and repeating the process. As my rhythm quickened, I could hear Liam's breath growing ragged, his body tensing beneath my touch. His hands found their way back into my hair, holding onto me as if I was a lifeline keeping him afloat in this sea of desire we'd created. Suddenly, he bucked his hips, forcing himself even deeper than before.

"Erica," he panted, desperation lacing his voice.

"Baby, please." Pulling away, I looked up at him to see his eyes alight with golden lust. It was as if he was teetering on the edge of ecstasy, and I held the power to either push him over or pull him back. My heart swelled with love for this man, my fated mate, whose trust in me was unparalleled.

"Alright, baby," I whispered, releasing him from my mouth. He grasped my hand and pulled me up to meet his lips in a searing kiss.

The warmth of Liam's body against mine grounded me as I clung to him, our lips not parting until the need for air overpowered us. Panting, we broke away from each other, and his eyes gleamed with a carnal hunger that mirrored my own. He tugged at my top, and I raised my arms obediently, allowing him to lift it off and cast it aside.

"Erica," he whispered, his voice thick with desire as he admired my breasts, now bare before him. The weight of his gaze sent shivers down my spine, and I could feel my nipples hardening under his watchful eye. With a growl, he unclasped my bra and tossed it carelessly onto the ground, leaving nothing between us but raw passion.

"Goddess, you're so beautiful," he murmured, taking my left breast into his mouth without any hesitation. I arched my back toward him, offering myself fully, a moan escaping my lips as his tongue traced delicate circles around my hardened nipple. My fingers tangled in his dark hair, holding him close as waves of pleasure coursed through me.

As if sensing my growing need for more, Liam shifted our positions, flipping us around so that I lay on the bed beneath him, my legs spread wide to accommodate his muscular form. Without wasting a moment, he slipped his hands into my shorts again, deftly removing them and my panties in one smooth motion. The sudden exposure left me gasping, my skin tingling where the cool air met my heated flesh.

"Please, Liam," I whimpered, my body trembling with anticipation. His mouth returned to my breast as his free hand ventured down between my legs, seeking out the throbbing core of my desire. When his thumb found my clit once more, I cried out, my hips bucking involuntarily at the electrifying touch.

"Such a sweet, desperate sound for me," he teased, adding a second finger to the mix as his skilled fingers began to build a relentless rhythm inside me. My mind went blank, consumed by the mounting pressure within my body. I gripped the blanket, my knuckles white as the tension coiled tighter and tighter, threatening to shatter me into a million pieces.

"More," I managed to gasp between heavy breaths, my voice barely audible over the pounding of my heart.

"Please, Liam, more."

"Anything for you, my love," he promised, his fingers delving deeper into my core as he expertly massaged my swollen clit. In that instant, the dam broke, and I screamed his name, my vision blurring as tidal waves of pure, red-hot desire washed over me again and again.

As Liam's fingers continued their relentless dance within me, I couldn't help but clutch at his head, pulling him up to me and crashing my lips against his once more. The taste of his desire mingled with mine as I bit down on his bottom lip, a bold move that seemed to fuel the flames of our passion even further. He responded by driving his fingers deeper inside me, making me scream into his mouth as another orgasm tore through me.

"Goddess, Liam," I gasped, struggling to catch my breath between waves of pleasure. "I don't know how much more I can take."

"Let me take care of you, baby," he murmured huskily, slowly withdrawing his fingers from my quivering core. My body felt sensitive to the touch, every nerve ending alight with the aftermath of our intense union.

For a moment, he moved away, leaving me feeling empty and disoriented. Then, I heard a rustle in the background before Liam repositioned himself above me, his eyes burning with golden intensity. As the tip of his cock grazed my entrance, I gasped, my body instinctively craving more.

"Are you ready?" he asked, his voice rough with need. Unable to form coherent thoughts beyond the overwhelming desire for him, I simply nodded. In one swift, powerful motion, he thrust himself deep inside me. The force of our connection sent shivers down my spine, and I arched my back, welcoming him even closer. For a moment, he stilled, allowing us both to adjust to this new level of intimacy. Emerald eyes met molten gold as he began to move again, his pace growing more fluid and urgent with each passing second. His lips found the tender skin of my neck, nipping and biting along my collarbone in a carnal dance that drove me wild.

"Erica," he breathed, his voice laden with desire. "There's something so incredibly powerful about you, about us. I can't get enough of you."

"Neither can I," I whispered, my mind reeling from the all-consuming passion that seemed to bind us together in a web of fate and desire. As

Liam's thrusts grew more powerful and relentless, I realised this was far from over. The sensation inside me was unlike anything I had ever felt before; it was darker, more primal. My body ached to be free from the confines of my own skin as the pleasure built to unbearable heights.

"More, Liam," I panted between gasps, feeling myself teetering on the edge of oblivion.

"Are you sure?" he asked hesitantly, his voice strained with the effort of holding back his own desires.

"This... this is different, Erica."

"Please!" I cried, desperate for release. As if sensing my need, Liam began driving into me even harder, each powerful thrust sending shockwaves through my very core.

"Erica!" he moaned, his voice thick with need. "Something... something incredible is happening." I could feel it too, a feral energy coursing through our joined bodies, growing stronger with each passionate collision. The intensity of our connection seemed to defy the boundaries of reality, forging an unbreakable bond between us.

"Can't... hold on..." I whimpered, my nails digging into his back as I rode the waves of ecstasy washing over me. With a final, resounding scream of his name, I felt the dam within me burst, releasing a torrent of unimaginable pleasure that threatened to consume me entirely.

"Erica!" Liam cried out, his voice breaking as he continued to pound into me, his own orgasm imminent. "I can't... I can't hold back any longer!"

"Let go, Liam," I urged him breathlessly, my mind swimming in a haze of passion and desire.

"Erica, goddess, I love you." Liam's voice was raw and thick with emotion as he whispered the words against my skin. With a final thrust and a roar, he climaxed inside of me. He collapsed onto me, both of us panting, his cock still inside me twitching and sending smaller aftershocks through my body.

We stayed there connected in body for I don't know how long, as we both took time to come back down to our bodies. At some point, he lifted his head and looked at me with glazed eyes before kissing me on the nose. I smiled up at him, feeling so complete and so loved at this moment.

"Wow," I breathed out, my chest heaving with the effort to regain my normal breathing. "That was... incredible." He moved and pulled himself out, and I felt empty suddenly. I noticed him reach down and pull a now full condom away. That must have been the rustling from earlier. I winced, geez I'm glad one of us had the foresight to think of that, werewolves couldn't get STD's but we could get pregnant and even though I was on the pill, it was significantly less effective with our metabolism and I certainly was not ready for pups yet. He dropped the used condom into the picnic basket before coming back to the blanket and joining me once more.

"Thank you," I murmured, appreciating his thoughtfulness.

"Anything for you, baby," he replied, his voice husky and warm. Beneath the moonlit sky, the waterfall's cascading water sang softly in the background, and the air was filled with the intoxicating scent of night-blooming flowers. The powerful bond that had formed between us tonight seemed to shimmer around us, an invisible force that drew us even closer together.

The moon cast a soft glow on the waterfall's glistening surface, bathing us in its ethereal light. I lay there, my body still tingling from the intensity of our lovemaking, trying to catch my breath and process what had just happened between us.

"Are you okay?" Liam asked with concern, his voice a seductive rumble that sent shivers down my spine.

"Better than okay," I admitted, unable to suppress a contented sigh. "That was... incredible."

Lying there on the blanket, my body still tingling from our passionate encounter, I could feel the damp grass beneath us and the cool night air brushing against my exposed skin. The sound of the waterfall crashing down in the distance was soothing, enveloping us in our own little world.

"Are you alright?" Liam asked, concern lacing his voice as he noticed my struggle to move.

"Exhausted, but in a good way," I admitted, feeling a bit embarrassed by my inability to do anything more than lie there in his arms.

"Do you need help?" he asked, an amused grin on his face. I realised I hadn't moved, and I wasn't sure if I could. I felt heavy and empty at the same time. I nodded complacently in the spent state. He laughed and pulled on his jeans and scooped me up. I vaguely remember him carrying back through the woods with my head on his chest, hearing his heartbeat as I began to drift off into an exhausted but satisfied sleep.

"I love you," I mumbled and felt him kiss the top of my head.

"Love you too, baby." Liam murmured into my hair, his chest rumbling with each word. His strong arms held me close, making me feel safe and protected. I could feel the warmth of his skin seeping through the thin fabric of my shirt, sending shivers down my spine. As my eyelids grew heavier, I struggled to stay awake, wanting to savour every moment spent in Liam's embrace. But exhaustion gripped me, pulling me closer and closer toward the edge of consciousness.

"Rest, Erica," Liam whispered softly, sensing my internal battle. "I'll be here when you wake up." And so, I surrendered myself to slumber, allowing the darkness to wash over me like a warm, comforting blanket. Liam's steady heartbeat lulled me deeper into sleep, drowning out the soft sounds of the waterfall nearby.

Just as I felt myself slipping away completely, an unfamiliar voice reached my ears. It was distant and faint, like a whisper carried on the wind.

"Erica..." it called out, weaving itself seamlessly between the rustling leaves and the gentle splashing of water. Though I couldn't quite place the voice, there was something strangely familiar about it – a quality that sent shivers down my spine and set my heart racing. "Who's there?" I wanted to ask, but my body refused to cooperate, weighed down by a heavy cloud of fatigue. Panic threatened to claw its way to the surface, but Liam's presence anchored me, keeping me from being swept away by fear.

"Sleep, love," he soothed, pressing another tender kiss to my forehead, as if to banish the disquieting voice from my thoughts. And like a spell, his words washed away my anxiety, leaving only the peaceful sound of his breathing as I succumbed to the pull of slumber. The last thing I heard was the unfamiliar voice again.

"So close..."

Chapter 34

Erica

The lingering warmth from last night's date with Liam wrapped around me like a soft, comforting blanket as I sat at my office desk, finishing up the day's work. His touch still danced on my skin, sending shivers down my spine at the memory of our passionate encounter. My heart swelled at the thought of waking up in his arms this morning, feeling safe and loved for the first time in ages.

A smile crept onto my face as I recalled my conversation with Imogen earlier. She had gushed about her new home and how things were finally looking up for her family. It was such a relief to know that she was happy and settling in well. The thought of my friend finding peace brought me a sense of contentment and joy that I hadn't felt in a long time.

"Erica, are you daydreaming again?" Lucy teased, poking her head into my office. "You've got that goofy look on your face."

"Shut up, Lucy," I retorted playfully, shaking my head. "Just finishing up some work."

"Whatever you say." She winked and disappeared back into the hallway.

I glanced at the clock and realised I was running late for my first day of warrior training. Panic bubbled up inside me as I scrambled to shut down my computer, eager not to miss a single moment. I was ecstatic to start training; it was an opportunity to protect myself and those I cared about. Given my past experiences, I knew I couldn't rely on anyone else to keep me safe.

"Come on, come on!" I muttered under my breath, tapping my foot impatiently as the computer took its sweet time shutting down. Finally, the screen went black, and I grabbed my bag, rushing out of the office.

"Bye, Lucy!" I called out as I raced from the office. My heart still swelled with the lingering happiness of last night's date with Liam. The memory of waking up in his arms filled me with warmth and safety. As I glanced through a nearby window, I spotted Liam in his office, phone pressed to his ear. He looked up, catching my gaze, and smiled so tenderly it made my stomach flutter. Despite my eagerness to share another moment with him, I knew I couldn't stop now, warrior training awaited, and I was already late. I sprinted across the pack grounds, the wind whipping through my red hair, and skidded into the changing rooms just as Gen and the others were leaving for training. Their laughter and friendship echoed through the halls, reminding me that I had finally found a place where I belonged.

"Erica, you're late!" Gen scolded playfully, but her eyes held concern. "Don't worry, I'll let Grayson know you're on your way."

"Thanks, Gen," I panted, leaning against the wall for support. I darted into a changing cubicle, my heart still pounding from the sprint across the pack grounds. The memory of Liam's smile lingered in my mind, warming me from within. Shaking off the thought, I quickly changed into my sportswear, a pair of black shorts and a matching sports bra. My fingers deftly tied my red hair into a high ponytail, securing it tightly as I prepared for the physical exertion that lay ahead.

"Focus, Erica," I muttered to myself, steadying my breath. "You're here to train, not daydream about your boyfriend." Ha, boyfriend. I had a boyfriend, that sounded funny. With newfound resolve, I stepped out of the cubicle and hurried to stash my belongings in a locker. As I locked it, the sound of metal clicking into place seemed to echo through the empty locker room. With one last deep breath, I turned to head into the training room. But before I could take more than a step, my momentum carried me straight into someone. "Oof!" I gasped, stumbling back and clutching my arm where the impact had occurred. "I'm so sorry! I didn't see you there."

My apologies died in my throat when I realised that the person I'd collided with was none other than Grant. His blue eyes bore into mine, a storm of emotions swirling beneath the surface. For a moment, neither of us spoke, and the tension between us was palpable.

"Grant," I managed to say, my voice barely above a whisper. "What are you doing here?"

"Shouldn't I be asking you the same thing?" he replied, his tone guarded. It was clear that our complicated relationship weighed heavily on him too.

"Look, about what happened the other night..." I began, feeling the need to address the elephant in the room. But Grant cut me off before I could continue.

"Erica, not now," he said firmly, though his eyes softened with a vulnerability that tugged at my heart. "We have other things to focus on."

"Grant, are you okay?" I asked, concern lacing my voice. There was something off about him, the way his blue eyes seemed to bore into me like I was prey. It sent an uncomfortable shiver down my spine.

"Erica," he began, his voice low and intense, "do you have any idea how long it took me to get here, to become who I am now?" I blinked in confusion, unable to comprehend the meaning behind his words. Grant's behaviour was so far removed from the understanding friend I had known. I just wanted to get past him and start my first day of warrior training.

"Grant, I don't understand what you're talking about," I said, attempting to sidestep around him. But he swiftly blocked my path, his expression stormy.

"Everything I've done, all the work and sacrifices I've made, were all for this," he ranted, his eyes blazing with a barely contained fury. "But then you came along, and everything changed. You messed everything up!"

"Grant, I never meant to -" I tried to interject, but he cut me off, his anger only intensifying.

"Then I found out that you betrayed me!" he spat, his face contorted with rage.

"Betrayed you? How?" My mind raced, trying to make sense of his accusations. Was he talking about Liam? If so, it wasn't betrayal. We hadn't even established anything between us. My heart still pounded with exhilaration from my night with Liam, the warmth of his touch lingering on my skin. Yet a twinge of guilt surfaced as I stared into Grant's tormented eyes.

"Grant, you need to calm down," I pleaded, my voice shaking. "I don't know what you think happened, but we can talk about it. Please, let's just talk."

He stared at me for a moment, the storm in his eyes seeming to subside slightly. But as I tried to step around him once more, he moved back in front of me, his voice rising as he continued his tirade.

"Erica, you have no idea what you've done," he growled, his face inches from mine. "The things I've risked for you, and you just throw it all away."

"Grant, please," I whispered, tears stinging my eyes. "I never wanted to hurt you." But my words seemed to have little effect on him, as he continued to rant about betrayal and expectations.

"Grant, I don't understand what you're talking about," I said, my voice wavering as fear and confusion gripped me. "You're scaring me."

His eyes softened, and he seemed to deflate, suddenly looking vulnerable and lost.

"I'm sorry, Erica," he murmured, his voice hoarse with emotion. "My head's just... it's all messed up right now. I can feel this connection between us, and it's confusing the hell out of me." Hearing the pain and confusion in his voice, my heart went out to him. Despite the tumultuous emotions swirling inside me, I wanted to comfort him, to reassure him that we could figure things out together. Tentatively, I reached out and placed a hand on his arm.

"Grant, we'll get through this," I whispered, trying to convey the sincerity of my words through our touch. "We'll find a way to make sense of everything." He looked at me for a long moment, his blue eyes searching mine, before he pulled me into a tight embrace. As his arms wrapped around me, I felt a strange sense of safety and familiarity, even as my heart still ached for Liam.

"I just want you to be safe, Erica," Grant muttered into my hair, his voice thick with emotion.

But then, without warning, he stiffened in my arms. His grip on me tightened painfully before wrenching me away from him with such force that I stumbled backward, crashing into the row of lockers behind me. Pain shot through my skull, and I crumpled to the floor, clutching my throbbing head.

"Grant... what are you doing?" I gasped, barely able to breathe from the impact.

"Can't you smell it?" he snarled, his nostrils flaring as he glared down at me. "His scent is all over you. Are you already fucking him?" His eyes blazed with fury, and I realised he was talking about Liam.

"Grant, please," I whispered, my voice trembling. "It's not what you think."

"Isn't it?" he spat, his anger boiling over as a new realisation dawned on him. "Liam's trying to get rid of me. He's sending me on that away mission because he knows I'm competition for your heart!"

"Grant, no," I protested, tears streaming down my cheeks. But he wasn't listening, consumed by his own rage and jealousy. My heart pounded in my chest, echoing the throbbing pain in my head as Grant's rage continued to pour from him. His words were a chaotic mess of accusations and confusion, a storm that threatened to engulf me whole.

"Erica, you don't understand!" he shouted, his voice barely recognisable through the venom coating each syllable. "You're in danger! And with Liam... it's only going to get worse!"

"Grant, I just..." I tried to reason with him, but my own emotions were teetering on the edge of despair. How could someone I felt so connected to suddenly become this unrecognisable monster?

Seemingly out of nowhere, Grant grabbed my arm, yanking me to my feet with a strength that sent fear coursing through me. My legs wobbled beneath me, weak from the pain and shock of the situation. He shook me violently, his grip bruising my skin as he screamed his frustration into my face.

"Stop it!" I cried out, tears streaming down my cheeks as I fought to free myself from his grasp. "You're hurting me, Grant!" It was as if those words finally pierced through the fog of his rage.

A look of horror crossed his face, and he dropped me as if I were a hot coal. I crumpled back to the floor, gasping for breath and struggling to contain my sobs.

"Erica... I'm so sorry," he whispered, his blue eyes wide with regret. "I didn't mean to hurt you. I just... I'm scared for you. You don't know what kind of danger you're really in."

"Is that why you're doing this?" I asked, my voice trembling with both anger and sadness. "Because you're scared?"

"Erica, now that you're Liam's fated mate, things are more dangerous than ever," Grant said, the urgency in his voice only adding to my own turmoil. "I just want to protect you."

"By hurting me?" I choked out, tears streaming down my face as I stared up at him, searching for the person I thought I knew beneath the fury and desperation.

"Erica, please," he pleaded, reaching out a hand as if to offer me comfort. But I couldn't bring myself to accept it.

"Grant, I don't know what's happening to you," I whispered, my heart aching with the weight of betrayal and unmet expectations. "But this isn't right. We can't... I can't do this."

Pain coursed through my body, making every breath a struggle as I glared back at Grant. His expression shifted from remorse to determination as he tried to lift me back to my feet, but I refused his help.

"Stay away from me," I hissed, my voice shaking with anger and pain. "You need to leave me alone." Grant's face fell for a moment before it was replaced by a sudden hopefulness. Ignoring my words, he grabbed hold of my arm and pulled me closer.

"Erica, I can fix everything. You just need to come with me."

"Come with you? On your mission?" Confusion clouded my mind as I tried to understand what he was saying.

"No, not the mission," he replied, his grip tightening on my arm. "I'll help you escape the pack. We can live as rogues, or I know another pack that will take us in. I just want to protect you." I struggled against his hold, feeling the sting of his fingers digging into my skin.

"I don't want to escape. I have friends here, and I love Liam," I snapped, my anger flaring up once again.

The mention of Liam seemed to ignite something within Grant, as his face twisted with rage.

"Of course you do," he spat, his voice laced with venom. "You're just like all the others, wanting the Alpha title and nothing more. You don't care about being a pack whore!" Fury surged through me, drowning out the pain as I snarled at him. With all my strength, I managed to wrench my arm free from his grasp. Pushing him hard, I shouted,

"You have no say in my life or who I love! You don't have the right to pass judgement on me!" My heart pounded in my chest as I stared him down, betrayal and disappointment churning within me. The anger coursing through me grew wilder, unchecked, like a feral beast clawing at the cage of my chest. I could feel it straining to break free, to take over completely.

Grant's eyes widened as he began backing away, panic etched into his features.

"Erica, we... we can figure this out," he stammered, trying to find some way to defuse the situation. There was something in my face that seemed to shock him, but I couldn't focus on anything except the rage that consumed me. It drowned out all rational thought, all compassion, leaving only a primal instinct to protect myself and destroy the threat before me. In that moment, Grant wasn't my friend, my confidant. He was prey, and I was the predator. My vision tunnelled, focusing solely on him as I stalked closer, every muscle tensed and ready to strike.

"Stay away from me!" I snarled, my voice hardly recognisable even to myself.

"Erica, please-" Grant pleaded, his back pressed against the wall, leaving him nowhere to run. But his words fell on deaf ears as I prepared to lunge at him, to tear out his throat and end his betrayal once and for all.

I sprang forward, but my attack was thwarted before I could reach him. An arm wrapped around my waist, holding me back with unexpected strength. The restraint only fuelled my fury, and I struggled against my captor, desperate to sink my teeth into Grant's flesh.

"Get Damon! Get Liam!" someone shouted nearby, but the voice sounded muffled, distant. Whoever held me must have been another member of the pack, but I didn't care. All that mattered was the seething rage within me, demanding release.

"Let go of me!" I screamed, thrashing wildly in an attempt to break free. But the arm held me tight, refusing to relent.

"Erica, calm down!" a familiar voice called out, but the words barely registered in my feral mind. I only had one goal, one desire: to rip Grant apart for his lies and deception. I growled through clenched teeth.

The scent of gingerbread and fire filled my nostrils, cutting through the fog of rage that clouded my mind. It was a familiar, comforting scent, one that I associated with safety and love. My mate, Liam. My focus shifted from Grant to Liam as I turned and lunged at him. The anger that had consumed me moments before transformed into raw, primal lust. My mind felt less human, more feral animal as I growled, clawing at both his clothes and mine, desperate to feel his bare skin against mine.

"Erica, please," Liam whispered softly, trying to soothe me while holding me back. But it did little to quell the insatiable desire burning within me. I could only think about how much I needed him, how much I craved his touch, his warmth.

Suddenly, an intense cooling sensation washed over my body like a tidal wave. It spread through every nerve and muscle, extinguishing the fiery passion that had taken hold of me. I blinked, my surroundings coming back into focus as if waking from a dream.

"Erica?" Damon stood beside me, eyes filled with concern. He must have used his supernatural gift to calm me down, to bring me back to my senses. My heart began to race as I looked around, taking in the chaos I had caused. Grant huddled against the wall, shock etched on his face. Jacob clutched his arm, blood streaming between his fingers. And there was Liam, his clothes torn and blood staining his chest. I had done this. I had hurt them all.

"No," I whispered, horror and despair settling heavily on my chest. Tears welled up in my eyes, spilling over and streaming down my cheeks. "I didn't mean to... I don't want to hurt anyone."

"Everyone out, now!" Liam barked, his Alpha command silencing the room. The others hesitated, casting worried glances my way before obeying and filing out one by one.

"Erica," Liam's voice softened as he lowered us both to the floor, cradling me in his arms. I sobbed against his chest, my body wracked with guilt and fear over what had just happened.

"Shhh, it's okay," Liam murmured, stroking my hair as he held me close. "We'll figure this out together, I promise." As my sobs subsided, exhaustion crept over me. The emotional turmoil had drained me, leaving me weak and vulnerable. My eyelids grew heavy, and I finally succumbed to sleep, safe in the arms of my mate.

Chapter 35

Erica

The sensation of soft lips on my neck gently stirred me, the warmth of a strong body pressed against mine, enveloping me in luxurious comfort. I inhaled deeply, and the scent of gingerbread and fire filled my senses, Liam's unique aroma.

"Wake up, sleepyhead." A tender murmur danced through the air; Liam was coaxing me out of my slumber. As I gradually opened my eyes, the tantalising smell of freshly cooked bacon wafted into my nostrils.

"Goddess, I don't know what smells better, you or the bacon," I joked, rubbing the sleep from my eyes.

"Are you comparing me to bacon? How dare you!" Liam feigned offence, his brown eyes sparkling with mischief. Then he began tickling my sides, eliciting peals of laughter from me. I tried squirming away, but he was relentless, and soon we were tangled in each other's arms, our lips meeting in a passionate kiss.

As we kissed, the heat between us intensified, our bodies pressed together, our desire for one another growing stronger. But just as our hands began to roam, my stomach rumbled loudly. Our eyes met, and we both burst into laughter.

"Clearly, the food has won this round," Liam teased, "but I'll win the war." He grinned as he jumped off the bed, revealing that we were in his room at the pack house. My heart raced, both with excitement and nerves, as I watched him retrieve a large tray piled high with food from a nearby table. Rushing to sit up, I marvelled at the feast before me: crispy bacon, fluffy scrambled eggs, buttery toast, and fresh fruit. My mouth watered, and I realised just how famished I was.

As I eagerly tucked into the food, it occurred to me that Liam must have planned this all along, the breakfast in bed, the closeness, the growing intimacy.

"Enjoying yourself?" Liam asked, watching me with a soft smile as I took another bite of bacon. His gaze was tender, and I could see the genuine happiness in his eyes.

"Definitely," I replied between bites, feeling grateful for this thoughtful gesture. I polished off the last bite of buttery toast, feeling full and content. Liam chuckled as he took the tray from my lap and set it back on the side table.

"Wow, you really were hungry," he said with a hint of admiration in his voice. I shrugged, not thinking much of it. Hunger was just another part of life, especially for a werewolf, and I had learned to listen to my body's needs.

My eyes drifted down to the oversized T-shirt I wore, realising for the first time that it was one of Liam's. The soft fabric carried his comforting scent, but I couldn't help wondering why I was wearing his clothes. As my memories began to surface, the warmth of the moment faded, replaced by a wave of regret and shame. The events in the training grounds locker room came crashing back into focus, my anger at Grant, the feral rage that consumed me, and how close I'd come to ripping out his throat. If Jacob hadn't intervened, things would have ended so much worse. Tears welled up in my eyes as I looked over at Liam, noticing the fading remains of scratch marks across his chest. My heart ached, knowing I was responsible for them.

"Liam..." My voice cracked as the tears began to fall. "I'm so sorry for what happened. I hurt people... I hurt you." He reached out to me, pulling me into his embrace.

"Hey, it's okay," he whispered soothingly into my hair.

"We're all alive, and we'll heal."

But his words did little to console me. How could I have let myself lose control like that? Was I truly a danger to those around me? The weight of these thoughts crushed me, making it hard to breathe.

"Erica," Liam said softly, his warm breath tickling my ear. "You're strong, and that strength can be scary sometimes. But you didn't let it destroy you. You're here, with me, and we'll figure out what happened together." I wanted to believe him, but the image of Grant's terrified face haunted me. How could I ever regain their trust? The tears flowed freely as I clung to Liam, my anchor in this storm of doubts and fears. Liam's hand gently cupped my face, wiping away the tears with his thumb.

"Look at me, Erica." His voice was firm but gentle as he tilted my chin up to meet his gaze.

"Everyone is fine. No one was seriously hurt. Hell, I've had more damage in a regular training session." My eyes flicked down to the scratch marks on his chest, a fresh wave of guilt washing over me. He followed my gaze and smiled, touching the marks lightly.

"See? Werewolf healing has its perks." I tried to smile, but it felt more like a grimace. Somehow, knowing that they would heal didn't erase the fact that I had caused them.

"Come here," Liam murmured, pulling me into his embrace once more. His strong arms wrapped around me, offering comfort and protection. As much as I wanted to believe that everything would be okay, the fear that I was a danger to those I cared about still gnawed at me.

Finally, I pulled away from him, taking a shaky breath.

"What happened with Grant?" I asked, needing to know that he was alright.

"Grant's fine," Liam reassured me, though there was a hint of tension in his voice. "He's already gone."

"Gone? Did he leave the pack?" The words rushed out of me, my heart pounding in my chest.

"What?" Liam sounded genuinely confused. "No, he hasn't left. He's gone on a mission. Why would you think he left the pack?"

"Yesterday, he... he tried to get me to leave with him." I admitted hesitantly, unsure how Liam would react. His eyes darkened, and his jaw clenched as anger flared within him.

"Why would he do that?"

"Grant said it wasn't safe for me to be your mate," I whispered, feeling the weight of those words between us.

"Damn him," Liam growled, his anger barely contained. But as he looked at me, his expression softened, and he pulled me close again.

"Erica, you are not a danger to anyone," he murmured into my hair. "And I'll do whatever it takes to keep you safe." I wanted so desperately to believe him, to find solace in his embrace. But the lingering doubts and fears still clung to me, like shadows I couldn't quite shake.

Liam's eyes bore into mine, searching for the truth as he asked,

"What made you so angry with Grant?" I hesitated for a moment before starting my explanation.

"He was acting weird at first, but then he calmed down. I thought everything was fine, so I gave him a hug." I paused, remembering the feel of Grant's arms around me. "But then... he could smell you on me and got violent."

"Violent?" Liam's voice was low and dangerous, his protective instincts clearly triggered.

"Y-yes," I stammered, looking away from his piercing gaze. "He slammed me into the lockers. He said it was dangerous to be your mate and wanted me to leave with him."

"Son of a..." Liam clenched his fists, anger radiating off him in waves. "If he hadn't already left, I would have killed him for hurting you like that." Despite the situation, I felt a warmth spread through me at Liam's fierce protectiveness. But I needed him to understand the depth of what had happened, how my own anger had spiralled out of control.

"Before I knew it, I was furious with him," I continued, my voice barely above a whisper. "And it wasn't just normal anger, Liam. It grew so fast, and I started to feel... feral. Like I was losing myself to something primal." Throughout my confession, Liam listened intently, nodding occasionally as if piecing together a puzzle. When I finished speaking, he leaned over and pressed a gentle kiss to my forehead.

"Erica, you're safe with me," he murmured, his breath warm against my skin. "I won't let anything happen to you." I closed my eyes, desperately wanting to believe in the sanctuary he offered.

Our lips met again, tender and sweet, a balm for the hurt we'd both endured. Liam's hands cradled my face, his thumbs brushing away the last of my tears. The kiss deepened, our breaths mingling, and I felt myself losing control once more. But this time, it was to the heat building between us, a fire stoked by our shared concern and relief. Liam pulled away abruptly with a groan, leaving me breathless and wanting.

"Erica," he said, his voice strained. "My father just mind-linked me. He wants to see you." My heart dropped into my stomach, a heavy weight of dread settling there. The Alpha's arrival brought forth a fresh wave of anxiety, but there was no escaping him now.

"I need better clothes, then," I murmured, glancing down at the oversized T-shirt I wore - one of Liam's. Without hesitation, Liam reached down beside the bed and produced a bag that I immediately recognised as mine.

"I asked Gen to pack a few things for you," he said, a soft smile playing on his lips.

"Thank you," I whispered, feeling an overwhelming sense of gratitude wash over me. In the midst of everything we'd faced together, Liam still found small ways to care for me. It reminded me that despite the chaos around us, there were still moments of solace to be found in each other.

With the bag in hand, I darted into the bathroom and locked the door behind me. The cool tiles beneath my feet grounded me for a moment as I took a deep breath. The gravity of the situation weighed heavily on me, but I knew I had to face it. Rummaging through the bag, I found black jogging pants, a white loose-fit t-shirt, and fresh underwear. My fingers lingered on the soft fabric, grateful for the thoughtfulness Liam had shown by packing these items for me. Glancing at the shower, I considered indulging in the warm spray to wash away my lingering unease, but time was not on my side. I dressed quickly, feeling more secure with each layer of clothing that covered my skin. As I brushed my hair, the strokes felt like a soothing balm against the tumultuous thoughts swirling within my mind. I couldn't help but think about the conversation that would soon take place, the Alpha's grim expression haunting my thoughts. The bristles of the toothbrush scrubbed away the staleness in my mouth, leaving behind a minty freshness that momentarily distracted me from the tension building in my chest. I needed to be prepared for whatever the Alpha had to say, even if my heart quivered with trepidation.

As I stepped out of the bathroom, my eyes met Liam's concerned gaze. His presence was both a comfort and a reminder of the stakes at hand. Standing beside him were Alpha Declan and Beta Gregg, their expressions serious and unreadable. I could feel the weight of their expectations, heavy on my shoulders like a thick fog.

"Erica," Alpha Declan said, his voice low and grave, "we need to talk." I swallowed hard, my throat suddenly dry.

"Of course, Alpha," I replied, trying to steady my voice. Beside me, Liam's presence offered a semblance of solace, but I knew that I would have to face this conversation head-on. "Is this about... what happened with Grant?" I asked, my heart thudding in my chest. The memory of the altercation was a raw, open wound – one that still bled with regret and guilt. Alpha Declan exchanged a glance with Beta Gregg, and I braced myself for their response, my stomach twisting into knots.

Chapter 36

Erica

"Erica, please, come and sit down with us," Alpha Declan said, his voice firm but gentle. I couldn't help but notice that he didn't answer my question about Grant. Was this meeting because of what I did to him?

I glanced around the room, taking in the expressions on their faces. Beta Gregg looked serious, his arms crossed over his chest as he leaned against the wall. Liam appeared tense, trying to keep his anger in check. The atmosphere in the room was heavy, as if a storm was brewing. My heart raced as I took a seat on the sofa, the leather creaking beneath me. Liam sat down next to me, his body rigid and his jaw clenched. Alpha Declan pulled up a desk chair, sitting directly in front of me while maintaining eye contact. The intensity of his gaze sent shivers down my spine, and my anxiety skyrocketed.

"Alright," Alpha Declan began, his voice steady and deliberate. "We need to talk." As I sat there, surrounded by these powerful werewolves, I couldn't shake the feeling that my world was about to be turned upside down. My mind raced, grasping at any possible explanation for this meeting, yet coming up empty. What could they possibly want from me that required such an ominous gathering? A bead of sweat trickled down my temple, and I wiped it away with the back of my hand..

"Whatever you have to say, just say it," I spoke up, my voice shaking despite my best efforts to sound strong.

"Erica," Alpha Declan began, his voice even and formal. "I need to discuss an incident that occurred at the Barking Brews last week. Heidi has informed me that you attacked her." My blood ran cold at his words, my heart pounding in my chest. The accusation was so absurd, I couldn't help but let out a bitter laugh.

"That's ridiculous. Heidi is lying, she's had it out for me since before I got here. You believe me, don't you?" I desperately looked over at Liam, seeking reassurance, but he continued to avoid my gaze, his eyes distant and unreadable. Alpha Declan leaned back in his chair, steepling his fingers in front of him as he considered my response.

"You've only been a pack member for a short time, whereas Heidi has been a loyal member for four years. It's difficult to ignore such a disparity. Furthermore, I've heard rumours that you've been attempting to enlist others in the pack to help you escape." The disbelief and betrayal twisted in my gut like a knife, making it hard to breathe. I tried to defend myself, my voice cracking with emotion.

"Those rumours are completely unfounded! I don't understand why you're so quick to believe them instead of me!" But every time I tried to argue my case, he shut me down, his tone growing colder and more commanding.

"Enough, Erica! I am still speaking, and you will not interrupt me." His words lashed out like a whip, leaving me feeling small and powerless.

As the moments stretched on, my anger bubbled up from within, mingling with the hurt and confusion festering inside me. I clenched my fists, nails digging into my palms, desperate for some semblance of control. Why was I being treated this way? Were friendships and alliances so fickle in this world? I had thought Liam, and I were growing closer, yet here he was, silent and detached in the face of my distress. The room seemed to close in on me, the weight of their stares and judgments suffocating. I couldn't understand why they would deliberately twist my actions and intentions, painting me as some sort of traitorous villain. As much as I tried to keep a lid on the turmoil raging within me, I could feel it seeping out, darkening the atmosphere even further.

"Please," I whispered, my voice barely audible over the pounding of my heart. "Liam, look at me. Tell them this isn't true." But still, Liam remained quiet, and I knew then that I was truly alone in this fight. The crushing weight of their expectations and my own shattered trust bore down upon me, threatening to break me entirely. And as the storm continued to brew around us, I braced myself for the tempest to come.

Alpha Declan's expression shifted to one of disgust as he looked back and forth between Liam and me. His head shook, disappointment radiating from him like a cold breeze.

"Given the trouble you've caused with Heidi, and now attacking not one, but three members of my pack, including my own son, yesterday," he began, his voice low and menacing, "I have decided that you are clearly not stable or fit enough to be a mate for my son." His words felt like they were ripping my heart apart, leaving me breathless and numb. I couldn't believe what he was saying. Desperation clawed at my chest, and I turned to Liam, hoping for some sign of support.

"Liam, please, help me," I begged, my voice trembling with emotion. But Liam offered no comfort. He clenched his jaw and looked away, leaving me feeling unbelievably betrayed by his inaction. The anger that had been simmering beneath the surface of my heart began to boil over, threatening to consume me entirely.

"Despite being more trouble than I want," Alpha Declan continued, his eyes locked on mine like a predator sizing up its prey, "I do now own you, and you will work for your place in this pack or find yourself in silver chains." My voice rose in defiance, fuelled by the injustice of his accusations.

"It was you who made me join this pack, and you who made me spend time with Liam! And now you want to rip everything away from me?"

"Miss Hallows," Alpha Declan roared in his Alpha tone, silencing my protest. "I have told you repeatedly that I am speaking and I am your Alpha, and when I am speaking, you will listen to me." He stepped closer, his dark eyes boring into mine as he continued to berate me.

"And what is more, Miss Hallows, you will learn to submit to me, or so help me god I will have you living in silver chains for the rest of your years here." His words wrapped themselves around my heart like a vice, squeezing until it felt ready to shatter. The unfairness of it all was overwhelming, and I could feel hot tears pricking at the corners of my eyes. How could he judge me so harshly for trying to survive in a world where everyone seemed determined to tear me down? As Alpha Declan's tirade continued, my mind raced with thoughts of betrayal and shattered expectations. The friendships I had sought to build were crumbling around me, leaving me feeling more alone and vulnerable than ever before. And as anger and despair threatened to consume me.

"I have opened my home to you, and brought you into my pack and you have spat on my kindness the whole time," Alpha Declan seethed. "You might have been allowed to grow up like a filthy rogue, but that stops here." I was shaking, not from fear, but from fury. How dare he speak to me in that way? My chest tightened as anger swelled within me, making it difficult to breathe. It took all of my self-restraint not to lunge at him. The Alpha held my stare for a good minute, his disgust palpable.

"Pathetic runt," he scoffed before turning his back on me and walking away.

Big mistake. With a furious growl, I lunged at his back, unable to contain the rage inside me any longer. But I didn't get far. Beta Gregg jumped into action, grabbing me around the waist just in time. I struggled, trying to reach the Alpha, my desperation and fury mounting with each passing second. The Alpha spun around, and I was taken aback by the excitement lighting up his face. His phone was in his hand, and he quickly snapped a picture before nodding to Beta Gregg. Suddenly, I felt a rush of cool calm coursing through my body. My growls turned to sobs, and I drooped in Gregg's arms. Why was this happening to me? What had I done to deserve this? I thought back to the relationships I'd tried to build since joining the pack. The friendships that were crumbling around me, leaving me feeling more alone and vulnerable than ever before.

Beta Gregg lowered me gently to the ground, my sobs still echoing through the room. Liam appeared at my side in an instant, trying to pull me into a hug. I pushed him away, tears streaming down my face, as I choked out,

"Leave me alone!" But he persisted, his strong arms finally enveloping me and pulling me onto his lap. Shame and desperation clawed at me, but I couldn't help clinging to him. Liam's warm voice reassured me,

"I'm here, Erica. I've got you." A gentle touch on my arm made me look up, and I saw Alpha Declan gazing at me with something akin to sympathy in his dark eyes. In a low, calming tone, he said,

"I'm so sorry, child. But I had to find out for real, I needed you to see it. This was the only way I could think of." Confusion swirled within me, mixing with my lingering anger.

"What are you talking about?" I demanded, my voice ragged. Alpha Declan sighed.

"We need to talk about your wolf, Erica."

"Wait," I interrupted, my heart pounding. "This isn't about Heidi?" The Alpha shook his head.

"No, this is all about you." Liam's irritation flared up as well.

"So why did we just piss her off on purpose?" My gaze snapped back to the Alpha, annoyance rising within me.

"Am I some sort of toy or something?" He smiled, glancing at Beta Gregg.

"You might want to be ready, just in case." Gregg laughed out loud.

"Nah man, this was your dumbass idea. I told you, I don't protect you from stupid." He winked at me, and despite the tension, I felt a flicker of gratitude towards him. The Alpha shot Gregg a frustrated look, but I could see the hint of a smile in his eyes.

"Erica," he began anew, "we've been watching you since you arrived, and one thing that stood out was your quick temper. Then last night, I was told about the incident with Grant."

"Okay," I said, my impatience growing. "But what does this have to do with my wolf?" The Alpha suddenly pulled out his phone and handed it to me. My breath caught in my throat as I saw the picture he had taken. It was horrifying – my face twisted in an almost unrecognisable rage, teeth bared and lips curled back in a snarl. But what drew my focus were my eyes, no longer their usual green but rather the shining eyes of a wolf that I didn't even know for sure that I had.

"Look at your eyes, Erica," the Alpha instructed softly. I couldn't tear my gaze away from the photo, my heart pounding in my chest. The colour of my eyes wasn't the copper hue of a Gamma rank that they should have been; instead, they were a bright white gold colour. The realisation hit me like a ton of bricks, and I could feel the blood drain from my face. The only rank that had a colour that bright was...

"Erica dear," the Alpha said with solemn conviction, "you are without a shadow of a doubt a pure Alpha."

Chapter 37

Liam

"I'm sorry, what now?" I watched as Erica's green eyes widened, struggling to process the revelation my father had just dropped on her. I already knew that she was an Alpha rank, but I hadn't realised she had no idea herself.

"Are you saying... I have a wolf?" Erica asked, turning to me with a mixture of disbelief and elation. Her light red hair framed her face, making her eyes stand out even more.

"Of course you do," I smiled warmly at her, feeling the weight of my own protective instincts for her. I pulled her into a tight hug, breathing in her citrus scent. "You're stronger than you know."

My father and Gregg chuckled softly at Erica's happiness. It was a rare sight to see her this vulnerable, but it warmed my heart knowing that she trusted us enough to let her guard down.

"Erica," my father said, his voice steady and authoritative, "not only do you have a wolf, but you've been communicating with it on some level. It's trying to break free."

"Then why can't I shift?" Erica inquired, her brow furrowing as she tried to understand the situation. I could sense her frustration building, and I reached out, placing a comforting hand on her shoulder.

"Your wolf is undoubtedly powerful, but it seems to be restrained somehow," my father explained, his gaze filled with concern. "We believe that's why you're getting angry so easily, your wolf is fighting to break free from whatever is holding it back." I squeezed Erica's shoulder reassuringly, my thoughts racing alongside hers. How could we help her release the power within her? The responsibility weighed heavily on my chest, but I knew I would do anything to aid her.

"Baby," I said softly, my eyes locked onto hers, "we'll figure this out together. You have the strength of an Alpha, and we'll help you harness that power. We just need to find a way to free your wolf."

"Thank you, Liam," she whispered, her voice filled with gratitude and determination.

"Erica, it's possible that the greater the danger, the more your wolf can push," my father suggested, his voice deep and commanding.

"Could that be why I might have shifted when I was attacked a couple of years ago?" she asked hesitantly, her green eyes searching for answers in my father's face. I could almost see the gears turning in her head as she tried to piece together the puzzle of her past. My father exchanged a glance with Gregg before returning his gaze to Erica.

"If you had truly shifted back then, your wolf would know how to break free from whatever is holding it back now." He sighed, running a hand through his dark greying hair. "Unfortunately, that doesn't help us understand what happened during the attack, or how the Alpha who assaulted you was ripped apart." I could practically feel the frustration radiating off of Erica as she absorbed this new information.

Unable to stand her distress any longer, I reached out and gently touched her arm. The simple contact sent a jolt of electricity through my body, stirring my own protective instincts.

"Baby," I began softly, trying to ease her tension. "This is a good thing. We can learn to control the power you have. Together." She scoffed at my words, her eyes flashing with defiance.

"I must be pretty pathetic if I can't even control it myself."

"Erica, you don't understand," my father interjected, shaking his head. "You possess the power of an Alpha, a very powerful Alpha at that. Even my wolf is apprehensive around you." I couldn't help but nod in agreement, adding with a mischievous grin,

"Although, my wolf thinks it's sexy." The comment earned me a groan from my father, but I could see a faint smile tugging at Erica's lips.

"Both my parents were Gamma rank," Erica argued, her brow furrowing in disbelief. "There's no way I could be an Alpha."

"Erica, the proof is in the picture," my father insisted. I nodded in agreement, remembering the day we met and the undeniable power she exuded.

"Trust me, I saw it too." My voice was gentle, trying to ease her confusion. I could tell she needed comfort, so I pulled her onto my knee. As she snuggled into me, her citrus scent enveloped me, sending a wave of warmth through my body.

Suddenly, my father's expression shifted, and he looked uncomfortable. I raised an eyebrow, urging him to continue.

"Spit it out, Dad."

"Erica," he began hesitantly, "I think you should be taken out of warrior training for now." Her eyes widened, and she protested immediately.

"No!"

"Listen to me," my father reasoned. "You're struggling to control your power, and the volatility of warrior training isn't helping. Instead, you should train with Liam, Jacob, and Damon."

"Training with them?" Erica asked, her voice laced with suspicion. "What does that have to do with controlling my anger? And what do you mean by 'other things'?" My father's discomfort increased, and he stuttered as he tried to find the right words. I couldn't help but be amused by his awkwardness, and even Gregg chuckled at the scene unfolding before us.

"Wh-what I mean," my father stammered, "is that Damon has a calming power that could help with... other aspects of your abilities."

"Like what?" Erica pressed, her frustration mounting. As my father continued to fumble over his words, I struggled to hold back laughter. The sight of the usually unflappable Alpha flustered like this was too rich.

Gritting his teeth as he tried to maintain composure, my father finally found the words that had been escaping him.

"Erica, have you noticed an... abundance of potential, well, erm... suitors?" I couldn't help but growl at the idea of other men pursuing Erica, and her confusion was evident on her face. But as realisation dawned, her eyes widened, and she narrowed them, fixing my father with a glare.

"What does my sex life have to do with anything?"

"Ah, well," my father stammered, still flustered. "You've mentioned having issues with other Alphas, and it seems they often revolve around... sexual matters." It took all my strength not to burst into laughter at my father's awkwardness. With a smirk, I turned to him.

"I'm glad mum knew how to give us the birds and the bees talk," I quipped, causing Gregg to lose his battle against laughter.

As the chuckles subsided, Erica's confusion remained. I sighed and decided to lay it out for her.

"The power you give off baby, it's immense and carnal. It's likely attracting aggressive Alphas because of how strong it is." The words fell heavily in the room, and I could see the horror creeping into her expression. "They feel a need to protect or covet you."

"Wait," she said, her voice shaking. "So, basically, I'm some kind of Alpha magnet? And it's making me a target?"

"Something like that," I confirmed, trying to soften the blow. "But we'll figure it out, I promise. That's also why we want guards on you." I looked over at my father, my resolve firming. "Damon and Jacob will be your main guard detail." She considered this for a moment, her brow furrowed. I could see the gears turning in her head as she processed everything we had just told her. Her fear and frustration were palpable, but beneath it all, I sensed her determination to overcome these newfound challenges.

"Alright," she finally said, steeling herself. "We'll do this. But I won't let this define me or control my life." I smiled at her, pride swelling in my chest.

"That's the spirit."

I couldn't help but notice Erica's drooping eyelids and the weight of all we had just discussed pressing down on her. She was exhausted, both mentally and emotionally.

"Hey," I said gently, reaching for her hand. "Why don't we table this conversation for now? You need some rest." My father nodded in agreement, his eyes softening with concern.

"Yes, Erica, let's continue this another time."

"Okay," she agreed, her voice barely above a whisper. I guided her off my knee and onto the sofa and wrapped a warm blanket around her shoulders. As I made sure she was comfortable, I felt an overwhelming urge to protect her from anything that would hurt her further. With one last squeeze of her hand, I turned to leave the room.

"Sleep well," I whispered as I stepped out into the hallway, making sure to close the door softly behind me.

"Son," my father began, clearly noticing my worry. "You know this is only the beginning, right? There's still much more to learn about Erica's situation."

"I know, Dad," I sighed, running a hand through my hair. "It's just... I feel like there's something we're missing. Something important." He placed a comforting hand on my shoulder.

"Perhaps it's time for us to visit Erica's old pack. They might have more information that could help us understand what's going on."

"Maybe you're right," I conceded, my brow furrowed in thought. My mind raced with possibilities, questions, and concerns for the woman I cared so deeply about.

For now, though, I needed to focus on keeping her safe and helping her navigate the challenges that lay ahead.

"Let's make plans to visit her old pack soon," I suggested, determined to uncover the truth. "The more we know, the better equipped we'll be to handle whatever comes our way."

"Agreed," my father replied, his expression resolute. "We'll face this together, Liam. As a pack, as a family."

"Thank you, Dad." I offered him a grateful smile.

The soft sound of Erica's breathing filled the room as I stepped back inside, the dim glow from the moonlight casting a serene ambiance. Her peaceful expression tugged at my heartstrings, and I couldn't help but feel a swell of protectiveness for this strong-willed woman who had been through so much. Gently, I scooped her up in my arms, her body fitting perfectly against mine as if we were two halves of a whole. She stirred slightly, her breath hitching as she snuggled closer to me. The sweet scent of citrus wafted up, filling my senses and making my wolf purr in contentment.

"Shh," I whispered, trying not to wake her as I carried her toward the bed. "I've got you, baby." As I carefully laid her down, the soft sheets rustled beneath her. I took a moment to appreciate the sight of her nestled among the pillows, her red hair fanned out like a fiery halo. Despite all the uncertainties and challenges that lay ahead, I knew I would do anything to keep her safe. Slipping off my shoes and climbing into bed beside her, I wrapped my arms around her, pulling her close to my chest. Her warmth seeped into my skin, and I revelled in the sensation. It felt like coming home after a long journey, comforting, familiar, and right.

"Is everything okay, Liam?" she murmured, her voice still thick with sleep. "Everything will be fine," I reassured her, the words heavy with promise. "We'll figure this out together."

"Promise?"

"Cross my heart," I whispered, pressing a soft kiss to her forehead. Her eyes fluttered closed again, and I could feel the weight of her trust settle on my shoulders. As her breathing evened out and she drifted back to sleep, my mind raced with thoughts of our next steps. Visiting Erica's old pack could be the key to unlocking the answers we needed, but it was also a journey fraught with potential danger.

Chapter 38

Erica

I stumbled through the dark woods, my heart racing with fear. Tears streamed down my face as I tried to wipe them away with my small, trembling hands. The night was filled with the sounds of screams and the smell of burning wood. Fires raged around me, painting the trees in eerie shades of orange and red.

"Mummy?" I called out, desperately hoping she would hear me. "Daddy?" I felt so alone, just a little girl lost amidst chaos.

My chest tightened at the realisation that I couldn't find my parents. But then, like an answer to my prayers, I heard my mummy's voice.

"Erica!" she cried out, and without hesitation, I ran towards the sound. Through the smoke and fire, I saw her standing beside my dad, who was in his great big wolf form. Their backs were turned to me, facing off against another large black wolf that I had never seen before. Panic surged through me as the unknown wolf lunged towards my dad. Mummy's hands seemed to glow, and she threw something that looked like a fireball at the attacker.

"Run, Erica!" she screamed as she turned to face me, her eyes wide with terror. I did as I was told, running away from the horrifying scene before me.

Suddenly, the world shifted, and I found myself standing in a circle of ancient stones, surrounded by a serene silence that contrasted sharply with the chaos I had just left behind.

"Christian?" I whispered, recognising his scent before I even saw him. He stood with his back to me, but I knew it was him, the Alpha heir of our pack. Relief washed over me, knowing that he would protect me.

"Erica," Christian said softly, his voice reassuring. "I'll always protect you." I didn't understand what was happening or why we were here, but I trusted him. As I looked beyond Christian, I saw a tall, shadowy figure lurking in the darkness. Somehow, I knew it was the black wolf from earlier.

Fear gripped me again as the figure rushed forward, hurling Christian into one of the standing stones. I screamed, my heart lurching at the sickening crunch that followed. Christian crumpled to the ground, his body twisted at an unnatural angle, unmoving. The shadowy figure closed in on me, and as he neared, I could see the gold flecks in his eyes.

"I've found you," he growled before grabbing me roughly. I screamed for Christian, even though I knew he couldn't save me now. The man carried me away from the stone circle and the hidden cove, my cries echoing through the night. "Christian!" I sobbed, unable to fathom what had just happened and my world shattered around me.

I bolted upright, a scream tearing through my throat. The darkness of the room closed in on me, suffocating my senses. Panic surged through me as I felt arms holding me down, trapping me in this nightmare. My heart raced, and I struggled to break free from their grip. A soft glow filled the room suddenly, illuminating Liam's concerned face. The scent of gingerbread and fire filled the air, calming my racing heart as I realised I was safe in bed with him. He loosened his hold on me, and I collapsed against him, my body wracked with sobs.

"It's all my fault," I choked out between heaving breaths. "Everything that happened... It's because of me."

"Baby, slow down. What are you talking about?" Liam asked, a frown creasing his brow as he tried to make sense of my words.

"Everyone who died... My parents, Alpha Trenton... I'm the reason they attacked us." I babbled, my thoughts a jumbled mess of guilt and fear.

"We had to live in hiding because of me."

"Hey, hey," Liam soothed, his hands rubbing circles on my back as he attempted to calm my hysteria.

"Tell me what happened in your dream. Maybe it'll help you understand why you're feeling this way." With Liam's gentle reassurance, I managed to piece together the horrifying details of my dream. As I recounted the events that unfolded in the standing stones, I saw Liam's expression darken.

When I mentioned about Alpha Trenton had been killed in an accident, he went quiet.

"Is something wrong?" I demanded, my eyes searching his face for answers.

"Erica..." Liam hesitated, clearly unsure of how to proceed. "Alpha Trenton didn't die in an accident. He was tortured and killed." My stomach churned at his words, and I couldn't hold back the horrified gasp that escaped my lips. This new information only served to confirm my deepest fears: I was a magnet for pain and suffering, and everyone around me would pay the price.

"God, this just proves it," I whispered, tears streaming down my cheeks. "Maybe I'm just poisonous," I whispered, my voice hoarse from crying. "Everyone I love seems to get hurt or killed because of me."

"Baby, you can't think like that," he insisted, his warm brown eyes filled with concern. He pulled me closer into his embrace, and I felt the steady rhythm of his heart against my cheek.

"You're not responsible for what happened." But the guilt weighed heavily on me, settling deep in my chest like a stone. The deaths of my parents, Alpha Trenton, and who knows how many others – it was all connected to me somehow. My inability to shift, the hidden power inside me... It was too much.

"Who's Christian?" Liam asked softly, breaking through my thoughts.

"Christian..." I choked out, fresh tears springing to my eyes. "He was Alpha Trenton's and Luna Becca's firstborn. He was supposed to be the Alpha heir of Moon Key pack." I paused, my breath hitching as memories of Christian flooded my mind.

"He died right in front of me, trying to protect me from the leader of the pack that attacked us." Liam's arms tightened around me, offering comfort as sorrow washed over me again.

"I'm so sorry, baby. I didn't know."

"Every time I think about him, I can't help but cry," I confessed, my body shaking with sobs. "He was so brave, and he didn't deserve what happened to him."

"Hey," Liam murmured, tucking a strand of my light red hair behind my ear. "It's okay to grieve. But you can't let this guilt consume you. We'll figure this out together, alright?" I nodded, my vision blurry with tears. Despite the overwhelming grief and guilt coursing through me, I couldn't deny the sense of warmth and security that Liam provided.

"Wait a second," Liam said, his eyebrows furrowing in thought. "Christian... was he the blond-haired lad with piercing blue eyes?"

"Y-yes," I stuttered, shocked that Liam would know him. "How do you know Christian?" A smile tugged at the corner of Liam's mouth as he looked at me warmly.

"We met before, when you were just a little girl." His brown eyes sparkled with nostalgia. "I used to call you 'kitten' back then. You'd follow me around everywhere, your light red hair bouncing as you tried to keep up." My eyes widened in realisation. I remembered the boy who called me 'kitten,' but I never knew it was Liam. How could I not have recognised him?

A flood of memories rushed back, filling me with warmth and longing for simpler times.

"Maybe we were always fated to be together," Liam continued, his voice soft and tender. "Even if we didn't know it yet." His words hung in the air between us, making my heart race.

"Erica?" Liam asked, concern etching his features as I pulled away from his embrace. "What's wrong?"

"I..." My voice trembled as I tried to find the right words. "I need to go back to my place. I need time to think."

"Think about what?" Liam's expression shifted to one of confusion, hurt flickering in his eyes. "About everything," I replied, barely managing to hold back tears.

I grabbed my duffel bag, hastily stuffing clothes and personal items inside as I tried to ignore Liam's gaze on me. It felt like a thousand needles pressing into my skin, each one pricking at my already fragile heart.

"How long will you need?" he finally asked, his voice strained.

"I don't know," I admitted with a heavy sigh, the weight of uncertainty crushing me.

"Are you going to your room, or... are you leaving me?" The hurt in his voice was almost too much for me to bear.

Unable to look him in the eye, I whispered, "I don't know that either." Gathering the last of my belongings, I pulled the zipper shut on my bag with a soft click. The sound seemed to reverberate through the room, echoing the finality of my decision.

"Sorry," I managed to choke out before slipping out the door, not daring to look back.

The moment I was outside Liam's room, I leaned against the wall, tears streaming down my face as if someone had opened a floodgate within me. All I wanted was to run back into his arms and tell him how much I loved him, but I couldn't. Not until I knew if our bond was real, and if he was safe around me. My mind raced with thoughts and doubts, spinning in circles like a whirlwind threatening to tear me apart. Was this fated bond genuine, or was it just an Alpha attraction? Did Liam truly love me, or was it my power that drew him in? As I stood there, my heart ached with longing and fear.

With shaky steps, I left the pack house and made my way to my apartment, the weight of my decision heavy on my chest. The cold night air stung my tear-streaked face as I crossed the distance between the buildings, but it did nothing to numb the pain in my heart. Upon entering my apartment, I saw Gen and Frankie sitting together in the living area, chatting animatedly. Hearing the door open, they both turned to greet me, their smiles quickly fading when they saw my distraught state.

"Erica?" Gen asked, concern etched on her face.

"Are you okay?" Frankie added, her rebellious exterior cracking slightly as she looked at me with worry. I ignored their questions, unable to form words with the lump in my throat.

Instead, I rushed past them and slammed the door to my room shut, immediately collapsing against it as uncontrollable sobs racked my body. In that moment, all the pent-up emotions I had been holding back came pouring out, leaving me feeling raw and vulnerable. As I cried, my thoughts raced with uncertainty and guilt, wondering if I was making the right choice by distancing myself from Liam. The gentle sound of my own breathing eventually lulled me into a fitful sleep, still slumped against the door.

A soft knock stirred me from my uneasy dreams. Blinking away the remnants of sleep, I slowly opened the door, revealing Gen standing there with a piece of paper in her hand. Her expression held a mix of understanding and sadness, and without saying a word, she pulled me into a comforting hug.

"Here," she whispered, handing me the paper before stepping back and leaving me alone once again. I closed the door behind her and sat down on the edge of my bed, unfolding the paper with trembling hands. Inside, I recognised Liam's familiar handwriting, each word written with care and love.

"Erica,

I don't know what happened, but I will do my best to respect your space, for now. But know that I have vowed to protect you, and I take that vow seriously. I also know that I said I would respect your decision about us either way, but I don't want that. I have never wanted that, not since the first moment I saw you. I want you, all of you. I want you to be mine and me to be yours.

Again, I will respect your request to stay away, for now, but I mean what I said tonight, I will protect you with everything I have. I will try to find out more information to help you figure this out so you can come home to me.

Sweet dreams, baby,

Liam x."

Chapter 39

Liam

The weight of the note in my hand felt like a heavy stone as I handed it to Gen. She forced a smile onto her face as she turned to go to Erica's room, leaving me with an unmistakable feeling of dread. My heart pounded in my chest as I sat in the living room, trying to make sense of the situation.

"Maybe I shouldn't have given it to her," I muttered under my breath, casting a sidelong glance at Frankie. She was sprawled on the nearby couch, arms crossed over her chest, staring into space. Her black dyed hair with purple tips framed her rebellious face, and her tattoos seemed to tell their own story.

"Perhaps," she replied absently, lost in thoughts I couldn't read.

The door creaked open, and Gen emerged from Erica's room. As soon as I saw her tear-streaked face, my heart sank.

"She okay?" I asked, though I already knew the answer. Gen shook her head, wiping her eyes with the back of her hand.

"She's hurting, Liam...badly. And so are you. I can see it." I let out a long sigh, my fingers drumming against my thigh. Guilt gnawed at me, consuming me like wildfire. This whole mess started because of me, and here I was, unable to fix it.

"Listen," I began, steeling myself for what I was about to say. "I need both of you to look after Erica while I'm gone."

"Where are you going?" Frankie asked, sitting up straighter.

"North, with my father," I replied, avoiding meeting their eyes. "But I'll be back. I promise."

Despite the uncertainty swirling inside me, I wanted them to believe that I would return and make things right again.

"Erica needs her friends more than anything right now, and I trust you two to be there for her."

"Of course, Liam," Gen said softly. "You know we would do anything for her."

"Good," I murmured, a faint smile touching my lips. "I haven't given up on our love, not yet." As the words left my mouth, I felt the familiar knot of determination tighten in my chest. Erica was everything to me, and I would fight through hell and back to protect her.

"Take care of yourself too," Frankie chimed in, her voice solemn but supportive. "We'll be here when you get back."

"Thank you," I whispered as I stood up, feeling the weight of their expectations resting on my shoulders. With one last glance at Erica's closed door, I stepped out into the night..

The cool night air wrapped around me like a shroud as I walked back to the pack house, my thoughts a whirlwind of emotions and memories. The moon cast eerie shadows across the ground, reflecting my tumultuous state of mind. I clenched my fists, trying to contain the anger and pain building inside me. Upon reaching the pack house, I hesitated for a moment, taking a deep breath before entering. The scent of pine and earth filled my nostrils, grounding me momentarily. I made my way to my father's office, where I knew he'd be discussing the upcoming trip with my mother and Beta Gregg. It was time to face them and announce my decision.

"Father," I said, stepping into the dimly lit room. The soft glow from the fireplace cast flickering shadows across their faces, highlighting their concern.

"I'm coming with you on the trip." My father eyed me carefully, his gaze piercing through the darkness. I could see the questions swirling in his eyes, but he remained silent. Relief washed over me as he didn't press for answers. He simply nodded, acknowledging my choice.

"Very well, Liam," he finally responded, his voice low and steady. "We leave at dawn tomorrow."

"Thank you," I murmured, feeling a weight lifted off my shoulders.

"Son," my mother began, her voice soft yet firm. She placed a gentle hand on my arm, her brown eyes warm and comforting. "You must have faith in this journey and in yourself. Things will work out, I promise." I looked at her, searching for any hint of doubt, but found only reassurance and love. Her words were cryptic, as always, but they brought comfort nonetheless.

"Remember what the witch told us about the curse?" she continued. "It's a fated love that will break it. And she also said the world is powered by puzzle pieces, and the butterfly is the key that will unlock everything." I frowned, trying to decipher the meaning behind her words. The witch's words had always seemed like an enigma, something my mother would tell me as a child, before I even knew she was talking about me, but I couldn't deny the pull it had on me. It felt as though she was speaking directly to my soul, urging me to uncover the truth hidden beneath the surface.

"Have faith, Liam," my mother whispered, squeezing my arm before releasing it. "You're not alone in this struggle."

"Thank you, Mother," I said softly, feeling a renewed sense of determination course through me. I turned to leave the room, pausing at the door to glance back at my father, who gave me a nod of approval. Beta Gregg met my gaze with a silent understanding, his loyalty unwavering.

The first light of dawn filtered through the curtains as I threw my bag into the trunk of our SUV. My father stood beside me, his face a mixture of concern and determination.

"Don't worry, Liam," he said, clapping me on the back. "I've arranged for a security detail to watch over Erica while we're gone. She'll be safe."

"Thank you, Father." The weight of his reassurance brought a small comfort, but it couldn't quell the gnawing guilt that chewed at my insides. We embarked on our long journey north, the landscape shifting from dense forests to rolling hills as we approached the Scottish-English border. The silence between us was heavy, charged with unspoken questions and fears. It wasn't until we neared our destination that my father spoke up, his voice low and measured.

"Why did you leave Erica behind?" he asked. I knew it was coming. I just didn't want to say the words out loud.

"She needs time," I said and my father glanced at me before looking back at the road. "Erica believes she's the reason for the attack on her old pack, that they're living in hiding because of her." My father didn't look over this time, but I could tell that there was more he knew that I didn't.

"And she's right, Liam," he finally said. I clenched my fists, trying to contain the anger that surged within me.

"Why?" I demanded, my voice shaking. "Why would anyone want to hurt her?"

"Whoever is hunting down the Moon Key pack, they want Erica," my father explained, his expression grim. "I don't know much more than that, but it factored into why Beta Marshall didn't fight for her when you took her away."

My heart raced, the gravity of the situation sinking in. Erica, my fated love, was being hunted. And there was still so much we didn't understand about the curse, the witch's cryptic prophecy echoing in my mind: the world is powered by puzzle pieces, and the butterfly is the key that will unlock everything.

"Father, what if we can't protect her?" The question slipped from my lips before I could stop it, the vulnerability in my voice revealing the depth of my fear.

"Have faith, Liam," he said softly, his hand briefly gripping my shoulder. "We'll find a way to keep her safe." I stared out the window, watching the vibrant green hills blur into a single streak as we sped by. My thoughts were a storm of emotions: anger towards those who sought to harm Erica, guilt for not being able to shield her from the darkness, and a desperate hope that our love would be strong enough to weather the challenges ahead.

The late afternoon sun cast long shadows as we pulled up to a large Victorian house nestled in the heart of a small town. The ivy-covered facade gave it an air of aged grandeur, contrasting with the quaint and charming surroundings. My heart raced with anticipation, knowing that we were on the brink of uncovering vital information about Erica's past. As my father and I stepped out of the car, the heavy wooden door of the house creaked open to reveal Beta Marshall standing in the entrance. He was a tall, imposing figure, but his face bore the marks of hardships and secrets that weighed heavily upon him. My father approached him with a warm smile, and they exchanged pleasantries before shaking hands.

"Good to see you again, Marshall," my father said, his voice filled with genuine warmth. "I hope you have all settled in."

"Indeed, Alpha, and we have, thank you for your assistance in the matter," Marshall replied, his eyes flickering briefly to me. As I reached out to shake his hand, he fixed me with a grim expression, one that sent a shiver down my spine. It was clear that dark times lay ahead, and whatever news awaited us within these walls would not be easy to digest.

"Please, come in," Marshall gestured towards the interior of the house. "I've put the kettle on. I imagine you could use a cuppa after such a long journey."

"Did you phone ahead?" I asked my father, confused by Marshall's apparent preparedness for our arrival. My father shook his head, a bemused smile playing on his lips.

"No, I didn't." Marshall grinned.

"No need for that when there's a seer in the house." And with that cryptic statement, he turned and walked back inside, leaving my father and me to follow in his wake.

Stepping further into the house, I was immediately struck by the warmth and friendly atmosphere that greeted us. Rich vibrant colours adorned the walls, and the tantalising scent of freshly baked apple pie wafted through the air, filling my senses and offering a strange sense of comfort. "Please, make yourselves at home," Marshall gestured towards the plush couches in the living room, his demeanour relaxed and welcoming despite our unannounced visit. As we settled into the cosy space, Becca entered the room with an infectious smile, carrying a tray laden with steaming cups.

"I'm glad you made it before the storm," she said, her eyes sparkling with an unreadable glint as she handed me a cup of tea. Confused, I glanced out the window, the sun still shone brightly overhead, not a cloud in sight. Turning back to Becca, I caught her wink and couldn't help but feel that there was more to her statement than met the eye.

"Are you here about Erica?" Becca asked my father directly, her smile fading into a sombre expression. He nodded gravely, his gaze locking onto hers.

"Yes, we're concerned about her recent outbursts, and we've discovered that she's an Alpha rank werewolf." Becca's eyes flickered with a mixture of sadness and resignation.

Glancing towards Marshall, she sighed, "It's time to come clean." At that moment, another woman descended the staircase and offered us a warm greeting. Marshall introduced her as his wife, Charlene.

With introductions complete, my father relayed the details of Erica's struggles and what little we knew about her past. As I listened to their conversation, my chest tightened with a mix of guilt and concern. I felt responsible for Erica's pain, and I was desperate to shield her from any further harm. But how could I protect her when I was so entwined in the darkness that threatened to consume her?

"Erica's past is more complicated than any of us realised," Becca said, her voice heavy with emotion. "But there are things you need to know if we're going to help her." My heart raced, and my hands tightened around the warm cup of tea as I braced myself for the revelations that were about to unfold.

"Get comfortable, because this is a long story," Becca said, her voice thick with emotions I couldn't quite decipher.

Chapter 40

Erica

Two Months Later

TWO MONTHS HAD PASSED since I got the note from Liam, and life had taken on a rhythm of its own. Sweat dripped down my forehead as I landed a solid punch on the training dummy in front of me. I couldn't help but smile at my progress.

"Nice hit," Jacob praised, a slight grin tugging at the corners of his mouth. He was Liam's Gamma-to-be, and a formidable warrior in his own right. It felt good to have him on my side.

"Thanks," I replied, panting slightly. "I'm getting better, huh?"

"You're a natural, Erica," Damon chimed in, clapping me on the back. His dark eyes sparkled with pride. "You've come so far in such a short time."

"Still have a long way to go before I can match you two," I said with a smirk, wiping the sweat from my brow. As much as I enjoyed the friendship and the physical challenge, a small part of me couldn't forget that I hadn't seen Liam in weeks. He'd been on one trip after another since leaving me that note, and it left an ache in my chest that I couldn't ignore.

"Hey," Damon said gently, catching the change in my mood.

"Liam's just giving you space, like you asked. He's still struggling, but he cares about you, Erica."

"I know," I sighed, unable to completely hide the longing in my voice. "It's just... hard, not seeing him."

"Give it time," Jacob suggested wisely. "You're both strong individuals, and you'll find your way back to each other when the time is right." I nodded, knowing they were right. But that didn't make the absence any easier.

"Alright, warriors," Jacob announced, clapping his hands together. "Enough talk. Let's get back to training."

The scent of jasmine filled the air as we gathered in our cosy apartment, the excitement for a night out at Barking Brews palpable. Gen and Frankie lounged on the couch, sharing stories from their week while Kaitlyn and Verity sat cross-legged on the floor, flipping through gossip magazines.

"Erica, you have to wear this dress!" Kaitlyn exclaimed, holding up a scandalous piece of black leather that looked more like straps than an actual dress.

"Absolutely not!" I laughed, shaking my head. "I'll stick to my skinny jeans, thank you very much."

"Come on," Verity chimed in, her pale grey eyes twinkling with mischief. "It's been ages since we've had a proper girls' night out. Live a little!"

"Fine, but I'm not wearing that death trap," I said, pointing at the dress. "I'd trip and break my neck before we even left the apartment."

"Alright, alright," Kaitlyn conceded, tossing the dress back into her bag. "But promise me you'll wear something fun and flirty, okay?"

"Deal," I agreed, rummaging through my closet for an outfit that would satisfy my friends without making me feel too exposed.

As I changed, I couldn't help but think about Liam. The ache for him in my heart only seemed to grow stronger with each passing day. I pushed the thought aside, focusing on the moment as I slipped into a pair of dark denim jeans and a deep red off-the-shoulder top that hugged my curves just right.

"Perfect," Verity declared when she saw my outfit, giving me a thumbs up.

"Let's do this!" Frankie shouted, grabbing her purse and heading for the door. We made our way downstairs, laughter and playful banter filling the air as we walked arm in arm. I couldn't help but feel grateful for the friendships I'd formed within the pack, and as we made our way to Barking Brews, I decided to let go of my worries for one night and simply enjoy the company of my friends.

"Remember," Kaitlyn whispered in my ear as we entered the bustling bar, "tonight is about having fun, letting loose, and showing off that gorgeous outfit!"

"Got it," I replied with a smile, trying to ignore the small voice in my head that wondered what Liam would think if he saw me now.

"Ugh, I miss Red Bank," Gen lamented as we entered the bustling bar. I shot her an apologetic glance, remembering how often they used to visit when I worked there. I knew they hadn't been going because of my restriction from leaving pack territory.

"Cheer up," Frankie said with a smirk, "We'll go again soon, once Erica here isn't grounded anymore." She playfully nudged me, and I stuck my tongue out at her in response, making her laugh.

"Why can't you leave the pack?" Verity inquired curiously. She had vented about her overbearing father and brothers earlier in the evening, and it still amazed me that she was not only the Commander's daughter but also the youngest of six kids. Her combat skills were nothing short of incredible, and she could take down elite recruits twice her size with ease.

"Erica tried to pull off a jailbreak," Kaitlyn interjected with a grin. Verity's eyes widened as Frankie cackled.

"Really? When?" Gen asked, her eyes fixed on me. I winced under their collective gaze.

"I didn't want to join the pack," I admitted. "So during my first week here, I tried to escape. Even enlisted Grant for help."

"Badass!" Frankie exclaimed, laughing even harder. Gen frowned, clearly hurt.

"Why didn't you want to join?" I smiled warmly and pulled her into a hug.

"Because I didn't know you'd be here, silly. If I'd known that, I would've happily joined." Gen giggled and hugged me back. Our friendship had grown strong over the past two months, and she was one of my closest confidants, along with Imogen. I kissed her cheek, and she giggled again.

Finally ready, our group ventured deeper into Barking Brews. The bar was packed with singles from the pack, and rock music pulsed through the speakers. People were already dancing and enjoying themselves. I took a moment to appreciate my friends' outfits: Verity wore a form-fitting emerald green dress that highlighted her pale grey eyes; Frankie had on a black leather skirt paired with a band tee and her signature purple-tipped hair; Gen donned a flowy white blouse tucked into high-waisted jeans, which accentuated her curves; Kaitlyn looked stunning in a sleek burgundy jumpsuit that hugged her tall and slender frame.

"Alright, ladies, let's show 'em what we've got!" Kaitlyn proclaimed, and we wasted no time joining the throng of dancers, getting lost in the rhythm of the music and the friendship of our newfound sisterhood.

Gen grabbed my hand, pulling me onto the dance floor as the bass thumped through my veins. Frankie, with a cheeky wink, disappeared into the crowd to fetch us drinks at the bar. Kaitlyn trailed after Gen and me, her hips swaying to the beat. Before Verity could join us, two large men blocked her path. Even from behind, I recognised them as her older twin brothers, both blond, short-haired, and built like tanks. A mixture of concern and annoyance flitted across Verity's face, but she squared her shoulders and faced them head-on. My gaze flicked around the room, and my heart skipped a beat when I spotted Liam leaning against the bar. He was surrounded by a group of warriors, including Damon and Jacob. His eyes locked onto mine, and I couldn't help but notice how his hair had grown a bit longer, giving him an even more rugged appearance. He looked tired, but every bit as hot as the last time I'd seen him. In that moment, I realised just how much I'd missed him. Reluctantly, I broke our eye contact and returned my attention to my dancing friends. Kaitlyn caught my glance, grinning and wiggling her eyebrows suggestively. That's when it hit me, she'd been trying to get me to dress up for Liam's return.

As we danced together, I couldn't help but steal glances at Liam. The pull towards him was undeniable, but I remained focused on enjoying the night with my friends. Our laughter mingled with the music, drowning out any lingering thoughts of the complicated relationships within our pack.

"Let's show them what we're made of!" Kaitlyn shouted over the music, her eyes sparkling with excitement. The vibrant energy on the dance floor was intoxicating, but I couldn't shake the sensation of Liam's gaze following my every move. I tried to focus on my friends and the music, letting my body sway to the beat. Laughter bubbled up within me as Frankie pulled a ridiculous dance move, but her expression suddenly turned sour.

"Ugh," she scowled, glancing at Kaitlyn before peering over my shoulder. Kaitlyn's face mirrored Frankie's disgust, and even Gen looked worried. Curiosity piqued, I spun around to see what had caught their attention.

My blood boiled the moment I saw Heidi draped all over Liam like a cheap shawl. Her hands roamed his chest as she whispered something in his ear, a smug smile plastered on her face. The primal growl that erupted from my throat took me by surprise, and the three girls stared at me with wide eyes.

"Erica, don't let her get under your skin," Gen warned, biting her lip.

"Play her at her own game," Frankie suggested, her eyes narrowing as she watched the scene unfold.

"Rip her apart," Kaitlyn added, her glare fixed on Heidi. Somewhere deep within me, the bond between Liam and me flexed, and I realised there was no denying it. Our fates were intertwined, and it was time for everyone to know who their Alpha heir belonged to.

My heart pounded in my chest as I locked eyes with Liam, who was trying his best to be polite to Heidi despite her overly forward advances. He noticed my deliberate approach, and the way I put a little extra sway into my step, and his uncomfortable smile slowly morphed into a wicked grin, full of anticipation for what I was about to do. Heidi's voice carried over the music, irritatingly sweet as she promised Liam a "special" homecoming gift. As I came to stand just behind her, she caught sight of me in her peripheral vision and whipped around. "What the fuck do you want?" she sneered, amber eyes flashing with anger. I spared Liam a quick glance before turning my attention back to Heidi. At that moment, I knew exactly what I wanted, and who I wanted it with. My voice rang out clear and strong, fuelled by the bond that had grown between Liam and me.

"Mine," I declared, and all chatter ceased as the entire bar turned to watch the unfolding drama. Heidi's face turned an ugly shade of red, but I ignored her, looking straight at Liam instead.

"Mine," I repeated, the word heavy with meaning.

"Yours," Liam agreed, his brown eyes locking onto mine. With surprising strength, he pulled me towards him, my hands instinctively grabbing at his shirt as our lips collided in a passionate kiss that seemed to set the world ablaze.

The fire within me roared, driving away any lingering doubts or fears. Liam lifted me up, my legs wrapping around his waist as he held me close. I buried my face in his neck, nipping at his marking spot, eliciting a low groan that vibrated against my lips. As Liam pressed me against the bar, I could feel his arousal, a testament to the undeniable connection between us. It was exhilarating and terrifying all at once, but I knew one thing for certain, I wasn't going to let anyone, especially Heidi, stand in our way.

The scream of rage that pierced the air made my heart skip a beat, and I barely had time to react before Liam was violently ripped away from me. The force of the sudden separation sent me tumbling to the ground, my legs no longer wrapped around him. My head spun with shock as I tried to process what had just happened.

"Did you really think you could steal the Luna title from me?" Heidi's voice was dripping with venom as she loomed above me, her face contorted in fury. "I'll rip your filthy omega ass apart!" As I struggled to catch my breath, the anger that had been simmering below the surface took hold and surged through my veins like wildfire. I felt an unfamiliar sense of control over the rage inside me, and a fierce determination to protect what was mine, Liam.

"Try it," I growled, my voice low and menacing. I could feel the change deep within me and knew without looking that my eyes had shifted to the pale gold of my wolf. The power and confidence that flowed through me was unlike anything I'd ever experienced. Heidi didn't hesitate. She lunged at me like a wild animal, her nails aimed for my throat. But I was faster, fuelled by my newfound control and the love I felt for Liam. I reached out, my fingers wrapping around her throat with surprising ease, and slammed her to the floor with a force that shook the entire room.

The rush of something feral deep inside me, guiding me, helping me control the rage. I could feel the fury of cold ice flowing through me, powering me. I could feel it try to take hold, to take over and exact the revenge that I wanted. I knew now what this was; it wasn't my wolf trying to take over. This was something different, something more ancient, more feral. This was some birthright that I knew was mine to control, and not to be controlled by. There was no denying right now that I was anything other than pure Alpha blood, but Alpha what? What had previously felt hot as it burned through my system taking me over stayed cool while in my control. I could see Heidi's eyes widen again, this time in fear, and I knew she could feel every ounce of this raw power coursing through me. And deep down in the depths of me, held captive in a prison of unknown origins, I heard her again after two months.I recognised her voice instantly from my first night with Liam. I saw and heard my wolf; she paced the prison looking for a weak spot but for just a moment we saw each other and I heard one word.

"Finally."

Chapter 41

Erica

The thick scent of alcohol and sweat filled my nostrils as I held Heidi pinned to the floor of the crowded bar. My heart pounded in my chest, a combination of anger and adrenaline coursing through my veins.

"Do I look like an Omega to you?" I snarled, my voice dripping with contempt. Heidi's amber eyes widened in terror, flickering between my pale gold wolf irises and the sea of curious onlookers surrounding us. The room had grown eerily silent, no doubt due to the spectacle we were providing. She looked like a deer caught in headlights, her body rigid with fear beneath mine as she finally began to grasp the extent of my power.

"Answer me," I demanded, my grip tightening on her wrists which were pinned above her head. The force of my words made her wince. Despite my inability to shift, the raw strength radiating from me was palpable. It was a reminder that I was not weak, despite what others may have thought. I felt my blood boil at the memory of Heidi's constant belittling, her insistence on referring to me as an Omega.

"Y-yes," she stammered, her voice barely audible. "You're not an Omega, Erica."

"Good," I replied, my tone icy. I wanted to make sure she understood the gravity of the situation, that she would never dare underestimate me again.

I felt a warm hand on my shoulder. It was Damon, his dark eyes filled with concern as he tried to help me get the Alpha power under control, something we had been working on for the past two months.

"Erica, how are you doing?" he asked, his voice soft and steady. I wanted to respond calmly, to reassure him that I could handle this surge of power coursing through me, but all I could manage was an involuntary growl. My body tensed at the sound, threatening to unleash the full force of my abilities if provoked further. Liam, sensing the danger and feeling possessive of me, his mate, matched my growl with one of his own, directed at Damon. As much as I appreciated Damon's assistance, a primal part of me understood Liam's need to protect what was his.

"Wait a minute, Liam," Damon said, holding up his free hand in a placating gesture. He never broke eye contact with me, trusting that I wouldn't lash out. A couple of guards stepped closer, their wary expressions telling me they were ready to intervene if necessary.

Damon tried to push his calming cool gift in to me.

"Come back to us, Erica," he urged gently. "You're stronger than this." I glanced at him, forcing a grin while keeping Heidi pinned to the floor with one hand.

"Does it look like I'm not in control?" Damon raised an eyebrow and smirked, trying to lighten the tense atmosphere.

"Well, you're in some sort of scary control. In fact, I'm not sure which one scares me more right now. Uncontrolled gold-eyed Erica or controlled gold-eyed Erica." His words sparked a flicker of amusement deep within me, momentarily distracting me from the burning desire to assert my dominance over Heidi. I knew he was joking, but there was an underlying truth behind his words, the power coursing through me was both intoxicating and terrifying. It was a double-edged sword, one that could either protect those I cared for, or destroy them. Damon glanced up at Liam, seeking approval and permission to continue. Liam's eyes locked on mine for a moment, filled with a mix of concern and trust before he gave Damon a subtle nod.

"Alright, Erica," Damon said, resuming his role as the calming force in my life, "why don't you show me how in control you are and bring back those pretty green eyes of yours?" My grin widened almost manically, the thrill of power coursing through me like lightning.

"Hold on just one moment," I told him, voice laced with a dark edge that even I could barely recognise.

I turned my attention back to Heidi, who was still pinned beneath my grasp. Her amber eyes were wide with terror, the helpless look of a cornered animal. As my gold wolf eyes bore into her, I felt the satisfaction of asserting my dominance. It was a sensation that was both intoxicating and terrifying, and I knew I had to tread carefully.

"Please," Heidi whimpered, the sound so pitiful it almost made me want to release her. Almost. A growl rumbled deep in my chest, the raw power within me demanding submission. With a wicked smile still plastered on my face, I focused on the trembling figure beneath me. Heidi's eyes widened in terror, her breath hitching in her throat as she realised that she was the object of my attention once more.

"Listen closely, Heidi," I hissed, my voice laced with venom. "Liam is mine. He belongs to me, and you need to stay far, far away from him." Heidi whimpered again, and I could feel her body shaking under my grip. But I wasn't done yet.

"Furthermore," I continued, my tone colder than ice, "if I ever hear that you've gone near Liam, or any of my friends for that matter, or if you cause even the slightest bit of trouble... I will hunt you down and rip you apart, piece by agonising piece. Understand?" As if her life depended on it, which, let's be honest, it did, Heidi nodded frantically, tears streaming down her cheeks. Satisfied, I released her and stood up, revelling in the power coursing through my veins.

"Fuck off," I spat at her, watching as she scrambled to her feet and practically tripped over herself in her haste to escape. Within moments, she had disappeared out of the bar, leaving nothing but the lingering scent of her fear behind. I couldn't help but smirk at her retreating form, feeling a surge of triumph as the room remained silent in the wake of my outburst.

The air crackled with tension as I stood, the remnants of Heidi's fear still tangible in the atmosphere. I looked around the room, my gaze drifting over the myriad of faces watching me intently, their expressions a mix of fear, concern and, in some cases, excitement.

"Damn, Erica," Frankie breathed, her eyes shining with admiration as she took a step towards me. "That was... intense." I glanced at her, noting how her tattooed arms seemed to vibrate with energy, as if she were eager to join in on whatever chaos I had just unleashed. It wasn't surprising, given her penchant for getting into trouble. My eyes found Liam, his expression a mixture of awe and pride, and my heart clenched. This was the man who mattered most to me, the one whose opinion carried more weight than anyone else's. And if he was proud of what I'd done, maybe it wasn't so terrible after all.

"Are you okay?" he asked softly, stepping closer until our bodies nearly touched.

"I'm fine," I replied, forcing a smile. "Just trying to get used to this... power."

"Take your time," he murmured, his handsome face etched with concern. "You don't have to master it all at once."

I closed my eyes, focusing on drawing the alpha power back into myself, feeling it recede like a tide pulling away from the shore. The warmth of Liam's presence served as an anchor, keeping me grounded as I navigated the unfamiliar territory of my newfound abilities. When I opened my eyes again, I knew they had returned to their usual green, reflecting the calm that had settled within me.

The room seemed to sway as the last remnants of the alpha power ebbed away, leaving me drained and vulnerable in its wake. My limbs felt heavy, my head clouded with fatigue that threatened to pull me under like a riptide.

"Erica?" Liam's voice came from somewhere far away, his concern lapping at the edges of my consciousness. I tried to keep my gaze focused on him, but even that took more effort than I had left to give.

"Ti-tired," I mumbled, feeling every ounce of my exhaustion in that single word. The world around me blurred and darkened, and I could sense the impending collapse before it happened. But just as my knees buckled beneath me, Liam was there, his strong arms catching me before I could hit the unforgiving floor. His embrace was like a lifeline, steadying me even as everything else threatened to crumble.

"Easy now," he murmured into my hair, his breath warm against my scalp. "I've got you."

"Thank you," I whispered, grateful not only for his physical support but also for the unwavering love that shone through each and every one of his words. It was a beacon in the storm, guiding me back to shore when I felt lost at sea. As he lifted me into his arms, I nestled against his chest, the steady thrum of his heartbeat lulling me into a fragile sense of security. Though my body ached and my mind reeled, I knew that I was safe with him, and that he would protect me, no matter what the future held.

"Rest," Liam urged softly, pressing a tender kiss to the top of my head. "We'll figure everything out together, but for now, you need to heal." And then, feeling safe and protected, I allowed myself to be swallowed into the darkness.

Chapter 42

Liam

The weight of Erica's unconscious body pressed against my chest, her soft curves fitting perfectly into mine as I carried her through the dark corridors of the pack house. The whole way there, I struggled to focus on anything other than her. Her chest rose and fell in a steady rhythm, each breath a delicate sigh that sent shivers down my spine. It had been two months since I'd been able to touch my mate, my forbidden desire. And now, all I wanted to do was worship her like the queen she was in my eyes.

"Almost there," I whispered to myself, trying to ignore the growing need inside me. My heart pounded in my chest, anticipation and desire twisting together as we reached my room.

I pushed open the door, revealing the dimly lit sanctuary I called my own. The moment my bedroom door closed behind us, a wave of desire and anticipation washed over me like a tidal wave. I couldn't help but drink in every inch of her as I laid her gently on the bed, her unconscious form still radiating an undeniable allure that threatened to consume me entirely.

"Baby," I whispered, my voice husky with need, as I admired the way her red hair framed her face, the curve of her neck leading down to her breasts. My inner beast roared its approval, urging me to take her, to claim her as mine and mine alone. I hesitated for just a moment before giving in to my primal desires, climbing onto the bed beside her. My hands trembled slightly as they made their way down her top, fingers brushing across the swell of her breasts as I traced the outline of her curves. A groan escaped my lips, unable to resist the magnetic pull she had on me, even in her vulnerable state.

"Please forgive me," I murmured, not knowing if she could hear me or if it was just a futile offering to the universe. But I knew I couldn't stop myself now; my body craved her too deeply. My hand continued its journey down her body, fingertips grazing the smooth skin of her stomach before reaching her dark jeans. I hesitated once more, my beastly instincts warring with the part of me that wanted to protect and care for her.

"Mine," I growled under my breath, feeling the raw lust building inside me. It was almost unbearable, this hunger that clawed at my very being, demanding satisfaction.

Closing my eyes, I allowed the images of our past encounters to fuel my desires. I remembered the taste of her lips, warm and inviting, the feel of her soft skin beneath my touch, the sounds she made when I brought her pleasure. The memories only served to fan the flames, and in that moment, I knew that there was no turning back.

"Baby," I breathed out, my voice thick with desire as I pressed my hand against her jeans, restraining myself from ripping them off of her. Instead, I leaned down and captured her lips in a searing kiss, my tongue slipping past her parted lips to taste the sweet nectar within. My fingers hovered at the waistband of her jeans, aching to explore further. The moment I touched the skin beneath, Erica let out a small, sensual moan that sent shivers down my spine and ignited something primal within me.

"Mine," I growled against her lips, capturing her mouth in a bruising, passionate kiss. My hand slipped into her jeans and panties, seeking out the source of her pleasure. Finding her clit, I began to rub slow circles, letting the sensation build as our kisses grew more desperate.

The exact moment Erica woke up was like electricity coursing through me. Her moan filled the room as my fingers continued their dance on her clit. It was intoxicating - every movement, every sound she made as she surrendered to the intensity of our connection.

"Harder," she panted, her green eyes locked onto mine, full of raw desire. "Don't stop."

"Goddess, yes," I managed to choke out, picking up the pace as I felt her growing closer to the edge. She reached for my hair, pulling me in for another searing kiss, while bucking her hips up into my hand, trying to get as much friction as she could.

"Come for me, baby," I whispered against her ear, feeling her body tighten as she approached her climax. The sight of her, lost in pleasure, was enough to make me want to lose control myself.

"Almost... there," she breathed heavily, the words barely escaping her lips.

"Let go," I encouraged, my own breath hitching as my fingers kept working her sensitive bud. "I've got you."

"Ah... Liam!" she cried out, her body shuddering as the wave of ecstasy washed over her.

"Beautiful," I murmured between kisses, as she pushed against my fingers "You're so perfect, baby."

"Yours," she whispered in response.

I reluctantly pulled away from Erica's hungry lips, the taste of her still lingering as I gazed upon her beautiful face. Her green eyes shone with unmistakable lust, and it was nearly impossible to resist diving back in for another heated kiss. But I had other plans for my feisty mate. My hand slid out from between her legs, earning a frustrated whimper from Erica. Her cheeks flushed a deep shade of pink, making my wicked grin grow wider.

"Patience, love," I teased as my fingers deftly worked on the button of her jeans. "I'm going to make you feel even better." Her chest heaved with anticipation, her breaths coming out in shallow pants. Moving down her body, I couldn't help but admire her curves, the way her hips flared out from her waist, the enticing dip of her collarbone. With one final primal look, I gripped the waistband of her jeans and panties, yanking them both down in one swift motion. Erica's sharp gasp turned into a surprised scream as the cold air hit her exposed flesh.

"Fuck, Liam!" she managed to choke out before I silenced her with my mouth once more, stealing another passionate kiss. Pulling back, I glanced down at her beautiful pussy, glistening with arousal, beckoning me closer. I didn't give her time to react, my tongue darted out, eagerly tasting her essence.

"Goddess, you taste incredible," I groaned, flicking her clit with my tongue, causing her to buck her hips wildly, desperate for more contact. She screamed again, her voice raw and full of need.

"More...please," she begged, her hands gripping the sheets tightly. I couldn't deny her anything, especially when she looked so fucking sexy like this. Smirking up at her, I slowly slid one finger inside her tight wet heat, eliciting a throaty moan from Erica.

"Is this what you want, baby?" I asked, my voice low and husky as I pumped my finger in and out of her. Her eyes rolled back in her head, unable to form words, only managing breathy gasps and moans.

"Answer me," I demanded, my inner Alpha emerging, hungry for her submission.

"Y-yes, Liam," she stammered, finally finding her voice.

"Don't... don't stop."

"Good girl," I praised, watching as her cheeks flushed with pride and arousal. I had every intention of driving her wild, making her scream my name over and over again. And by the time I was done, there would be no doubt that she was mine. My finger slid in and out of her with ease, feeling the tight walls of her pussy gripping me, urging me to go deeper. I added a second finger, stretching her further, causing her back to arch off the bed as she cried out for more.

"Oh goddess, More, Liam... please," Erica whimpered, her voice breathy and desperate. My inner Alpha revelled in her submission, even as my human side longed to give her everything she asked for. I slowly pushed a third finger into her tight wet heat, watching her body shudder from the sensation.

"You feel so fucking good, baby," I growled, my eyes locked on hers.

"Fuck me, Liam. Please," she begged, her green eyes clouded by lust. And who was I to deny her? I began to slowly fuck her with my fingers, lapping at her clit with my tongue, driving her wild, her moans filling the room like music to my ears. Her hands gripped my hair, holding me in place as her hips bucked, seeking more contact, more pleasure.

"Goddess, yes, don't stop..." she gasped, her body trembling beneath me. I could tell she was close; her breaths had become ragged and her thighs were quivering around my head.

"Come for me, baby," I commanded, my voice rough and primal, leaving no room for doubt or hesitation. And she did, screaming my name as she came, her orgasm washing over her in waves, her sweet juices coating my fingers and face. I eagerly lapped up every drop, unable to get enough of her taste.

As her climax subsided, I slowed down, but pushed deeper inside her, curling my fingers upwards. I knew I'd found her sweet spot when she let out another scream, her body thrashing beneath me. She was a frenzied mess, completely lost in the pleasure I was giving her.

"Fuck, Liam... I can't take much more," she panted, her chest heaving, but her eyes pleading for me to continue. I couldn't help but feel a swell of pride at having my beautiful mate so thoroughly undone by my touch.

"Are you mine, baby?" I growled, needing to hear her say it, needing that reassurance deep within my soul.

"Yours," she whispered, her voice shaky but full of conviction.

As Erica lay panting beneath me, I slowly withdrew my fingers from her slick heat, savouring the sensation of her trembling around them. I placed a gentle kiss on her inner thigh before making my way up her body, pushing her top up as I went. With each kiss, I felt her shiver, her nails digging into my forearms, urging me to continue.

"Please, Liam," she whimpered, her green eyes darkened with need, "I need you inside me."

"Patience, love," I murmured against her skin, finally reaching her top and pulling it off over her head. I unclasped her bra and discarded it, taking in the sight of her flushed cheeks and heaving chest. She was breathtakingly beautiful, even more so now, completely exposed and vulnerable to me. I quickly stripped off my own clothes, my cock painfully hard and aching for her. As I settled myself between her legs, I couldn't help but admire the contrast of her pale thighs against the darkness of my own skin. Our bodies seemed to fit together like pieces of a puzzle, destined to be connected.

"Are you ready?" I asked, my voice rough with desire, even as I tried to give her some semblance of control in this intimate moment.

"Goddess, yes. I've been ready for so long, Liam," she breathed, her hips arching towards me, seeking the connection we both craved. That was all I needed to hear. I lined myself up with her entrance, the tip of my cock teasing her wet folds as I hesitated for just a moment, giving us both time to prepare for what was to come. Finally, unable to wait any longer, I thrust forward, burying myself deeply within her tight, welcoming heat. A scream tore from Erica's lips as I hit her sweet spot once more, her hands flying to my back, her nails digging in as she clung to me. The feeling of her nails raking down my skin only fuelled the primal, possessive need I had to claim her, to brand her as mine in the most intimate way possible.

My thrusts grew more forceful, driven by that instinctual desire for domination and possession.

"Baby," I growled, "you feel so fucking good." Her whimpers turned into moans, each one a beautiful symphony of pleasure and need. Our bodies moved in sync, sweat slicking our skin as we chased that elusive peak together.

"Harder, Liam," she pleaded, her voice raw with passion, "I need more!"

"Anything for you, love," I swore, my breath coming in ragged gasps as I drove into her with renewed fervour, determined to bring her to heights she'd never before experienced. As Erica's moans grew louder and more desperate, I knew she was close, we were close. That knowledge tipped me over the edge, sending me spiralling into my own release just moments after she cried out my name one final time.

As I continued to thrust inside her, the overwhelming urge to mark Erica as mine surged through me. The primal instinct was nearly impossible to resist, but I knew I had to maintain control for her sake. She deserved nothing less than my complete devotion, and I wasn't about to let my inner beast take over.

"Erica," I panted, each forceful thrust eliciting a gasp or moan from her beautiful lips.

"I want... I need to mark you."

"Please, Liam," she begged between breaths, her green eyes blazing with desire. But I couldn't, not yet. Instead, I channelled my feral need into every movement, fucking her with a ferocity that left us both gasping for air. Her nails dug into my back, each scratch stoking the fire within me, pushing me closer to the edge.

"Goddess, Liam!" Erica cried out, her voice breaking as our bodies collided in a symphony of passion and lust.

"Don't stop!"

"Never," I promised, my climax building like a tidal wave, threatening to crash down and consume me entirely. My grip on her hips tightened, fingers digging into her flesh as I drove into her with every ounce of strength I possessed.

"Erica," I snarled, the animal within me rearing its head as I finally succumbed to the pleasure coursing through my veins. I released myself deep within her, filling her with my seed as we clung to one another, riding out the aftershocks of our passion. Exhausted, I collapsed beside her, our sweat-slicked bodies heaving as we struggled to regain our breath. Turning my head to look at her, I couldn't help but growl possessively, "Mine."

Her smile was radiant, even in the aftermath of our heated coupling. "Yours," she agreed, sealing our fate with a single, powerful word.

Chapter 43

Erica

The sun pierced through the curtains, bathing my body in a warm golden light. I stretched languidly, feeling the soreness of last night's passion engulf me. A smile touched my lips as memories of Liam and me intertwined, our bodies seeking the pleasure we found in each other. It had been rough, intense, and filled with a hunger that couldn't be satiated, yet every touch spoke of love. My thoughts drifted back to the bar, where I'd claimed Liam as mine in front of everyone. I could still feel the adrenaline coursing through me as I stood up to Heidi, her jealousy palpable in the air. That bitch had it coming. By now, the entire pack would know about us; an Alpha heir finding their mate was no small news.

"Goddess, what have I got myself into?" I muttered under my breath, reflecting on the implications of being mated to an Alpha heir. The pack would expect me to fall in line, to become the perfect Luna they envisioned. But that wasn't me. I valued my freedom, my independence, and the thought of losing that made me uneasy.

As I lay in bed, tormented by the changes I knew were going to happen, I couldn't help but notice the emptiness beside me. The sound of running water from the bathroom told me that Liam was taking a shower. The shower stopped, and moments later, Liam emerged, wearing nothing but a towel wrapped low on his hips. My eyes were drawn to his toned muscles rippling with each step he took. His chiselled abs, powerful arms, and strong legs made my heart race and my body ache with desire.

"Morning," I said, trying to sound casual despite the heat building within me.

"Good morning," Liam replied with a wicked grin. He seemed to sense my arousal, his nostrils flaring as he sniffed the air. Maintaining eye contact, he slowly walked towards the end of the bed like a predator stalking its prey.

"Like what you see?" Liam asked smugly, his eyes twinkling with mischief as he stood at the end of the bed, completely exposed.

"Seen better," I replied, feigning disinterest even though my pulse quickened at the sight of his muscular frame and hardened arousal.

"Really?" He raised an eyebrow, clearly amused by my attempt to rile him up. My heart raced as I jumped off the bed, eager to put some distance between us.

"Yep. I'm going for a shower," I announced, turning my back to him. But before I could take more than a step, Liam's arm snaked around my waist and yanked me back, pinning me to the bed. His body pressed against mine, trapping me beneath him. I struggled to catch my breath, my chest tightening with a mixture of desire and apprehension.

"Are you sure you've seen better?" he whispered into my ear, his warm breath sending shivers down my spine. He nipped at my neck playfully with his teeth, teasing my skin just enough to make me squirm. I tried to maintain my facade of indifference, but it was quickly crumbling under the weight of his touch.

"Maybe not," I gasped as Liam's fingers deftly traced across my wet folds, causing my hips to buck involuntarily. He slid a finger inside me, making me moan in response. The familiar battle within me raged on, was it worth losing control to experience this undeniable passion?

"Thought so," he murmured before crashing his lips onto mine, swallowing my moans as our tongues danced together. I gripped his shoulders, torn between wanting to push him away and pull him closer.

The pleasure Liam was giving me came to an abrupt halt as he groaned and pulled away from me. I looked up at him, a mix of annoyance and frustration evident on my face. The fire in his eyes had been replaced with something else.

"Damn it," Liam muttered, running a hand through his dishevelled hair. "My mum just mind-linked me. She wants us both at family breakfast."

"Seriously?" I groaned, not even trying to hide my disappointment. It seemed the universe was intent on keeping my needs unmet today. I glanced down at my naked body, then back at Liam.

"And what am I supposed to wear? My clothes from last night are hardly appropriate for a family gathering." Liam's gaze softened slightly as he took in my dishevelled appearance. His smile was infuriatingly charming as he kissed my nose. He pointed to a bag by the door, and I couldn't help but feel grateful when he told me that Kaitlyn had brought it from the bar, along with some clean clothes from my apartment.

"Thank her for me," I said, trying to keep my voice steady despite the rising tension in the room.

"And we can pack the rest of your stuff later," Liam added. "Wait, what?" I asked, my eyebrows shooting up in surprise.

"The rest of my stuff?"

"Of course," Liam replied, his tone casual. "You'll be moving in with me now."

"Excuse me?" I snapped, feeling my anger flare. "Where was I when you made that decision?"

"It's normal for the Alpha's mate to move in with him," Liam argued, his own frustration evident. "And I have no plans of letting you leave my sight without full security detail."

"Wow," I scoffed, crossing my arms over my chest. "Nothing like a little control-freakery to kick off the morning after our great night together."

"Erica, don't make this more difficult than it has to be," Liam growled, clearly not appreciating my sarcasm. "This is for your safety and the sake of the pack."

"Right, because nothing says 'I love you' like stripping away my autonomy and freedom," I retorted, my heart pounding with a mixture of anger and fear.

"Damn it, Erica!" Liam shouted, his patience wearing thin. "Why are you being so stubborn about this? This is how things work in our world!"

"Your world, Liam!" I shot back. "Not mine! Just because you're suddenly a part of my life doesn't mean I'm ready to give up everything I've known!" He stared at me, his eyes filled with a mix of frustration and hurt. I knew he was trying to do what he thought was best for both of us, but the idea of losing my freedom, my independence, terrified me.

"Fine," Liam finally said through gritted teeth. "We can discuss this further after breakfast. But you're still coming with me."

"Whatever, I'm going for a shower," I announced, my voice trembling with barely contained anger. Liam growled low in his throat, a primal sound that sent shivers down my spine.

"You're to listen to me, Erica. Do you understand?" I didn't respond, continuing my march towards the bathroom. The weight of his stare bore into my back like a branding iron.

"Erica!" he growled again, demanding an answer. I halted, taking a deep breath as I turned to face him.

"I understand," I gritted out, my heart pounding in my chest.

"Good girl," he replied condescendingly, riling me up even more. Opening the bathroom door, I shot him one last defiant look.

"But I don't agree," I spat before slamming the door shut. The lock clicked into place just as I heard Liam's weight crash against the other side. The sound of his frustration only fuelled my own, and I leaned against the closed door, struggling to catch my breath. I knew that Liam was just doing what he thought was best, for me, for the pack, but it felt suffocating, like a cage closing around me.

As I stepped into the shower, the hot water cascaded over my body, washing away the lingering touches from last night. But it couldn't wash away the feelings of anger and claustrophobia that had taken root in my chest. My thoughts raced, trying to find a way to reconcile the life I'd known with the world Liam wanted to pull me into. Was there any room for compromise? Or would I have to sacrifice my hard-earned independence for the sake of love and pack loyalty? With each passing moment, as the water continued to pour down, I felt the pressure mounting. The contrast between the intimacy we had shared then and the anger that simmered between us now left me feeling raw and exposed. After rinsing the soap off, I reluctantly turned off the water and stepped out of the shower. The cold air hit me like a slap across the face. I wrapped a towel around myself and rummaged through the bag Kaitlyn had brought, pulling out clean clothes. As I dressed, I caught sight of my reflection in the mirror, my green eyes blazing with defiance and my light red hair damp and tousled.

"Let's see him try to control this," I murmured, a sarcastic smile tugging at the corners of my mouth.

With one last deep breath to steady my nerves, I unlocked the bathroom door and stepped back into the bedroom. Liam sat on the edge of the bed, his sculpted body still naked, his brown eyes fixed on me with an intensity that sent a shiver down my spine.

"Enjoying the show?" I asked, trying to keep my voice light and casual, even as his gaze made my heart race.

"Erica," he growled, his voice low and dangerous. I ignored him, walking around the bed to gather my discarded clothes from the previous night and stuff them into the bag.

"Is there anything you want to say to me?" I asked, my tone dripping with sarcasm as I continued to pack. "Or are you just going to sit there and glare?"

"Erica," he repeated, his voice strained. The silence that stretched between us was thick with tension, a palpable reminder of the struggle for control that had left us both battered and bruised. Liam's low, dangerous voice broke the tense silence.

"I'm ready for you to stop acting like a brat, Erica." My blood boiled at his words, and I turned on him, my green eyes blazing with fury.

"And I'm ready for you to stop acting like an Alpha dick," I spat out, my hands clenched into fists.

"Damn it, Erica," Liam growled, his brown eyes flashing with anger. "I'm just trying to keep you safe."

"No," I shot back, my voice shaking with barely contained rage. "You're trying to control me." I turned towards the door, my heart pounding in my chest. Liam's voice echoed after me, desperate and confused.

"Where do you think you're going?"

"Home," I replied curtly, stalking out of his room without looking back. The corridor outside Liam's bedroom was empty except for his mother, who stood there with a smile on her face. But when she caught sight of my stormy expression, her smile dropped, replaced by concern.

"Oh dear," she murmured, watching me closely as I approached.

"I am sorry, Luna," I said, pausing briefly in front of her. "But I am unable to come to breakfast." Her eyes flicked to Liam's bedroom door just as he emerged, now fully clothed and visibly frustrated. I rolled my eyes and stepped past Luna, making my way down the stairs as quickly as I could. Behind me, I heard Liam call out my name again, his voice strained with emotion.

"Let her cool down, son," his mother advised, her calm tone carrying just far enough for me to hear before I distanced myself from them.

The wind tousled my hair as I rushed across the park to my apartment block, each step fuelled by a potent mix of anger and indignation. I could feel Liam's presence receding behind me like a fading echo, but the memory of our heated confrontation still burned hot in my veins. As I made my way to the apartment, I silently thanked the universe that both Gen and Frankie were away visiting their families this Sunday morning, it was a small mercy that the place would be empty. I stormed into my apartment, slamming the door shut with a satisfying bang, the sound resonating loudly throughout the otherwise quiet space. But before I had a chance to relish the solitude, I walked straight into someone. My breath caught as I looked up to see Grant standing there, his eyes wild and intense, as if he'd been waiting for me all night.

Chapter 44

Erica

When I walked into my apartment, the last person I expected to find was Grant. His eyes were wild and searching as though he'd been hunted for days. As soon as he saw me, a mixture of relief and excitement washed over his face.

"Erica!" he exclaimed, rushing towards me like an eager puppy. "I'm so glad you're safe."

"Stay back," I warned, holding up a hand. My heart raced in my chest.

"Erica," Grant breathed, appearing shocked that I didn't trust him. "What's wrong? Why are you acting so strangely?"

"Me?" I scoffed, shaking my head in disbelief. "You're the one who's acting strangely, Grant. Where the hell have you been?" I remembered Damon telling me that Grant had gone on a mission but disappeared after going psycho on one of the kidnappers they'd pursued.

Grant's lips curled into a smile, as if he held some secret knowledge. "I've had some major revelations, Erica. Things make sense now, our connection, everything."

"Revelations?" I questioned, my brows furrowing. The anger inside me simmered, tired of being at the mercy of others' decisions. My green eyes bore into his blue ones, demanding answers.

"Yes," he said, his voice filled with conviction. "But we can discuss it more later. Right now, I just need you to trust me."

"Trust you?" I laughed bitterly, crossing my arms over my chest. "You vanish without a word and then show up in my apartment unannounced, and you expect me to trust you? You've got to be kidding me, Grant."

"Please, Erica," he pleaded, desperation etched on his face. "I know I don't deserve your trust right now, but if you just give me a chance, I promise everything will make sense."

"Make sense?" I muttered under my breath, my thoughts racing. What could he possibly know that would explain our connection and his sudden disappearance?

"Grant, why are you even here?" I asked, trying to keep my voice steady. "I thought you were gone for good. Damon told me that you had disappeared."

"I wasn't planning on coming back so soon," he admitted, running his fingers through his dirty blond hair. "But I heard about you publicly claiming Liam last night. I had to come."

"Is that what this is all about?" I scoffed, crossing my arms over my chest. "You're just jealous of Liam?" Grant laughed bitterly, the sound echoing through my apartment.

"Jealous? Erica, I have nothing to be jealous of when it comes to Liam. He's caused enough trouble already."

"Trouble?" I repeated, my brows knitting together in confusion. "What do you mean?"

"Erica, please," Grant begged, his eyes pleading with me. "Publicly unclaim Liam. You don't know what you've got yourself into."

"Grant, you're not making any sense," I snapped, my patience wearing thin.

He paced my apartment like a caged animal, the muscles in his arms flexing with each step. "There's so much at stake, and they're watching us. The things I've discovered... Erica, you need to trust me." As he rambled on, I tried to make sense of his words, but they seemed to slip through my fingers like sand. What secrets could he possibly hold that would put me in danger? Why was he so insistent on getting me away from Liam?

"Who are 'they', Grant?!" I demanded, my voice cracking under the weight of my frustration.

"Erica..." he hesitated, looking at me with a mix of anguish and desperation. "I can't tell you everything right now. But you have to believe me when I say that your life is in danger."

"From who?" I asked, my heart pounding in my chest. "Liam?"

"No," he whispered, shaking his head. "Not Liam. But claiming him has put you in their crosshairs."

"What Crosshairs," I asked, "Grant, what are you talking about?"

The flicker of excitement in Grant's eyes was unsettling, like a storm brewing on the horizon.

"Erica," he said, his voice barely containing the urgency he felt. "I know you said no, but if you leave with me right now, I can keep you safe. It's what I've always been meant to do."

"Safe?" I scoffed, my heart racing at the intensity in his gaze. "What are you talking about? You're not making sense."

"Look," he said, swallowing hard. "I'll explain everything once we're out of here. But trust me when I say that staying here with Liam isn't safe anymore."

"Are you talking about your pack?" I asked, trying to piece together his cryptic words.

"No, that place isn't safe either," he replied, shaking his head. "We need to go somewhere they won't find us."

Before I could respond, Grant darted into my bedroom and grabbed one of my bags from the closet. He began frantically shoving clothes inside, his movements growing more erratic by the second.

"I know where we can lie low," he continued, his voice almost breathless. "And I know how to get you out of this territory without being noticed."

"Grant, stop!" I shouted, my chest tightening with anxiety and confusion. "I can't just leave with you. I love Liam, and despite everything, I don't want to leave him behind."

"Erica, please!" Grant's voice was frantic, his agitation growing as he grabbed my wrist, yanking me out of the bedroom and into the main living area. "I'm trying to protect you!"

"Grant, you're hurting me," I choked out, wincing as his grip tightened. But it seemed as if he wasn't even listening.

"Taking you away from here is the only way I can keep you safe," he insisted, repeating his plea over and over like a broken record. I could sense the desperation behind his words, but it only served to fuel my anger and confusion.

"Let go of me!" I demanded, tears streaming down my cheeks. But before he could comply, the door to the apartment burst open with a bang that echoed through the room like a gunshot.

Liam stood in the doorway, his face contorted with rage as his eyes locked onto Grant's hand clamped around my wrist. Time seemed to slow as his gaze flicked between us, taking in the scene.

"Get your hands off her," Liam snarled, fury pouring off him in waves.

"Stay out of this, Anderson," Grant spat back, not releasing his grip on me.

"Stay out of it?" Liam roared, and in an instant, he was barrelling toward us, slamming into Grant with enough force to knock both men flying and wrenching me free from his grasp.

As they crashed to the floor, I stumbled backward, gripping my throbbing wrist. My heart pounded in my chest, my breath coming in ragged gasps. How had everything spiralled so far out of control?

"Enough!" I screamed, my voice filled with desperation. "Just stop it, both of you!" But they didn't seem to hear me, their bodies tangled together as they grappled, fists flying and snarls filling the air. I stood there, helpless and trapped in my own home, the weight of their violence pressing down on me like a vice. The sound of shattering glass filled the apartment as Liam and Grant continued their ferocious battle. They were like two wild animals, snarling and clawing at each other with a primal fury that sent chills down my spine. My heart raced in my chest, and I could feel the adrenaline coursing through my veins as I watched them tear apart the place I called home.

"Enough!" I shouted again, clenching my fists in frustration. This time, however, something was different. The word seemed to carry an electric charge, a force that resonated through the room and slammed into both of them like a tidal wave.

"STOP!" I commanded, my voice laced with power I had never felt before. And just like that, they froze, their bodies suddenly rigid and immobile.

Liam looked over at me, his eyes wide with surprise and something else, pride. Grant stared at me too, but his gaze held only awe and confusion.

I exhaled slowly, feeling the energy drain from my body as though I had been holding my breath for hours.

"Grant," I said, my voice shaking slightly, "I think you should go."

"Erica, I'm not leaving without you," he replied, his voice firm and resolute. His blue eyes bore into mine, pleading for understanding. Liam's growl reverberated through the room like a warning siren, making me shiver despite myself.

"This is the last straw, Grant," he snarled, his eyes flashing dangerously. The door to my apartment swung open once more, and two burly guards entered, their expressions grim and resolute.

"Wh-what's going on?" I stammered, fear knotting my stomach as I glanced between Liam, Grant, and the guards. My heart pounded in my chest like a prisoner desperate for escape.

"Grant has not only gone AWOL on a mission," Liam began, his voice cold and authoritative, "but he has also now attempted to kidnap you, the future Luna of our pack." His eyes bored into mine, heavy with unspoken accusations. "These acts are an attempt at weakening the pack, Erica. They're punishable by death."

My breath caught in my throat, the words striking me like a physical blow. I could see my guilt and devastation reflected in Liam's eyes, and it hurt me to know he didn't want to cause me pain. But I couldn't shake the feeling that I was somehow responsible for this disaster.

"However," Liam continued, turning back to Grant with a steely glare, "since your service has been exemplary up until recently, I'm willing to show some leniency. Instead of death, you'll be exiled from the pack. Should you ever set foot in our territory again -" He paused, the threat hanging in the air like a guillotine blade poised to fall. "- it will be an instant death sentence."

Tears pricked my eyes, hot and bitter, as I stared at Grant. His face was a storm of emotions: anger, confusion, and worst of all, betrayal. I couldn't help but feel that this was all my fault, that I had somehow failed him. But the weight of Liam's gaze and the expectations of our pack held me in place, tethering me to a decision I wasn't sure I could live with.

Grant's eyes bore into mine, desperation and determination battling for dominance.

"Erica, Liam is keeping things from you, and you can't trust him," he said urgently. My heart raced as I tried to process his words, but the raw intensity of his gaze made it difficult to think clearly.

"Grant, stop," I whispered, my voice shaking with fear and confusion. But he refused to back down. Instead, he took a step closer, his hands clenched into fists at his sides.

"Erica, he'll get you killed," Grant insisted. "Come with me. I can protect you, like I was born to do." His voice cracked, the weight of his emotions threatening to shatter his composure. A growl erupted from Liam, and he pulled me in closer, wrapping a protective arm around me. I could feel the anger radiating off him, and for a moment, I thought he would strike Grant without warning. Instead, he raised his head and spoke in a booming voice that echoed through the room.

"I, Alpha Liam Anderson of the Silver Stone pack, banish you, Christian Grant. Never return or the punishment will be death."

"Christian?" The name slammed into me like a tidal wave, knocking the breath from my lungs. As the bond between Grant and the pack shattered, a scent I hadn't experienced in nearly twenty years permeated the air, the scent of loss, of home, and of a life long since buried beneath the weight of time and grief.

The realisation hit me like a bolt of lightning, electrifying my entire being. Suddenly, everything clicked into place, the pieces of the puzzle fitting together with terrifying clarity. How could I have been so blind? How could I have not recognised him? How could I have not realised why I had felt so comfortable around him? But it couldn't be possible. He was dead. I had recurring nightmares about his death my whole life.

Christian.

Grant.

I knew him as Christian Grant Hughes. Alpha heir of the Moon Key pack.

Chapter 45

Liam

I stood there, watching with grim determination as the two guards gripped Grant's arms tightly, beginning to drag him away. The air was thick with tension and unspoken words. I had never really liked Grant, he always seemed standoffish, distant. But until Erica joined the pack, he had been an outstanding warrior, loyal and dedicated. Now, though, he had crossed the line. He tried to persuade Erica to leave with him, betraying the pack and, more importantly, me. I couldn't help but feel a sense of satisfaction in finally being able to block any sort of interaction between him and Erica. Part of me would have preferred to put him to death for his betrayal, but for some reason Erica had become attached to him and I couldn't bear to upset her in such a way.

"Wait," Erica suddenly cried out, her voice shaking with panic. "Please, Liam, don't exile him!" Her eyes were wide and pleading as she turned to face me.

"I'll do anything if you let me explain first," she continued desperately, her green eyes filling with tears. "I'll even move in with you." The words hung heavy in the air between us, and I couldn't help but feel a flutter of confusion mixed with hope. After our argument this morning, I hadn't expected her to make such an offer. Something serious must be happening.

"Tell them who I am!" Grant's voice rang out, his screams echoing throughout the room as he struggled against the guards. Over and over again, he repeated those five words, each time more desperate than the last.

"Alright," I finally conceded, my own voice strained as I fought to keep my emotions at bay. "Take him to the Pack Cells until I decide otherwise." As soon as the words left my lips, Erica rushed towards me, her arms wrapping tightly around my waist as she sobbed into my chest. I held her close, doing my best to calm her trembling form despite the torrent of questions and worries that plagued my thoughts. "Thank you," she whispered between sobs, her grip on me never wavering. "Thank you, Liam."

"Liam," my father approached us as we entered the pack house, his brow furrowed in concern. "I felt the bond break, but I can still feel him. Why is he still on our territory?" I didn't even have a chance to get any words out before Erica stepped forward with a determined look.

"Alpha," she began, hesitating briefly before continuing. "It was me. I asked Liam to hold off on the exile. I need to be sure about something first and I need Marshall and Becca here to do it."

"Marshall and Becca?" My father looked puzzled but nodded. "Very well, I'll call them immediately." As he moved away to make the call, I couldn't help but feel a mixture of protectiveness and worry wash over me. What did they have to do with this situation?

The sun dipped low in the sky, casting long shadows across the pack house grounds. It had been a long stressful day. Erica had barely spoken and seemed to be lost in thought the whole time. We tried filling time with helping Erica pack up some of her belongings at the apartment. And I helped the girls to clean up the mess that my fight with Grant had caused. Gen had tried to talk to Erica, but all Erica would say was that she needed to be sure. I didn't like whatever it was that was causing her to act like this. It was like she was in some sort of shock. Erica and I returned to the pack house, her belongings in tow. Her eyes were rimmed with red, evidence of the tears she had shed earlier, but her jaw was set in determination. It was clear that whatever was going on; it mattered deeply to her.

The fire crackled softly in the corner of the Alpha living room, casting flickering shadows on the walls. But the warmth it provided did little to ease the heavy tension that hung in the air. Erica's lithe form paced back and forth like a caged animal, her light red hair swaying with each frantic step. Her green eyes darted between the windows and the door, as if willing Marshall and Becca to appear. I could feel her frustration and anxiety churning through our bond, a palpable storm of emotions that left me feeling helpless.

"Come on, sit down for a moment," I urged her, reaching out to touch her arm. But she shrugged me off, resuming her restless pacing.

"Any word yet?" she asked again, her voice tight and strained. "Are they here?" I shook my head, unable to hide a grimace as I watched her wear herself down with worry. My mother had made several attempts to offer Erica food, but every plate remained untouched, a collection of abandoned sustenance on the coffee table.

"Erica, please," I pleaded, standing up to block her path. "You need to rest."

"Rest?" she scoffed, her eyes flashing with anger. "How can I rest when everything is so uncertain? I need to know Liam. I need to know that I am not going crazy."

"Whatever happens, I will protect you," I promised, my voice firm and unwavering. "No one is going to hurt you while I'm here." For a moment, something flickered in her eyes – a glimmer of gratitude, perhaps, or a hint of trust.

The distant rumble of a car engine caught my attention, pulling me from my thoughts. Peering out the window, I saw headlights approaching through the thickening twilight. Relief washed over me as Marshall and Becca's vehicle came to a stop outside the pack house.

"Erica," I called softly, "they're here." She whirled around, her eyes wide and hopeful. The moment the door to the Alpha apartments opened, Erica dashed out of the living room, her desperate need for answers driving her forward like a relentless force. I followed closely behind, concerned for her well-being never far from my mind. As Marshall and Becca stepped inside, their expressions shifted from worry to shock at the sight of Erica's dishevelled appearance.

My father cleared his throat, drawing their attention.

"Thank you for coming so quickly," he said, his voice tinged with both gratitude and unease. "We've had some...troubling developments with one of our warriors, Grant Davis. He tried to convince Erica to leave with him. We suspect he may have been affected by Erica's Alpha power somehow, but we can't be certain." Marshall frowned, clearly disturbed by the news, while Becca glanced over at Erica. Before they could respond, Erica threw herself into their arms, embracing them tightly.

"I need your help," she choked out, tears streaming down her face. "I can't explain it; you just have to see for yourself. Please." Their concern deepened as they exchanged glances, silently agreeing to support her no matter the circumstances. With a nod, I led the group back to the Alpha living room, watching as Erica clung to Marshall and Becca as if they were her lifeline.

"Can we go see him now?" she implored, turning her tear-streaked face toward me. Her desperation was palpable, a tangible weight in the room. I hesitated for a moment, feeling torn between my instincts to protect her and the need to uncover the truth. I glanced at my father and he nodded to say that it was my decision.

"Alright," I finally consented, my heart heavy with apprehension. "Let's go."

As we made our way toward the cells, I couldn't shake the nagging sense of unease that settled over me like a shroud. Whatever secrets lay hidden within Grant's actions, they threatened to change everything. The doors to the cells slid open, and we stepped into the brightly lit corridor, the air thick with tension. My father, Erica, Marshall, Becca, and I made our way toward where Damon, Gregg, and Gideon stood waiting. Their expressions were a mixture of concern and confusion, and I could tell they were eager for answers.

"Alpha," Gregg greeted my father with a nod before turning to me. "What's going on, Liam? Why is Grant back? And why is he in a cell?" I explained briefly about Grant's actions and his subsequent return to pack territory, trying to keep my voice steady despite the turmoil raging inside me. Gregg's eyes widened in shock as he processed the information.

"Grant disappeared mid-mission," he confirmed what I already knew, disbelief evident in his voice. "We had no idea where he went."

As we spoke, I noticed Erica fidgeting; her gaze constantly drawn toward the cells. Her anxiety was palpable, and it only served to heighten my own. Erica turned to me with a determined look.

"I think that Marshall, Becca and I should see him alone first," she said, her eyes pleading.

"Absolutely not!" I said.

"Fuck that," from Damon.

"Not a chance," from Gregg.

"I think not," from my dad, all of us at the same time. Erica looked at the four of us and smiled, the hint of amusement playing on her face.

"Thank you, all of you," she said. "I appreciate your protection." She hugged into me before sighing.

"Ok then," she sobered with a worried look on her face. "We all go," she clasped my hand as Gregg led us into the cell area.

Gregg keyed in the code that opened the door to the inner hallway, where all the cells were. Marshall, who had been quiet until now, suddenly stopped in his tracks and sniffed the air. His eyes widened, and he looked at Becca in confusion.

"What?" she asked, confused at his reaction.

"No," he said, "it can't be?" His eyes tearing up, and he looked at me and then at Erica. I looked at her and she was crying again.

"Marshall," she said, "I don't understand it, but it is, isn't it?" Marshall pushed past Gregg towards the cell and stopped and stared.

"Marshall?" Becca ran to him and he whispered something to her. She looked in the cell. A strangled cry came out of her mouth as she stared. Then I heard Grant speak from the cell.

"Hi Marshall," and then there was a pause. "Hi mum." My eyes widened as Becca broke down in tears and Marshall rushed to catch her. My heart skipped a beat, realisation crashing down like a tidal wave. All the pieces of the puzzle fell into place, yet the picture they formed seemed too surreal to comprehend. This was what Erica had been so desperate to confirm. This was the secret she had been carrying around all day. No wonder why she was so distracted.

"Erica!" I called out, but it was too late. She was already running towards the cell, tears streaming down her face. Her arms reached through the bars, wrapping tightly around Grant as if she feared he would disappear again.

"I didn't want to believe it until I knew for sure," she choked out, her voice strained by emotion.

"It's okay, beautiful," Grant said, smelling her hair. He looked up at me as I glared at him.

"I'm here, I got you," he smirked at me over her shoulder. "I'm never letting you go again, I promise."

Chapter 46

Liam

The bars of the cell were cold and unforgiving, but Erica's embrace was warm as she hugged Grant through them. Their whispers drifted to my ears despite their attempts at discretion.

"Erica, I can't believe it's you," breathed Grant, his voice thick with emotion.

"Grant... I never thought I'd see you again," Erica replied, her green eyes shimmering with unshed tears. Feeling a knot of anger and jealousy twist in my gut, I called out to her.

"Erica." She turned to face me, offering a tear-stained smile that pierced my heart. My father and Gregg looked just as confused as I felt. The air hung heavy with questions and uncertainty, but one thing was clear - our lives had just become a lot more complicated.

"Hey, Liam," she said softly, stepping towards me. I opened my arms, pulling her in for a tight hug. In that moment, I wanted nothing more than to shield her from the pain and confusion that surrounded us. I could feel her body trembling gently, her warmth seeping into me as we held each other. As I glanced over her shoulder, my eyes met Grant's. His smirk taunted me, darkening the cloud of suspicion that already hovered in my mind. I tightened my grip on Erica, vowing inwardly to protect her from whatever secrets Grant might be hiding. This reunion was far from a happy coincidence; something darker lay beneath the surface, and I would do everything in my power to uncover it before it affected my family or my pack.

My father cleared his throat, drawing our attention to him.

"Erica, we need some answers. What's going on here?" Before she could speak, Marshall interjected. "Alpha, you've met Grant before. You would have known him as Christian Hughes. He's Becca and Trenton's first son."

"The Alpha heir of the Moon Key pack." Erica said, her gaze shifting over to Grant. The room was thick with disbelief as everyone tried to process this revelation. Shock rippled through me, and I could see a similar reaction in my father and Gregg's expressions. Damon, however, looked suspicious.

"That's impossible," he said, eyeing Grant warily. "Erica told us that Christian was dead. She said she saw him die." Erica nodded, her voice barely above a whisper.

"I did... I thought he was dead. It happened when I was just a child. That awful day has haunted my nightmares ever since." Her eyes were distant, reliving the horror of her past. Despite the emotional turmoil, I kept my face stoic, my eyes never leaving Grant. There was something about his reappearance that gnawed at me, and I couldn't shake the feeling that there was more to this story than met the eye.

"Is it really you, Christian?" Becca asked, her voice choked with emotion. The weight of the revelation seemed to press down on her, threatening to break her spirit. Grant nodded, his eyes shimmering with unshed tears.

"Yes, mum, it's me. I'm here now, and I want to make things right." His words did little to ease my suspicions. Deep down, I knew that I had to find the truth before it threatened the safety of those I held dear. And while I couldn't deny the connection between Erica and Grant, I couldn't help but worry about the impact his return would have on her. My fingers curled into fists at my sides, the anger and disbelief simmering just below the surface. Grant's revelation left everyone grasping for answers, and I couldn't shake the feeling that something wasn't right.

"Where have you been for almost twenty years?" Marshall asked and Grant looked over at him.

"Until recently, I had very little memory before joining Silver Stone," Grant spoke up, his voice laced with vulnerability. "But on the recent mission... it all came flooding back." I studied him, noting the strained expression on his face as he turned to Erica.

"I was chasing after a werewolf who had kidnapped a pup, and suddenly, images of trying to protect you in the stone circle filled my mind." My heart clenched at the raw emotion in Grant's eyes. A part of me wanted to believe him, but the overwhelming need to protect Erica and my family urged caution. Gregg chimed in, his tone thoughtful.

"A similar situation triggering repressed memories makes sense." He paused, his gaze shifting between Grant and me. "Grant went berserk on the kidnapper, nearly beating him to death."

"Then I disappeared," Grant admitted, his eyes downcast. "My memories were flooding back, and I didn't know what to do with them. I know I shouldn't have left, but I wasn't thinking straight." As much as I wanted to dismiss his words, there was a ring of truth to them. Memories could be powerful, even destructive, I knew that all too well from my own experiences.

But there was still something gnawing at me, a nagging doubt that refused to settle.

"Grant," I began, my voice tight with emotion. "It's a lot to take in, and I need to know that my family and pack are safe. You have to understand that we can't just accept your explanation without question." He held my gaze, and for a moment, I saw a flicker of understanding in his eyes.

"I know it's hard to believe, I am still trying to wrap my own head around it. But I'm telling you the truth. All I've ever wanted was to protect Erica and make up for what happened in the past." As I stared into Grant's eyes, searching for any hint of deception, I knew that the answers we sought would not come easily. I eyed Grant warily, my heart pounding in my chest as I struggled to make sense of his revelations. Around me, the room seemed to hum with tension and unspoken questions. I needed to know more, to understand how someone I had considered a loyal pack member could have such a hidden past.

"Where were you all this time?" I asked, my voice steady despite the tumultuous storm of emotions coursing through me. "What do you remember now, Grant?" Grant's gaze flickered to Erica and Becca before settling on me with a haunted expression.

"After being thrown against that wall," he said quietly, "I woke up cuffed in silver chains in a dark, damp place that reeked of blood and... other things." He trailed off, shuddering at the memory. Erica and Becca gasped in unison, their eyes wide with horror. My own heart clenched in sympathy, but I couldn't shake my suspicions. I needed to hear everything.

"It was complete hell," Grant continued, his voice strained. "For over a year, I was beaten, tortured, and subjected to things I can't even bring myself to say out loud."

"Grant..." Erica whispered, reaching for him through the bars, her touch gentle and comforting. He looked back at us, his eyes filled with pain.

"At some point, I woke up in a bed, no longer chained. A woman was caring for me, she told me her Alpha had brought me there to be nursed back to health. There were some tattered remains of clothes with the name Grant on them, so that became my new identity."

"Was this another pack?" my father asked.

"About fifteen years ago," Grant confirmed, nodding. "But then we were attacked about six years ago, and I managed to escape with a few others. It wasn't long before I crossed paths with Alpha Declan." I clenched my fists, trying to make sense of it all. My father cleared his throat, drawing my attention back to the present.

"Five years ago, Grant saved me from a rogue attack when I was returning from visiting my brother," he recounted, his voice steady but serious. "He fought bravely and without hesitation. It was then that I offered him a place in Silver Stone."

I glanced at Damon, whose expression mirrored the unease gnawing within me. Despite the confirmation of Grant's loyalty, I couldn't shake the feeling that something was amiss.

"Perhaps we should call it a night," I suggested, my eyes flicking between Erica and my father. "Erica's had a long day, and it might be best for everyone to get some rest." I held my father's gaze, willing him to understand that I wanted to give Erica some space from Grant, a chance to clear her head and regain her bearings.

"Agreed," my father nodded, catching my unspoken message. "I've arranged guest rooms for Becca and Marshall. We can continue this discussion tomorrow."

"Wait," Grant interjected, glaring at me with undisguised animosity. "I need to be out there, protecting Erica. I won't let anything happen to her."

"Erica's safe with me," I assured him firmly, trying to keep my tone level despite the anger simmering beneath the surface.

"Safe?" Grant scoffed, his blue eyes flashing with disdain. "You think you can protect her? With everything that you know. The last thing I want is for her to end up like..." His voice trailed off, and he shot me a pointed look that sent a cold shiver down my spine. Jessica. He was talking about Jessica, the girl I had failed to save before Grant had even joined our pack. My jaw tightened, and my hands clenched into fists at my sides.

"Erica's safety is my number one concern," I bit out through gritted teeth. "I promise you that."

In the hallway of the cells, a sombre atmosphere fell over the group as Erica, Marshall, and Becca exchanged tearful goodbyes with Grant. I watched from a distance, my chest tightening at the sight of Erica's raw vulnerability.

"Take care of yourself, Grant," she whispered, her voice cracking with emotion. "I can't lose you again."

"Neither can I, Erica," he replied, his eyes never leaving hers. "But I'll find a way to make this right, I promise." As the farewells lingered on, I couldn't help but wonder what hidden truths still lurked beneath the surface. Finally, Erica returned to my side, her green eyes glistening with unshed tears.

"Come on," I murmured softly, wrapping an arm around her shoulders as I guided her back toward our room at the pack house. Her body was heavy with exhaustion, and every step seemed to sap more energy from her already weary frame.

"Everything's just so... messed up," she mumbled into my chest as I helped her into bed, her words slurring together in a sleep-induced haze. I brushed a strand of her light red hair away from her face and pressed a tender kiss to her forehead. As she succumbed to the embrace of sleep, her breathing became slow and even, a testament to the trust she placed in me.

With Erica safely asleep, I stepped out of the room, my footsteps echoing softly down the hall as I made my way to the Alpha living room. My father, Gregg, and Damon were already there, each nursing a drink as they contemplated the evening's revelations.

"Are Becca and Marshall settled in?" I asked, my gaze fixed on my father. He nodded, extending a glass toward me.

"They're resting now. It has been a long day for everyone." Taking the offered drink, I took a sip before Damon suddenly blurted out,

"I don't like this, Liam. I don't trust Grant."

"Neither do I," I admitted, swirling the amber liquid in my glass. "Dad, I want to investigate Grant's story further. Something just doesn't add up." Declan met my gaze with understanding.

"You're right, Liam. We need to get to the bottom of this."

"Also," I continued, feeling a wave of protective concern wash over me, "I think it's best if we keep Erica away from Grant for now. There are too many inconsistencies and unanswered questions." Damon frowned, his eyes narrowing in thought.

"Like how he knew about Jessica. What's that all about?"

"Exactly," I replied, taking another sip of my drink as I contemplated the ever-growing web of uncertainty that surrounded us.

"Agreed," my father said, his jaw set with determination. "We'll ask more questions and make sure Grant doesn't spend time alone with Erica until we get some answers."

"Thank you," I replied, feeling a small sense of relief at my father's support. The weight on my shoulders lessened just a bit, but the worry for Erica still gnawed at me.

"Get some rest, son," Declan urged, placing a hand on my shoulder and giving it a reassuring squeeze. "We'll figure this out together."

"Thanks, Dad," I said, finishing my drink and setting the empty glass down on the table.

As I made my way back to our room, the soft light from the hallway cast elongated shadows on the walls, their eerie shapes mirroring the dark unknown that surrounded us. My mind raced with possibilities and potential dangers, each more chilling than the last. Pushing open the door, I was greeted by the sight of Erica, her chest rising and falling in the rhythm of peaceful slumber. I crossed the room, taking off my shoes and shirt before sliding into bed beside her. As I lay there, I couldn't help but watch her sleep, marvelling at the serenity that graced her features. It was a stark contrast to the turmoil that had enveloped us earlier in the evening.

Erica shifted slightly, unconsciously moving closer to me, seeking warmth and comfort even in her unconscious state. I wrapped an arm around her, pulling her close as if I could shield her from any harm that might come her way. I knew all too well how fragile life could be, and I was determined to protect her and the pack from whatever danger lurked in the shadows. With every beat of my heart, I whispered silent promises to her. Promises to keep her safe, to fight for our love, and to never let go.

Chapter 47

Erica

The last week had been crazy busy. My body ached from the relentless warrior training sessions Jacob had been putting me through lately. Four times this week alone, and that didn't even include the sudden increase in my workload at the office.

"Damn it, Liam," I whispered under my breath. I knew he was behind all of this. He was trying to keep me so busy that I wouldn't have time to visit Christian, who was still locked away in the cells after revealing his true identity. I had managed to see him twice, despite Liam's efforts. Both times our conversations ended in arguments, with Christian insisting that I was in danger but refusing to explain why. He just told me to ask Liam about it. As much as I wanted to believe Christian was wrong, I couldn't shake the feeling that there was something he wasn't telling me. But confronting Liam... I wasn't sure if I was ready for that.

Sweat dripped down my forehead as I focused on my opponent. Jacob's hazel eyes gleamed with determination as he circled me, waiting for the perfect moment to strike. We had been sparring for what felt like hours, and my sore muscles were screaming for a break.

"Come on, Erica," Jacob taunted, smirking. "You're getting slower by the second."

"Shut up," I huffed, trying to ignore the throbbing in my legs. "I'm just giving you a chance to feel good about yourself."

"Ha! Like I need your help with that." He lunged at me, his movements swift and precise. I barely managed to dodge, feeling the brush of air as his fist sailed past my face.

"Close one," I grumbled, gritting my teeth. But even in the midst of our intense training session, I couldn't help but appreciate the friendship we had built. It was a welcome distraction from the turmoil that had consumed my life recently.

"Alright, I think we can call it a night," Jacob finally announced, stepping back and wiping sweat from his brow. "I'd hate for Jenna to kick my ass for being late to dinner again."

"Can't have that happening," I agreed, panting slightly. "So, same time tomorrow?"

"Sure thing," he nodded, grabbing his towel from a nearby bench. "But don't expect me to go easy on you just because you're tired. I'll be expecting nothing less than your best, Luna."

"Wouldn't dream of slacking off," I replied, rolling my shoulders to ease the tension. As much as I appreciated Jacob's dedication to helping me improve, I couldn't shake the nagging suspicion that Liam was using these training sessions to keep me from seeing Christian. The thought made me clench my fists, worry gnawing at my insides.

"Before I forget," Jacob said, pausing at the door. "Liam's on his way to pick you up, right?"

"Yep," I confirmed, absently rubbing my sore shoulder. "So you'd better hurry before Jenna decides to kick both our asses for keeping you late."

"True that," he chuckled, then disappeared through the doorway.

I let out a small sigh and made my way into the changing room. My muscles ached from the intense workout, but it was a good kind of pain, an ache that reminded me I was growing stronger. I thought about all the times I'd spent at Jacob and Jenna's place for dinner, feeling grateful for their company. Liam had increased my security detail recently, so Jacob was almost always around. As I began grabbing my things, I heard the door creak open. Turning with a smile, expecting to see Liam's ruggedly handsome face, I found myself met with empty space. No one was there. I frowned slightly, shrugging off the odd moment, and continued gathering my belongings.

"Must've been the wind," I whispered under my breath, despite the fact that we were indoors and there shouldn't have been any drafts. But the alternative, someone lurking in the shadows, watching me - sent a shiver down my spine that I couldn't quite shake.

"Get a grip, Erica," I muttered, chastising myself for letting my imagination run wild. I couldn't afford to be paranoid, not with everything else going on. And besides, Liam would be here soon, and he always knew how to make me feel safe.

I zipped up my gym bag, my thoughts drifting back to Christian and the cryptic warnings he'd given me during our last encounter. He seemed so certain that I was in danger, but he wouldn't tell me why. The frustration of not knowing gnawed at me, fuelling the ever-present worry for my family and friends.

As I went to pick up my bag, a whirlwind of pain exploded through my body as I was suddenly slammed face-first into the cold metal lockers. Shock and agony coursed through me, the impact sending stars bursting across my vision.

"Time to finish what I started," came a menacing voice in my ear, hot breath tickling my neck. My heart froze, and I realised who it was, Louis. Heidi's brother was here, and I was all alone.

"What the fuck," I choked out, the sour taste of fear flooding my mouth. "What do you want?"

"Isn't it obvious?" His cruel laughter rang out like nails on a chalkboard as he pressed his much larger body against mine, trapping me. "You think you're safe with your precious Alpha? You think you can just forget about what happened before because of you? Or that you can talk to my sister like you did?"

"Get off me!" I snarled, desperately trying to break free from his vice-like grip. But it was no use; he was too strong, and the pain in my chest only grew with each futile attempt.

"Ah, Erica," Louis taunted, his voice dripping with malice. "You are a feisty one aren't you. But it won't save you this time."

My mind raced, frantically searching for a way out of this nightmare. Liam was on his way, but would he get here in time? And even then, would he be able to protect me from the monster that had returned to finish what he'd started?

"Please," I whispered, hating the tremble in my voice, but unable to hide the fear that gripped my heart like a vice. "Don't do this." If I kept him distracted for long enough, maybe Liam would get here in time.

"Too late for begging, sweetheart," Louis sneered, tightening his hold on me, crushing my spirit along with my body. Despite my best efforts to wriggle free, I was no match for Louis's strength. His grip on me only tightened, and my heart pounded in terror. My breath came in short, shallow gasps as panic threatened to overwhelm me.

"Listen closely, bitch," Louis hissed in my ear. "You're going to pay for the hell you put me through while I spent those two weeks in silver chains."

"You brought that on yourself, " I snarled. Louis grabbed my hair and yanked my neck back causing an involuntary yelp from me.

"Here's how it'll go," he continued menacingly. "You can be good, maybe even enjoy this... or it can get real bad, real quick." As he spoke, he yanked at my shorts, pulling them down my legs. I could feel his arousal pressed against me, and my stomach churned with revulsion.

"Never fucked a Luna before," he growled. "I'm going to have my fun with you before delivering you to him." Him? Who him?

As Louis fumbled with my shorts, I knew it was now or never. Summoning every ounce of courage and determination, I slammed my head back into his face, feeling his nose break under the force. The metallic scent of blood filled the air, and he cried out in pain, releasing me from his grip.

Seizing the opportunity, I sprinted out of the changing room and into the training area, screaming at the top of my lungs for help. My voice echoed throughout the empty space, and I prayed that someone would hear me in time.

"Help!" I screamed again, the raw desperation in my voice nearly breaking me. "Somebody, please help me!" My heart hammered in my chest as I sprinted towards the exit door of the training room, panic clawing at my throat.

"Please," I whispered, praying that it would open. But when I reached for the handle, it refused to budge. Desperation surged through me as I threw my weight against the door, but it remained stubbornly locked.

"Damn it!" I cursed, feeling tears prick at the corners of my eyes. My mind raced, searching for a way out, an escape from this nightmare.

"Thought you could get away from me, bitch?" Louis's voice was a snarl, filled with rage and pain. He stumbled out of the changing room, blood streaming down his face from his broken nose. "I'll still deliver a dead body, but I'm going to fuck you first!"

"Stay away from me!" I shouted, trying to sound more confident than I felt. As he lunged towards me, I dodged to the side, adrenaline fuelling my movements. He slammed into the door with a vicious snarl, momentarily stunned by the impact. Spotting a chair nearby, I grabbed it and swung it with all my strength at Louis's head. It connected with a sickening crack, and he crumpled to the ground, dazed.

"Go to hell!" I yelled, my voice trembling with emotion. Dropping the chair, I turned and ran back towards the changing room, hoping to find another way out. As I sprinted across the cold floor, my thoughts raced. Who could I trust? Who could I turn to for help? My heart pounded in my chest as I raced back towards the changing room, the echoes of Louis's furious threats still ringing in my ears. The fear and dread that had gripped me moments before now morphed into a desperate determination to escape this nightmare. I hadn't made it far when a guttural snarl pierced the air behind me. My instincts screamed at me to turn around, but in my haste, I twisted my ankle, sending me crashing to the ground.

"Shit!" I hissed through gritted teeth, the pain in my ankle momentarily dulling the terror that threatened to consume me. I struggled to catch my breath, my pulse hammering against my temples. I heard a snarl again and turned in time to see Louis shift into his wolf before he started stalking towards me with fury in his eyes, baring his teeth.

Chapter 48

Erica

The room seemed to shrink as Louis, in his wolf form, stalked slowly towards me. Fear clutched at my chest, making it difficult to breathe. I tried to stand up to get away, but the moment I put weight on my injured ankle, a searing pain shot through it. My legs buckled beneath me, and I collapsed back onto the cold, hard floor. Desperation clawed at my insides as I inched backward, never taking my eyes off the snarling beast. His amber eyes were filled with rage and something darker, more sinister. He bared his teeth at me, saliva dripping down his powerful jaws. My heart pounded so hard in my chest; I was sure he could hear it.

My ankle throbbed with pain, but I forced myself not to cry out. I had to stay strong and focused. The fear that gripped my heart began to morph into determination. I wasn't going to let Louis win. I wouldn't allow him to destroy the family and pack I had come to love. But how could I fight back when I was unable to shift into my wolf form?

"Think, Erica, think," I muttered under my breath, trying to come up with a plan. The snarling beast continued to close in on me, every step sending a shudder of terror down my spine. Time was running out, and I needed to act fast.

My heart pounded in my chest as I glanced down at my ankle, already swollen and discoloured. The pain was almost unbearable, and I knew there was no way I could stand on it, let alone run from the snarling beast that was once Louis.

"Okay, Erica," I thought to myself, trying to calm my racing thoughts. "What are your options?"

Option one: sit here and wait for him to reach me and rip out my throat. Yeah, pass on that. The image of my lifeless body lying on the cold floor sent shivers down my spine. Option two: jump up and run for the door behind me, hoping that it was unlocked, and that my ankle wasn't broken and could take my weight. I gritted my teeth, forcing back tears as I considered the likelihood of outrunning a vicious wolf on a broken ankle. Again, the chances were leaning away from slim and towards none that I would make it in time before he attacked. So that was out. Option three: try to stall until Liam gets here.

"Where the fuck is he, anyway?" I muttered, frustration bubbling up inside me. Anyone know how to distract a rage-filled wolf? Anyone? Nope, me neither. I took a deep breath, trying to steady my nerves. So far, my options all seemed to end with me dead. The thought was sobering, but I couldn't allow fear to consume me. There had to be a way out of this. There just had to be. And with that beast getting closer by the second, I was running out of time to pick which death I wanted. I stared into Louis's wild, bloodthirsty eyes, desperately searching for any sign of humanity, but seeing none. It was in that moment that I heard it, the faint sound of someone trying the locked door. My heart leapt into my throat. Could it be him? It had to be.

"LIAM!" I screamed, praying that he could hear me, that he would burst through the door and save me from this nightmare. But my desperate cry seemed only to spur Louis on, his wolf eyes narrowing as he prepared to lunge.

I didn't have time to think; my instincts kicked in. As Louis launched himself at me with a ferocious snarl, I threw my legs out, making contact with his underside. I tried to use his momentum to propel him over me, but the weight and speed of the beast sent pain shooting up my already injured ankle. I could hear and feel a snap, and I couldn't help but scream out in agony. My vision blurred, and I fought for consciousness, knowing that I needed to stay alert if I had any hope of surviving. I clenched my teeth and blinked away the tears, trying to focus on the sound of the struggle at the door.

The agony in my ankle was a consuming fire, making it nearly impossible to focus on anything else. I tried to blink away the tears that blurred my vision, but all I could see was the twisted shape of my foot, now at an unnatural angle. My heart raced as panic began to set in, and each thud against the locked door only heightened my sense of urgency.

"Please... let it be Liam," I thought desperately, praying for his strength and determination to save me from this nightmare. As if sensing my growing terror, Louis closed in on me, his hot breath tickling the back of my neck like tendrils of fire. He was so close; I knew I had run out of time.

Just when I thought it was over, a sudden crash shattered the oppressive silence. Glass rained down like icy daggers, and a large black shape hurtled through the broken window. In a blur of fur and fangs, Liam's wolf form threw himself at Louis, snarls and growls echoing throughout the room as they collided. He fought viciously to protect me, forcing Louis further away, but the other wolf refused to be deterred. They circled one another, teeth bared and hackles raised, their eyes locked in a deadly dance.

A sudden, sharp tug to my side sent a fresh wave of agony shooting up my leg, and I couldn't help but cry out in pain. Blinking through the tears that clouded my vision, I saw Frankie's familiar face, her eyes filled with concern as she tried to pull me away from the fight.

"Erica, we need to get you out of here," she said urgently, her voice strained as she struggled to drag me across the floor. I nodded through gritted teeth, trying to focus on anything other than the searing pain in my ankle.

My gaze was drawn back to the snarling wolves, their bodies a whirlwind of fur and fangs as they fought for dominance. Panic rose in my chest when I saw Louis's powerful jaws close around Liam's neck, his teeth sinking into the vulnerable flesh.

"No!" I screamed, my heart thundering in my ears. But before Louis could do any further damage, another dark brown wolf crashed through the window, slamming into him and knocking them both apart. Relief washed over me as I recognised Damon's familiar form, his eyes burning with a fierce determination.

"Stay with me, Erica," Frankie murmured, her grip tightening on my arm as she continued to pull me towards the safety of the far corner. My body trembled with pain and fear, but I forced myself to stay focused on the battle unfolding before us. Liam and Damon worked seamlessly together, their movements fluid and coordinated as they circled around Louis, trapping him against the wall. The air crackled with tension, the room filled with snarls and growls as they closed in on their opponent.

The room seemed to come alive as pack warriors flooded in, their faces etched with concern and determination. Alpha Declan and Beta Gregg stormed in, their eyes immediately locking onto the snarling wolves before them. I could feel the power radiating off Declan, his alpha authority commanding attention as he strode forward.

"Louis, shift now!" His voice boomed, an undeniable force that sent shivers down my spine. I watched as Louis struggled against the command, fighting the natural instinct to obey his Alpha. His body trembled, caught between his desire for revenge and the powerful influence of the Alpha's order.

"Shift!" Declan roared again, his frustration palpable.

Just when it seemed like Louis might finally succumb to the command, something changed. Frankie gasped beside me, her grip tightening on my arm as she stared at the scene unfolding before us. The air was thick with tension, and I could sense the weight of everyone's gazes on us. Liam and Damon both snarled viciously, and without hesitation, they lunged at him. Every muscle in my body tensed, fear and hope warring inside me as I watched the attack unfold. Liam reached Louis first, his powerful jaws closing around the other wolf's throat. I could almost hear the sickening crunch as he tore through flesh and bone, ending Louis's threat once and for all. My heart pounded wildly, relief and shock coursing through my veins. As the lifeless body of Louis crumpled to the floor, I allowed myself a shaky breath. The room seemed to hold its collective breath, the sudden silence deafening in the wake of the brutal battle.

My thoughts were a swirling mess, trying to piece together the whirlwind of events that had just unfolded. I knew we had won, but the cost was still uncertain. My attention was suddenly drawn away from my internal chaos as Beta Gregg approached me, his brow furrowed with concern.

"Let me see your leg, Erica," he said gently, kneeling beside me. I could feel his worry for me, and it only served to heighten my own anxiety.

"Is it bad?" I asked, already knowing the answer. I could see the bone protruding through my skin, the pain nearly blinding as it radiated up my leg.

"Definitely broken," Gregg confirmed, swallowing hard. "We need a medic over here!" His voice carried across the room, and within moments, a young woman in white scrubs rushed to our side.

As she reached out to examine my injury, her touch seemed to ignite the pain even further. I couldn't help but scream, the sound tearing through the air like a banshee's cry. The snarl that followed was unmistakable; Liam, still in his wolf form, lunged at the medic with an intensity that made my heart race. But before he could reach her, Damon intercepted him, his ebony form crashing into Liam's and sending both wolves skidding across the floor. Alpha Declan stepped forward, his powerful voice cutting through the chaos.

"Get yourself under control, boy!" he barked, his dark eyes locking onto his son's fierce gaze.

I could see the poor medic trembling, her eyes wide with terror as she stared at Liam. It was clear she had never expected to find herself facing down an enraged werewolf while simply doing her job.

The medic's hands shook noticeably as she glanced between my mangled leg and Liam's warning growl. I could see the fear in her eyes, but she was obviously trying to maintain a brave face for my sake. I admired her courage and hated that this situation was putting her in harm's way.

"Her leg..." She swallowed hard, and looked up at Beta Gregg, her voice wavering slightly. "It's healing crooked. It'll need to be... re-broken." My stomach churned at the thought, bile rising in my throat. My body already felt like it had been through hell, and the thought of enduring even more pain made me light-headed. But I knew she was right; if I wanted any hope of walking normally again, it had to be done.

Liam growled low in his throat, his hackles raised and teeth bared. He didn't trust anyone to hurt me, even if it was necessary. That protective streak was both endearing and terrifying, and right now, it was making life difficult for the poor medic.

"Enough, Liam," I hissed through gritted teeth. "She isn't hurting me on purpose." As if understanding my words, Liam's wolf form pressed itself against me. His warm fur provided a small amount of comfort, and I buried my face into his neck, inhaling his familiar scent of gingerbread and fire. It brought back memories of safety and solace, helping to calm my frayed nerves.

"Alright," I whispered, my voice barely audible. "Do it." Beta Gregg exchanged a nod with the medic, giving her the go-ahead. I tightened my grip on Liam's fur, preparing myself for the inevitable wave of pain that would follow.

"Okay, Luna, on three," the medic announced, her voice steady despite the tension in the room. I nodded, focusing on Liam's fur as I clutched it tightly in my hands, feeling the softness and warmth against my skin. The scent of gingerbread and fire filled my nostrils, providing a small measure of comfort amidst the impending pain.

"Are you ready?" the medic asked softly, her fingers lightly brushing my swollen ankle. Even that slight touch sent a jolt of agony up my leg, and I gritted my teeth, trying to mentally prepare myself for what was coming. My heart hammered in my chest, anxiety coiling like a snake in my stomach.

"Alright," she breathed, gripping my leg firmly. "One." Before I even had time to brace myself for impact, an almighty crack rang through the room, and with it came a tidal wave of searing, unbearable pain. It felt as if hot iron rods were being driven through my bones, setting every nerve on fire. I screamed, the sound raw and primal, tears streaming down my face as I clung to Liam's fur for dear life.

The room seemed to spin around me, disorienting and terrifying, making it nearly impossible to concentrate on anything but the throbbing agony radiating from my broken leg. My strength was dwindling rapidly, sapped by the relentless pain. The darkness at the edges of my vision began to swallow me whole, and I knew I was slipping away. It wasn't long before the edges of my vision started to darken and I was swallowed into the black sea of unconsciousness.

Chapter 49

Erica

A MUFFLED BEEPING SOUND roused me from my drug-induced slumber. My eyelids fluttered open, the harsh lights above me momentarily blinding. A tangle of tubes and wires snaked their way across my body, connected to machines that monitored my every breath and heartbeat. The sharp scent of antiseptic filled the air, reminding me of a sterile emptiness. Where am I? My eyes adjusted to the brightness, and I saw Liam sitting beside my bed. His head was tilted back, resting against the wall while he slept, one hand holding mine. The sight of him brought an odd sense of comfort, even as my memories remained hazy.

Just then, the door opened with a soft creak, making me wince at the intrusion of noise. Damon strolled into the room, his dark eyes alive with mischief. Instinctively, I lifted a finger to my lips, urging him to be quiet so as not to wake Liam. Damon just grinned and sauntered over to the foot of my bed.

"Good morning, Erica," he said in a voice louder than necessary. He nudged Liam's leg with his foot.

"Hey, Sleeping Beauty, wake up. Your damsel is conscious." Liam jolted awake, his eyes wide with confusion before they landed on me. Relief flooded his features, and he grinned.

"Baby, you're awake."

"Hi, Liam," I whispered, my throat dry and scratchy. "How long have I been here?"

"Almost twenty-four hours," he answered, concern etching lines into his handsome face. "You had us all worried."

"Sorry," I muttered, guilt settling like a stone in my chest.

"None of that," Damon chided, waving a finger at me. "None of this is your fault." Liam's warm lips pressed gently against mine, and I couldn't help but smile through the kiss. The familiar scent of his cologne enveloped me, providing a sense of safety amidst the sterile hospital surroundings.

"How are you feeling?" he asked softly, his brown eyes filled with genuine concern.

"Okay, I guess," I admitted. "Groggy, but not really in pain."

"Good," Damon chimed in, leaning against the doorframe. "The doctors have you on a pretty strong cocktail of medications. You should be feeling better soon."

"Thanks," I murmured, my eyelids heavy as I fought to stay awake. I needed answers, and despite the overwhelming urge to succumb to sleep, I knew I couldn't let this opportunity slip away.

"Erica, do you remember what happened?" Liam questioned, his fingers tracing comforting circles on the back of my hand. I shook my head, my heart pounding in my chest as I tried to recall the events that had led me here.

"No, everything's still a blur."

"Louis attacked you," Liam explained, his voice strained. As he spoke, memories from the previous night rushed back to me, the snarling wolf stalking me, ready to kill. My breath caught in my throat, and I felt a shiver run down my spine.

"Louis..." I whispered, my voice barely audible. The thought of that monster bearing down on me, his teeth inches from my throat, sent tremors through my body. I'd been so close to death, and the realisation was almost too much to bear.

"Hey, it's okay," Liam reassured me, pulling me closer. "He can't hurt you anymore."

"But how did he get so close?" I asked, my mind reeling with questions. "Why did he attack me?"

"We're still piecing everything together, Erica," Damon cut in, his dark eyes filled with worry. "But don't worry, we'll make sure nothing like this ever happens again."

As my memories slowly pieced themselves together, I recalled the horrifying scene of Liam's wolf leaping at Louis, tearing into him with a ferocity that both terrified and awed me in equal measure. The image was so vivid, it felt like it had been etched into my very soul.

"Wait," I said, interrupting the silence that had settled over us. "I remember now... Liam, you killed Louis." My heart raced while I tried to process the gruesome event I'd witnessed. "You had him cornered, but then you just attacked. Why did you do that?" Liam's eyes darkened, and his jaw clenched as if he was trying to hold back a tidal wave of anger. He looked away from me, unable to meet my gaze. A tense silence hung in the air, and Damon shifted uncomfortably in his seat.

"Louis knew he was losing, Erica," Damon finally said, breaking the silence. "He realised that facing Alpha Declan would mean certain death, so he chose to die quickly rather than endure the humiliation of submission."

"Submission?" I questioned, still puzzled by the chain of events that led to Louis' demise. "What do you mean?"

"Louis understood that if he submitted to my father, he would be at the pack's mercy. He likely feared that his punishment would be drawn out or particularly cruel," Liam explained through gritted teeth, his voice laced with contempt. "So he decided to take the coward's way out."

"How?" I asked and Liam and Damon exchanged looks. Liam's jaw clenched, and I could practically hear his teeth grinding together.

"Louis...he sent out a mass mind link to everyone in the room," he said through gritted teeth. "He showed us his intentions towards you."

"His intentions?" I asked, my stomach churning with dread. Liam stared at me, pain and anger flickering in his eyes.

"He showed himself killing you. And..." His voice trailed off, the fury on his face growing more intense.

"Tell me," I demanded, needing to know what else haunted him. Damon stepped forward, resting a hand on Liam's shoulder as if trying to dissipate some of the rage building inside him.

"You don't want to know, Erica," he said gently. But I did need to know. My memories flashed back to that terrifying moment when Louis, in his human form, had tried to rape me. I shuddered at the thought, my heart pounding in my chest. The crude images he must have sent to everyone made bile rise in my throat.

Liam reached out to me, his fingers brushing against my arm, and I shuddered at the contact.

"You're safe now, baby," he said, his voice low and soothing. "Louis is dead. He can't hurt you anymore."

"Before it happened," I whispered, my voice shaky from the memories that threatened to overwhelm me, "he said he was going to deliver me to some guy." The words felt surreal as they left my lips, and I tried to focus on Liam's face instead of the terror that clawed at my insides.

"Who?" Liam asked, his brow furrowing in concern.

"I don't know." My hands were trembling, and I clenched them into fists to try to stop the shaking. "I don't have any idea who he was talking about." Liam's eyes darkened, and for a moment, I saw a flicker of something, conflict or fear, maybe, pass through his expression before he carefully schooled his features back into a mask of calm reassurance.

"You should get some rest, baby," he urged gently, squeezing my hand. "We'll figure this out, but right now, you need to heal."

As much as I wanted answers, I couldn't deny the heaviness that weighed down my eyelids, my body craving sleep after the assault it had endured. But there was something Liam wasn't telling me, a hidden truth that lingered just beneath the surface of his carefully controlled exterior. I knew he was trying to protect me, but I was tired of secrets and half-truths. I needed to know what was going on, even if it hurt.

"Promise me you'll tell me everything when I wake up," I murmured, my eyes drifting shut despite my best efforts to keep them open.

"Promise," he whispered back, his breath warm against my skin.

With that reassurance, I allowed myself to drift into the darkness of sleep. The nightmares that awaited me there would be nothing compared to the reality I'd just escaped, but at least in my dreams, I could fight back. And when I woke up, I'd have Liam by my side, ready to face whatever demons we had to conquer together. As I surrendered to the pull of the medication and exhaustion, I held on to that thought, the idea that no matter what lay ahead, I wouldn't have to face it alone.

When I awoke, the room was bathed in soft morning light. The beeping machines and tangle of wires that had been my companions were gone, replaced by an eerie silence. With Liam and Damon absent, Jacob occupied a chair in the corner, his attention focused on his phone.

"Morning," he said, looking up as I stirred. His voice was gentle, but I could hear a hint of unease beneath the surface.

"Hey," I replied groggily. "How long have I been asleep?"

"Almost 12 hours," he informed me. My eyes widened at the revelation, I hadn't realised how much time had passed. Jacob's expression turned sombre as he continued.

"Erica, I'm so sorry I left you alone. I put you at risk before Liam got there."

I studied him, taking in the bruising around his left eye and the cut on his lip. A surge of annoyance bubbled inside me; I had a strong feeling those injuries were Liam's doing. Despite my anger, I knew that Jacob didn't deserve to be blamed for what happened.

"Jacob, it's not your fault," I reassured him. "Louis probably would've found another opportunity if you hadn't left. It might have ended much worse." He looked down, his face contorted with guilt.

"Still, I should've been more careful."

"It's done now," I said firmly, trying to push past the lingering sense of unease. "We need to focus on what comes next." Jacob nodded, but I could see the worry etched into the lines of his face. He was a loyal friend, bound by duty and honour to protect those he loved and his potential future Luna. And I knew, deep down, that he would never forgive himself for the part he'd played in my ordeal.

I tried to change the subject so that Jacob could feel better.

"Jacob, where's Liam?" I asked, my voice groggy from the lingering effects of the medication. He shifted uncomfortably in his seat before responding,

"There's been an emergency at the pack house. Liam and Damon are in a meeting with Alpha Declan."

"An emergency? What happened?" I pressed further, my concern mounting. Jacob hesitated, avoiding my gaze.

"I was tasked to protect you and take you home when you woke up," he said, dodging my question entirely. "The doctor cleared you, and your leg has already started healing. You can go home whenever you want." His evasion piqued my curiosity even more, but I knew I wouldn't get any straight answers from him right now. My body still felt heavy, weighed down by exhaustion and pain, but I needed to know what was happening.

"Alright," I sighed, conceding for the moment. "I want to go home."

As Jacob and I exited the hospital room, two other warriors joined us, their expressions grim but determined. A third warrior awaited our arrival outside in a pack SUV, his eyes scanning the surrounding area for any potential threats.

"Is all this really necessary?" I asked as we approached the vehicle, feeling slightly overwhelmed by the security measures in place.

"Precaution," Jacob replied tersely, opening the door for me. "We can't take any chances right now." I climbed into the SUV, followed by Jacob, my mind reeling with unanswered questions. One of the warriors slid in beside me while the other took a seat up front, effectively sandwiching me between them. Their presence should have been comforting, a reminder that I was under their protection; instead, it only served to heighten my sense of unease.

The drive up to the pack house passed in tense silence, broken only by the quiet hum of the engine. As we pulled through the gates, I couldn't help but notice the eerie stillness that seemed to permeate the air. It was morning, and yet the grounds were devoid of the usual bustle of activity. The ominous atmosphere weighed heavily on me, like an unwelcome shroud that threatened to suffocate everything in its path.

"Jacob, what's going on?" I demanded, unable to contain my worry any longer. "Why is everything so...quiet?"

"Like I said before, there's been an emergency," he replied, avoiding my gaze. "That's all I can tell you right now." His evasiveness only fuelled my growing anxiety, but I knew better than to press him further. We parked in front of the pack house, and without another word, Jacob led the way inside.

Climbing the four flights of stairs to the Alpha floor felt like scaling a mountain, my legs growing heavier with each step. I clung to the railing for support, my heart pounding in my chest as I forced myself to keep moving. It was a struggle but, finally; we neared the top.

"Erica," Jacob said quietly, his tone laced with concern and a hint of regret. "I'm sorry I can't tell you more right now, but trust me when I say that we're doing everything we can to keep you safe."

"Thank you," I whispered, my voice barely audible even to my own ears. Though I still didn't know what was happening, I had no choice but to place my faith in those who were sworn to protect me – and hope that it would be enough.

The moment I stepped onto the Alpha floor, a cacophony of raised voices reached my ears. My heart raced in anticipation as I followed the sound, Jacob trailing silently behind me. When we reached the doorway to the Alpha living room, I paused, taking in the tense scene before me. Alpha Declan stood tall and imposing, his dark eyes narrowed in frustration. Beside him were Beta Gregg, Luna Fallon, and Gregg's wife and mate, Astra. Gamma Gideon and his wife, Jacob's wife Jenna, Kaitlyn, and Damon filled the rest of the room. But it was Liam who caught my attention, sitting on the opposite sofa to his father, his jaw clenched and a storm brewing in his brown eyes.

"Putting every pack member under investigation is not a viable solution!" Declan argued, his voice booming throughout the room.

"Then what do you suggest, Father?" Liam snapped back, his anger palpable. "We have a territory full of spies, and if we don't find out who they are, Erica or someone else could get hurt!"

"Maybe we should consider more subtle approaches," Gregg suggested, trying to diffuse the escalating tension between father and son.

"Subtlety hasn't exactly been effective so far," Liam retorted, his gaze lingering on me for a brief moment before returning to his father.

"Excuse me, but what's going on?" I asked, my voice cutting through the heated argument. Liam was on his feet and by my side in an instant.

"Baby, you should be resting. How are you feeling?"

"I'm fine, Liam," I replied, brushing off his concern with a small wave of my hand. "Now tell me what's going on."

"Nothing for you to worry about, love," he said, trying to placate me. "Everything's under control." I raised an eyebrow at him, unimpressed.

"Liam, if you want me to be your Luna someday, you need to actually tell me things. I'm sick of secrets."

"Ha, that's a Luna right there for you!" Fallon chimed in, her grin wide and proud. Damon chuckled in agreement, earning a glare from Liam.

"Erica has a point," Alpha Declan conceded, his gaze shifting between Liam and me. He shared a knowing look with his wife before turning back to his son. "Liam, tell her." Liam sighed, clearly unhappy with the decision, but he nodded. I could see the struggle in his eyes as he tried to find the right words to explain the situation.

Chapter 50

Liam

The room was tense, the air thick with anticipation as I prepared to reveal my family's secret. Erica sat across from me, her green eyes glistening with curiosity and concern. My mother and father flanked her, their expressions a mixture of support and unease. This was the moment of truth.

"Baby," I began, my voice unsteady, grappling with the weight of my words. "There's something you need to know about my family. Something that could affect us all." Her gaze never wavered, but I sensed her growing anxiety. Taking a deep breath, I continued.

"There's a rival pack, originally led by Felix Blackwood, who wants to destroy the Silver Stone pack. We've had... issues with them for years."

"Wait, Felix Blackwood?" Erica interrupted, her brow furrowing. "That name sounds familiar."

"Let me explain," my mother chimed in, her voice soft yet determined. "Felix had a crush on me when we were younger. Our packs were neighbours, and he wanted to bring mine into his and make me his Luna."

"Then Fallon met me," Declan added with a hint of pride, placing a hand on my mother's shoulder. "We were fated mates. I still remember the overwhelming feeling of finding her, like every fibre of my being aligned perfectly with hers." My mind flashed back to the first time I laid eyes on Erica, and I knew exactly what he meant.

"Anyway," my mother continued, "my father agreed to merge our pack with Declan's. That's when Felix became furious. He accused me of betraying him, even though I never intended to complete the mate bond with him."

"His anger turned into an obsession," I added, clenching my fists at the thought of our enemies threatening our pack and Erica's safety. "Which only got worse when my mother became pregnant with me," I began, my voice wavering slightly. "It was far from an easy pregnancy. Her body seemed to be rejecting it, and she became incredibly ill." My father took over, his eyes distant as he recalled those harrowing days.

"We sought help from a local witches' coven, desperate for any kind of relief or answers. The daughter of the Coven Priestess came to our aid, and after examining Fallon, she informed us that the cause of her illness was magical in nature. There was a curse on our family."

"Upon further investigation," I continued, feeling the weight of the curse bearing down on me as I spoke, "the witch deciphered that the curse had been placed specifically on the unborn baby, on me. She revealed that I would need to complete the mate bond by the time I turned thirty years old, or everyone connected to me, through blood, bond, or pack, would die."

The room fell silent as I finished speaking, the heaviness of the revelation settling around us like a thick fog. Erica's eyes were wide with shock and worry, her hand gripping mine even tighter.

"Is there any way to break the curse?" she asked, her voice barely above a whisper.

"We've spent years searching for a solution," my father answered grimly, "but nothing has proven successful. The only hope we have is for Liam to complete the mate bond within the allotted time."

I could see Erica's eyes welling up as we told her about the curse, her green irises shimmering in the dim light of the room. She had been so strong until now, but the weight of this revelation seemed to be too much for her. My heart ached at the sight of her pain, and I wished there was something I could do to take it all away.

"Erica," I began softly, my voice cracking under the strain of my emotions, "I didn't tell you because I wanted you to want to complete the bond, not feel obliged to." Her gaze snapped to mine, those emerald eyes now brimming with tears.

"That's the problem, Liam," she whispered, her voice trembling. "I have no choice. I can't be responsible for the deaths of three thousand lives."

The atmosphere in the room grew heavy as her words hung in the air like a thick fog that threatened to suffocate us all. As I looked into her eyes, searching for some semblance of comfort or understanding, I saw a flicker of doubt cross her face. It was as if she sensed there was more to the story than what we had told her so far.

"Something else is going on, isn't it?" she asked, her voice barely above a whisper, yet somehow, it managed to echo throughout the room, making everyone shift uncomfortably.

My throat tightened as I tried to find the right words to explain the situation without causing her further distress. But how could I sugarcoat the fact that our enemies were closing in and that we were losing more pack members by the hour?

"Erica," my father said, his voice heavy with the weight of the news he was about to deliver, "in the last twelve hours, we've lost over half the pack warriors and their families." This was a devastating blow to us. Of the three thousand pack members eight hundred were trained warriors. Since we had pulled in Aldrich, and then Grayson, whole families seemed to have fled. We couldn't say for certain if they were involved but from the pack members we had been able to investigate there was an alarmingly high percentage that had been planted into the pack. Erica's horrified gasp cut through the air like a knife, her green eyes brimming with unshed tears.

"How?" she choked out, her voice barely a whisper. I clenched my fists at my sides, anger boiling within me at the thought of our enemies picking off our pack members one by one.

"After Louis attacked you," I began, struggling to keep my voice steady, "we brought in Aldrich, his father, for questioning. We needed to know why Louis would have such a vicious vendetta against you." As I spoke, I recalled the sheer hatred that had radiated from Louis during the attack, an intensity I couldn't quite comprehend. It was during Aldrich's interrogation that Erica had told me about Louis's declaration, that he was to deliver her to someone. I had passed this information onto my father immediately, desperate to understand the connection.

The air in the room grew heavy with tension, a suffocating weight pressing down on all of us. The roaring fire offered no comfort, only emphasising the stark contrast between its warmth and the chill that had settled in my bones.

"Alpha, what else did Aldrich say?" Erica asked, her voice barely audible, trembling under the strain of her emotions.

"Using my Alpha tone, I forced him to tell us everything," my father began, his voice laced with anger and disgust. "Aldrich admitted to working with the Shadow Night pack from the beginning. Felix Blackwood came to him and offered a deal, he would find a way to join our pack and provide information on us." Erica's eyes widened in shock and betrayal, her hands clenching into fists at her sides.

"Did Louis and Heidi know about this?"

"Unfortunately, yes," my father replied, his jaw clenched tight. "They both agreed to Felix's terms. Only Aldrich's mate refused, and for that, Felix killed her."

"Those bastards," I growled, my own rage simmering beneath the surface. I could feel my wolf pacing restlessly within me, wanting nothing more than to tear apart those who had betrayed our pack. But now was not the time for bloodlust; we needed answers, and we needed them fast.

"Who else, Alpha? Who else is involved?" Erica demanded, her voice cracking but strong.

"From what Aldrich told us, there are others," my father said, hesitating for a moment before looking down at the floor. "One of the names he mentioned was Grayson Thompson."

"Grayson?" Erica gasped, her heartache evident in her wide, disbelieving eyes. "He's the Warrior Commander! His job is to keep the pack safe!"

"Believe me, Erica, we were just as shocked," I reassured her, trying to keep my own emotions in check. "Grayson is currently being interrogated, and we won't rest until we've rooted out every last traitor." Erica's horrified gaze bore into me, and I could see the moment she realised the full extent of what we were dealing with.

"Warriors and their families," she whispered, shaking her head in disbelief. "You can't possibly think that Verity is a spy..." My heart clenched at the pain laced through her voice, and I struggled to find the right words to comfort her. "It might not be the case, baby," I tried to reassure her gently. "But it doesn't look good. The Thompson family has disappeared, all except for Grayson."

Her eyes filled with tears, and I could feel her devastation as if it were my own. But it wasn't just Erica who was hurting; Kaitlyn, my little sister, was also quietly crying, her shoulders trembling with each sob. My anger surged, building like a storm inside me. How dare they infiltrate our pack and threaten the people we loved? They would pay dearly for this.

The weight of the room grew heavier as Erica's expression shifted into one of deep concern. She looked up at me, her green eyes searching for something to cling to amidst the chaos.

"Did you say Felix Blackwood?" she asked, her voice barely a whisper. I nodded reluctantly, bracing myself for whatever questions might follow.

"Yes, that's right."

"Is he related to Jasper Blackwood?" At the mention of Jasper's name, a sudden surge of anger coursed through me, my hands clenching unconsciously. That bastard had been causing trouble for far too long, and now it seemed, his reach extended even further than I'd initially thought.

"Jasper is Felix's son and now the Alpha of the Shadow Night pack," I told Erica, struggling to keep the bitterness from my voice. "He's made it his mission to make my life miserable."

"Jasper was in Red Bank," Erica revealed, her words sending a shiver down my spine. "The bar I used to work at." Damon chimed in, nodding his agreement. "I remember seeing him there. I warned Erica to stay away from him." My jaw tightened, I had already heard this , but it felt like we were under attack from all sides, and the need to protect those I loved became increasingly urgent. I turned to my father, frustration bubbling beneath the surface.

"We need to clear some more warriors first, so we can protect Erica." But Erica wasn't satisfied with my answer.

"Why me in particular?" she demanded, her confusion evident.

My thoughts raced, trying to find a way to explain without revealing too much. The uncertainty gnawed at me, fuelling my determination to keep her safe. But I didn't want to overwhelm her with the disaster that was my life either.

"Because..." I hesitated, searching for the right words. There was a sudden mind link from the warrior guarding Grayson, which interrupted our discussion, and I knew we couldn't afford to waste any more time. I looked over at my father and could tell he had received the same message. I shared the information with everyone in the room; their faces were a mixture of shock and suspicion.

"Grayson wants to talk to me. He says he'll name more spies, but only if it's me who goes to see him." Damon frowned, his dark eyes narrowing as he crossed his arms over his chest.

"That sounds suspicious, Liam. It could be a trap."

"Maybe, but we have no choice. We need to know who we can trust." My voice was firm, resolute. Inside, though, I battled with conflicting emotions: anger at the betrayal within our pack, worry over Erica's safety, and a gnawing dread that things were about to get much worse.

"Jacob, don't fuck up this time. Stay with Erica and keep her safe," I ordered, my tone leaving no room for argument. Jacob nodded, his hazel eyes locked on mine as he understood the gravity of the situation.

"Let's go," I said, and Damon, Declan, Gregg, and Gideon fell into step beside me, as we headed to find out how fucked we really were.

Chapter 51

Erica

The pit in my stomach grew deeper and more nauseating with each tick of the clock. I couldn't shake the gnawing fear that crawled up my spine, making me restless as I paced back and forth across the room. It was suffocating, like a poisonous fog wrapping around me, squeezing the breath from my lungs.

"Erica, you need to calm down," the Luna said, her voice laced with concern. She knew how anxious I was about Liam interrogating Grayson, but there was nothing she could say to ease my mind.

"Sorry, I just... I can't help it," I murmured, pausing for a moment to lean against the wall. The cold plaster pressed against my forehead, offering little comfort. "What if Grayson's information is even worse than we thought?"

"Whatever it is, Liam will handle it," Kaitlyn reassured me, placing a hand on my shoulder. But her eyes betrayed her own worry, and I knew she didn't fully believe her words either.

I let out a shaky breath, trying to focus on the present, on the familiar surroundings of the pack house. But all I could see was the image of Liam, his dark brown hair dishevelled, his strong hands gripping Grayson's prison bars, his intense brown eyes searching for answers.

"Erica, come sit with me," the Luna offered, guiding me towards the couch. My knees felt weak, and I gratefully sank into the cushions, still feeling the relentless ticking of the clock echoing through the room.

"Grayson must have had a good reason to speak with Liam directly," I whispered, my voice barely audible above the oppressive silence. "But what could be so important? Why put Liam at risk like this?"

We lapsed into silence, the tension in the room was palpable, like a thick fog that clung to every surface and stifled any attempts at conversation. Kaitlyn and Jenna tried to fill the silence with small talk, but their voices were strained, their forced laughter hollow.

"Erica," Jenna began hesitantly, her gaze flicking between me and Jacob. "I'm so sorry that Jacob didn't stay with you the other night." Jacob managed a grim smile, his eyes apologetic.

"Yeah, Jenna kicked my ass for that one. I should've been there for you."

"Hey," I said softly, reaching out to touch Jacob's arm reassuringly. "I don't blame you or anyone else. The only person responsible for what happened is Louis." Jacob nodded, grateful for my understanding, but the guilt still lingered in his eyes. We fell into an awkward silence, each of us lost in our own thoughts, the weight of the situation pressing down on us like a suffocating blanket. As the minutes dragged on, we continued to discuss trivial matters, desperately trying to distract ourselves from the gnawing unease that settled in our stomachs. It felt as if the walls were closing in, trapping us in this nightmare with no escape in sight.

Suddenly, Jacob stiffened, his eyes widening. He quickly stood up, his face pale and alarmed.

"I won't be long," he announced, his voice tight with urgency. Without waiting for a response, he rushed out of the room, leaving us all to exchange concerned glances. I watched Jacob's retreating figure, my heart pounding with a mix of worry and frustration. I turned to face the others in the room, noticing their concerned expressions.

"Okay, what's going on?" I demanded, unable to hold back any longer. "Why is everyone so worried?" The Luna hesitated before replying, her voice tense.

"Liam and his father are back from their meeting with Grayson."

"What about the others?" I asked.

"They went off to collect some more names that Grayson had given them," Jenna said.

"Then why do you all look like someone just died?" I snapped, my patience wearing thin. No one answered, their silence only fueling my unease. It was maddening, being left in the dark while everyone else seemed privy to some crucial information. I knew they had likely received mind links about the situation, but that knowledge only served to remind me of my own inadequacy. The fact that I couldn't connect to them in the same way weighed heavily on me, further isolating me from the pack.

"Fine," I gritted out, pushing myself up from my seat. "If no one is going to tell me anything, I'll find out for myself." Determination and anger flared within me as I asked, "Where's Liam?" The room remained silent, but I wasn't backing down. I locked eyes with the Luna, silently pleading for her to give me something, anything to ease my growing panic.

"Erica, please understand it's not our place to—" she began, but I cut her off. "Tell me where he is," I insisted, desperation seeping into my voice. "I need to know."

"He's in my father's office," Kaitlyn said, which earned her a glare from her mother.

"Thank you," I said tersely, already heading towards the door. My chest tightened with apprehension, but I couldn't sit idly by any longer. I needed answers, and I needed them now.

"I'm coming with you," Kaitlyn announced, standing up and displaying a fierce determination. Her loyalty to me was unwavering, and I appreciated it more than she could ever know. The Luna shot her a disapproving look, clearly unhappy with Kaitlyn's decision.

"Kaitlyn, you know this isn't your place."

"Enough," Kaitlyn snapped. "We're all sick of the secrets, and whatever's going on affects all of us, not just Erica. If Liam has information that concerns the pack, we all deserve to know." The Luna's expression softened slightly but didn't argue any further. Instead, she gave me a nod of understanding, silently urging me to be careful.

"Thank you," I whispered to Kaitlyn, feeling a small flicker of hope in the midst of my unease. At least I wouldn't have to face whatever awaited us alone.

Together, we left the room and made our way through the main pack house. As we descended the stairs, the atmosphere grew heavier with each step, as if the very walls were closing in around us. The unnerving silence only added to my anxiety, making the pit in my stomach grow deeper.

"Something's definitely wrong," Kaitlyn murmured, echoing my thoughts. "I've never seen everyone so on edge."

"Neither have I," I admitted, my voice barely audible. Fear twisted inside me, coiling around my heart like a venomous snake ready to strike. As we neared the Alpha's office, I couldn't help but recall the countless times I'd been in there before, usually for some kind of reprimand or meeting. But this time felt different; the stakes seemed so much higher now that Liam was involved.

As we turned the corner into the hallway leading to the Alpha's office, the sudden sound of raised voices shattered the eerie calm. My heart leaped into my throat, adrenaline coursing through my veins as I braced myself for the confrontation ahead.

"LIAM, WILL YOU CALM DOWN?" The Alpha's voice boomed, carrying a note of authority laced with concern. My pulse quickened, anxiety gnawing at my insides.

"Calm down?! How can I calm down when everything is against me?!" Liam's response was filled with desperation and rage, his words slicing through the tense atmosphere like a knife.

Kaitlyn and I shared a look of alarm before hastily moving towards the door. As we reached out for the handle, I heard footsteps approaching from behind us. I turned my head to find Damon, his expression a mixture of confusion and worry.

"What the hell is going on now?" he asked, his dark eyes scanning our faces for answers. Before I could respond, another crash resonated from within the office, followed by a guttural growl. My heart clenched with fear as I turned back to the door, gripping the handle tightly. With bated breath, I opened it just as Liam spat out his next furious words.

"I mean, if she can't even shift, then it's useless!" The venom in his voice caught me off guard, causing me to gasp involuntarily. As my eyes met his, the pure fury painted across his face cut me to the core.

The world seemed to slow down around me, every nerve in my body pulsing with raw emotion as I struggled to process the implications of Liam's words. My breath hitched in my chest, and a whirlwind of thoughts swirled through my mind, fear, hurt, and the crushing weight of inadequacy. The icy weight of Liam's gaze bore into me, leaving me paralyzed as my heart thudded painfully in my chest. A cacophony of emotions surged through us both, but it was his wrath that dominated the air between us. I searched his face for any sign of remorse or understanding, but all I found was cold, unrelenting anger. Part of me hoped that this was some sort of misunderstanding. But deep down, I knew the truth; he believed I was useless, broken, less than what he needed and deserved.

I felt as if I'd been plunged into an arctic ocean, the frigid water stealing my breath and numbing my limbs. I wanted to scream, to protest, to convince him that I was more than my inability to shift. But the raw pain in my chest rendered me speechless, choking on the devastating truth he had laid bare. My hands trembled at my sides as I forced myself to turn away from Liam, unwilling to bear the brunt of his piercing stare any longer. Damon had moved to stand beside his father, his dark eyes filled with a mixture of concern and anger. He glanced at me, clearly torn between his loyalty to Liam and his desire to protect me from this emotional onslaught.

"Erica," he murmured, reaching out tentatively to touch my arm. I flinched as I heard Liam growl behind me. I couldn't help it, the intensity of the sound had me turning back to face him.

My heart shattered into a thousand pieces at the look of pure fury directed at me. I could barely breathe as the air around me grew thick with anguish and betrayal. As I slid to the floor, tears blurred my vision and a painful sob welled up in my chest, making it hard to breathe. The cold tiles beneath me offered no comfort; they were as unforgiving as the truth that now haunted me. I was lesser, defective. My world seemed to crumble around me, leaving me broken.. I sat there, feeling the cold floor beneath me, the chill seeping into my bones as I waited, waited for what was to come. Who was I, a defective wolf, to think that I could be a Luna, especially not one to the Alpha of a pack this size? My heart ached with the weight of my own inadequacy. Tears streamed down my face, hot and unforgiving, as I waited for the one thing I feared the most in my life, the one thing that would confirm everything I already knew about myself.

The air crackled with tension, thick and suffocating. I felt Liam's anger build like a dark storm cloud, ready to unleash its fury upon me. And then it came: a full primal roar of pain and betrayal that shook me to my core. The room seemed to vibrate with the intensity of his emotion. He lunged forward, and I flinched instinctively, but he didn't touch me. Instead, I saw the legs of the Alpha's desk disappear, followed by a crash on the other side of the room. Splintered wood and shattered glass littered the floor, a testament to the destruction his anger had wrought.
"Enough, Liam!" the Alpha shouted, but his words fell on deaf ears. Liam rushed past me, his breath hot and heavy, and stormed out of the room. A door slammed in the distance, followed by more smashing and roaring, each sound tearing at my heart like claws on flesh.

I looked up, my vision blurry through the tears that refused to cease, and saw the shocked faces around me. They stared at me with a mix of pity and fear, unsure of what to say or do. It was then that I realised how truly alone I felt in that moment, surrounded by people who were supposed to be my family, my pack.

All I could do now was to await my fate. Await to be rejected or killed by the person I loved most in the world. And I deserved it because I was lesser, I was defective.

I was broken.

Chapter 52

Liam

As I stormed into my room, the vile taste of fury and defeat clung to the back of my throat. Each breath came in ragged, angry bursts, and my heart pounded like a war drum in my chest. How was I supposed to deal with everything when it all seemed to be designed to fuck me over? Was this some sort of sick test?

"Dammit!" I yelled, slamming the door behind me so hard it shook on its hinges.

My hands clenched into fists as I surveyed the room, feeling the anger rise like a tidal wave from deep within me. I kicked the nightstand, sending books flying and scattering across the floor. The pain barely registered - it was nothing compared to the torment in my soul.

"Fuck!" I shouted again, hurling a decorative vase against the wall, watching as the glass shattered into a thousand pieces, each one reflecting the chaos in my mind.

In the midst of my destruction, my gaze landed on a framed photograph sitting innocently atop the dresser. It was a picture of Erica and me, taken not long ago during a rare moment of happiness and peace. Her light-red hair shimmered in the sunlight, her green eyes sparkling with life. The sight of her beautiful face ignited a mixture of emotions - love, longing, frustration, and helplessness.

"Erica," I whispered, my heart aching with an intensity that threatened to consume me.

"Everything is just so fucked up," I muttered, feeling the tears prick at the corners of my eyes. I grabbed the frame, gripping it tightly until I could feel the cold metal digging into my skin. With a roar of rage and anguish, I hurled it against the wall by the door, watching as it smashed into pieces on impact, the sound echoing through the room like a gunshot. The broken shards of glass and wood lay scattered on the floor, a cruel reminder of the mess my life had become. As I stared at the wreckage, my chest heaved, and I fought to catch my breath.

The door burst open and Damon barged in, his face contorted with anger. He surveyed the room, taking in the destruction I had wrought. His dark eyes fell upon the torn picture on the floor, glass shards glinting menacingly around it.

"What the fuck do you think you are doing?" he shouted at me, his voice cutting through the tense silence like a knife. My chest tightened at the sound of his voice, and my fingers curled into fists. I didn't need him here right now; I couldn't handle anyone else's bullshit piled on top of mine.

"Back the fuck off, Damon," I growled, my voice low and dangerous. I could feel the tension in the air, prickling at my skin like static electricity.

"Really, Liam?" he snapped, stepping further into the room. "You think destroying everything is going to solve your problems? You think this is helping Erica?"

"Leave her out of this!" I snarled, my temper flaring like a wildfire as my heart twisted painfully in my chest at the mention of her name. The thought of her suffering because of me was too much to bear.

"Stop being so goddamn selfish, Liam!" Damon spat, his own anger boiling over. "We're all worried about you, but you can't just shut everyone out and break shit when things don't go your way!" I clenched my jaw, my vision blurring as hot tears threatened to spill over. I knew he was right, deep down, but admitting that felt like a betrayal to myself.

"Fuck you, Damon," I whispered hoarsely, my voice cracking under the weight of my emotions.

Damon's snarl grew louder and more menacing, his eyes flashing with rage as he suddenly charged at me. I barely had time to react before he slammed me into the wall, the impact rattling my bones and causing a cascade of framed memories to shatter around us. Broken glass littered the floor, reflecting the chaos that filled the room. I could feel the anger surging through me, fuelled by confusion and despair. My heart pounded in my chest, adrenaline coursing through my veins as I clenched my own fists, preparing to defend myself. Instinctively, I pushed back against him, each of us snarling and throwing punches that landed with painful force. Our swearing echoed off the walls, adding to the cacophony of destruction.

"Stop it, Damon!" I warned, my voice strained with the effort of holding back my rage. "You don't want to do this!"

"Bring it on!" he roared, his face contorted with fury as he landed another punch, this one catching me square in the jaw. The pain shot through my skull, momentarily stunning me, but I couldn't understand why he was attacking me like this.

"What the fuck is wrong with you?!" I shouted, my breath ragged as I struggled to keep my emotions in check. "Don't I have enough to deal with already?!"

In that moment, I realised how much damage we were doing to each other, both physically and emotionally. My chest tightened with the weight of regret, and I couldn't help but wonder how we'd got to this point. We were supposed to be allies, friends even, yet here we were, tearing each other apart. But instead of backing down, Damon's expression only hardened further, his eyes wild with anger. I braced myself for another blow, my body tensed and ready for the impact that seemed inevitable.

"Self-entitled prick!" Damon shouted, his face contorted with anger. "I'm ashamed to call you my friend! You left your mate sobbing and broken on the floor, and you don't deserve someone as amazing as Erica!" His words cut deep, but I refused to let him see how much they hurt. My heart raced as fury boiled within me. Instead of letting it show, I snarled back at him, my voice dripping with sarcasm.

"Is that what you think? Playing the white knight, are you?" I mocked him, my eyes narrowing. "You think you can be the hero, swooping in to save her from the big bad Alpha?" Damon's jaw clenched, his eyes flashing dangerously.

"Damn right I could treat her better than you do," he shot back, his voice low and venomous.

"Watch your words, Damon," I warned, my voice barely a growl. The tension between us was palpable, a storm ready to break.

"Fine," he spat out, his eyes never leaving mine. "I'll say it: I would love Erica better than you ever have." My blood ran cold at his declaration, but rage quickly pushed its way back through my veins. How dare he claim that? The connection between Erica and me went beyond anything Damon could understand. With each word he spoke, my anger grew, fuelling the primal instincts inside me. I snarled, my anger reaching a boiling point as I charged at Damon, screaming,

"Erica is my mate, and you need to stay the hell away from her!" My fists clenched, ready to strike.

"Both you and Erica have been miserable since you met," Damon shot back, his voice cold and harsh. "She smiled more when she was with me, and she was in less danger." The truth in his words stung like a thousand needles piercing my heart. My hand collided with the wall in frustration, leaving a deep imprint. As the pain radiated up my arm, I slid down to the floor, feeling the weight of my failures crushing me. Tears streamed down my face, my vision blurring.

"Dammit, don't you think I know that?" I shouted, my voice cracking. "Why does it have to be so hard? Why do they all hate me so much?"

Damon's expression shifted to one of shock, his eyes wide as he took in the shattered mess I'd become. For a moment, he seemed lost for words, taken aback by the raw emotion spilling from me. Kneeling down beside me, Damon's eyes searched mine, as if trying to decipher the storm of emotions raging within me.

"Who are you talking about?" he asked, his voice strained with concern.

"Jasper fucking Blackwood, the Moon Goddess, and every other fucker who wants to tear me down," I spat out, bitterness tinging my words. Damon's brows furrowed in confusion.

"Why would you think the Moon Goddess hates you?"

"Because she paired me with a mate who can't shift!" I exploded, anger and frustration boiling over. "What kind of sick joke is that?"

The moment the words left my mouth, Damon's expression darkened, and before I knew it, his fist connected with my face, sending me sprawling back onto the floor.

"What the fuck, man?" I yelled, clutching my throbbing jaw and glaring up at him.

"How dare you say that Erica is less than perfect," Damon seethed, his chest heaving with barely contained rage.

"Where the hell is this coming from?" I demanded, struggling to sit up. "I'd tear apart anyone who says my mate is less than perfect."

"Explain to me then," Damon demanded, his voice tense and strained, "why you just blew up at Erica and called her useless?" His words were like a punch to my gut. My anger subsided, replaced by a dawning realisation of the consequences of my outburst. I had let my rage consume me, and now Erica was paying the price.

"I... I didn't mean it like that," I stammered, searching for the right words to defend myself. "I wasn't angry at her. It's this fucking curse and the Shadow Night pack." Damon's eyes narrowed, suspicion still evident in his gaze.

"What does that have to do with Erica?"

"The message that Grayson had for me," I explained, my voice heavy with regret. "The curse isn't on me—it's on my wolf. In order to break it, I have to complete the bond in wolf form."

"Are you sure about that?" Damon questioned, doubt lingering in his voice.

"Louis mentioned something similar in the mind link before... before I killed him," I admitted, the bitter taste of hatred filling my mouth. "So yeah, I'm sure."

The heavy silence between us stretched on, my thoughts consumed by the impossible task before me. As I studied Damon's face, I saw the moment realisation struck him, his eyes widening with understanding.

"If Erica can't shift, then you two can't complete the bond in wolf form." I nodded, my heart aching at the seemingly insurmountable obstacle that stood between Erica and me.

"Yeah," I murmured, feeling more defeated than ever. "Exactly."

"Fuck, man," Damon breathed, running a hand through his dark hair.

But as he looked at me, a grin slowly spread across his face, the corners of his eyes crinkling with mischief.

"Hey, don't you dare give up hope yet," he said, his voice firm yet encouraging. "We're going to find a solution, Liam. And I think I might have an idea. Or at least a witch with an idea."

"An idea?" I couldn't help but feel sceptical, given our current predicament. "I've consulted a hundred witches, Damon, and none of them have been able to help." His grin only widened, a spark of excitement lighting up his dark eyes.

"Yeah, well, you haven't consulted a high priestess from one of the most powerful covens in the world, have you?"

"Are you serious?" I asked, hope flickering to life within me like a candle in the darkness.

"Damn right I am."

"Alright, if it'll help, I'm willing to try anything," I agreed, desperation clawing at my insides.

Damon nodded, determination set in his features. "I'm gonna make a phone call. But first, you need to find Erica and make sure she knows you're not going to reject her."

"Reject her?" I asked, confusion and hurt welling up within me. "Why would she think that?"

"Because, Liam," Damon's voice softened, concern etched across his face, "it's one of her fears, that she's less than other wolves. She was devastated when you called her useless earlier."

"Shit," I muttered, my heart pounding wildly in my chest. Without another word, I bolted out the door, my footsteps echoing down the hallway as I sprinted towards my father's office. Bursting inside, I found the room empty, devoid of any signs of life.

"Where are you?" I mind-linked my father, anxiety gnawing at me as I awaited his response.

"Away from you," he spat back, his anger palpable even through our mental connection.

"Please," I begged, desperation and regret twisting together in a bitter concoction. "Tell me where you are, and I'll explain everything." My father's voice finally broke through the strained silence.

"we're in the Alpha living room."

With renewed determination, I raced back up the stairs to the fourth floor, my heart pounding in my ears. As I burst into the living room, I found my parents sitting there, their expressions tense and wary. My father scowled at me, his eyes filled with disappointment.

"Where's Erica?" I demanded, my voice cracking under the weight of my concern.

"Resting in Kaitlyn's room, after what you did," my father snarled, not bothering to hide his disdain.

"Listen, I wasn't angry at Erica," I tried to explain quickly, desperate for them to understand. "I need her to know that." Without waiting for a response, I sprinted towards Kaitlyn's room, hope and fear warring within me as I slammed the door open. But to my dismay, the room was empty.

"Kaitlyn, where is she?" I mind-linked urgently, but all I received was a cold, furious response.

"Fuck off, Liam," she snapped, shutting down our mental connection before I could plead my case any further. Cursing inwardly, I stepped back into the hallway, feeling helpless and lost. It was then that Damon emerged from my room, a small smile playing on his lips. Confused by his unexpected expression, I turned towards him.

"We have to go now if we want my friend to help us," he informed me, optimism shining in his eyes.

"But I can't find Erica," I said, frustration bubbling beneath the surface. As if on cue, my father rounded the corner, his face etched with concern. "Where are you going?"

"Damon has a witch friend in Cornwall who might be able to help us."

"Fine," my father relented. "You two go, and I'll find Erica. I'll explain everything to her and make sure she's safe."

"Thank you," I said, and he shook his head.

"I'm doing it for her son. When you get back, you will need to do some serious grovelling," My father said. I nodded. I would do anything that Erica wanted me to do to show her how much she meant to me.

Chapter 53

Erica

Tears rolled down my cheeks as I sat on the cold floor, feeling the weight of rejection crushing me. I was certain that Liam would cast me aside once he had the chance, and I didn't want to make it easy for him. Desperation clawed at my chest as I looked up from my huddled position, finding sympathetic faces surrounding me. But their well-meaning attempts at consolation only made me feel more suffocated.

"Erica," Alpha Declan's voice broke through the haze of my misery. "Come, let's go back upstairs to the Alpha floor. You'll be more comfortable there." His words sent a jolt of panic through me. The thought of returning to the place where I had felt so exposed and vulnerable made my heart race with dread. My fight-or-flight instincts kicked in, and despite the tears still streaming down my face, I pushed myself off the ground with surprising force.

"No!" I screamed, my voice shaking. "I can't go back there! I won't!" Without thinking, I bolted down the hallway, ignoring the shocked expressions of those around me. I needed to get out of the Pack house, away from the constant reminders of my impending rejection, but my escape was short-lived.

Alpha Declan and a few others intercepted me before I could reach the exit, their faces etched with concern. Their hands gripped my arms firmly but gently, holding me back from running further.

"Erica, please," Alpha Declan implored, his dark eyes filled with sincerity. "It isn't safe for you to leave right now. We need to stick together." My breaths came in ragged gasps as I struggled against their hold. The fear of staying and the desperation to leave waged war within me, but ultimately, I knew I couldn't simply flee the situation. With a resigned sob, I stopped struggling and nodded, feeling the crushing weight of my reality settle back onto my shoulders.

"Erica," Alpha Declan said softly, his voice a soothing balm on my frayed nerves. "You need to come upstairs. It's not safe for you to be down here." Beta Gregg nodded in agreement, his warm brown eyes filled with understanding. I hesitated, torn between the urge to flee and the knowledge that they were right. With a shaky breath, I finally gave in, my heart thudding painfully in my chest.

"Ok," I whispered, allowing them to lead me back to the Alpha floor. As we climbed the stairs, every step felt like another nail in my coffin, driving me closer to the inevitable rejection that awaited me at the end of this tragic tale.

Entering the Alpha living room, I found Luna waiting for me, her arms open in a welcoming embrace. Despite my fears, I couldn't help but be drawn to her warmth, as if she were a beacon in the stormy sea of my emotions.

"Everything is going to be okay, Erica," she murmured into my hair as I clung to her, my teardrops staining her shoulder.

"How can it be?" I choked out, my voice barely audible even to my own ears. The weight of my situation bore down on me, making it difficult to breathe, let alone speak.

"Sometimes, things have a way of working themselves out," Luna replied softly, her words offering a glimmer of hope amidst the darkness. "For now, why don't you get some rest? You've been through so much." Kaitlyn, who had been standing nearby, stepped forward with a gentle smile.

"You can stay in my room, if you'd like," she offered, her dark eyes radiating warmth and support.

"Thank you," I whispered.

Kaitlyn's bedroom door clicked shut behind us, the sound echoing in the dimly lit space. The room was cosy and inviting, but my heart still pounded with anxiety.

"Kaitlyn, you don't have to stay," I murmured, my voice barely audible as I stared at the plush carpet beneath my feet. "I can manage on my own." Her grin was both playful and understanding.

"Why? So you can leave when no one is watching?" She raised an eyebrow, her dark eyes dancing with amusement. Despite my worry, a reluctant smile tugged at my lips. Kaitlyn had seen right through me; she knew running away had crossed my mind more than once since coming to the pack house. I couldn't deny it, that was my plan.

"Doesn't matter," Kaitlyn said with a shrug, her tone suddenly serious. "We're leaving, anyway." My eyes widened in surprise.

"What?" She nodded, determination etched across her features.

"I know you don't want to be in the pack house, Erica. I'll take you somewhere in the pack territory where no one will look."

As Kaitlyn began packing a few essentials into a bag, my chest tightened with a mix of gratitude and fear. I knew how much trust she was placing in me by choosing to help me escape, and with that trust came the weight of responsibility and expectation.

"Are you sure about this?" I asked hesitantly, my voice trembling.

"Positive," she replied without a moment's hesitation, slinging the bag over her shoulder. "Now come on, let's get out of here before anyone notices we're gone."

We moved stealthily through the quiet corridors, my heart pounding in my ears with every step. Kaitlyn's confidence seemed unwavering, but I couldn't shake the feeling that we were walking on a tightrope, one misstep away from falling into an abyss of consequences. As we slipped out a side door and into the cool night air, I couldn't help but feel a pang of guilt.

I was leaving behind the safety and support of the pack house, but at the same time, I was escaping the judgement and potential rejection that loomed over me like a shadow.

"Are you okay?" Kaitlyn asked softly as we made our way deeper into the pack territory, her voice barely more than a whisper.

"Am I making a mistake?" I questioned, my thoughts spinning with uncertainty. The idea of being alone in the world again terrified me, yet the thought of facing the pack, and Liam, filled me with dread.

"Only you can answer that," Kaitlyn said gently. "But remember, you're not alone. You've got friends who care about you, and no matter what happens, we'll be there for you."

The cold wind whipped at my face as Kaitlyn and I crossed the narrow bridge that connected the pack house to the main part of the territory. The moon hung low in the sky, casting shadows on the ground that seemed to dance with every gust of wind.

"Where are we going?" I asked, trying to keep my voice steady despite the uneasy feeling that settled in the pit of my stomach.

"To my fated mate's place," Kaitlyn replied, her eyes fixed on the path ahead. "No one knows about them yet, so they won't know to look for us there."

"Are you sure your mate isn't a spy?" I couldn't help but ask.

"Absolutely," Kaitlyn assured me, her voice firm and confident. "My mate is safe. You'll see."

We continued walking through the deserted streets of the pack town; the silence amplifying my anxiety. With the pack on lockdown, there were no people milling about or laughter filling the air. Instead, the atmosphere was heavy with tension, leaving the place feeling cold and unwelcoming. I glanced at Kaitlyn, who walked beside me with determination etched on her face. She had risked so much to help me escape, and I wondered if I was worth the trouble. Was I simply dragging her down with me, forcing her to make sacrifices she shouldn't have to make?

"Kaitlyn," I began hesitantly. "Thank you. For everything." She turned to me, offering a small, reassuring smile. "You don't need to thank me,

Erica. You're my friend, and I'm here for you, no matter what." Her words stirred something deep within me, easing some of the pressure on my chest. Despite my fears and uncertainties, I knew that I wasn't alone. Kaitlyn had shown me that there were people who cared, even if I couldn't see it myself.

"Let's keep going," she urged, taking my hand and pulling me forward. "We're almost there."

We finally arrived at a house nestled on the edge of the forest. The modern design and warm lighting emanating from within provided a stark contrast to the surrounding darkness. I admired the architecture, feeling a sense of hope that this place could offer me sanctuary, if only for a brief moment.

The front door opened, revealing Frankie standing in the doorway with her signature mischievous grin plastered across her face. My eyes widened in shock as Kaitlyn let go of my hand and sprinted towards her, enveloping her in a passionate embrace before sharing a deep, loving kiss.

"Frankie...is your fated mate?" I stammered, struggling to grasp the revelation.

"Surprise," Kaitlyn replied, still intertwined with Frankie, their connection undeniable. I couldn't help but feel a pang of envy, longing for the same kind of love they shared.

"Come on in," Frankie beckoned, guiding us into the warm, inviting interior of her home. The door clicked shut behind us, locking the cold world outside.

"Never a dull moment around you, eh?" Frankie teased, smirking at me. Despite the heaviness weighing on my chest, her playful demeanour managed to coax a small smile onto my lips.

"I try my best," I responded, trying to keep things light even though my thoughts were racing. Here was a secret relationship hidden away from the pack, defying societal norms. It made me question everything I thought I knew about the world I had been thrust into.

My gaze wandered over the cosy living room, taking in the comfortable furniture and personal touches, paired with bold colours and exciting looking artwork.

"Whose place is this?" I asked, my curiosity piqued by the unique blend of styles.

"It's my mom's," Frankie replied, her tattoos catching the light as she gestured around the room. "She's away on pack business right now. They called everyone to go to their family homes or stay in their own housing a few hours ago. Kaitlyn filled me in about the spies earlier through mind link." Frankie cast a sidelong glance at Kaitlyn. "It's definitely a tense situation."

My gaze shifted between the two of them, noting the way they gravitated toward each other even when they weren't touching. Their connection was palpable, and I felt a pang of envy deep within my chest.

"How long have you two known you were fated mates?" I asked, unable to suppress my curiosity any longer. Kaitlyn exchanged a look with Frankie before answering, her voice soft yet steady.

"We found out when I turned eighteen, about eight months ago."

"Wow," I breathed, marvelling at their ability to keep such a monumental secret hidden from the pack. "Why didn't you tell anyone?"

"We had to be careful, we didn't know how people would react," Frankie chimed in, her eyes darkening for a moment. I nodded in understanding, feeling the weight of their secret pressing down on me. They had chosen to keep their love hidden in order to protect themselves and each other; it was a decision I couldn't fault them for but hated that they had to do it. Even though the world is slowly catching up to more acceptance, the Werewolf community seems to be particularly lagging behind.

"Living a double life must be exhausting," I said quietly, my heart aching for the sacrifices they'd made. "I hope one day you won't have to."

"Us too," Kaitlyn murmured, reaching out to grasp Frankie's hand. The simple gesture spoke volumes about the depth of their bond, and I couldn't help but feel a swell of emotion rise within me.

Sitting in the cosy living room, I felt a strange mixture of comfort and unease. The warmth of friendship radiated from Kaitlyn and Frankie, but my own dread threatened to smother it. My thoughts were consumed by the looming spectre of Liam's potential rejection, the fear that gnawed at the edges of my heart.

"Hey, Erica?" Kaitlyn's voice cut through my reverie, her eyes glazed over with the telltale sign of a mind link conversation. She frowned slightly, her brow furrowing in concentration.

"My dad is trying to get me to tell them where we are. Apparently, Liam's looking for you." My breath caught in my throat, panic constricting around me like a vice.

"Please don't tell him!" I begged, certain that if Liam found me, it would only lead to my inevitable rejection. "I can't face him yet." Kaitlyn's eyes cleared, and she looked at me with sympathy.

"I had to tell my dad, but I also told him not to let Liam know. If he shows up here, he won't be allowed in, okay?" Frankie chimed in, her voice firm and resolute.

"I won't let him through the door, Erica. You're safe here."

Despite their assurances, my heart still raced with apprehension. I knew it was only a matter of time before my sanctuary crumbled, leaving me exposed and vulnerable once more. But for now, I clung to the solace they offered, like a drowning woman grasping at a lifeline.

The black SUV pulled up outside the house a few moments later, its dark windows tinted like the murky depths of uncertainty that clouded my thoughts. I watched as the Alpha stepped out from the passenger side, his authoritative presence seeming to eclipse the sun itself. My heart pounded in my chest, a staccato rhythm that matched the rapid succession of knocks on the door.

"Frankie," I said, my voice barely audible above the cacophony of fear ringing in my ears. "You have to let him in." She hesitated for a moment, her rebellious spirit warring with her duty to obey, but ultimately nodded in agreement. The door creaked open, revealing the Alpha's imposing figure, his eyes scanning the room as if searching for something, or someone, out of place.

As Frankie led him inside, I caught snippets of their hushed conversation, my curiosity piqued by the intensity of their whispers. I threw Kaitlyn a puzzled look, but she just shrugged, her face a perfect mask of neutrality.

"Kaitlyn," the Alpha growled as he entered the living room, his gaze boring into her like twin daggers. "You're in serious trouble, young lady." My stomach churned at the admonishment, guilt gnawing at my insides like a ravenous beast. This was my fault. I had dragged her and Frankie into this mess, and now they were paying the price for my cowardice. But then, the Alpha's expression softened as his eyes fell upon me. He crossed the room in three long strides, his towering frame dwarfing my own as he knelt down before me.

"Erica," he asked gently, concern etched into the lines of his face. "How are you holding up?" I wanted to scream, to unleash the torrent of emotions that threatened to overwhelm me, but all I could muster was a feeble shrug. How could I possibly put into words the crushing weight of fear, the suffocating sense of unworthiness that held my heart in an iron grip?

"Talk to me, Erica," he urged, his voice a soothing balm against the raw wounds of my soul. "I can't help you if you don't let me in." His sincerity pierced through the fog of my despair, and for a moment, I allowed myself to believe that perhaps there was still hope. But then the bitter sting of reality reared its ugly head, reminding me that no matter how much the Alpha cared, he couldn't save me from the truth.

"Alpha," I whispered, tears streaming down my cheeks. "I'm so afraid."

"Of what?" he asked gently, his hand resting comfortingly on my shoulder.

"Rejection," I admitted, the word tasting like ash on my tongue. "I feel so unworthy, so... unlovable."

"Erica," he said, his voice thick with emotion. "You are not unworthy. You are not unlovable. And you are certainly not alone. Please sweetheart, come home." I couldn't meet the Alpha's gaze as I shook my head.

"I can't go back," I murmured, my voice barely audible. "Liam will reject me."

"Erica, Liam isn't at the pack house," the Alpha said, his tone gentle yet firm. "He and Damon are on a trip to speak to a witch about the curse. And I can assure you, he isn't angry with you, nor does he want to reject you." Despite his reassurances, doubt gnawed at me like a persistent itch. How could he be so sure? I tried to swallow the lump in my throat, my heart heavy and aching.

"I... I don't know if I can believe that. I can't go back yet."

"Would you consider returning tomorrow?" The Alpha's eyes sought mine, filled with understanding and concern. He knew how much this meant to me, and it was comforting to know he wanted what was best for me.

"Only if Frankie is okay with it," I replied hesitantly, casting a glance toward her. She gave a small nod, a reassuring smile gracing her lips.

"Of course, Erica. You're welcome here." The Alpha nodded, his expression softening.

"Stay the night, then come back tomorrow." He reached over and gently kissed my forehead, his touch surprisingly tender. As he stood up, his eyes locked onto Kaitlyn. "We'll have words tomorrow, young lady." Kaitlyn winced but didn't argue. The Alpha then turned to Frankie, a hint of warmth in his eyes. "Look after my girls, Frankie."

"Yes, Alpha," she replied dutifully, her posture straightening. With one last warm smile for me, the Alpha stepped out of the house, leaving us to watch as he climbed back into the SUV and drove away. The hum of the engine faded into the distance, leaving an eerie silence in its wake.

As I sat there, surrounded by the comforting presence of Frankie and Kaitlyn, I couldn't help but feel a flicker of hope. Maybe there was a chance for me to find acceptance in this pack, and maybe, just maybe, Liam wouldn't reject me after all.

But as that tiny spark of hope began to grow, so too did my fear. What if it was all a lie? What if I was setting myself up for heartbreak once again? My chest constricted with anxiety, my thoughts spiralling out of control.

The hum of the television served as background noise while Kaitlyn and Frankie chatted, their laughter mixing with the movie's soundtrack. They seemed so at ease in each other's company, a stark contrast to the storm brewing within me. I tried to focus on their conversation, but my thoughts were relentless, dragging me back into the depths of my own fears. Liam had gone away, off to consult a witch about his curse. My heart ached at the thought of him, his absence leaving an indelible emptiness inside me. Would he reject me when he returned? Or was the Alpha sincere when he said Liam held no ill will towards me?

The pack house, my home, as the Alpha had called it, suddenly felt distant, as if I didn't belong there. But then there was Frankie, Gen, and Verity; I refused to believe Verity was a spy until I saw proof. And Damon, Beta Gregg, Jacob, Jenna, even Christian, who had just come back into my life. Most of all, though, was Liam. The mere thought of losing him was devastating, a crushing weight on my chest.

As I mentally listed the people I had come to care for, the thought of being separated from them filled me with dread. A sense of isolation enveloped me, tightening its grip until it became stifling. Tears pricked at the corners of my eyes as sobs threatened to break free.

"Erica, are you okay?" Frankie asked, concern etched on her face.
"Yeah," I choked out, trying to smile through the tears. "Just...thinking."
"About what?" Kaitlyn inquired gently, moving closer.
"Everything that's happened. All these people I've come to care about, and..." My voice faltered, betraying the overwhelming emotions that welled up inside me.
"Hey," Frankie said softly, wrapping an arm around my shoulders. "We're here for you, no matter what." Kaitlyn nodded in agreement, offering her own comforting embrace. "You're not alone, Erica. We'll face everything together."

As I lay there, sandwiched between their warmth and care, I wondered how many times a heart could break before it was beyond repair. If the pain of rejection felt anything like the crushing sadness that consumed me now, I wasn't sure I'd survive it.

Chapter 54

Erica

The night had been a nightmare, in more ways than one. As I lay on my bed, the darkness of the room seemed to close in on me like an oppressive weight. My heart ached with the fear that Liam might reject me and take all my friends away in the process. Unable to bear the pain any longer, I let the tears flow freely as I cried myself to sleep.

My dreams were no refuge. Liam haunted me there too, his normally kind brown eyes filled with cold rejection. He pursued me relentlessly through a twisted landscape, snarling accusations and brandishing claws that threatened to tear me apart. It was as if he'd become a monster, bent on destroying everything I held dear.

"Please, Liam," I begged him in the dream, "I don't want to lose you or our friends!" But he only laughed cruelly, baring his fangs in a terrifying grin.

"You're not worthy of them, Erica," he spat. "And you're certainly not worthy of me."

I woke up with a start, gasping for breath as if I'd just narrowly escaped drowning. The sheets were tangled around me like a net, slick with my sweat. My heart pounded in my chest, the residual terror from the dream still gripping me. I felt as if I hadn't slept at all, my body heavy with exhaustion. I blinked back tears, swallowing the lump in my throat, and stared at the ceiling for a moment before pulling myself into a sitting position.

The smell of coffee wafted through the air as I made my way into the kitchen. My stomach rumbled, reminding me that I hadn't eaten much the night before. Frankie stood by the stove, flipping pancakes with a practised ease, while Kaitlyn set the table. The sight of them working together so seamlessly should have warmed my heart, but instead, it only served to remind me of what I was afraid to lose.

"Morning, sleepyhead," Kaitlyn greeted me with a smile, placing a steaming mug of coffee in front of me. "Frankie made breakfast."

"Thanks," I mumbled, taking a sip of the bitter liquid. It jolted me awake even further, chasing away some of the lingering cobwebs from my fitful sleep.

"Hey, Erica," Frankie said, sliding a plate of pancakes onto the table. "I wanted to let you know something. Last night, after you got here, the Alpha used his Alpha command on me." I blinked at her, confused.

"Why would he do that?"

"He wanted to make sure I was loyal to the pack," she explained, her voice carefully neutral. "That's probably why he allowed you both to stay last night."

"Wasn't it obvious?" I asked, feeling a twinge of indignation on their behalf. "You have been nothing but supportive of me."

"Sometimes appearances can be deceiving," Kaitlyn replied softly. "But we all know how much we care about each other, and that's what matters."

"Yeah and I would rather them be suspicious of me and clear me, than either of you end up dead. Which reminds me I have my meeting with the Alpha in thirty minutes so eat up."

We ate our breakfast in companionable silence for a few minutes, allowing the conversation to shift to the events that had transpired recently. As we discussed Verity's situation, I couldn't help but feel a pang of empathy for her. She was being accused of something that seemed so utterly out of character for her.

"Verity's not a traitor," I declared, my voice firm. "I've seen her in action, and she's always been dedicated to the pack. There's no way she would betray us."

"Agreed," Frankie chimed in, her fork stabbing into a piece of pancake. "And if anyone tries to hurt her because of these accusations, they'll have to deal with me first."

"Same here," Kaitlyn added, her eyes darkening with determination. "I just hope that wherever she is, she is okay." I nodded, feeling a swell of gratitude for their unwavering loyalty. Despite the turmoil churning inside me, I knew that I could rely on them. No matter what happened between Liam and me, I couldn't let it affect the bond we shared.

"Okay, let's get moving," Frankie announced, glancing at the clock on the wall. "I've got to meet with the Alpha soon."

"Once that's done, you'll come back to the pack house, right?" Kaitlyn asked, her eyes filled with concern.

"Of course," Frankie reassured her, giving her hand a quick squeeze under the table. "I just need to get through this meeting first. Alpha stuff, you know?"

"Maybe we can invite Gen to join us too," Kaitlyn suggested, knowing how much I missed my best friend. "She's always been there for Erica and it might help to have her around." Frankie hesitated before responding.

"I'd love to, but we can't invite her until she's been cleared by the Alpha as well. You know how it is, everyone needs to be checked out before they're allowed in."

"Right," Kaitlyn sighed, disappointment evident in her voice. "Well, hopefully it won't be too long then."

"Hopefully," I echoed, trying to push down the nagging feeling of dread that had taken root inside me.

We finished our breakfast and piled into Frankie's car, a sleek black vehicle that matched her rebellious personality. As we drove back to the pack house, I couldn't help but notice the way Frankie and Kaitlyn interacted. They had grown more touchy-feely over time, their fingers brushing against each other as they adjusted the radio or shared a private smile when they thought I wasn't looking. It warmed my heart to see them so happy together, even if it was tinged with sadness. They felt the need to hide their love from the world, and it made me ache for them. My own heart still lay shattered and bruised, but I could appreciate the beauty of theirs. As the car pulled up in front of the pack house, Frankie and Kaitlyn seemed to snap back into "friend" mode. Their touches ceased, their smiles dimmed, and they looked like two people who merely tolerated each other's presence.

"Alright, I'll see you girls later," Frankie said, a forced casualness in her voice. "Remember, if you need anything, just call me."

"Thanks, Frankie," I murmured, feeling the weight of my own troubles pressing down on me. As much as I wanted to be there for my friends, I couldn't shake the feeling that I was drowning, sinking deeper with every passing moment.

As Kaitlyn and I approached the front door of the pack house, my eyes fell upon Wes, one of the guards that I recognised from before. He stood there, his usually stoic expression marred with worry and sadness. I couldn't help but think of how he must be feeling, knowing that Verity, who had just told us that Wes was her fated mate but her dad was kicking off about it, was potentially missing and presumed a traitor.

"Hey, Wes," I said softly, forcing a small smile to my face despite the ache in my heart. "How are you holding up?"

"Erica," he replied, his voice strained as he tried to maintain his composure. "I'm... surviving." My chest tightened at the sight of his pain. "I'm so sorry about Verity," I whispered, feeling the weight of his loss. "If there's anything we can do..."

"Thank you," he said, nodding curtly. "I appreciate it." Kaitlyn and I exchanged worried glances, but there was little else we could say or do to console him. As we entered the pack house, I couldn't help but think of how fragile happiness seemed to be in our world, so easily snatched away by fate, leaving only shadows in its wake.

"Frankie will be back soon," Kaitlyn murmured as she held the door open for me. Her face was pale, her eyes shadowed with concern for both Wes and our other friends. Together, we climbed the stairs to the Alpha floor, the weight of our own troubles pressing down on us with each step. When we reached the living room, we found the Alpha, the Luna, and the Beta huddled together over several piles of papers, deep in discussion. Their faces were drawn and serious, hinting at the gravity of the situation that had befallen our pack. The moment the Luna noticed us, she sprang up from her seat, concern etched across her face. She reached me in an instant, wrapping her arms around me in a comforting embrace.

"Erica, honey, is there anything we can do to help?" I leaned into her warmth, my heart aching as I whispered, "I just need my friends, and maybe some rest."

"Of course, dear," she replied, giving me one last squeeze before releasing me. The Alpha, who had been watching our exchange, turned his attention back to the papers strewn about the table. He rifled through them with purpose, finally extracting one and handing it to Gregg, the Beta.

"Call in the Sinclairs straight away."

"Thank you, Alpha," I managed to choke out. My gratitude was genuine; he knew how much I needed Gen's support right now. As Gregg left to make the call, Kaitlyn seized the opportunity to ask about Verity.

"Dad, has there been any word on Verity or her family?" His features tightened, and I could sense his frustration.

"No news yet, Kaitlyn. It seems that all of them, except for Grayson, are confirmed missing." Kaitlyn nodded solemnly, but her eyes were clouded with worry. The Luna, sensing the heaviness settling in the room, attempted to steer the conversation toward more practical matters.

"Erica, we've prepared a guest room for you and moved some of your belongings in there. Of course, once we've cleaned up the broken furniture in yours and Liam's room, you're welcome to move back in." My chest tightened at the thought of returning to that shattered space, where fragments of my life with Liam lay strewn like wreckage after a storm.

"Thank you, Luna," I said, my voice barely audible, "but I think... I think I should stay in the guest room for now."

"Whatever you need, dear," she replied gently, her eyes filled with understanding.

With a heaviness in my chest, I excused myself from the Luna's comforting presence and retreated to the guest bedroom. The moment I crossed the threshold, I felt the weight of my emotions pulling me down like quicksand. Shadows seemed to creep from every corner of the room, their tendrils reaching out, whispering that I was unworthy and undeserving of love.

"Enough," I muttered, trying to dispel the dark thoughts swirling around me. I climbed into the bed, the cold sheets enveloping my body as if they were trying to shield me from the pain outside. My eyes stung with unshed tears that threatened to spill over, but somehow, I managed to drift off into a dreamless sleep.

The buzzing of my phone tore me from my slumber. Groggy, I blinked at the screen and saw Liam's name displayed. My heart leaped into my throat, choking me with fear and anticipation. Could he reject me over the phone? Would he? As the call rang off, I noticed eight other missed calls from him. My hands trembled, and just as I considered turning off the phone to silence its insistent demands, it started buzzing again. Liam's name taunted me from the screen, and something inside me snapped.

"Leave me alone!" I screamed, hurling the phone against the wall with all the force I could muster. It shattered into pieces, scattering across the floor like shards of my broken heart. Tears streamed down my face as I stared at the wreckage, my chest heaving with sobs that shook my entire body.

The bedroom door burst open, startling me from my thoughts, and Frankie came rushing in, her black hair flying wild around her face. Jacob followed close behind, looking concerned.

"Erica!" Frankie exclaimed, her eyes flicking between me and the shattered remnants of my phone on the floor. "What happened?" I couldn't speak, choked by the sobs that still racked my body, so I just pointed weakly at the broken mess. Jacob crouched down to examine the wreckage, his hazel eyes narrowing as he pieced together what had transpired.

"Ah, I hate cold callers too," he quipped, trying to lighten the mood. But it was the wrong thing to say, and Frankie's fist shot out, connecting with his arm in a hard punch.

"Idiot," she muttered, glaring at him. "This isn't the time for jokes." Although I couldn't help a small smile for his efforts.

"Clear!" Frankie called out, and Kaitlyn entered the room, her worried expression replaced by relief when she saw me. Gen followed closely behind her, and as soon as she laid eyes on me, she rushed forward, her arms outstretched.

"Erica!" she cried, wrapping me in a tight embrace. I clung to her desperately, burying my tear-streaked face against her shoulder as I sobbed. She held me close, her warmth seeping into my chilled bones, and whispered soothing words into my ear.

"Hey, it's going to be okay," she murmured, her voice steady even as her own emotions threatened to overwhelm her. "I'm here for you, Erica. We all are." Through my tears, I looked up at my friends, their faces etched with concern and love. In that moment, I realised just how much they cared for me, and it was both comforting and heartbreaking. Comforting because I knew I wasn't alone in my pain, but heartbreaking because I didn't want them to suffer with me.

"Thank you," I whispered, my voice barely audible even to my own ears. "I don't know what I'd do without you guys."

"You'll never have to find out," Gen promised, her grip on me tightening as if to shield me from all the hurt in the world.

"Come on, Erica. Let's watch a movie together," Gen suggested gently, her eyes filled with understanding and concern.

"Fine," I muttered, wiping the remnants of my tears away with the back of my hand. I knew she was only trying to help, but every part of me felt heavy, as if weighted down by the burden of my own emotions. We settled down on the bed, while Jacob and Kaitlyn grabbed chairs from around the room, pulling them closer so we could all be together. Frankie dimmed the lights, and the movie began to play on the screen across the room. It was an old favourite, one that usually made me laugh, but tonight, the familiar scenes only served to remind me of happier times. As the movie played, I couldn't help but get lost in my thoughts. My heart ached for Liam, for the love I thought we had, and I couldn't shake the fear that he would reject me, leaving me alone and broken. I tried to focus on the film, to let the laughter of my friends wash over me and bring some light into the darkness, but it felt like I was being swallowed whole by despair. The hours slipped away, and we watched movie after movie, none of them managing to lift the heavy cloud that hung over me. Eventually, exhaustion claimed me, and I drifted off into a fitful sleep, haunted by dreams of Liam hunting me down, his face twisted with anger and disgust. I woke the next morning, my body tangled in sweat-soaked sheets again, and my heart pounding in terror. The nightmares had been relentless, tormenting me with visions of rejection and abandonment. I glanced over at my friends, still asleep in their chairs or curled up beside me on the bed, and wondered how they could stand to be around me when I was such a mess.

This same cycle went on for around a week. My friends hung out in my room, watching movies and trying to keep my spirits up, but I couldn't escape the horrible nightmares that filled my nights. Day after day, I would drag myself out of bed only long enough to shower and change into fresh nightclothes, before retreating back into the safety of my blankets.

Liam had resorted to calling Kaitlyn's phone since mine was destroyed. But no matter how much he begged I still wouldn't talk to him.

"Erica, look at me," Kaitlyn pleaded, her voice thick with concern. I reluctantly dragged my gaze away from the closed bedroom door and met her eyes. She held her phone in one hand, Liam's pleading voice still echoing in my ears.

"Please don't let his absence destroy you," she said softly. "You're stronger than this."

Later that day, I found myself accidentally overhearing the Alpha speaking on the phone with Liam. My heart pounded in my chest as I pressed my ear closer to the door, desperate to understand what was going on.

"Liam, you need to be patient. Wait till you come back. This isn't a conversation you have over the phone." The Alpha's words sent a shiver down my spine, confirming my worst fears. Liam was coming home, but not to comfort me, he was returning to reject me, to tear my world apart.

"Come on, get up!" Gen barged into my room later that evening, her eyes sparkling with determination. She began rummaging through my closet, tossing aside various articles of clothing with a mission in mind.

"Gen, what are you doing?" I asked, feeling a mix of curiosity and annoyance.

"We're going out to Barking Brews for a night out," she replied, her voice firm. "You need to get dressed and put on a smile. It's your birthday party, and you have to be there."

"Gen, my birthday isn't until next Thursday," I protested weakly, but she merely shot me a stubborn look.

"Then we're celebrating it tonight," she declared, tossing a dress in my direction. "No arguments, Erica. You need this, we all do."

Reluctantly, I allowed myself to be dragged out to Barking Brews. The dim lighting and lively atmosphere were a stark contrast to the dark cocoon of my bedroom that I had become accustomed to. My friends surrounded me, their laughter and lighthearted banter slowly chipping away at the walls I had built around myself.

"Come on, Erica! You need to dance!" Gen urged, pulling me onto the crowded dance floor as cheesy pop songs blared through the speakers. Despite the turmoil within me, I couldn't help but smile as we danced together, momentarily forgetting about the crushing weight of the inevitable rejection looming over me. Kaitlyn handed me a drink, her eyes filled with concern and love.

"You're doing great, Erica," she said softly, offering a reassuring smile. We clinked our glasses together, and I took a long sip, feeling the liquid courage warm my insides. As the night wore on, I became increasingly aware of the two guards stationed nearby, their watchful gazes never straying far from me. It was clear that the Alpha had assigned them to keep an eye on me, and I appreciated his eye for protection.

"Excuse me for a moment," I muttered to my friends, making my way toward the restrooms. The guards followed closely behind, their presence both comforting and suffocating.

"Are you planning on coming into the bathroom with me?" I asked them, my tone dripping with sarcasm. One of the guards met my gaze, his expression impassive.

"We'll wait outside the door," he replied. "But if you're longer than two minutes, we'll come in looking for you."

"Fantastic," I muttered under my breath as I pushed open the restroom door and rolling my eyes. I went into the bathroom and did what I needed to do. With a sigh, I washed my hands and glanced at my reflection in the mirror, trying to ignore the gnawing feeling of fear and unworthiness that clung to me like a heavy shroud.

When I stepped back into the dimly lit hallway, I immediately noticed that the guards were gone. Panic spiked in my chest as I scanned the area for any sign of them. Just as I turned to head back into the bar, a strong hand clamped over my mouth, muffling my scream. Another arm wrapped around my waist, pinning my arms to my sides as I was dragged away from the safety of the bar. I struggled wildly, kicking and thrashing against my captor as they pulled me through the back door and out into the cold night air. My mind raced with terror, wondering if this was some cruel twist of fate, Liam's rejection made physical in the form of an attacker.

"Be quiet!" a familiar voice hissed into my ear, and I stilled in shock. The person released their grip on my mouth, and I whipped my head around to see Christian standing behind me.

"Christian?" I breathed, relief and confusion warring inside me. "What are you doing? When did you get released from the cells?"

"Shh," he said, glancing around nervously. "I'll explain everything, but we need to be quiet." I nodded, tears pricking at the corners of my eyes.

"Erica, I had to see you," Christian confessed, his voice strained. "You were holed up in the pack house all week, and I didn't think they'd let me in." I stared at him, trying to process his words. My heart ached with the weight of everything that had happened, but part of me was relieved to have someone familiar to lean on.

"Christian, I... I don't know what's going on anymore," I admitted, my voice trembling. "Everything has gone so wrong."

"I know," he whispered, pulling me close. "I heard about Louis and Liam. I wish I could've been there to kill Louis myself."

I flung myself into his arms, desperate for the comfort and safety he provided. Christian wrapped his arms around me, holding me in a tight embrace.

"Erica, I love you," he said earnestly, his breath warm against my ear. "I'll protect you, no matter what it takes. Everything I do is for your protection, even if it doesn't seem like it."

"Wh-what do you mean?" I tried to pull away, needing to see his face, but he tightened his hold on me, refusing to let go.

"You'll understand soon," he murmured, just as I felt a sharp sting in my neck. I jerked away from him, confusion and betrayal flooding through me. Turning, I saw Heidi standing there, syringe in hand and a sinister smile on her face.

"Christian? What's going on?" I slurred, as a burning sensation flooded through my body, making my limbs heavy and unresponsive. I swayed dangerously, feeling faint, but Christian caught me before I fell. He cradled me in his arms, and my vision began to blur.

"Shh, it's okay," he whispered, his voice filled with an odd mix of love and determination. "I just want to protect you."

"Stop making lovey eyes at her, Christian," Heidi sneered, her amber eyes cold and unfeeling. "We still have a lot to do."

As my consciousness slipped away, I desperately tried to cling to the last threads of awareness, feeling an overwhelming sense of betrayal and abandonment. The darkness won, swallowing me whole as I fell into a black abyss.

BOUND BY RIVALRY

ERICA

I COULD HEAR THE steady hum of a car as I tried to claw myself out of an unconscious black hole. I managed to open my eyes and the first thing I saw was the scenery outside the wind of the car rushing past. I realised I was laid down in a back seat and tried to sit up. I felt the heavy pressure of arms holding me down and then heard a familiar voice.

"It's okay, beautiful. Just rest, we have a little way to go yet." I look up and see the face of Christian looking at me with warm affection, but then movement draws my attention to the front seat and my gaze meets the smirk of Jasper Blackwood.

"Well, good morning there sweetheart," he purrs, his voice low and menacing. "It's lovely to see you again. I just wished that it could be under better circumstances. But don't worry we'll have plenty of time for fun later." Icy fear engulfs me as Jasper sneered down at me, promising 'fun' that will do anything but make me smile. Then I felt a sting in my neck and suddenly everything was going black before I could ask why Christian would betray me. I was spiralling into a dark abyss of fear, not knowing what horrors await me on the other side.

Bound by Rivalry – Book 2 in The Key Stone Pack Series will be released on Amazon 2nd October 2023

Pre-Order it here –
books2read.com/TKSPBBR

Read where it all began

When powerful witch Andriana receives a call for aid from a local werewolf pack pack, she is thrust into a world of ancient prophecies, dangerous sorcerers, and unexpected love. As she races against time to break a curse threatening an entire pack, Andriana is targeted by the enigmatic Myron, a sorcerer who harbours dark plans surrounding a prophecy about her unborn child.

Forced to confront the intersections of witch and werewolf worlds, Andriana and her newfound mate, Alpha Nathaniel, must navigate trust, power, and the looming threat posed by Myron. When their very survival is at stake and futures uncertain, alliances are forged, loyalties tested, and destinies revealed. In a climactic clash that will determine the fate of the Moon Key pack and a prophecy child, choices will be made, sacrifices endured, and a new legacy born.

Dive into a tale where love battles fate, prophecies beckon, and darkness seeks to consume the light of hope.

This is a Prequel short novel in The Key Stone Pack Series and revolves around Erica's parents, Andriana and Nathaniel.

Sign up for this free short novel HERE – https://dl.bookfunnel.com/krwz00niyx

About Aisling Elizabeth

Hey there! I'm **Aisling Elizabeth** (yep, that's pronounced ASH-Ling). A Yorkshire lass through and through, I juggle the fun chaos of two kids and two mischievous cats. I've always been the storytelling type. Before getting my name on an actual book cover in 2022, I dabbled with sharing my tales on reading apps. Turned out, people kinda liked them!

Dark paranormal romance is my jam. In my stories, you'll find threads of resilience in the face of tough times, characters whose lives are all tangled up (in the best way), and some nods to mental health – something close to my heart, given my own ups and downs.

My first published piece? "Beyond Beta's Rejection", kicking off The Divine Order Series. But trust me, my brain's always buzzing with a bunch of new story ideas.

Outside of spinning tales, I'm all about belting out songs (quality not guaranteed), hopping into gigs, and geeking out at TV and Film fan conventions. If you share my love for any of the above, we'll get on just fine!

AISLING ELIZABETH

Website - www.aislingelizabeth.com

Facebook Reader Group – www.aislingelizabeth.com/puzzlepieces

Also By Aisling Elizabeth

Current and future releases by Aisling Elizabeth. Please check www.aislingelizabeth.com/books for more updates and release dates.

The Divine Order Series
Beyond Beta's Rejection
The Alpha's Tainted Blood
The Gamma's Shattered Soul *(coming soon)*

The Key Stone Pack Series
Bound by Prophecy (Prequel)
Bound By Fate
Bound By Rivalry *(coming soon)*

Bound by Curse *(coming soon)*

Dark Heath University
Dark Ashes (Prequel Novella) *(coming soon)*
Dark Flame *(coming soon)*
Dark Inferno *(coming soon)*

Claimed by the Curse Series
Claimed by the Pack *(coming soon)*

Printed in Great Britain
by Amazon